The Root of All Evil

CW00552583

Trevor Negus

© Trevor Negus, 2019

Published by Bathwood Manor Publishing

A CIP catalogue record for this book is available from the British Library.

ISBN 978-1-9996885-2-3

Book layout by Clare Brayshaw

Prepared and printed by:

York Publishing Services Ltd
64 Hallfield Road
Layerthorpe
York YO31 7ZQ

Tel: 01904 431213

Website: www.yps-publishing.co.uk

PROLOGUE

15th June 1982
Wireless Ridge, Falkland Islands

'Okay men gather round, come on look lively.'

The voice belonged to Lieutenant Ian Findlay and he was addressing the men of B Platoon, 3rd Parachute Regiment.

The early light of dawn was breaking over the rugged, windswept terrain as the soldiers urgently gathered around the young officer. Satisfied that the entire platoon was within earshot, Lieutenant Findlay raised his voice against the wind and said loudly, 'Gentlemen, I've just received the following signal from headquarters; The Argentine Forces that were illegally occupying these islands have now agreed to an unconditional surrender and have laid down their arms.'

As one voice the gathered assembly let out an almighty roar of approval followed by differing yells of delight at the prospect of going home and of surviving the conflict.

After the initial euphoria, the mood among the gathered soldiers changed back to one of sober reflection. The young men standing in the early mist began remembering their fallen comrades, those who would never make the long journey home from the South Atlantic.

As the men quietened their officer continued, 'In effect gentlemen, what this signal means is this; as of this minute all hostilities against our enemy have ceased. You will not engage the Argentine forces in any way, shape or form other than to protect yourself against immediate aggression. Basically, if they're not shooting at you, they will be treated as prisoners of war and given all the protection offered by the Geneva Convention. Does everybody understand the importance of what I've just said?'

A resounding, 'Yes. Sir!', broke the silence as the men shouted loudly that they had understood the order.

Raising his hand for quiet, the Lieutenant then smiled and shouted loudly, 'Gentlemen, never mind all that POW bollocks! We are 3 Para! The finest regiment in the British army and we're not interested in gathering up a multitude of sad, beaten, disconsolate Argies. We're going to be the first troops marching into Port Stanley. Get your gear together gentlemen, we move out in five minutes.'

Like every other man there, Tom Naylor was overjoyed at the prospect of going home and the thought of no more conflict. At nineteen years of age and in the space of just three and a half weeks, he had experienced the magnitude of war and all its horrors at close quarters.

All the training in the world cannot prepare a man for actual armed conflict and now that the end was in sight his overriding emotion was of relief. He had no idea how many men he'd killed or wounded during that short period of time and he didn't want to dwell on the thought. He was more concerned with how many close friends and comrades he had lost to care about the enemies' losses.

The weather that morning was typical of the islands for that time of year. It was bitingly cold with a strong wind. Low on the horizon, a pale, almost insignificant sun tried its best to break through the grey leaden skies. Showers of sleet and hail, propelled by the strong winds came biting in, between the fleeting moments of sunshine.

Tom had quickly gathered his equipment together and now started the familiar routine of placing one foot in front of the other, gradually working into a steady rhythm.

It had been this way ever since the regiment had come ashore at Port San Carlos.

Alongside his brothers in arms, he had tabbed from one side of the island to the other, fighting the enemy along the way.

He could feel the heavy weight of his Bergen back pack squarely on his shoulders and the lesser weight of his L1A1 SLR weapon cradled across his arms and he felt strangely comforted.

The pack and his rifle had been his constant companions throughout his time on the islands and he now found it difficult to imagine a day when it wouldn't be so.

The kit and the rifle were now an extension of the man.

With the announcement of victory from Lieutenant Ian Findlay, Tom, like every other man in the platoon, had replaced his combat helmet for the famous maroon beret of the Parachute Regiment.

The men had then set off down the ridge for the final, triumphant push into the Falkland Islands capital, Port Stanley.

As he trudged relentlessly on following his comrades in Indian file, Tom felt an overwhelming sense of loss as he reflected on those comrades that were missing for this final push. Some of his closest friends would lie in this cold, unforgiving landscape forever, having been killed in the fierce fighting necessary to secure the last two areas of high ground that overlooked Port Stanley.

The air was still thick with the heavy smell of cordite and now as the early dawn light grew brighter, Tom became aware of the numerous bodies strewn across the down slope of the ridge. These were the twisted, damaged corpses of young Argentinian soldiers who would also never see their homeland or loved ones again.

Looking at the multitude of dead Argentine soldiers, frozen forever in an instant of time, Tom couldn't help but experience a sense of futility.

Had it all been worth it? Countless lives lost on both sides, and for what?

With just his thoughts for company, steadily he tabbed down the ridge. He maintained a position in the line twenty metres behind the soldier in front of him with a similar gap to the one behind him.

To his left, just a couple of yards off the track Tom saw yet another dead Argentine soldier. The dead man looked to be a similar age to Tom. A look of permanent surprise, etched forever onto his boyish features.

The childlike expression on his face was in stark contrast to the enormous gaping exit wound that had ripped open most of his chest. The Argentine had obviously been shot in the back as he ran down the steep incline, fleeing the final onslaught from the Paras.

For a fleeting second, a macabre thought flashed into Tom's head. He wondered if it had been a bullet from his rifle, that had abruptly ended the Argentine's life on that dark, cold mountain.

In the mayhem and chaos of the battle there was no way he could ever have known.

Apart from the initial ferocious and bloody hand to hand fighting on parts of Mount Longden, the majority of the battle was spent laying down arcs of fire into shapes moving around in the darkness below their position.

As he glanced down at the dead soldier, Tom could see that he had been a signaller. He saw the discarded, damaged radio laying smashed on the floor beside him. The radio set was equipped with a long whip like antennae which was undamaged.

Tom exclaimed, 'Perfect!', before bending down and unscrewing the antennae from the radio.

Slipping his heavy Bergen from his shoulders he quickly tied the aerial to his backpack before reaching into the thigh pocket of his combat trousers and retrieving a Union Jack flag. He tied the flag to the aerial and hoisted the Bergen back onto his shoulders before regaining his place in the line of paratroopers heading into Port Stanley.

As he resumed his steady march, he said quietly to himself, 'There you go mucker, I promised you I'd fly your flag as we marched into Stanley.'

Walking slowly in file, with his head bowed against the bitingly cold wind, his thoughts turned to the events of the last three weeks. After the epic journey from the UK on the Navy auxiliary ship, down through the mountainous, heavy seas of the South Atlantic, Tom could easily recall the sense of relief he'd felt after finally coming ashore at Port San Carlos on the 21st of May.

Like a lot of the troops not used to heavy seas, Tom had suffered badly from sea sickness in the rough swells, especially over the final days of the voyage. He had been extremely pleased to once again feel solid, if not slightly boggy, ground beneath his feet.

After six days of planning and equipment preparation, his platoon had finally moved out from the beachhead at Port San Carlos, tabbing all the way across the sodden landscape.

As he had taken those first steps towards liberating the islands, immediately in front of him was one of his closest friends in the Regiment. A man who had gone through the rigours of selection at the same time as him and who shared his all-consuming passion for Liverpool Football Club.

Gary 'Apples' Mercer was a born and bred scouser, having been raised on the notoriously tough streets of the Toxteth area of Liverpool.

The Liverpudlian was only five feet eight inches tall, but he was very stocky and immensely strong. He had an unruly mop of yellow blonde hair that constantly strove to creep out from below the maroon beret and he spoke with the thickest scouse accent Tom had ever heard.

Gary Mercer had earned the nickname 'Apples' during the tough training at the initial selection stage, after his mates noticed that whatever he was doing at some point he would shout loudly in his broad scouse accent, "How do you like those apples, mate!"

Whether it was throwing a grenade, hitting the centre of the target firing his rifle or some other action, it would always be followed by the same triumphant shout.

By the end of training, if Gary didn't shout it himself the rest of his platoon would. After he had passed through training and been rewarded with the coveted maroon beret, he had been posted to B Platoon in 3 Para, his nickname of 'Apples' had stuck and travelled with him to his new platoon.

Tom had also been posted to B Platoon and the two men became firm friends.

The recollections of Gary Mercer brought a grim smile to Tom's face as he continued steadily placing one foot in front of the other. As he trudged down the slope towards Port

Stanley in the distance, visions of previous fighting filled his thoughts.

His head was filled with images of the fierce fighting 3 Para had been involved in, to secure first Teal Inlet and then later Estancia House. Before the conflict Tom had never heard of the Falkland Islands and now these place names would be forever etched in his memory.

The battles for Teal Inlet and Estancia House had been short but fierce firefights with losses on both sides.

Glancing back over his shoulder towards the ridge of high ground behind him, Tom recalled the mixture of emotions he had felt as 3 Para attacked the Argentine defences on Mount Longden on the evening of June the 11th.

He had felt a jumbled mess of excitement, fear, pride and above all else an overwhelming sense of comradeship. At his side throughout the fierce firefight to take the high ground had been his friend, Gary Mercer.

A vivid, technicolour memory now flashed into Tom's head.

It was the first night of the battle, he and Gary along with other members of the platoon were making their way between some large boulders of rock that formed the last barrier to the summit of Mount Longden. As the group of soldiers began to move stealthily around a natural curve in the rocks, they suddenly came under withering automatic fire from an Argentinian heavy machine gun that had been set up above them.

It was a perfect ambush and two men from B Platoon had been cut down instantly in the first salvo. Had it not been for the lightning speed of Gary Mercer, barging Tom out of the line of fire and behind cover, it would have been three.

As soon as they were in cover, Gary was once again on his feet and skirting his way back around the rocks the other way. This manoeuvre enabled him to emerge on the blind side of the Argentinian machine gunners who continued to lay down heavy machine gun fire at the natural opening where the Para's had been ambushed.

As Tom and the rest of the platoon remained totally pinned down, Gary had managed to crawl within metres of the machine gun nest. Without a thought for his own safety, the stocky scouser, then hurled a fragmentation grenade at the Argentine's before rolling off the rock and dropping ten feet onto another rock.

There was a deafening roar as the grenade exploded, killing the Argentine machine gunners instantly.

Tom smiled as he recalled, how following the ear-splitting noise of the exploding grenade, he'd heard a familiar shout in the darkness, 'How do you like those apples mate!'

With that memory fresh in his mind, Tom chuckled as he continued the downhill slog towards Port Stanley.

As the procession of soldiers began to reach the outskirts of Port Stanley and they could finally see the buildings of the capital with their brightly coloured rooves and white rendered walls, Tom felt the bitingly cold wind strengthen and the cold sleet sting as the wind drove it almost horizontally into his face.

He could hear the Union Jack flag on his Bergen flapping noisily in the strengthening wind.

Hearing the noise made by his friends' flag, the expression on Tom's face changed to one of grim determination as he recalled the final part of Gary Mercer's involvement in the battle for Mount Longden.

Having taken Mount Longden, the men of 3 Para had then repelled numerous counter attacks from the Argentine forces for the ensuing forty-eight hours. The Argentine commanders had quickly realised that if this high ground overlooking the islands capital fell into British hands, then effectively the brief war was lost. They had ordered their troops to fight hard to try and retake the mountain.

The Argentine forces had used artillery to try and dislodge the paratroopers and had mounted a sustained heavy barrage pounding the positions occupied by the British forces.

It was during one of the last salvos of this artillery barrage that Gary Mercer had been hit by shrapnel from an exploding shell. The red-hot metal had caused a severe injury to his right leg. The shrapnel had shattered the femur and caused massive damage to the right knee.

Tom had managed to staunch the blood flow with an improvised tourniquet and had then used Gary's own SLR rifle as a makeshift splint in an attempt to hold the shattered right leg together. Although in obvious agony from his wounds, Gary's only concern was to thrust a neatly folded Union Jack flag at Tom. As he passed over the flag, he said in his thick scouse accent, 'Make sure you fly this fucker as you and the boys march into Stanley, okay mate?'

Tom had taken the flag but before he could reply, the attending medics plunged two vials of morphine into Gary's good leg before hauling him away from the front line to the casualty evacuation area.

Tom had heard no news of his mate since.

As the paratroopers started to walk into the centre of Port Stanley to be met by the grateful islanders, Tom wondered how his mate was doing.

He was surprised by how quickly what seemed like the world's media had got into the capital. Didn't they realise there was a war on? he thought to himself.

Suddenly, a very large Falkland Islander emerged from the crowd lining the road and made his way directly towards Tom.

The man had a huge smile on his ruddy face.

He warmly shook Tom's hand and said, 'Alright lad? It's great to see some scousers here mate. Thanks for everything you and your mates have done.'

Tom was puzzled, the look of incredulity must have been apparent to the Islander as he burst out laughing and said, 'I'm sorry lad, but you've got to be a scouser with that flag!'

Pulling the flag over his shoulder, Tom saw for the first time that right in the centre of the Union Jack flag was a golden Liver Bird.

Immediately below the Liver Bird, were three large gold letters that simply said, L. F. C.

Tom joined in the laughter with the red faced Falklander. He realised that Gary Mercer, in his own inimitable way had managed to proudly fly a Union Jack flag, emblazoned with the Liverpool FC badge as the world's media captured the very moment the British armed forces made their triumphant entry into the Falkland Islands capital of Port Stanley.

Millions of people watching the coverage on their tv sets would have seen the young paratrooper with the Liverpool FC Union Jack flag marching proudly with his comrades into Port Stanley.

CHAPTER 1

31ˢᵗ July 1986
Cheltenham, Gloucestershire

Nearly six hours had passed since the two police officers had left her house.

Having delivered the devastating news, they had remained for fifteen minutes trying to comfort her, before excusing themselves and leaving.

The two uniformed officers had explained that their colleagues from Nottingham CID would be travelling to Cheltenham later that morning to speak with her and that those detectives would provide transport to take her back with them to Nottingham.

After the two officers had left the house, a shell shocked and totally stunned Angela Hincks had slumped to the floor in the hallway. She had remained there motionless, sitting on the thick hall carpet.

Angela remained sitting on the floor with tears streaming down her face, her eyes were stinging and she had a feeling of nausea deep in the pit of her stomach.

The tears welling in her eyes made it difficult for her to focus on the features of her beloved daughter Jenny, constantly smiling down at her from the photograph on the sideboard.

Even now after almost six hours, she still found it difficult to believe what the young policewoman had so calmly told her.

How could it be true?

How could her beautiful, intelligent, nineteen-year-old daughter be dead?

A terrible accident, the policewoman had said.

How could that be?

The young officer had held Angela's hand as she told her how Jennifer had been struck by a Land Rover being driven by security guards inside the secret compound of a private pharmaceutical company based in the Nottinghamshire countryside.

Angela knew that her daughter was actively engaged in protesting against animal cruelty. She had been involved with the Animal Liberation Front, since she was fifteen years old. Her pet Beagle, Molly, had been snatched off the street and sold by the thieves to a laboratory owned by one of the major tobacco companies. The dog had then been used for experimentation by the tobacco company.

By the time the police had apprehended the thief and realised what was going on it had been too late to save her beloved Molly.

Angela and Jenny had gone with the Police to the laboratory but it had been impossible to identify their pet from the scores of other tortured animals found both dead and alive at the laboratory.

The surviving dogs had been in such poor condition, that the vets employed by the RSPCA had taken the decision to euthanise the surviving animals

Even after all this time, Angela still felt nauseous recalling the sight of all those dead, brutalised animals.

Following this harrowing experience, Angela had actively encouraged her daughter to protest against animal cruelty in all its forms.

As Jennifer grew from teenager to young adult, she regularly went on demonstrations against the fur trade and the cosmetic industry. She was also an avid anti-hunt protester and would join hunt saboteurs at fox hunting meetings.

Suddenly, Angela felt racked with guilt. Had the encouragement she had shown to her daughter's stance against animal cruelty been the reason for her untimely death?

This feeling of guilt was almost instantly replaced by another emotion.

Anger.

An inner rage now coursed through her body and she vowed through gritted teeth to find out exactly how and why her precious daughter had died.

The policewoman had also told Angela that the pharmaceutical company involved was UK Pharmaceutical Ltd, a company funded almost entirely by the government. The Nottinghamshire based company specialised in carrying out research into new drugs used to fight motor neurone disease.

Jennifer had been knocked down and killed inside a compound in their secretive establishment, located just outside the Minster town of Southwell.

At the time of the incident several other people had also broken into the compound, but they had fled the scene and made good their escape after the tragic accident. The young policewoman delivering the awful news could only speculate as to the purpose of the intrusion at the compound. She had told Angela that apart from a small hole cut in the perimeter wire there had been no damage to the laboratories and that

UK Pharmaceutical Ltd were not looking to press charges against anybody.

The security guards had been questioned about the events leading to Jennifer being struck by their vehicle, but the whole incident appeared to be a tragic accident.

When given this information so matter of factly, Angela had stiffened.

She knew it would be down to her to find out what had really happened in that compound and why her daughter had died. Her ex-husband, Jennifer's father, was useless and had played no part in their lives for many years, having walked out when Jennifer was five years old.

No, it would be down to her to find out the truth.

At least her job would help in her quest for answers.

Angela Hincks was a high-ranking official at the top-secret GCHQ building just outside Cheltenham. She could access any files held on the top-secret laboratory at Southwell. Her clearance level would also mean she could access all memos sent between the government and top officials of UK Pharmaceutical Ltd.

This was her daughter, her Jenny.

There would be no cover up, a mother's anger and determination would see to that.

Once again, she felt a volcanic surge of anger building within her and this time she felt strangely comforted by it. While ever that rage was burning, Jennifer still felt close.

Finally, Angela stood up and made her way upstairs to shower and get dressed.

The CID officers would be arriving at ten o'clock, in less than an hour, to take her to Nottingham.

She had made the trip to that particular city on many occasions, ever since her daughter had been accepted into Nottingham University to study for a law degree.

This time, instead of travelling to the beautiful University buildings, the Nottinghamshire detectives would take her directly to the mortuary at Nottingham City Hospital so she could identify her daughter and begin to make the arrangements to bring her home.

Jennifer's dream had been to continue the fight against animal cruelty through the courts, prosecuting multi national companies that were all too eager to brutalise and exploit animals.

She had wanted to become a champion for animal welfare.

Angela realised that she would now have to undertake her daughters dream, she would become that champion and ensure her daughter had not died in vain.

She stood motionless in the shower, allowing the hot water to cascade onto her face, washing away her tears.

CHAPTER 2

11.00am 21st November 1987
Clifton Estate, Nottingham

Dave Wakefield was totally pissed off.

He was having a shit life and he didn't care who knew it. His wife had disappeared three months ago, taking their three-year-old daughter with her.

Dave had done what he thought was the decent thing and married Maggie when she fell pregnant. Every one of his mates had warned him at the time that she'd been seeing other blokes behind his back and there was every reason to think that the kid wasn't his.

For Dave, all those niggling, worrying doubts had disappeared the moment Jessica was born. He doted on his beautiful, enchanting daughter.

His love for Maggie and Jessica had counted for nothing when he lost his job as a delivery driver for Boots in Nottingham.

As soon as the money ran out so had Maggie, the heartless cow.

After he had lost his job, she had constantly nagged him about money to buy new clothes for her and little Jessica. After yet another row, he'd told her to stop nagging and fuck off.

He'd been more than a little surprised when his wife had done just that.

Maggie had quickly packed what little clothes and belongings they had left, dressed Jessica, put the baby in her pram and did exactly what she had been told to do.

She had fucked off.

Dave hadn't seen his wife or daughter since. One of his mates told him he'd seen Maggie in town having a drink with a bloke he thought was a fireman.

A month after she left the flat, Dave had gone to the local police station on the vast Clifton estate to report his wife and daughter missing.

Two days later the police came to his flat and informed him coldly, that they had located his wife and baby and that they were both well. They also told Dave Wakefield that his wife didn't want him to know where she was living. The officers had made it clear to him that if he harassed his wife it would lead to his arrest.

From the hostile attitude of the police officers, it was obvious that she'd spun them some bullshit story about him beating her up. The two cops had told him the whole thing was now a civil matter and that if he wanted to get access to his daughter, he would need to do it through the courts and that he should employ the services of a solicitor.

What a joke that was, he had no money for a solicitor.

What little money there was from his job seekers allowance was soon swallowed up on his rent and other bills. There was barely enough for food, let alone fags and booze.

For Dave Wakefield, today was just another day in paradise.

He had spent another pointless morning at the "No Job Centre" before trudging along to the local supermarket where he spent the last of his money on a packet of ten,

Park Drive fags, a disposable lighter and a two-litre bottle of White Lightning cider. He didn't buy any food, he couldn't be arsed to eat, he just wanted to have a smoke, get shitfaced and forget his troubles.

He stopped walking and took a long swig from the big brown bottle of cider. It was still another five-minute walk to his flat at Fenchurch Walk on the Clifton estate.

The small flat was all he had left.

It was barely furnished now. He had been forced to sell off everything but the bare essentials. All he had left in the flat was a small television and a tatty three-piece suite in the living room, a double bed and an old double wardrobe in the bedroom and a gas cooker and fridge in the kitchen.

As he climbed the two flights of grey, concrete stairs that led to the landing of his first floor flat, the strong cider was starting to take effect.

A thought rushed into his head that very soon everyone would know the name Dave Wakefield. He would make sure of that. He didn't know how yet, but pretty soon he would make everybody pay for forcing him to have such a shit life.

As he walked along the landing to his flat, he fumbled for his door key.

Slowly, he raised the key to the lock. As he went to insert the Yale key, he noticed for the first time that the front door was already open. He could now see that the lock had been smashed.

He muttered a single word, 'Bastards!'

Very carefully he opened the door wide. It took him less than a minute to see that his television had been stolen. The one little luxury he had left was gone, nicked by some low life scumbag.

He walked around the flat, all that was left was the heavy furniture and the gas cooker. Even the fridge had been nicked. The last photograph he had of beautiful Jessica was now on the floor of the bedroom, ripped in two. The thieves had ripped it out of the silver frame it had been in.

'Bastards!' he roared, before slumping down onto the floor in the hallway of his flat.

He took out a fag from the packet, lit up and took a deep drag of the strong cigarette before taking a long swig of cider. At his side on the floor, he saw a single white envelope with his name typed on it. He opened the envelope and read the top line of the letter inside.

There it was in black and white, the letters leaping off the page and hitting him like a sledge hammer.

The top line said 'Notice of Eviction'.

Tears started to stream down his face, he felt crushed. The last semblance of self-respect he had was about to be ripped away from him.

He took another long drink of White Lightning and felt the intoxicating effect of the strong cider rush instantly to his brain.

Something inside him snapped and he started to shriek and howl like some demented banshee. His rage now out of control, he started to smash up the few pieces of furniture he had left in the flat. He began to pull the old kitchen units from the walls and emptied their contents over the floor. He found a large carving knife and a heavy meat cleaver at the back of one of the cupboards. He stuffed the weapons into the waistband of his jeans and began to drag the smashed furniture towards the front door of the first floor flat.

He completed the job the burglars had started and ripped the front door off its hinges. He then used the door to form the base of a barricade. Once the door was in place, he piled whatever else he could find behind it and in no time he had formed a sturdy obstruction.

He returned to the kitchen intent on dragging the gas cooker into the hallway to add to the barricade. He found that the cooker was still connected and the gas pipe wouldn't stretch that far.

A plan started to form in his alcohol befuddled brain.

He went into the cupboard under the stairs where all the junk was kept. Right at the back of the cupboard under a pile of rubbish, he found a green petrol can. He stood up and began shaking the can vigorously. He allowed a wide grin to spread across his features, when he realised the can was still almost full of petrol.

Now everyone would know the name Dave Wakefield, he thought to himself.

He continued to howl and scream until eventually he achieved the response he wanted. The neighbour from the flat below, after initially bellowing at Wakefield to shut the fuck up, had become concerned enough about his weird behaviour to call the police.

Dave Wakefield grinned malevolently as he watched the young police woman park the panda car outside the flats.

As quickly as it had appeared the grin disappeared and he growled out loud, 'Fucking typical. They send one of their bitches to start bossing me around again. Well not today sunshine!'

Having climbed the stairs to the first floor flat, WPc Carson was surprised to see the makeshift barricade.

She shouted, 'Mr Wakefield is everything okay? Are you in there?'

Wakefield approached the barricade from inside the flat, held out the green petrol can in one hand and the disposable lighter in the other.

He shouted, 'Fuck off bitch! Take one step closer and I'll blow you to pieces. I've switched all the gas hobs on and if you lay one finger on that barricade, I will torch us both!'

The young policewoman was desperately trying to think on her feet, 'It's alright Mr Wakefield, put the lighter down, we can talk about this. I'm sure things aren't as bad as you think.'

A low growl started to escape from the curled mouth of David Roger Wakefield as his mind finally slipped over the edge of reason. He put the petrol can down and his free hand moved towards the waistband of his jeans.

Still growling he took another step closer to the barricade and beckoned the policewoman to come closer. To her credit, in view of the situation confronting her. Very bravely, WPc Carson stepped closer, thinking she would be able to engage Wakefield in some meaningful conversation to try and resolve the situation.

Suddenly, the demented Wakefield lunged forward and let out a blood curdling high pitched scream as he thrust the large blade of the carving knife towards the policewoman's throat.

The young policewoman's life was saved by the same letter that had helped tip Wakefield into madness. As he thrust the knife towards the policewoman, his foot slipped on the shiny envelope containing the Notice of Eviction and the point of the knife fell inches short of its intended mark.

The horrified policewoman staggered back along the landing of the flats desperately reaching for her personal radio. As soon as she reached what she felt was a safe distance away from the barricade, she spoke quickly into the radio, 'Sarge, I need back up at Fenchurch Walk immediately! This bloke's a bleeding nutter. He's just tried to stab me in the throat and now he's pacing up and down, howling like some bloody Werewolf!'

CHAPTER 3

3.00pm 21st November 1987
Orrell Park, Liverpool

The three men had spent days watching the Tesco Superstore, all three of them were itching to get the job over and done with. The time spent painstakingly observing the area around the superstore was vital. It didn't come without risk though. For every hour they spent in the area, there was an increased risk of some nosy member of the public seeing them and more importantly remembering them.

It had been difficult to keep eyes on the security van when it arrived each day to collect the takings.

The three men had regularly carried out anti-surveillance drills when they approached the supermarket, as well as the time they were actually on the car park.

Even after taking all these precautions, there was still always the risk of the unknown. The one in a million chance that some nosy old bastard with nothing better to do, would remember seeing the same person hanging around.

All three men knew the risks.

All three were more than willing to accept those risks, in the pursuit of easily acquired wealth.

Over a period of days, each of the men had taken it in turns to watch the arrival of the security van, tasked with collecting the store's takings for the day. Each day, the security van had been observed from a different vehicle and an alternative location.

The gang had quickly established that the best time to target the security van would be on a Friday evening. The takings were the highest and the security van didn't arrive to make the collection until five thirty in the evening, when it was already dark.

The leader of the armed robbers had chosen this Friday to carry out the armed robbery. The decision had been made after The Ace had provided information on police activity for that specific time and day.

The gang had been informed by The Ace, that a large police operation was planned for the other side of the city during the early evening so any police resources in this part of Liverpool at that time would be extremely sparse. This meant that any interference from the police during the planned robbery was virtually non-existent.

The gang of three men had previously carried out five cash in transit robberies in as many months. On each occasion, the raids had been executed with a military precision and had gone like clockwork. Nobody had been hurt and, on each occasion, they had got clean away with very large sums of cash.

The success of their offences, was due in a very large way to the input of The Ace. To have the Chief Inspector in the Police Control Room at Canning Place Police Station, providing up to date information on police movements prior to the offences was a massive advantage.

The gang knew this information was worth every penny they had to pay the grasping, bent bastard.

The leader of the armed robbers was a softly spoken scouser who the other two knew only as Gadge. They were unaware of his real name and knew nothing about him.

The other members of the gang knew exactly where they stood and although they were both extremely violent individuals with long histories of uncompromising violence, they both knew better than to give any lip or backchat to Gadge. He was one hard bastard, who you crossed at your peril.

The getaway driver was Stevie Key, a twenty-year-old part-time bouncer from the Croxteth area of Liverpool. Stevie was a gifted driver who would back himself to outrun and outmanoeuvre any police drivers.

The reason for his confidence was simple.

Basically, Stevie didn't give a fuck; he would quite happily run over a granny or a kid to get away.

He was also very adept at stealing high performance cars and could always find a way to bypass the extra security measures these types of vehicles came fitted with, such as trackers and smart alarms.

The third member of the gang was Micky Stone.

Stone was a businessman who ran a successful scrap metal business called Delta Scrap Metal Limited on Rock Park Road, Tranmere.

He was a complete psychopath who revelled in physical violence. He was very muscular and a regular on the underground bare-knuckle fighting scene. The scrap metal business he owned was one of the most successful in the north west region, but Stone had realised at an early age that being wealthy and successful was not enough for him.

He committed armed robberies for the adrenalin rush it gave him and also because he loved the sense of power he felt over members of the public and the police.

Like all true psychopaths, Stone was an extremely intelligent, articulate individual and he always played a major role in the planning and execution of the robberies. Even so, it was always down to Gadge to have the final word on when and where the robbery would actually take place.

The reason for this was that it was only Gadge who had access to the information from The Ace.

Gadge was the only one who knew the true identity of the gang's police informer.

Being an intelligent individual, Stone readily accepted this pecking order. He secretly admired Gadge for the meticulous way he planned every robbery, leaving nothing to chance.

Conversely, Gadge merely tolerated Micky Stone.

He would never understand the mindset of a person who would take all these risks with their liberty, just for kicks.

For Gadge it was always risk versus reward, it was all about the money, strictly business.

Now that the planned day of the robbery had finally arrived, the three men arrived in the superstore car park at three o'clock in the afternoon. They had parked up on the very edge of the car park, well out of the way.

At four fifteen, Stevie Key moved the car into its final position. He parked the black Subaru, two parking bays down from where the security van would be parked while the day's takings were collected.

Stevie had stolen the four door Subaru earlier that week from a housing estate in Manchester. It was now showing bogus registration plates. Following the robbery, it would be dumped three streets away and torched. The team would then transfer to a nearby Ford Sierra, another stolen car on false plates. This vehicle would end up in one of the crushers at Stone's scrap yard in Tranmere.

The three men were all dressed identically in navy blue boiler suits, fluorescent yellow tabards and black ski masks.

Gadge and Micky would be carrying Remington pump action shotguns. The weapons could be shortened as they had a folding metal stock. Both men knew that if push came to shove and their escape was in any way compromised, they would not hesitate to use the weapons.

On the back seat of the Subaru were three large nylon holdalls. These would be used to hold the cases containing the bundles of banknotes they would soon be liberating from Tesco's Superstore.

Gadge glanced at his watch. Five more minutes and the security van would arrive.

CHAPTER 4

3.00pm 21ˢᵗ November 1987
Clifton Estate, Nottingham

Dave Wakefield settled down on the threadbare carpet of the now totally trashed living room of his soon to be repossessed flat. He took another long drink from the bottle of White Lightning, belched loudly and grinned to himself. His eyes darted around the scene of chaos, flitting from one piece of smashed furniture to the next and he began to laugh maniacally.

He thought to himself that very soon his plan would come to fruition, then the world would finally sit up and take notice.

It had been his bitch of a wife that had caused all this trouble. It had been Maggie's face he could see as he thrust the knife forwards, trying to slice open the throat of that bothersome, cocky policewoman.

How dare they send out a woman to deal with him? It was just one more occasion when he'd been shown a total lack of respect.

After the policewoman had backed off, Wakefield had looked down from the lounge window of his first floor flat as other police cars started to arrive. First to pull up outside had been the burly, thick set sergeant who obviously considered himself to be God's gift to policing.

The sergeant had rapidly backed off though.

Scuttling quickly back along the landing of the flats, after he'd been told by the bare chested, wild looking Dave Wakefield that all the gas taps of his cooker had been left turned on and that once the flat was full of gas, he intended to blow up the block of flats, along with everyone in them.

How gullible was that burly sergeant?

There was no gas escaping into the flat. Not yet anyway. He was saving that for the grand finale later.

Gradually more and more police cars arrived, but now all the officers were keeping a respectful distance.

That is all Dave Wakefield had ever wanted.

Respect.

Then the Fire Brigade had arrived. The bright red tender screeching to a halt outside the flats with all the blue lights flashing and two-tone horns going full blast.

What a bunch of pricks, he thought to himself.

He hated firemen with a passion. Especially after one of his mates had told him his wife had been out on the town with one a few months before she had left him.

He watched them closely as they got out of the tender and began setting up their equipment. Rolling out the thick hose jets ready to deal with the anticipated explosion and subsequent fire storm.

Dave hoped like hell that the wanker who had dated that bitch of a wife of his was out there so he could get what was coming to him.

If everything went to his deranged plan, he knew that it would probably end up costing him his own life. He didn't care; if he died in the explosion then that was all good too.

Who wanted to stay living in a shit tip like this?

He took another drink, lit another cigarette and contemplated his master plan.

19

His eyes took on a wild stare and the same maniacal grin appeared on his face, as he thought about what he was going to do.

Sooner or later the cops would have to try and get him out of the flat. He would let the dozy fuckers start to negotiate with him and while they were busy demonstrating to him how much cleverer than him they were, he would switch all the cooker gas taps on and quickly fill the flat with gas.

He knew, that just as soon as the negotiations started to fail, some idiot would make the decision to try and dismantle the barricades. He would then pour petrol all over the makeshift barricade, before throwing the lighter on to the petrol. He intended causing a massive explosion that would blow the coppers, the firemen and himself to kingdom come.

He settled down in the hallway with his cider and fags and waited for the negotiations to start.

He took a swig from the bottle, smacked his lips and said aloud, 'Perfect!'

CHAPTER 5

3.00pm 21st November 1987
Orrell Park, Liverpool

'Get ready, here comes the cash box', growled Gadge as the large navy-blue security van came into view. As expected, the security van pulled to a stop less than ten yards from the black Subaru containing the three robbers.

As always, the weak point in this kind of operation, as far as the security men were concerned, was that moment when the cash was being carried from the superstore towards the armoured van. At that instant the only thing standing between thousands of pounds in cash and the thieves were the unarmed security men.

The gang watched as the three security guards got out from the back of the armoured van. They were dressed in the uniform of the security company, wearing NATO style jumpers and NATO crash helmets that were the same maroon colour as the security company logo.

Finally, each man carried a large, black, hard plastic cash box.

Gadge knew that this type of cash box didn't carry the dye that was sometimes used to mark the banknotes in the event of someone unauthorised attempting to open it.

He also knew that when the three guards came out of the supermarket each box would contain approximately £100,000 in used banknotes of various denominations.

Between the three of them, the guards would be carrying just over £300,000 in cash that was virtually untraceable.

Not bad money for two weeks work.

The helmeted guards emerged from the building confidently. The three men chatted amiably among themselves as they walked towards the side door of the armoured van where the hatch was located.

As soon as all three guards were on the pavement, Gadge and Stone leapt from the Subaru. They were now fully masked up, screaming instructions and pointing the pump action shotguns at the shocked guards.

'Get on the fucking floor, NOW!' shouted Gadge.

'Do what he says, or I'll blow your fucking legs off!' shouted Stone.

Faced with the very real threat from the masked gunmen, without hesitation all three guards dropped to the floor. The plastic cash boxes had been handcuffed to the security men. Gadge stood menacingly over the prone guards, pointing his shotgun at each one in turn, growling at them to stay still.

With his own shotgun hanging from a lanyard around his neck, Stone moved swiftly between the guards using a pair of bolt croppers to sever the chain links of the handcuffs and release the cash boxes.

The bolt croppers went through the chains easily and Stone swiftly pulled the three plastic cash boxes away from the prone guards.

One of the guards looked up from the pavement and growled at Stone, 'You won't get away with this, you piece of shit!'

Beneath the black ski mask Stone smiled and said menacingly, 'Is that right, dickhead?'

He stepped forward and used the same bolt croppers to instantly sever two fingers from the mouthy guard's right hand.

The man screamed in agony and began to writhe around the floor, desperately trying to stem the spurts of blood that began gushing from the bloody stumps.

Suddenly, a man dressed in a stone coloured fleece jacket and blue jeans ran from the entrance of the store straight at Stone. As he closed on Stone he shouted, 'You fucking animal!'

Stone was taken by surprise as the man leapt at him. He had no time to raise his shotgun and the member of the public barged him to the floor scattering the cash boxes across the pavement.

Instantly, Gadge levelled his shotgun and discharged the weapon before swiftly using the pump action to reload. The cartridge full of searing hot buckshot hit the have a go hero in the left leg. The blast from the shotgun knocked the man to the floor.

Gadge looked down at the wounded man on the pavement and shouted, 'How do you like those apples hero? Move again and I'll put the next one in your head. Got it?'

The injured man tried to stand and began reaching for something in his fleece jacket pocket.

Gadge stepped forward and shouted, 'I said, don't move!'

There was a loud explosion directly to the left of Gadge.

Stone had got to his feet and from less than one yard away had fired his pump action shotgun directly into the face of the injured member of the public, killing him instantly and showering the pavement and one of the prone security guards in blood, brain and skull fragments.

'What the fuck are you doing? You maniac, he wasn't a threat!' yelled Gadge.

'No, he was a tiresome fucking prick! But he isn't any more', replied Stone icily.

Both men quickly gathered up the plastic cash boxes and threw them into the large nylon bag in the boot of the Subaru before jumping into the car themselves.

Stevie Key gunned the engine and the Subaru flew out of the car park, leaving a scene of utter devastation and carnage behind.

The audacious armed robbery had left one man dead and three traumatised and injured security guards in a state of shock, spread-eagled on the pavement outside the superstore. This sorry group of dead and injured people were slowly being approached by other shocked members of the public.

Lying on the pavement by the right hand of the dead man was a small black leather wallet that had fallen from his grasp as he was gunned down. The wallet had flapped open, on one side was a photograph of the man whose face was now unrecognisable and on the other side was the enamel badge of the Merseyside Police Force.

A woman picked up the wallet and reading the words beneath the photograph she said to the gathering crowd, 'It says, Detective Sergeant Brian Mayhew, he's a cop.'

CHAPTER 6

5.00pm 21ˢᵗ November 1987
Clifton Estate, Nottingham

Sgt Turner and four members of C Section, Special Operations Unit were on mobile patrol in Nottingham city centre. They were travelling towards the Meadow Lane ground of Notts County FC ready to police the evening kick off. Tonight's visiting team were Walsall FC, not a team renowned for having a large hooligan element within their meagre support.

They had just parked near the football ground on Cattle Market Road, when the radio in the van crackled into life, 'Control to Sgt Turner, over.'

Graham Turner answered immediately, 'This is Sgt Turner, go ahead. Over.'

'Divert immediately to Fenchurch Walk, Clifton and liaise with Superintendent Johnson who is Silver Commander on scene. There's a man with mental health issues barricaded in a flat who's threatening to blow up the entire block of flats. The Fire Brigade and Ambulance Service are already in attendance. Do you have an E.T.A. please?'

'We can be there in ten minutes. Travelling now. Over.'

Without being asked, Steve Grey gunned the van's engine, switched on the blues and twos and accelerated over Trent Bridge, heading for Clifton.

Ten minutes of impressive high-speed driving later and he parked the van at the designated rendezvous point, one hundred yards away from Fenchurch Walk.

Graham said quietly, 'Steve, Jack, I want you two to start getting all the gear ready. Tom and Matt, you come with me. Let's go and find Superintendent Johnson.'

They didn't have to look far. As soon as the three men got out of the van, they saw a very harassed and red-faced Superintendent heading their way.

'Hello gents, thanks for getting here so promptly. This is all a bit of a nightmare, I'm afraid. About two hours ago, one of my policewomen responded to this block of flats after the tenant on the ground floor called in to say she was concerned about one of her neighbours. She reported that the man who lived in the flat immediately above her had gone stark raving mad and was constantly howling like a dog. When WPc Carson arrived at the upstairs flat, the tenant, a bloke named David Wakefield, had already barricaded himself in and was threatening to blow the place up. This Wakefield character told my officer that he'd turned on all the gas taps and then threatened to ignite the gas with a lighter. When she tried to reason with Wakefield, the arsehole tried to put a knife in her neck. She's a very lucky young woman, it seems this bastard only missed her throat because he slipped on something as he lunged at her.'

A stern-faced Graham Turner said, 'Okay sir, exactly what do you want from my team? Including myself, I've only got five on board this evening, but I'm sure we can help.'

'This man, Wakefield, seems to be getting progressively worse sergeant. I think if we leave it any longer, he's likely to blow the flats up anyway. Obviously, all the flats in the block have been evacuated, but I've no idea how far the effects of such an explosion would spread. What I want you and your team to do, is dismantle the barricade, get inside the flat and detain him before anybody's injured. I've just been speaking to the firemen on stand by and Station Officer Jenkinson who's in charge, is of the opinion that the gas to air ratio inside a flat of that size would not be conducive to an explosion. But, and it's a big but, he says this isn't an exact science and it could be that the whole flat will explode while you're inside. Those are the risks.'

Graham Turner was thoughtful for a moment then said, 'Okay sir, I'll find Station Officer Jenkinson and talk to him myself. Depending on what he says, we'll then probably have a go at getting Wakefield out.'

The superintendent nodded and said, 'Let me know what you decide sergeant.'

The three men walked back to the van. Matt was the first to speak, 'If the gas is on already, won't he just pass out or something? You know, get overcome by the fumes?'

Tom looked at him incredulously and said, 'No, you doughnut! It's natural gas! It's not poisonous, you're thinking of Calor gas or something.'

'Oh right, how thick can you get?'

Graham looked at Tom and Matt, 'Enough of the wise cracking you two. Start getting switched on. If we do have to get into this flat and get this nutter out, it's going to be no picnic. I don't think either of you have grasped the fact that not only is the gas leak and fire risk a major problem, but you're also going to have to contend with a violent individual who's just tried to stab a young policewoman in the throat. If he's willing to try and do that to her, he'll take great delight in trying to gut either of you two ugly fuckers. Start thinking about what's going to be required to get this nutter out of there. Get your kit together, I want you in full riot protection gear including NATO helmets. I'm going to go and find Station Officer Jenkinson and make sure that our friend Superintendent Johnson isn't feeding us a load of bullshit.'

Ten minutes later and Graham returned to the van. Tom and Matt were kitted up in full riot gear ready to go.

Graham said, 'Right you two, it's on. Station Officer Jenkinson has deployed staff on the landing with a hose jet aimed directly at the barricade. You'll both be pleased to hear that the Station Officer's confident that there'll be no explosion inside the flat, as there are too many holes for the gas to escape. There's still a real concern for a major fire though, but he's briefed his men to be ready for any outbreak of fire. If it does go up just back off and they'll put the hose jet directly on it.'

Tom asked, 'Do we know what the barricade's made of?'

'As far as I can ascertain from his lads on the landing, it's made up of the front door tipped on its side and a load of household junk. By the sounds of it, it shouldn't take too much shifting.'

As Graham quickly donned his own riot protection gear, he said quietly, 'Me, Steve and Jack will be waiting on the landing, as soon as you've breached the barricade we'll steam in and deal with Mr Angry.'

Five minutes later Tom and Matt were on the first-floor landing of Fenchurch Walk. Stealthily they crept passed the point where the fireman had set up their hose jet and approached David Wakefield's flat.

Tom peered over the barricade trying to see inside the flat. Although he couldn't see anything there was an all-pervading stench assaulting his sense of smell. It wasn't the odour of gas. When Tom finally realised what it was, he involuntarily recoiled away from the barricade.

What he could smell was human excrement.

'Jesus! Matt can you smell that?'

'Can I smell it? He must have shit himself or something. That's gross.'

'Okay mate, try to ignore the stench and let's get on with it.'

Both men then began pulling in earnest at the various bits of debris that made up the barricade.

The noise came out of nowhere and made Tom and Matt flinch back fractionally from the barricade. Howling like a demented banshee, Dave Wakefield suddenly hurled himself at the obstruction screaming. He began throwing objects at the two men who continued trying to dismantle the blockage.

Matt suddenly realised what he was being pelted with and shouted, 'Fuck me! He's throwing lumps of shit at us mate.'

Tom kept his head down, 'Never mind that, keep going. Let's get in there.'

As he pulled a large drawer away from the barricade, Tom saw something that made his blood run cold. Wakefield was standing on the other side of the obstruction with a green petrol can in his hand. Tom looked on in horror as Wakefield began to splash the contents of the green can all over the remainder of the barricade.

Tom shouted, 'Watch it Matt, he's got petrol as well!'

Frantically, both men tried to pull down the remainder of the obstruction.

Out of nowhere, Tom felt a heavy blow land directly on the top of his NATO helmet. The force of the blow knocked him backwards and to the right. Tom's first thought was that a significant part of the barricade had fallen on his head. He quickly regained his footing and once more began pulling at the debris. As he removed more pieces of old furniture, out of the corner of his eye he saw a small flame glowing within the flat. The small flame was growing larger as Wakefield advanced back towards the barricade.

To his horror, Tom realised that he was staring at the small flame of a cigarette lighter, being held in Wakefield's left hand.

Suddenly, there was a blinding white light and a very loud whooshing sound as the petrol ignited and what was left of the makeshift barricade erupted into a ball of flame. The sudden fireball sent Tom and Matt hurtling backwards onto the concrete landing of the flats.

Landing heavily flat on his back, Tom looked straight up and saw a powerful jet of water arcing its way towards the fiercely burning obstruction.

The jet of water smashed into the barricade and dismantled it instantly, putting out the fire at the same time. With the barricade cleared, Tom began to slowly get to his feet. He heard the rumble of boots on concrete and saw Graham, Jack and Steve sprinting into the flat.

Tom looked across the landing and saw Matt slowly picking himself up off the floor, his overalls still smoking from the heat of the blast.

From inside the flat, came the sounds of a scuffle and shouts.

Seconds later Jack and Steve emerged with a still struggling David Wakefield. The two policemen unceremoniously dumped Wakefield onto the ground before handcuffing him.

Tom looked closely at Wakefield.

The man was in a very sorry state, he had obviously taken the full force of the fireball and now had some very severe burns to his face, arms and torso.

He was still snarling and cursing, but his eyes were far away. Wakefield was in a very dark place indeed. Tom wondered what had been the catalyst that had sent a normal, family man into such a nightmare world.

Jack and Steve bundled their prisoner down the stairs to the waiting ambulance and police officers.

Graham Turner emerged from the flat carrying a very large kitchen knife and an even bigger meat cleaver.

He looked concerned at Tom and Matt, 'Are you two okay? That was quite a fireball that went up.'

Matt replied shakily, 'I'm soaking wet, a little bit singed and covered in human shit. Apart from that I'm fine and dandy.'

With a horrified expression Graham stared at Tom, 'Christ Almighty Tom, have you seen the state of your helmet?'

Tom removed his riot helmet as the fire crew began to gather around. He could now see a seven-inch-long split that ran directly across the top of the helmet.

Matt asked, 'Didn't you feel that mate?'

'Yeah, obviously I felt it. I thought a part of the barricade had fallen on my head.'

'Something had fallen on your head alright, that nutter and his fucking meat cleaver', replied Matt grinning.

31

Graham Turner said seriously, 'If you hadn't been wearing that helmet, he would have split your head open like a water melon.'

Tom groaned, 'Fuck me, I think I need a cup of tea!'

As the three men made their way along the walkway, one of the fire crew turned to Tom and said, 'Are you blokes alright? Sorry we had to soak you down a bit there.'

'Pity you didn't turn the hose on the barricade straight away. If you had I wouldn't need a new helmet now.'

Tom held up the helmet, split by a blow from the meat cleaver.

The fireman whistled and said, 'Jesus mate, I wouldn't do your job for a pension!'

'And me yours mate. Cheers lads, have a quiet night. What's left of it.'

CHAPTER 7

6.00pm 21st November 1987
Orrell Park, Liverpool

The white tent erected in the car park of the superstore was illuminated by bright arc lights, the sides of the tent flapping slightly in the ever-strengthening wind.

Within the confines of the tent, Detective Superintendent Greg Mitchell looked down upon the shattered body of his colleague. The full forensic suit and overshoes he was wearing rustled as he squatted his huge frame down to examine the devastating wound to Detective Sergeant Mayhew's head.

He turned and spoke to the only other person inside the tent, 'Would death have been instantaneous?'

The Home Office pathologist, Professor Rachel York, nodded silently then added, 'Most definitely, Superintendent. The first shot fired hit him just above the left knee and would have incapacitated him immediately. The second shot was fired at his face from almost point-blank range while he was defenceless on the floor. There are a few pellets in both hands, so it looks as though he saw it coming and at the last moment raised his hands.'

In a voice shaking with rage, Greg Mitchell growled, 'Little more than a fucking execution!'

'Quite.'

'Anything else you can tell me Professor?'

'Nothing you don't already know Superintendent. Time of death was approximately four o'clock today and the murder weapon was a shotgun. It would appear that the shotgun was loaded with cartridges of buck shot. There are two empty cartridges that were ejected after being fired, which means it could have been some kind of pump action weapon. The criminals didn't bother to pick up the cartridges which probably means they haven't been handled at all, but you never know, they might be as stupid as they are callous. Looking at the spread of shot in the wound to the left leg, my educated guess would be that the shooter was probably three meters away whereas the head wound looks like the shooter was…..'

The pathologist didn't finish her summing up as she noticed the big detective's shoulders slump even further.

When he finally regained his composure, Greg Mitchell pinched the skin above the bridge of his nose and said quietly, 'Brian Mayhew was married with two young boys. When I leave here, I've got to drive to his home and break the news to his widow and sons. I still haven't worked out what I'm going to say to them, Rachel.'

Rachel York placed a consoling hand on the detective's wide shoulders and said quietly, 'I'll do everything necessary here, Greg. Who are you leaving to manage the scene?'

'Detective Inspector Jackie Blane is outside chasing up the witnesses, making sure we don't miss anyone.'

'Okay, leave Detective Sergeant Mayhew with me. I'll make sure he's conveyed to the mortuary with me and in a proper manner. I'll see you there later this evening, shall we say eight o'clock?'

'Right you are Rachel, thank you. Apologies for my bad language earlier, inexcusable.'

'You only said what I was thinking Greg, just do me a favour and make sure you catch these bastards.'

The detective nodded slowly then stood up and stepped outside the tent. He looked around until he saw his Detective Inspector and then shouted, 'Jackie, come here please.'

Detective Inspector Blane strode briskly across to her senior officer, her bright blue eyes sparkling in the stark white light of the arc lights, tufts of her short blonde hair sticking out from beneath the hood of the blue forensic suit.

'Right Jackie, I'm away to see Mrs Mayhew and the boys now. Professor York will liaise with you when she's ready to move the sergeant's body. What have we got so far?'

'We've got details of fourteen witnesses that saw some or all of the offence, three of those actually witnessed the shootings. Preliminary accounts suggest both the robbers shot at D.S. Mayhew. The first shot was fired immediately after he'd tried to intervene, the witnesses have described how that shot was aimed deliberately at his legs to put him down. All three witnesses say there was no need for the second robber to shoot. Detective Sergeant Mayhew was helpless and injured by that time and could do nothing to stop them.'

'What about the store's CCTV?'

'This is the one bit of good news so far, boss. The store has just had a major revamp of its CCTV system. Dc Wainwright and Dc Flowers are sitting upstairs now with the store's security manager, getting copies of everything relevant.'

'You're right Jackie, that's good news. Make sure they watch all the recordings from as far back as three weeks ago. No doubt these bastards will have been here scoping the place out on a regular basis. We might get really lucky and get some footage when they're not masked up.'

'Will do sir.'

'What about the getaway car?'

'Black Subaru. It's been found burned out three streets away. House to house on that street has turned up one witness that saw the three of them transfer from the Subaru into a silver-grey Sierra. We've got a partial registration plate for the Sierra, but all three offenders remained masked up during the swap. We found the chassis number still intact on the burned-out Subaru. It was stolen from Manchester last week and the plates fitted on it for today's job were false.'

'What do you think Jackie? Is this the same crew that's done our other cash in transit robberies?'

'I'd stake my pension on it boss. Everything's the same. The clothing worn by the gang, the type of cars stolen to be used on the jobs, the actual method of the robbery, the way the two offenders on the pavement control the guards. If Sgt Mayhew hadn't stepped in to try and stop them today, they would have been clean away again. The nearest police unit at the time of the offence was over ten minutes away. This lot have got a bloody charmed life.'

'It certainly seems as though they've got more than their fair share of luck. Okay Jackie, do you need any more resources here?'

'No boss. Everything's under control.'

'Right, the post mortem is scheduled for eight o'clock this evening. I'll see you at the mortuary when I get away from Brenda Mayhew's.'

Jackie Blane said nothing.

What could she say?

She watched as the bulky figure of Detective Superintendent Greg Mitchell walked slowly towards his car.

Speaking to the widow of a murdered colleague was the one thing no senior officer ever wanted to do. It was no wonder he looked as though he was carrying the weight of the world on his shoulders.

The radio she was holding suddenly crackled into life, disturbing her thoughts, 'Dc Wainwright to DI Blane over.'

'Go ahead Tom.'

'Ma'am you need to come up and have a look at this CCTV, it's horrific viewing, but it's clear as a bell.'

'I'm on my way Tom.'

CHAPTER 8

3.00pm 1st December 1987
M42 Services near Tamworth

Angela Hincks returned to the Formica table carrying two large mugs of coffee. She placed one of the mugs in front of the handsome, tattooed man with the ponytail, before sitting down opposite him.

The two of them had been inseparable ever since Jeff Wicks had first come into her life six months ago.

As she sipped her hot coffee, Angela thought back to the first time she had seen him.

Jeff had turned up one day at a run of the mill Animal Liberation Front demonstration in Bedfordshire. About fifty activists were protesting outside a small company they suspected of being involved in animal experimentation.

She had spotted him immediately, as theirs was a close-knit world where at most demonstrations the same faces would be seen. She had been drawn to him and had watched him closely, taking in his lean slender body, his beautiful coloured tattoo's, his long dark hair pulled back in a pony tail, his gold hoop earing's and most of all his soft brown eyes.

As she observed the handsome stranger, Angela had found herself experiencing feelings and emotions she thought were long since buried. At forty-two years of age she thought her chance of ever finding love again had passed her by. Her first marriage had been a total disaster, the only good thing to come from that ill-fated liaison was the birth of her beautiful daughter, Jenny.

Her husband had embarked on a string of extra marital affairs about a year into the marriage and eventually walked out on her and his young daughter. His departure came as a relief and since he left Angela had never even considered being with another man.

Following the death of her daughter, this had become even more the case for Angela. She just had no interest in the opposite sex, her all consuming passion since that tragic event had been to try and establish the truth about her daughters' untimely death.

As she watched him that first day she had been surprised at Jeff's quiet, unassuming nature. He was hardly speaking to anyone let alone joining in the raucous chanting and shouting of the other demonstrators.

That quiet, passive demeanour changed instantly as soon as the trouble had started.

As security men employed by the company had started to get heavy handed with some of the younger female protestors, Angela had watched in amazement as the slim stranger had intervened. Verbally at first and then physically.

She had been massively impressed by the speed and efficiency in which Jeff had dealt with the security guards. Within seconds, he had left the two guards bruised and unconscious on the ground.

As the crowd finally dispersed, Angela had found herself with Jeff and a few other protestors in a small pub in Bedford. Being of a similar age, the two of them had started chatting over a couple of drinks. Jeff explained to a rapt Angela, how he'd only just been released from prison for assaulting a police officer. This offence had occurred at a protest against a mink farm in the Lake District. He told her that he was now technically homeless as his landlord had thrown him out after finding out about his most recent conviction.

As they talked and the drink flowed, Angela had felt so totally at ease with the enigmatic stranger that she told him how her only precious daughter had been murdered by thugs working for UK Pharmaceutical Ltd and how there had been a massive cover up to prevent any sort of enquiry into her death.

She had found herself sharing secrets with him. She had told him quite openly about the official memos she had seen from Sir Jarvis Soames, the head of the pharmaceutical giant, demanding that the government supress any enquiry into the tragic events.

Angela had forcefully expressed her opinion that Soames was the individual solely responsible for her daughter's cold blooded murder. Towards the end of the drink fuelled evening she had even told the stranger of her long-time plan to avenge the death of her daughter. She looked into Jeff's soft brown eyes and could see the genuine sympathy as he listened to her story.

Without even really thinking about it, Angela had offered Jeff not only a lift back to Cheltenham but also a place to stay for as long as he needed one.

Jeff had moved in and was the perfect lodger, keeping himself to himself and helping out with all the odd jobs around the house. He offered money for the room but she had refused.

There was a mutual respect and a blossoming friendship developing but nothing overtly sexual had ever happened between them at Angela's house during the time Jeff had been staying there.

Following another demonstration, this time in Lincoln, they had decided that as it was so late and they were both exhausted, to stop overnight at a Premier Inn just outside Nottingham.

They had just been in time to get a couple of drinks at the bar before going back to the room. It had seemed pointless getting two rooms. As they walked into the room within seconds they were kissing passionately, frantically tearing at each other's clothes before falling naked onto the large bed.

Sex the first time had been frantic and fast.

The second time however was as slow and sensual as they could both make it and after two hours they had lay there, unmoving and entwined in each other arms, physically spent.

Angela had never experienced lovemaking like it and had been totally besotted with the tall, slim stranger ever since.

Jeff Wicks had readily gone along with her plans to achieve the retribution she desired so badly for the death of her daughter.

That was the reason, six months later, why they were now sitting in services on the M42 on their way to Nottinghamshire. It was finally time for Sir Jarvis Soames to pay for his crime.

It was Jeff's soft voice that pulled Angela out of her reverie, 'Have you finished your coffee, sweetheart? It's time we got back on the road. The others will be arriving in Southwell soon.'

Angela Hincks smiled and finished her coffee, she looked across at the relaxed Jeff and wondered what their future held.

In her bag were two tickets waiting to jet them off to start a new life in New Zealand. She hadn't yet shared all of her plans with Jeff. She would do that in the next couple of days as they prepared to carry out the raid on the home of Sir Jarvis Soames.

At the moment Jeff and the other activists believed that Soames was to be kidnapped and held captive in order to force concessions from the government over future legislation on animal experimentation.

The truth was far simpler and far more brutal.

CHAPTER 9

4.00pm 1st December 1987
Merseyside Police Headquarters

Detective Superintendent Greg Mitchell coughed, then knocked lightly on the door of Detective Chief Superintendent Jasmine Wallace.

'Come in'.

Greg Mitchell opened the door with his right hand, he was clutching a large bundle of files under his left arm. He walked in and said, 'Good morning Ma'am.'

Jasmine Wallace leaned back in her chair, indicated a chair the other side of the desk and said, 'Sit down Greg and put the files on the floor. Thanks for coming over to headquarters. I know you're busy, but I wanted to hear from you first-hand how things are progressing into the murder of Detective Sergeant Mayhew. It's been nearly two weeks since his death, people are starting to ask questions of the Chief Constable. It's important to the image of the Force that we're seen to be making progress. So, what exactly have you got for me?'

Greg Mitchell had been dreading this meeting.

He hated making the trek over to headquarters at any time, but today was even worse because the truth of the matter was, he had next to nothing to offer his boss. For all the endeavour and long hours spent by his team all their enquiries had drawn a blank. Information from informants and sources had led to nothing. There was no forensic evidence. The eye witness accounts, although useful, hadn't yielded any suspects. The second vehicle used in the getaway had never been found.

The only thing they had was the CCTV footage of the murder. He had taken the decision very early on in the enquiry not to release the footage to the public as he deemed the content to be too horrific.

He took a deep breath, looked Jasmine Wallace in the eye and said, 'My team have been working tirelessly around the clock to try and move the enquiry forward….'

Seeing through the early attempt at waffle, Jasmine Wallace never let him finish the sentence, 'I sense a huge "but" coming, Greg. Have we made any progress or not?'

Greg Mitchell knew all about Jasmine Wallace's reputation for a tough, no nonsense approach, so he gave up on the waffle and decided to give it to her straight.

'The enquiry is stalling ma'am. We've no new leads despite my teams' best efforts and hard graft. We've got nothing whatsoever forensically and even though we have turned up several good eye witnesses, they aren't any help when it comes to trying to establish genuine suspects.'

'What about this wonderful CCTV evidence I keep hearing about?'

Greg was shocked and dismayed that the head of CID hadn't taken the time to view the footage, but he kept his reply measured, 'I took the decision not to release the CCTV images to the public. They're simply too horrific, in my opinion, and I felt it would be unfair for Brian's widow to be confronted with those images again and again.'

'Have you brought a copy of the video with you?'

Greg opened one of the folders on the floor and took out a VHS video cassette. 'Yes ma'am'.

Jasmine Wallace stood up, walked round the desk and took the video cassette from Greg. She placed it in the video recorder and switched on the TV.

The two senior detectives sat and watched the fateful three minutes in complete silence.

When it finished Greg retrieved the tape and placed it back in the folder.

Jasmine Wallace sat deep in thought.

Finally, she looked up and said, 'I completely agree with you, Greg. We can't possibly release that footage for general viewing by the public. What I'm prepared to do, is get that tape copied and sent out to every police force in the country. I want every serving officer in the UK to watch that footage, including forces in Scotland. Somebody, somewhere may recognise something about those individuals, about their methods, their language. The speech used, the threats, it's got to be worth a try. You said yourself the enquiry was stalling, this might just turn something up.'

Greg wasn't too optimistic that this would be the case, but nodded in agreement.

'The language used might be a problem ma'am, there's no sound on the video.'

Jasmine Wallace was not put off, 'Do we have witness statements that describe what was said and by whom?'

'Yes, we do, some of the accounts are quite specific.'

'Right, I want you to arrange for the witnesses to be recorded on video reading their own witness statements, that way nothing will be lost in how the comments heard by the individual witnesses were actually said by the offenders.

When you send the video of Sergeant Mayhew's murder to each force, make sure copies of the video recordings of witnesses are also sent. I want people to know not only what was being said, but how it was said and by whom when they view the video.'

'Okay ma'am.'

'Let me know as soon as you've sent them out Greg, and let's hope something comes from this. I'll go and see the Chief Constable later today and let him know what we're doing.'

Greg stood up, gathered his folders from the floor and walked out of the office. He had a familiar nauseous feeling in his gut. It didn't matter how many times he viewed the footage of the cold-blooded murder of his colleague, it still felt raw.

He knew those dreadful images would stay in his mind for the rest of his life.

CHAPTER 10

10.30pm 3rd December 1987
Southwell, Nottinghamshire

Angela Hincks and Jeff Wicks were alone in the lounge bar of The Saracens Head guest house in Southwell. The rest of the small team of activists had already gone upstairs to their rooms. While ever they were in public, they never congregated as a group. They made sure there was no conversation between themselves as a group and sat in pairs for meal times. Anyone observing would not have been aware that they were anything other than three random couples.

The spacious, wooden panelled lounge was furnished with high back, very comfortable, red leather Chesterfield chairs. Angela and Jeff were sat in the two that directly faced the large open fireplace. Jeff stood and placed another log from the basket onto the glowing red embers. He turned to Angela and said, 'One more brandy before we turn in sweetheart?'

Angela held out her empty glass and smiled, 'That would be perfect, thanks.'

She watched as Jeff took her glass, picked up his own and walked to the bar. As she studied his slender, but muscular physique showed off perfectly by the snug fitting woollen jumper, she felt a familiar warm tingling glow running between her breasts, down towards her stomach and beyond as she anticipated Jeff in her bed later that night.

They had spent the last two days carrying out detailed reconnaissance of the large country house owned by Sir Jarvis Soames.

Soames owned a large Georgian style house set in three acres of beautiful grounds, just outside the neighbouring village of Farnsfield.

It had been a simple task to pose as ramblers, exploring the delightful winter countryside around the Southwell area when they carried out the reconnaissance. Everything had been completed and finally Angela felt able to relax. She had enjoyed a beautiful meal with Jeff and felt totally at ease.

Jeff returned with two large measures of brandy in large bowl like glasses. Angela whirled the dark coloured spirit around the edges of the glass before taking a small sip.

Instantly she felt the liquid warming her and felt her face flush.

The planning was now finished.

The time had now come for Soames to pay.

Tomorrow night, they would break into Soames house armed with pistols and kidnap the odious man. Anyone getting in the way would be taken out, simple. Nothing was going to be allowed to stop them; if deadly force had to be used, then so be it.

The plan was a good one, the preparation and planning had been intense. Angela was confident they would achieve their objectives easily and without the need for bloodshed. Nobody would expect their arrival and they would be long gone before the Police even knew they had been there.

The team all knew their individual roles and were prepared.

Angela had briefed the rest of the team earlier in the day, informing them that once they had captured Soames, they would transport him to a remote barn over the border in Lincolnshire where he would be held captive. A video of him tied up and gagged would be made and sent to the government. He would be held captive until the government agreed to their demands on the total ban of using live animals in pharmaceutical experimentation. Only Angela and Jeff would remain with Soames while they waited for the government to comply.

The team were happy with the plan, but did question how long they thought it would take the government to give in to their demands. Angela had told them confidently that it wouldn't take long as the government would be given a set time scale to comply or Soames would die.

None of the team believed it would come to that and were happy with the answer.

The reality of Angela Hincks plan was far less complicated.

Soames would be kidnapped, but then as soon as the other members of the team had left, she planned to execute the businessman in grisly style with a ritual beheading. The killing would be carried out in front of a video camera and relayed via mainstream media to a shocked and appalled nation.

The entire plan was all about her own personal revenge, pure and simple. In her mind, Soames had murdered her daughter and now she would murder Soames.

The only other person who would be there at the time Soames was killed would be her lover and confidant, Jeff Wickes.

Angela was sure Jeff would understand and support her plans for Soames, after all, they were soul mates.

She would tell him the real plan tomorrow morning, before they set off to abduct Soames. She didn't want anything to be on his mind tonight, she needed him to be able to concentrate solely on pleasuring her.

She looked across at Jeff smiled, drained the last of her brandy and said, 'Shall we go up sweetheart?'

Jeff finished his drink and stood up, 'Ready when you are, gorgeous.'

CHAPTER 11

12.30pm 4th December 1987
Nottinghamshire Police Ranges, Gonalston.

'You will be given three, ten second exposures to the target. Double tap for close quarter combat drill. Watch and shoot! Watch and shoot!'

The voice belonged to Instructor Terry Davidson.

The automated targets suddenly turned to face the four marksmen from C Section.

As one, the four men extended their arms towards the targets, holding their Smith and Wesson.38 revolvers in a double handed grip. In a fluid, well-practiced movement all four men quickly aligned their weapons to the centre mass of the target and fired two shots.

Almost immediately the targets turned away again.

This process was repeated two more times until each man had fired six shots and the revolvers were empty.

Terry Davidson removed his ear defenders and said, 'Right lads, prove weapons and then advance to target. Let's see who's fit to carry a weapon and who shouldn't be armed with anything deadlier than an unpeeled banana!'

The attempt at humour was ignored by the SOU men, who all had serious, concentrated expressions on their faces. The four men opened the chambers on their revolvers, ejected the spent casings and proved they were unloaded before advancing in a line to their respective targets.

The close quarter combat drills were the first element of the classification shoot.

This was the test that every member of the Nottinghamshire force's armed response teams had to take and pass every month. Failure in any aspect of the test could mean the removal of an individual's authorisation to carry weapons.

First to have their individual targets checked by Terry Davidson, were Tom Naylor and Matt Jarvis. Both men were excellent shots and formed the sniper team for C Section.

However, they were both only too aware that accurately firing a rifle fitted with a telescopic sight and being accurate with the Smith & Wesson handgun required totally different skills.

To remain on the Special Operations Unit, both skill sets needed to be mastered to a high degree, as well as an equally proficient use of the Heckler and Koch Mp5 semi-automatic weapon.

As they walked the few paces to their respective targets Tom and Matt were relieved to see that all six shots had fallen well within the circle indicating the centre mass of the paper targets.

Terry Davidson was unimpressed, 'It's a pass lad's, but let's face it the grouping is shit! Seriously, you both need to tighten it up. Once the rest of the lads have completed their classification shoots, I want you two to get some more practice rounds down range. Concentrate on these close quarter combat drills. Got it?'

Tom and Matt both nodded.

Terry now moved along to the two targets used by Eddie Keane and Steve Grey.

Smiling Terry said, 'That's more like it lads.'

Terry turned to Tom and Matt, grinned and said, 'You two snipers need to have a look at these targets, that's what I'm talking about.'

He pointed at the two targets and the neat clusters of six holes that could have been covered by a tea cup.

With smug grins on their faces Eddie and Steve turned to Tom and Matt. A grinning Steve muttered under his breath, 'Snipers my arse!'

Neither Tom or Matt were prepared to get drawn into heavy banter, their colleagues already knew exactly how good C Section's sniper team were with the long weapons.

Once all the classification shoots for the Section had been completed all the men remained at the ranges carrying out the extra drills and practices as had been stipulated by the instructors.

Tom and Matt were just completing the last of their extra CQC drills when they heard the sound of an approaching police motorcyclist.

The telephones at the ranges were temporarily out of order and there was no reception for hand held radios due to the large earth mounds that surrounded the firing range.

The men gathered in a group to await the arrival of the motor cyclist.

Having placed the motorbike on its stand the motorcyclist approached the group removing his helmet as he did so, 'I've got an urgent message for Sergeant Graham Turner.'

Graham Turner stepped forward and said, 'That's me, what's the problem?'

'No problem sarge. It's a message from Chief Inspector Jim Chambers. He needs you and your Section back at

Headquarters immediately. This was the quickest way to get the message to you as the phones are down.'

'Okay, thanks. We'll pack up and get on our way. Do me a favour, as soon as you get out of the ranges and back into radio contact, give the Force Control Room a shout and inform the Duty Inspector to let the Chief Inspector know we're travelling. Thanks.'

The officer replaced his helmet before saying, 'Will do sarge.'

He fired up his motorcycle and hurtled back down the cinder path to the road.

Graham Turner turned and was about to bark an instruction, but just stopped and smiled as he saw that C Section had already stowed all the weapons in the vans and were ready to move.

CHAPTER 12

12.30pm 4th December 1987
Southwell, Nottinghamshire

Jeff Wicks was totally stunned.

He still couldn't quite believe what Angela had told him as they lay in bed earlier. He had held her in his arms as she slowly outlined the real purpose of the plan to snatch Jarvis Soames from his home. How the businessman would be abducted, then beheaded. How they would never make any demands of the government. Soames would be left to rot in the disused barn while they fled to New Zealand to start a new life.

Jeff had never intended to, but he had slowly fallen in love with Angela after she had confided in him the tragic story of her only child. She had shown him so much compassion. At first, he had felt desperately sorry for her, he could see there was a deep-seated pain behind her eyes.

After he had moved into her home, he realised that those feelings were being replaced by a genuine fondness and a physical attraction for the beautiful, intelligent and strong-willed woman Angela was.

The time spent together at Angela's house had cemented those emotions and urges and it had taken a great effort on his part not take his feelings any further.

He had been unable and unwilling to resist those physical urges when they had stayed overnight at the Premier Inn near Nottingham. It had been the most intense, passionate night of his life and ever since he had been swept along on a whirlwind of romance and amazing sex ever since.

It was the most intense and pleasurable relationship he had ever known.

It was everything it should never have been.

As an undercover police officer, Detective Constable Jeff Wicks had broken every rule in the book and up until this morning, he had no regrets.

Now he was in way too deep. He couldn't figure out a way to try and rectify the situation. He wasn't even sure if he wanted to change anything.

He was totally confused and angered by his own feelings.

His brief had been a simple one. He was to infiltrate the group and get as close as possible to Angela Hincks. He was to gather intelligence with a view to permanently closing down her group.

He had always thought that he would be able to bring down Angela's radical group of animal liberationists quietly and without fuss.

He genuinely believed he would be able to maintain their relationship once he had the time to talk her out of her beliefs. He knew that the only thing driving those beliefs was her hatred for Soames.

He had badly underestimated just how deep that hatred was.

Now he had a major dilemma.

Now he knew the full horrific intentions of the woman he had fallen in love with, he had no idea how to respond to it.

He had to try and thwart the murderous plan before it was too late.

An hour earlier and with a heavy heart, he had made the call to his handler back in London and had betrayed Angela. He had outlined the plan to abduct and kidnap Soames. He had stressed to his handler that if the group were successful and Soames was abducted then he would be murdered.

The only thing he hadn't been able to pass on was exactly when the abduction was to happen. He had promised to call back before they set off.

He felt wretched.

He genuinely loved Angela but at the same time he couldn't allow a man to be murdered in cold blood, whatever the reason.

He hoped that after the plan had been stopped and they were all arrested she would understand and her obvious, deep feelings for him would remain.

When she had outlined the plan, Angela had shown him the two one-way tickets to Auckland in New Zealand.

He genuinely hoped that when the dust had settled and she realised his motivation, she would forgive him and they would still be able to make that trip and spend the rest of their lives together.

CHAPTER 13

12.45pm 4th December 1987
Nottinghamshire Police Headquarters

Without slowing down, the two SOU vans raced into the car park at Headquarters, both vehicles finally coming to a screeching halt outside The Huts.

Waiting in the doorway was Chief Inspector Jim Chambers.

'Christ! This must be urgent', muttered Steve Grey.

As the men started to get out of the vans Jim Chambers shouted, 'Bring all the weapons inside, don't take them up to the armoury. I want all weapons stripped down and cleaned. There will be a full briefing in thirty minutes. Get cracking!'

After half an hour of frenzied activity, the men of C Section had assembled in the large briefing room. Jim Chambers entered the room and gestured for the men to remain seated.

As soon as the men had settled and the room had quietened, he said, 'Right gents. Hot off the press. We've just received reliable information that a group of fanatics, that have splintered from the Animal Liberation Front, are planning a major spectacular tonight. This group are extreme in every sense of the word. They're planning to abduct Sir Jarvis Soames, the Chief Executive of UK Pharmaceutical Ltd from his home just outside Farnsfield tonight.'

Chambers paused before continuing, 'This is the same group that are believed to be responsible for the exhumation of a man's body from a grave in Enfield. This awful act was done just because the descendants of that man now run a breeding farm for rabbits used in cosmetic testing and experimentation. There's a very fundamental and frightening difference between this lot and the usual run of the mill animal liberationists. That difference being, this group have declared a willingness to use firearms and explosives to achieve their aims. The information received today is quite clear and specific. Firearms will definitely be deployed for tonight's planned attack on the home of Sir Jarvis Soames. From the intelligence we have it is also apparent that Soames will be shot dead there and then if he offers any resistance. It has been intimated that the same threat level will apply to anyone else who attempts to intervene and stop the abduction.'

Graham Turner used the natural pause between statements from the Chief Inspector to ask what most of C Section wanted to know, 'Just how reliable is this information boss? I've never heard of an Animal Rights group willing to go to the lengths you've described.'

With a worried expression Jim Chambers replied, 'Unfortunately sergeant, the information we are getting is one hundred percent accurate. Following the national outcry after the body was dug up in Enfield, the Metropolitan Police decided to take action and introduced an undercover officer into the group. Apparently, this officer is one of their best and over a period of approximately six months, he's completely infiltrated the group, becoming an integral part of their organisation. The information we're getting is coming directly from him.'

Graham asked, 'What other intel can he give us?'

'It appears that the raid on Soames house will be carried out by five individuals plus the undercover officer. There are three women and two men involved. The leader of the group's a woman by the name of Angela Hincks. All of them will be armed and carrying handguns. The idea is to take Soames alive and then blackmail both the company and the government, bargaining Soames' life against a total ban on the current practice of animal experimentation and testing. If this total ban isn't implemented, they plan to execute Soames and release a video of his murder.'

Steve Grey muttered under his breath, 'Jesus, it's like the IRA for hamsters!'

Jim Chambers instantly picked up on the flippant remark, 'I know exactly what you mean Steve, but let's not underestimate the threat to life here. These people are extremists, fanatics; who, according to the undercover officer, are constantly training in the use and handling of weapons. Their threat needs to be taken very seriously, do I make myself clear?'

The men all nodded.

Jim Chambers continued, 'It's now three o'clock, I want you all fully briefed on the layout of the Soames residence in Farnsfield, the threat, the identities of the individuals concerned and I want a full plan of action by no later than five thirty. I want you on plot in Farnsfield by no later than six o'clock this evening. Are there any questions?'

Tom Naylor spoke up, 'Just one question, boss. Does Soames know of the threat and if so, does he intend to remain at the house?'

'Sir Jarvis Soames does know of the threat but refuses to be forced out of his home by what he describes as a "few cranks that are out of their tiny minds". Now if there's nothing else, let's get moving. Time's pressing.'

CHAPTER 14

6.00pm 4th December 1987
Farnsfield, Nottinghamshire

Tom Naylor let out a low appreciative whistle. He'd never set foot inside a house that displayed such opulent luxury in his life.

From the outside, the home of Sir Jarvis Soames, appeared to be the same as many other imposing three storey Georgian manor houses. It had large oak double doors that were recessed back from the two impressive stone columns either side of the porch. There were four large sash windows either side of the doors that were replicated on each floor. It made the front of the building hugely grand.

The real splendour of the property however, could not be seen from the front. The real beauty of the property was at the rear and was masked by the front facade.

The building was set in three acres of beautiful, picturesque countryside just outside the small village of Farnsfield. The house sat on the top of a small hill overlooking the quaint village below and could only be accessed via a single-track cobbled driveway that ran from the road.

Where the lane met the road there were two very large, ornate, wrought iron gates waiting to be re-connected to the electricity supply. These gates had recently been refurbished and repainted in black and gold, but for the time being were propped against the two imposing brick pillars. The ornate gates would eventually form a substantial barrier to anyone wanting to gain access to the house via the cobbled driveway.

The only part of the house that could be seen from the village in the distance was the imposing three storey, front aspect.

At the rear of the house there were two huge extensions that formed wings from the main house and created a large, spacious courtyard immediately behind the property.

At the centre of this paved courtyard was a decorative stone fountain. On the terracotta coloured paving slabs sat several large earthenware pots planted with olive, lemon and orange trees. At various points of the courtyard there were a number of red brick, raised beds that contained various heathers and herbs. The entire courtyard had been designed to mimic the Mexican haciendas of a forgotten time.

In the extension on one side of this courtyard was a huge indoor swimming pool and state of the art gymnasium that boasted a solarium and steam room.

The other extension contained a large board room and office for when Sir Jarvis wanted to work from home.

The rear of the house had identical sash windows to the front on the first and second floors. The ground floor windows at the rear had been replaced by French doors allowing easy access on to the magnificent courtyard.

At the far end of this courtyard, directly opposite the rear doors of the house sat a navy blue, Augusta Bell 206 Jet Ranger helicopter, squatting idle on the helipad.

If Tom thought the outside of the house was impressive, he was totally amazed by the level of opulence and luxury on display inside.

As he and Sgt Turner walked in through the large double

doors at the front of the property into a spacious hallway with cream marble floor tiles and an enormous crystal chandelier hanging above their heads, they were met by the single member of staff Sir Jarvis employed.

The tall, thin, immaculately dressed man said quietly, 'Sir Jarvis will be with you shortly officers, please wait here.'

The accent was vaguely Eastern Europe, possibly one of the Baltic states, thought Tom.

As he pondered over the accent, he was suddenly confronted by a huge bear of a man with a shiny red face. His shoulder length, greying hair slicked back with so much hair gel that it looked wet. The larger than life character was dressed in a dark red, kimono style, silk dressing gown and wooden soled Japanese sandals. He was holding a huge unlit Cuban cigar in his right hand and an equally large glass of brandy in his left.

Sir Jarvis Soames looked at the two officers and barked, 'Come this way gentlemen.'

It was an instruction given in a voice that obviously did not take no for an answer.

Tom and Graham followed Soames into a lounge area.

Soames turned and said, 'Okay Sergeant, what's the plan?'

There were no pleasantries, no introductions and no offer of refreshments, just straight down to business.

That suits me just fine, the sooner this job is done and we're out of this place the better, thought Tom. There was something distinctly unpleasant about Sir Jarvis Soames.

After a ten minute no nonsense briefing with Soames, both Tom and Graham were back outside the house.

Only Pc Jack Rimmer and Pc Luke Goddard would remain inside the property. They would station themselves directly outside Soames' bedroom in case the unthinkable happened and the animal rights activists managed to get past the rest of C Section.

The remainder of the team had already been well briefed and were now outside covering all the access points to the house.

At the rear of the house, Sgt Turner took Tom and Matt to one side, 'Listen you two, if I was a betting man, I would stake my pension on this door being the selected point of access for these muppets. I expect there to be some sort of diversion on the far side of the property near the pool house, but I think this here will be the entry point.'

The sergeant turned and indicated a pair of wooden French doors at the rear of the main house adjacent to where the extension containing the office was.

In his gravelly voice Graham said, 'Whoever's coming to grab this bloated, egotistical twat, they aren't going to be messing about. It's vital that you two stay on your toes tonight. Keep your weapons to hand, keep them loaded and be ready. I've got a horrible feeling that tonight's going to be the night you're going to have to use them. Clear?'

Tom and Matt nodded, fully appreciating the seriousness of the situation.

Graham said, 'Have you got any questions?'

Tom said, 'Have there been any further updates from the undercover cop?'

'Nothing as yet. You've just finished your Undercover Course haven't you Tom? Well, as and when you get a deployment, you'll quickly realise just how difficult it is to get information out at times. Having said all that, are you both happy you'll be able to identify the undercover officer tonight when the shit hits the fan?'

Tom nodded, 'No problem on that score, I just wondered if there'd been any updates, that's all.'

'Not yet, if we get any you'll be told. If that's all, I want you two to get switched on. I expect the early warning that these lunatics have arrived to come from Steve, he's got eyes on the lane up to the house.'

With that, Graham left Tom and Matt to assess their location and to finalise a plan to engage the criminals as and when they arrived at the house to abduct Soames at gunpoint.

At least it's not raining, thought Tom, as he and Matt got down into cover behind a small brick wall that formed part of one of the raised flower beds approximately five metres from the French doors. The bushy heather planting, gave good concealment and the metre-high wall offered good cover.

The decorative lamps dotted around the courtyard meant they were in shadow while at the same time the French doors were illuminated.

Both men were happy with the location and felt they would be able to successfully engage any threat from where they were.

Tom once again eased the rounds from the magazine of his Heckler and Koch Mp5 to lessen the strain on the spring and checked his Smith & Wesson revolver. This would be a routine he would adopt every hour.

Once his weapon checks were completed, he got down behind the raised bed and settled down for what might be a long wait.

CHAPTER 15

10.00pm 4th December 1987
Southwell, Nottinghamshire

Angela Hincks was fretfully pacing up and down in the car park at the rear of The Saracens Head guest house. Jeff walked across to her and placed a hand tenderly on her shoulder. He applied just enough force to temporarily halt her perpetual motion.

In his soft cockney accent, he said, 'Take it easy sweetheart, it's not too late to call this whole thing off. What we're about to do is huge, it will cause a massive shit storm. We're going to have every copper in this country and beyond looking for us.'

She stared at him incredulously and snapped a one-word answer, 'Good.'

Staring into those soft brown eyes, she was studying him now.

Finally, she said, 'Are you still okay with all this, Jeff?'

He looked away, unable to stand her penetrating gaze. It was as if she could see right into his soul.

She took his arm, squeezed it and said, 'I need to know that you're one hundred per cent with me on this.'

He looked at her and turned on his default smile, 'You know I am babe, let me go and call the others, they should be here by now. I'll find out what the hold-up is.'

With that he walked back inside, leaving Angela to her frantic pacing.

He was torn.

His chest felt tight, he was having difficulty breathing. He felt as though he was between a rock and a hard place.

Part of him was screaming to get away from there, to just keep walking out of the front door of the guest house and into the night. That way he would never see Angela again.

Another part of him desperately wanted to spend the rest of his life with the enigmatic, beautiful woman he had fallen so deeply in love with.

He stopped and placed a hand against the wall, desperately seeking some clarity.

There was no way he could run and leave her to it.

If he called it in, they would be intercepted by the Police, nobody would get hurt. She would be thoroughly pissed off that her plan had failed, but it wouldn't be all over between them. He would refuse to testify against her. He knew he would have to resign from the police, but if that's what it took, he would do it. If he played it right, Angela need never know that he'd been a cop.

They could still be together.

His mind was made up.

He reached for his mobile phone and made a quick call to the other four activists. They had spent last night at a different guest house in the nearby village of Edingley, to avoid the suspicion of everyone leaving The Saracens Head on the same day.

The call was answered on the first ring and Jeff snapped, 'Where the fuck are you man? We need to go!'

With more than a note of irritation in his voice, the man who had answered the mobile said, 'We're on our way, we'll be there shortly, the fucking van wouldn't start. Five minutes!'

The phone went dead.

Jeff quickly looked around him before punching in another set of numbers.

The phone just rang.

'Come on, pick up', he growled.

Suddenly, a woman's voice answered, 'Hello?'

Jeff said urgently, 'Don't say anything. Just listen. It's Dc 171 Wicks. The job is tonight and it's still very much on. We're leaving Southwell in ten minutes time and we'll be hitting Soames just after three o'clock in the morning. I'll be wearing a bright red fleece. We're all armed with self-loading pistols. For fucks sake make sure the firearms team on the ground know who I am, because this lot will start shooting. Guaranteed. Don't fucking forget, I'm wearing a red fleece! Got to go.'

Jeff deleted the last number he'd dialled then ran out into the car park just as the Transit van containing the rest of the kidnap gang pulled in.

Angela and Jeff got into the front of the van and the van pulled slowly out of the car park, heading along the Farnsfield Road.

Angela was grinning from ear to ear and said triumphantly, 'Soames, you fat bastard, your time's almost up!'

There were loud murmurs of appreciation from the other activists.

Jeff stared straight ahead, plans spinning in his head.

He would make sure that he never left Angela's side all night, that way he would be able to ensure her safety as the firearms teams closed in. He could stop her doing anything stupid and make sure she was safe.

Everything would be okay.

After tonight they would be together.

He felt sweat trickle down his back and as he squirmed, he felt the handgun push into the small of his back.

His mouth felt dry and he swallowed hard. He was desperately trying to hold it together.

As the van was driven at speed through the country lanes, Jeff stared out of the passenger window at the black hedgerows as they sped past.

CHAPTER 16

10.00pm 4th December 1987
Delta Scrap Metal, Rock Park Road, Tranmere

The noise in the scrap yard was deafening as yet another wrecked car was crushed into a cubic metre of recyclable metal.

It was Gadge who had called the meeting with Micky Stone and Stevie Key, but it was Stone who had insisted the meeting take place at the scrapyard he owned in Tranmere.

He had also insisted that the meeting take place after ten o'clock at night as the night shift employed at the scrap yard was only a skeleton crew.

Delta Scrap Metal Ltd was one of the most successful scrap metal businesses in the North West. Cars were crushed down to scrap, twenty-four hours a day, by state-of-the-art crushers. The business was spread over a one-and-a-half-acre site and wrecked cars and recycled metal were constantly being transported to and from the site.

The three men were sitting in a portacabin, situated about fifty yards away from one of the huge crushing machines.

Gadge was starting to doubt the wisdom of the choice of location for the meeting as yet another scrapped vehicle was fed into the automated crushing machine. The air was filled with the screeching sounds of twisted, tortured metal as the crusher did its work.

He scowled at Stone and said, 'For fucks sake Micky, why did we have to meet here? I can't hear myself fucking think!'

'Exactly my point mate. No fucking bizzies are going to overhear this conversation are they!'

Stone burst out laughing as did Stevie Key, who always laughed at everybody's jokes, no matter how shit they were.

Gadge didn't join in laughing and held his dead pan expression.

He waited for the other two men to stop laughing then said, 'Let's get down to business, shall we? We need to decide how long we're going to keep our fucking heads down after that debacle two weeks ago? Now that we've got every fucking cop in the country hunting our arses.'

He stared hard at Stone as he made the comment.

Micky Stone momentarily glanced down at the floor averting Gadge's gaze before saying coldly, 'Look Gadge, that interfering twat got what was coming to him. How was I to know that he was fucking plod? It's just one of those things. It's done now and I can't turn the clock back. Not that I regret it, because I don't. Like I said, he asked for it.'

'What a face full of buck shot from point blank range, when he was already on the floor and fucked anyway? Oh yeah Micky, of course he fucking asked for it!'

'Fuck off Gadge, you know what I mean!'

'Do I Micky?'

Gadge shook his head slowly resigned to the fact that he would never get a nutter like Stone to change his mind and accept that he was bang out of order.

This wasn't the time for recriminations anyway. What was done was done and couldn't be changed.

Gadge continued, making the most of the brief moment of silence before another wrecked vehicle was loaded into the crusher, 'Before that fucking machine starts up again, my question was; how long should we keep our heads down before we go again?'

Stevie Key spoke for the first time, 'What does The Ace say Gadge?'

'He thinks we're all fucking mentalist and should call it time.'

Stone growled, 'Fuck him! You need to lean on that prick and let him know that he can't just walk away from us. We can drop him right in the shit and deep down he knows that.'

Gadge nodded, 'That's very true Micky. You leave The Ace to me. I can sort him out and get him back onside, no problem. My own personal opinion is that we wait at least another couple of weeks before we go again. Maybe have a little break? Let some of this heat die down? What do you all think?'

There was a pause before Stone broke the silence, 'Sounds like a plan. I'm catching a plane first thing tomorrow morning anyway, I'm fucking off to my villa in Lanzarote, for a bit of winter sunshine.'

Stevie Key nodded, but said nothing.

Gadge said, 'Right that's agreed then. We'll meet up again just before Christmas. There's bound to be some heavy takings being carted around at that time of the year and we'll just help ourselves to some of the action.'

'Amen to that', said a grinning Stone.

Their meeting finished, all three men left Delta Scrap Metal Ltd and went their separate ways.

Stevie Key made his way from the Wirral, using the Kingsway Tunnel to drive beneath the Mersey and head towards Croxteth.

As usual, Stevie was driving at speed along the A59. He pressed the accelerator of his Audi Quattro hard down to the floor and grinned as the speedometer nudged towards the ninety miles an hour mark.

He was pushing for the ton mark, when to his dismay he heard the sound of sirens behind him. Glancing in the rear-view mirror, he saw the blue lights of a Traffic Police patrol car gaining ground steadily.

Stevie muttered under his breath, 'Bollocks! Fucking bizzies!'

The thought of stopping never crossed Stevie's mind, instead he gunned the engine and accelerated harder. Instead of taking the turning towards Croxteth, he drove straight on heading towards Walton, intending to get onto the M57 motorway.

Stevie believed that once he got onto the motorway, he would easily be able to outrun the pursuing police vehicle and had it not been for the stray Labrador dog he would probably have been right.

Suddenly, just as his Audi reached 140 miles an hour, he saw the big, black dog appear in the headlights directly in front of his vehicle.

He had no chance to swerve and no time to brake.

The Audi hit the animal flush on the offside wing of the car. The impact at that speed was enormous and the large dog virtually disintegrated after the collision.

The force of the massive impact wrenched the steering wheel from Stevie's grasp and suddenly the car was spinning out of control. In desperation, he made one last grab for the steering wheel, but the speed was too great, everything happened too fast. In that final split second, as the metal crash barrier rushed towards him, he realised he was fucked.

The Audi hit the central crash barrier at just over 130 mph. The barrier flipped the car, sending it hurtling end over end down the empty road.

Finally, the car came to a mangled, jarring stop as once again it smashed into the central crash barrier. As soon as the car came to a stop it burst into flames.

Stevie Key had died during the first roll of the car, as his neck snapped against the restraining seat belt. He would never have felt the searing heat of the fireball that engulfed his wrecked car.

The two police officers in the pursuing Traffic Patrol car were both convinced that it was without doubt the most spectacular crash either of them had ever witnessed.

Both of them were in a state of shock and disbelief as they halted their own car, some fifty yards back from the crash site. Without speaking, they looked towards the blazing inferno, that was eagerly devouring what was left of the smashed Audi. The mangled, blazing wreckage had instantly become Stevie Key's funeral pyre.

Finally, the older, more experienced officer reached for the radio and said flatly, 'Control, this is Tango Mike Two One. We need a fire crew at this location, the A59 just before the turn off for Walton. The Audi we were pursuing has crashed at highspeed and is now a fireball. The driver is 1/1, dead as a doornail. You'd better send out a supervisory officer and the Accident Investigation Team as we were in active pursuit when it crashed. Looking at the wreckage we're going to need to close this stretch of the A59 for the foreseeable. Over.'

With a resigned air he turned to his younger colleague who had been driving the police vehicle and said matter of factly, 'That's you suspended from driving for at least a couple of weeks, while they sort this fucker out.'

The young cop punched the steering wheel and exclaimed, 'Shit! That's all I need!'

Neither of the cops realised that the dead driver of the Audi, was one of the men responsible for the cold-blooded murder of their colleague exactly two weeks ago.

CHAPTER 17

3.00am 5th December 1987
Farnsfield, Nottinghamshire

Steve Grey strained his eyes.

He was sure he'd seen movement down near the entrance of the cobbled lane that led from the road up to Sir Jarvis Soames' palatial Georgian house.

It was getting difficult to see anything clearly now. The rain was falling as a soft drizzle and meant the ground below the house was shrouded in a mist.

Staring hard towards the lane, he squinted, trying to employ his natural night vision to the best of his ability.

There it was again.

He could see the outline of a large van, being driven slowly through the entrance. There were no lights on the vehicle and it was moving at a crawl, he could hardly make out the soft rumble of the diesel engine.

Halfway along the cobbled lane the van stopped and he saw figures getting out. The only door that didn't open was the driver's.

He continued to watch the figures as they made their way from the van along the lane towards the house.

The figures passed a natural gap in the hedgerow. Suddenly, the darker shapes stood out against the lighter field behind the hedge. The dark hawthorn hedgerow had offered the perfect backdrop to hide their approach, but now he'd achieved that first visual recognition, the location and direction of the animal rights activists became clearer and clearer.

Convinced of what he was seeing, Steve picked up his radio and said quietly, 'Stand by, stand by. I think our company has arrived.'

Sgt Turner responded immediately, 'How many and where are they Steve?'

'I've got a clearer view now, sarge. There are five of them and they are walking up the lane towards the house, bold as brass. I think the sixth has remained with their vehicle which is parked on the cobbled lane about fifty yards from the house. They're walking in single file. I can't see if they're carrying anything at the moment. The one at the front is definitely female though.'

Without being instructed to do so, the remainder of C Section instantly went to the next level of alertness and quickly checked their weapons to make sure they were all in a state of readiness.

Like every other member of the team, Tom had heard Steve's radio message. He thought to himself that from what Steve was describing, it sounded as though the activists were going to go for the brazen, straight in and get the job done approach, not the diversionary ploy that Sgt Turner had predicted.

If all the activists headed straight for the French doors being watched by Matt and himself, Tom knew they were going to have their hands full trying to engage with five armed suspects.

As if anticipating what Tom was thinking, Sgt Turner spoke to him via the radio, 'Tom, it sounds as though they're all heading to the house together and not splitting up. If they do all appear at the French doors where you and Matt are, I want you to challenge them immediately and we'll back you up as soon as possible. In the meantime, until we know for sure what their point of entry is going to be, I want everyone to remain in their current positions. Is that understood?'

Tom replied, 'Understood sarge. No problem.'

Sgt Turner then said, 'Steve, I want you and Tony to make your way to their vehicle. If the driver is still with the vehicle, I want him or her detaining. Be mindful that the information is that all these people are armed. There's no reason to think the driver will not be armed, so deal with it as an armed stop. Understood?'

Steve replied, 'I'll monitor the group on foot, until they're in your view sarge, then move to the vehicle and take the driver. Over.'

Sgt Turner replied brusquely, 'Roger that, Steve.'

Matt looked across at Tom and whispered, 'We're definitely going to have our hands full here mate. You heard the last update from the undercover cop as well as I did. He's made it quite clear to his handler that he believes this lot will start shooting.'

Tom nodded and whispered a reply, 'Yes mate, I heard it. So, we'd better be ready and be in good cover when we make the challenge.'

Matt nodded grimly, before once again checking his weapon.

Steve maintained his observations on the group of activists as they approached the house.

Finally, he could tell what area of the house they were approaching. He quickly updated the team, 'Definitely coming your way Tom. You and Matt better be ready, they're all sticking together. From the description we've been given it looks as though the undercover cop is second in line. He's immediately behind the woman and wearing a bright red fleece. He sticks out like a sore thumb, from the rest of them. The woman will be in your visual in twenty seconds. I'm moving back to their vehicle now. Over.'

Tom didn't reply, he just checked that the safety on his Heckler and Koch Mp5 was off and that the weapon was ready to engage any threat offered.

He quickly glanced across at Matt who was doing exactly the same. The two men looked at each other and both nodded a silent affirmation that they were prepared for whatever the next few minutes brought.

Suddenly, the group of activists were at the French doors.

The woman barked an instruction, 'These are the doors, get them open Stan.'

A stocky male wearing a donkey jacket and carrying a small crowbar stepped in front of the woman and the man in the red fleece, then quickly got to work trying to force the doors.

There was no finesse to their approach and it was obvious that they weren't expecting any kind of security presence.

What Tom could clearly see now that the group were this close, was the self-loading pistols, they were in possession of. There was one man and one woman standing at the rear of the group. Each held a handgun ready in their right hands. The woman, the man in the red fleece and the man trying to force the doors all had weapons that were still holstered. The gun belts were being worn outside their clothing for quick and easy access.

Tom glanced at Matt and mouthed silently, 'Ready?'

Matt nodded and raised his H&K Mp5 into his shoulder.

Tom raised his weapon, allowing the butt to nestle into his shoulder avoiding the Kevlar body armour that protected his torso.

He centred the sights of the weapon between the shoulder blades of the woman who was at the rear of the group with her weapon drawn.

At the top of his voice he shouted clearly, 'Armed Police! Stay exactly where you are! Do not move!'

Instantly the two at the rear of the group spun round, firing their pistols as they did so. The bullets were aimed in Tom's direction, the two activists firing at the location where the command had emanated from.

The rounds smashed into the small brick wall that Tom was behind, the impact of the bullets showered him in brick dust, momentarily blinding him.

Tom ducked further behind the wall, blinking furiously in an attempt to clear the dust from his eyes.

Covering his partner, Matt instantly fired at the two shooters.

He watched as the four rounds he fired found their target.

Both of the activists were hit twice in the chest, they instantly slumped to the ground, dropping their guns as they fell.

With his eyes now free of brick dust, Tom saw the woman and the man in the red fleece entering the house through the now forced French doors.

The man who had successfully breached those doors, now dropped the crowbar and drew his weapon. He crouched behind a large earthenware plant pot and began firing in Matt's direction.

From his position, Tom had a clear view of the third shooter and took aim.

As the activist fired his third shot, Tom squeezed the trigger of his Mp5 twice, hitting the gunman in the throat and the chest. He watched as the man fell face first to the ground.

As he fell, he dropped his gun and clutched both hands to what was left of his shattered windpipe, desperately trying to draw what would be his final breath.

Matt was on the radio now, 'The house is breached, two activists have gained entry through our access point. One is believed to be the undercover officer, the other is Angela Hincks. We've been fired upon and there are three activists down at our location. We're now in pursuit of Hincks and are entering the house.'

Tom and Matt were moving quickly now. They covered the downed activists as they moved forward towards the open French doors. There were no signs of life being shown by the three shot activists.

They all appeared dead, their catastrophic wounds and blood loss clearly evident in the light.

Matt quickly scooped up the three handguns the activists had been carrying, before following Tom into the house through the French doors.

Once inside, Tom squatted down and listened for movement in the dark house.

Instantly, he heard voices and knew they weren't too far away.

They were coming from the large hallway.

Tom and Matt moved stealthily into the hallway and could see Angela Hincks and the undercover officer facing each other at the top of the stairs. They were illuminated by the single nightlight on the landing that had been left on.

As the SOU men moved towards the bottom of the stairs, Tom whispered, 'I'll cover the woman Matt, you take the cop.'

Matt nodded and both men raised their weapons to cover Angela Hincks and the undercover officer who were engaged in a heated argument.

The undercover officer shouted, 'It's no good sweetheart. It's gone to ratshit! Give it up, people are dying here Angela!'

She shrieked back, 'No way! Soames has got to pay for what he's done. If you don't want to see it through with me, just fuck off!'

'Please Angela, you've got to stop!'

'I'm going to kill that bloated pig, if it's the last thing I do. Don't try to stop me Jeff, I owe it to Jenny!'

From his position at the bottom of the stairs, Tom saw the undercover officer suddenly lunge forward and try to grab the pistol from Angela's hand.

He was a fraction too slow.

Angela Hincks had anticipated his move and managed to step back just out of reach.

She was now pointing the handgun directly at the face of the undercover cop.

Tom shouted, 'Armed Police! Drop your weapon now!'

Without averting her gaze from Jeff's brown eyes, Angela whispered, 'Why did you make me do this Jeff?'

From below, Tom never heard the whispered comment, but he saw Angela Hincks extend her arm a fraction, he saw her knuckles whiten as she gripped the pistol a little tighter.

Tom had to make an instant decision. Was this woman mad enough to pull the trigger? Had he got to fire his weapon to prevent her killing a police officer?

He felt the minimal recoil of the Mp5 kick into his shoulder as he fired twice.

He had made his decision.

The two bullets slammed into Angela Hincks, Tom watched as she seemed to pirouette in slow motion, before tumbling head over heels down the marble staircase, finally coming to a stop on her back, at Matt's feet.

Tom looked over and could see the large exit wound in her chest and the massive blood loss gushing from the wound. One of the two bullets had smashed through her chest directly into her heart, tearing it apart.

Her lifeless eyes were now gazing straight up towards the ornate chandelier.

Angela Hincks was dead.

Suddenly, there was an anguished cry from the top of the stairs, 'Bastard! What have you done? She was giving me her gun, you stupid fuck! She was giving up!'

Tom did not respond, he just stared at the lifeless body of Angela Hincks.

Matt remained in control, he shouted, 'Stand still! I want to see your hands. Get your hands where I can see them. Now!'

His Heckler and Koch Mp5 was aimed directly at the undercover officer's chest.

The man spread his arms wide and shouted back, 'I'm job too, my name's Dc Wicks. My gun was never loaded. It's on the floor in front of me. I'm unarmed. Why did you shoot her? She was giving up!'

Tom had now recovered and was concentrating fully again, he remained kneeling in the aim position covering the undercover officer, as Matt moved slowly up the stairs towards him.

Matt placed Dc Wicks in plasticuffs, then walked him back down the stairs.

As he reached the foot of the stairs and walked past the lifeless body of his lover, Jeff Wicks suddenly screamed, 'Bastard!' and aimed a kick at Tom, striking him on the thigh. Instantly, Matt pulled the undercover detective backwards, so he couldn't lash out further at his colleague.

The room was suddenly filled with a bright light as the large chandelier was switched on.

A gravelly voice shouted, 'Just what the fuck do you think you're doing officer?'

Sgt Graham Turner had arrived in the hallway just in time to witness the kick and the unexpected reaction of the undercover officer.

Dc Wicks shouted back, 'That cretin murdered her! She was giving up. She was just about to hand me her gun when he opened fire and killed her!'

Turner answered firmly, 'Now isn't the time or place for some half arsed debrief, detective!'

He turned to Pc Eddie Keane and said, 'Get him out of here.'

Another booming voice filled the hallway from the top of the stairs, 'Have you got the bastards, Sergeant?'

Graham Turner looked up to the top of the stairs and saw Sir Jarvis Soames wearing the same bright red silk dressing gown, he was flanked by Jack Rimmer and Luke Goddard, the two officers who had been guarding his bedroom door.

With a note of real irritation in his voice, Graham barked an order to Jack and Luke, 'Will you dozy pair get switched on and get that fucking civilian out of my crime scene and back to his fucking bedroom. NOW!'

Graham turned to Tom and Matt, 'Are you two okay? You both know the score and what's got to happen next. The CID will be here shortly to start the investigation into the shooting. Hand them your weapons. Let them clear them and make them safe. Tell them how many rounds are in and what state the weapon is. If you've already re-applied the safety then leave it where it is. Just tell them okay?'

Both men nodded.

Graham continued, 'Co-operate with them fully. They will want swabs from your hands and will take possession of all your equipment, they will probably want to take your clothes as well, just co-operate and let them do their job. Chief Inspector Chambers and I will be with you every step of the way. Any questions?'

Matt asked, 'What about the three outside?'

'They're all dead, Matt.'

'Bloody hell', whispered Matt.

'Steve and Tony have detained the driver, so at least the CID will be able to get a story of the activists plans from her as well as the undercover detective. Have you got any other questions before the CID get here?'

Matt and Tom shook their heads.

They had trained hard for this eventuality, but the act of actually engaging with a threat and shooting someone dead had still come as a huge shock to both men, especially Matt, who had never fired a weapon at a person before. Both men had followed their training to the letter and were convinced they had acted correctly when responding to the threat posed. They were aware of the procedure following a shooting, but it still came as a shock to realise they would now be treated as murder suspects until the CID had completed their enquiries.

Both men also knew that the Independent Police Complaints Commission would be all over the enquiry like a rash. Whatever happened now, however the CID enquiry went, they would both face a lengthy time suspended from duty.

CHAPTER 18

11.00pm 6th December 1987
Puerto Del Carmen, Lanzarote

Micky Stone was buzzing.

He had arrived in Lanzarote that afternoon. The sun had been shining, the sky was blue and he could hear the ocean.

Life was good.

He had strolled through passport control and got a taxi from Arrecife Airport to his villa in the hills behind Puerto Calero at La Asomada.

He only ever carried the bare minimum hand luggage, as he had wardrobes full of stylish clothes and a safe full of pesetas at his villa.

His white walled villa was located on the very outskirts of the tiny village of La Asomada. The village consisted of a row of small houses inhabited by locals and a sprinkling of luxury villas owned by foreigners.

The villa afforded spectacular views inland towards the hills and also out over the cobalt blue Atlantic Ocean.

Stone had purchased the property two years before, just as the town of Puerto Del Carmen was transforming into a lively tourist destination. He'd spent a small fortune renovating it and supplying it with all mod cons.

It was his bolthole to the sun, he loved the place.

As always, the first thing he had done after his arrival, was to make a quick check on the property. He always liked to make sure that everything was just as he'd left it after his last visit in October.

Stone paid an elderly couple from the village to check the property every day.

Mariana would clean the villa and ensure there was always fresh fruit, food and drink in the fridge. It was extravagant, but for the price of a few pesetas every month it meant that the villa was always ready for him to arrive whenever the fancy took him. Mariana's husband Mateo, maintained the grounds and the swimming pool.

After making his inspection, Stone had taken a cold beer from the fridge and walked out onto the balcony that looked out towards the Atlantic Ocean, the small town of Puerto Calero stretched down to the coast below.

He'd finished his beer and walked back into the villa, stripping off his sweaty clothes as he walked through to the shower room. The marble tiles had felt cool against the soles of his sweaty feet. He'd walked into the vast wet room that housed the power shower and took a long leisurely shower to wash away the sweat and the lethargy caused by sitting on the cramped package flight from Manchester Airport.

He'd towelled himself down and walked into the master bedroom, where he flung open the fitted wardrobe doors and took a pair of beige, lightweight Chinos and a white cotton shirt off the hangers.

He'd quickly got dressed, grabbed a bundle of five hundred Pesetas from the safe, slipped on a pair of brown, suede Abarca espadrilles before walking outside to the double garage.

After opening the garage doors he'd quickly removed the tarpaulin that covered the cream coloured Jeep Wrangler soft top. The keys were still under the sun visor.

A huge grin had spread across his face as the engine kicked into life first time. He had purchased the brand-new vehicle when he was last on the island, having got sick of waiting for taxis. It was his latest toy and he couldn't wait to take it for a drive. He'd left it with a full tank, so he had quickly driven out of the garage and through the metal gates into the village of La Asomada. His first stop had been Mariana and Mateo's decrepit house in the village. He'd jumped out of the Jeep, leaving the engine running before banging on the front door of the elderly couple's house.

Eventually the old lady had opened the front door. He'd told her that he was back and that she wouldn't be needed at the villa for a week. He'd handed her a fistful of Pesetas before jumping back into the Jeep.

Mariana had smiled broadly and waved as Stone accelerated away, heading for the coast and the town of Puerto Del Carmen.

Stone glanced at his Rolex watch, it was now almost eleven o'clock at night. He had been strolling around the town since six o clock that evening. He had eaten at a restaurant that overlooked the Playa Grande beach. He had dined on langoustine and lobster, washed down with a delicious, cold white wine.

After eating he had flitted from bar to bar just enjoying the vibe.

Now as it neared eleven o'clock, the long day of travelling was starting to catch up with him. He was totally chilled now, walking along the Avenue de las Playas next to the Playa Grande beach, listening to the surf wash over the sand.

He felt so mellow, he decided to have one more drink before heading back to his Jeep.

He walked into the next bar he came to.

The Hideaway Bar was very small and poorly lit. The latest hit song from Belinda Carlisle, "Heaven is a place on Earth" was belting out through the poor-quality sound system.

As he walked up to the glass topped bar, he mumbled to himself, 'Fuck me Belinda, this isn't my idea of heaven, love.'

He sat down on one of the four empty bar stools and looked around him. Now that his eyes had adjusted to the poor light in the dingy bar, he could see that he was the only punter.

Once again, he spoke out loud, 'Why doesn't that surprise me? What a frigging dump!'

Stone was just about to get up and leave, when the greasy, unkempt barman approached him, 'What can I get you Senor?'

Stone decide to stay and have that one last drink. He pointed at the optics behind the bar and said, 'Jameson, Irish Whiskey. Large. Por favour!'

The barman nodded and grunted, 'Si, Senor.'

Seconds later he placed a large tumbler, three quarters full of whiskey in front of Stone.

For the first time since he'd walked into The Hideaway Bar, Stone grinned and said, 'Fuck me Pedro! Large really does mean large over here mate!'

The barman ignored his comment and walked into the back room.

Ten minutes later and the whiskey was going down so well, that Stone was trying to decide whether to have another. He was just about to ask for the bill and go when another punter walked in.

The woman was very tall, very slim with long tanned legs and large ample breasts that were obviously unrestrained by a bra. She had long blonde hair, worn like the actress, Farrah Fawcett and a nice white smile. She wore a white cotton mini dress that fitted where it touched, gold coloured stiletto shoes that matched the copious amounts of gold jewellery she was wearing.

Probably in her late thirties, she had the look of a confident woman who knew a thing or two about life. She was also already quite tipsy.

The woman sat down on the bar stool beside Stone, placing her hands on top of the bar.

He glanced down and saw a gold wedding band on her left ring finger.

Stone was completely taken with the woman and said, 'Can I get you a drink luv?'

'Bacardi and Coke would be nice dahlin!' she said in a broad cockney accent.

Seeing that he had a second client, the barman walked over with a lecherous grin on his face and said to the woman, 'What can I get you, Senora?'

Stone growled, 'She'll have a Bacardi and Coke, large. I'll have another Jameson, large.'

The order was given in such a way that the barman instantly knew that once he'd served the drinks he could fuck right off.

The woman took a sip of the Bacardi and Coke and said, 'Thanks dahlin! I bloody well needed that. I'm Janice by the way.'

Stone smiled and said, 'Hello Janice, my name's Micky. On your own tonight then?'

'I bloody well am now, I'm over here on a Hen Party, but the girls have all cracked off with muppets in a sleazy bar down the road. I can't be arsed with all that malarkey, besides, there was no one in there as handsome as you dahlin.'

Again, Stone smiled and raised his glass. Janice raised her glass, they clinked them together and Stone said, 'Here's to happy holidays!'

Janice laughed and said, 'I'll drink to that dahlin!'

Stone bought a couple more rounds as he and Janice got to know each other better. There was obviously a mutual attraction and he and Janice engaged in some heavy flirting.

The new George Michael song was belting out and Stone finally gave up trying to be heard above the music. He leaned in close to Janice and said, 'Why don't we go back to my villa and have a few drinks up there, at least we'll be able to hear ourselves think.'

Janice also leaned in and said breathily in Stone's ear, 'I'd like that Micky, is it far?'

'Ten minutes. I've got a car outside.'

She giggled and said, 'Are you okay to drive sweetheart?'

He grinned held out a wad of notes and said, 'It's fine, if I get pulled over, I'll just bung the Guardia a couple of hundred pesetas. Nobody gives a fuck about drink drive over here luv.'

Her eyes widened when she saw all the cash and she said. 'Come on dahlin, let's get out of this dump.'

Stone put enough notes on the bar to cover the drinks, stood up and said, 'Okay luv.'

'What's all this luv business, where you from dahlin?'

'I'm a born and bred scouser who loves cockney women.'

'Looks like we're going to be in for a nice night then dahlin! You can be my long-haired lover from Liverpool, if you play your cards right', she winked and giggled at her own joke.

They both staggered out of the bar, Janice wobbled on her stiletto's when she took her first breath of the cool night air. Stone grabbed her round the waist and said, 'Come on Janice, the car's just down here.'

CHAPTER 19

3.00am 7th December 1987
La Asomada, Lanzarote

Micky Stone had a problem.

A big problem.

He sat on the edge of the king size bed in the master bedroom and looked down at Janice on the floor. The vibrant, sexy woman he had picked up in the bar was now very still and very cold, her staring eyes were wide open and unblinking, a distinctive blue tinge around her lips.

She was naked, her stiletto shoes and white dress were lying on the floor near the door to the bedroom where she had stripped off the night before.

As he looked at the crumpled dress, thoughts, memories began flooding back into Micky's head.

When they had arrived back at the villa everything had been fine. They both consumed more alcohol, began kissing and heavy petting until inevitably they ended up naked together in the master bedroom.

Micky Stone was a charmer.

He was a man who was never short of female admirers. Women constantly threw themselves at the handsome, muscular millionaire. As soon as they realised what the suave Liverpudlian was really like they retreated just as quickly.

Stone was a complete psychopath, he found it impossible to show any real emotion. His many girlfriends soon found out that lovemaking for Micky Stone meant hard, rough sex. The more brutal, the better he liked it. He had escaped complaints of rape to the police by a mixture of threats and bribes. The majority of the women he had sexually assaulted were dissuaded from contacting the police by his menacing presence. The harder faced ones were bought off with lump sums of untraceable cash.

A gold necklace around Janice's neck suddenly glinted in the glow of the bedside lamp and Stone recalled it shining when she had stood naked in front of him. The first time they had made love was fast and furious. The second time, Janice had protested that she was tired and wanted to go to sleep.

Stone had ignored her pleas and had taken her forcefully, pinning her face down onto the bed. As soon as he finished, he rolled off and Janice suddenly transformed into a wildcat. She was screaming abuse at him, calling him a dirty rapist. Stone had just grinned at her and slapped her hard across the face, becoming more and more aroused as she tried to fight him.

He threw her on her back and raped her again, violently. The slaps turned to punches. When he finally stopped, Janice got up off the bed and started to get dressed.

As she fumbled for her clothes in the dark, she had told Stone that she was going to the Guardia Civil and that he wasn't going to get away with what he had done.

Stone had leapt off the bed and grabbed at her, she pushed him away and raked her long fingernails across his face, drawing blood. He had instantly lashed out, his right fist landing a heavy blow on her windpipe.

Looking down at her body now he could see the livid, purple bruise that covered her smashed windpipe.

Unable to breathe, Janice had suffocated on the marble floor of Stone's villa.

Realising that Janice was dead, Stone said aloud, 'For fucks sake!'

He stood up, stepped over her body and started to get dressed.

His true psychopath nature had kicked in, he knew what he had to do.

It was still dark outside.

He needed to get rid of this inconvenience, before people started going about their business.

Carefully, he removed all of her jewellery and placed it in a small ornamental box on the bedside cabinet. He then dressed her and put on her stiletto shoes.

There was no blood, so he had no cleaning up to do.

He just needed something to wrap her in so he could carry her out to his Jeep.

There was a six foot by eight-foot Moroccan rug in the hallway, that would do the job.

Stone placed Janice onto the rug, then rolled her up in it before carrying it to the Jeep outside. He threw her body into the back and started the engine. He already knew exactly where he was going to take her.

After a fifteen-minute drive he stopped the Jeep at the side of the road.

He was deep inside the Timanfeya National Park, an area of volcanic wasteland that lies towards the north west of Lanzarote.

He had driven north from El Golfo, until he could hear the sound of the ocean crashing against the rocks a short distance away. This was the place where volcanic lava had met the ocean millions of years ago. There was a twenty-foot sheer drop from the sharp jagged rocks down to the ocean. The waves constantly pounded the rugged shoreline sending clouds of salty spray high into the air.

Stone unrolled the rug and picked up Janice's lifeless body. He carried her over his shoulder in a fireman's lift to the very edge of the cliff top.

He took one final glance around, then hurled the dead woman down into the sea.

He watched intently as the incoming waves picked up the body before smashing it into the sharp, unforgiving, black rocks. He continued to watch as this process was repeated a few times before grinning and walking away.

Even if her body was later found, he knew that it would be in such a state the authorities would never be able to determine exactly how she had died.

Her death would be written off as just another drunken tourist falling into the sea after drinking too much.

He rolled up the rug, threw it into the back of the Jeep and began the drive back to his villa, nonchalantly whistling as though he had just taken out the garbage.

CHAPTER 20

2.00pm 7th December 1987
Liverpool, Merseyside

Chief Inspector Noel Prime drove his car steadily through the afternoon traffic. It was his day off and the last thing he wanted to be doing was driving along the A565 from Liverpool, along the coast to Southport.

Finally, he got clear of the heavier traffic and started to make better progress. The sun was already low in the sky and was making driving very arduous. He found himself constantly squinting against the glare.

Even though it was mid-afternoon, Prime still felt nauseous.

Ever since he had first received the news about the murder of Detective Sergeant Mayhew during the armed robbery, he had felt this way.

Whenever he thought about that tragic event, he felt terrible and had been physically sick on countless occasions.

It was one thing taking a backhander from criminals to provide information, but it was a whole different level to be knowingly involved in something that had led to the cold-blooded murder of a fellow police officer.

Prime knew he was an accessory in what had effectively been the execution of Brian Mayhew, a man he had previously worked alongside.

Just the thought of it was enough for Prime to slow his vehicle, looking for somewhere to pull off the road.

He saw a layby approaching, indicated and pulled in, finally stopping the car well away from any other parked vehicles.

As soon as his Ford Granada came to a stop, he opened the door, leaned out and retched violently. On this occasion the spasms in his stomach only brought up an acidic bile.

After two minutes the retching stopped and he sat up straight again. He reached into the glove compartment and took out the bottle of Evian water he kept in there.

He took a mouthful of the cool water, rinsed his mouth and spat it out on the roadside. He then took small sips to try and get rid of the acid taste that was still prevalent in his mouth.

Noel Prime closed the car door, sat back and reflected on how he had come to be in this terrible predicament.

His thoughts were whirling around in his head, but every time they kept bringing him back to the same conclusion.

There was one very simple reason he was in this predicament.

Women.

It had been his overwhelming lust towards the fairer sex that had caused his downfall. Even as a young uniformed bobby and then a detective in Croxteth he had always had an eye for the ladies, the younger the better as far as he was concerned.

It had been his addiction to women that had caused that first fateful meeting with the gangster Gary Mercer.

In 1984, when they first met, Gary Mercer was a Jack the Lad character who was always on the cusp of criminality. He had never been arrested, but he lived a lavish lifestyle that appeared to be way above his means. All of his associates were criminals. These were the circles he frequented. He was a charismatic, good looking man, always surrounded by beautiful women.

On that night, three years ago, when their paths had first crossed, Prime was out partying in one of the many night clubs in Liverpool. He'd been out celebrating his recent promotion to Chief Inspector with a few colleagues. When the colleagues left to go home, Prime remained at the night club. He was already the worse for drink, when he was approached by Gary Mercer.

The two men had a couple of drinks together, Mercer had insisted on buying. Prime had been impressed by the beautiful women who were in the company of his new friend.

When Mercer invited Prime back to his house to continue the party, it was the four beautiful women in tow that had made his mind up. Even though he had a beautiful wife and teenage kids at home, he couldn't resist the temptation and quickly accepted the invitation.

With the benefit of hindsight, Prime now realised that this had all been arranged and set up by Mercer. The gangster had known full well that Noel Prime was a high-ranking police officer and had decided to try and set him up in order to extort information from him.

Now, as he sat in his car, feeling sick, Prime felt his shoulders sag as he recalled the events of that night, three years ago. The memories were fresh and vivid, as though it had happened only yesterday.

That night, all Prime had been interested in was the young blonde, who looked about seventeen but who had the longest legs he'd ever seen. Best of all, she couldn't keep her hands off him.

As soon as they arrived at Mercer's house the beautiful blonde had immediately draped herself all over a very flattered Noel Prime. In less than ten minutes the two of them were alone in one of the bedrooms. The young girl amazed Prime with the depraved sexual acts she was prepared to do with him.

Noel Prime had loved every second of it and was totally oblivious to the fact that every one of those seconds was being recorded. A video camera, hidden in the wardrobe had made a full colour recording of every different sexual position the young girl and the middle-aged police officer had tried.

After an hour with the girl, Prime had been exhausted. He got dressed and returned to the party downstairs.

Instead of finding a party in full swing all he found was Gary Mercer and two other men who were both built like brick shit houses.

Prime knew immediately what had happened. When Mercer had told him coldly that from now on, he would be providing information whenever he wanted it, Prime had got angry and refused. He had wrongly assumed that it would be his word against Mercer and that when it came down to it, he would be the one who was believed, not this scouse wide boy.

Having made his position known to Mercer, Prime had stormed out of the house thinking that would be the end of it.

Two days later a padded envelope addressed to Chief Inspector Noel Prime had been hand delivered to him at the police station where he worked. He took the envelope into his office and opened it in private. Inside was a video tape, another envelope and a typed letter instructing him to view the VHS video first and then open the envelope, then finally he was to call the telephone number at the bottom of the letter.

Chillingly, at the top of the typewritten note in large bold type were the words:

VIEW THIS VIDEO ALONE

Now, as he sat in his car in a layby on the road to Southport, Noel Prime shuddered at the memory of sitting alone at home watching the video recording of him performing every sex act imaginable with the young blonde girl. He had instantly recognised the bedroom he'd shared with the girl at Mercer's house.

If he thought the content of the video was bad, it was nothing like the shock he got when he opened the envelope. Inside the envelope were several photographs of the same blonde girl. These photographs showed her in a school uniform, there was no trace of the garish make up she was wearing at the club. Prime recognised the uniform; the blonde girl was walking into the gates of the same comprehensive school that his own teenage daughter went to.

He had sat in total shock for over an hour before he finally plucked up the courage to call the telephone number on the typewritten note.

Gary Mercer had answered the telephone on the third ring.

He had mockingly set out the ground rules to their business arrangement.

Prime would provide information to Mercer as and when it was requested, with no questions asked. Mercer told Prime not to think of it as blackmail, he was willing to pay handsomely for all the information he received.

As the months turned into years, Prime had become accustomed to the brown envelopes stuffed with cash and had almost forgotten about the video.

Until the day Brian Mayhew had been murdered, Prime had been quite happy to accept the ill-gotten gains from Mercer. Even before the detective sergeant had been gunned down, Prime was fully aware that the information he was providing was being used by a ruthless armed gang responsible for numerous offences of robbery across the city of Liverpool.

Now, as he sat in his car, he knew he had to try and think of a way to get out of his toxic arrangement with Mercer. There was no way he could continue to provide information to the men responsible for the murder of his colleague. No amount of threats or promises of cash could excuse that betrayal any longer.

Prime started his car and continued to drive slowly along the coast road. He only had fifteen minutes to get to the meeting with Mercer in Southport.

Prime was dawdling, because he was dreading the meeting with Mercer for three reasons; firstly, he was dreading telling Mercer their business arrangement had to stop, whatever the consequences, and that he was no longer prepared to pass on information either for payment or any other reason.

Secondly, he had to tell Mercer that a man by the name of Stevie Key had died. Prime wasn't a hundred percent sure but he believed that Key was the robbery gang's getaway driver.

Stevie Key had been killed instantly, when his Audi had been involved in a devastating crash on the motorway two days earlier.

The third and final reason was the fact that Noel Prime was physically scared of Gary Mercer. There was something about the gangster's cold, aggressive demeanour that terrified him.

Fifteen minutes later, Prime drove his Ford Granada into the car park next to the boating lake at Victoria Park in Southport. He began to physically shake involuntarily, when he saw Mercer's black, Mercedes SLK parked in the corner of the car park.

Prime tried to compose himself and took deep breaths. Gradually the shaking subsided.

Having parked up, he got out of his car and walked across the car park to the Mercedes.

He opened the passenger door and got in.

Without looking at Prime, Mercer growled in his soft scouse accent, 'Good of you to join me Mr Prime, I was beginning to think you weren't coming.'

Prime blustered, 'Well I'm here now, but I haven't got long. It's my wife's yoga class this afternoon and I need to get back home for the dog.'

Mercer allowed a faint smile to cross his lips before saying, 'Look Prime, I really don't give a fuck about your domestic life. I just wanted you to know that in light of the little accident that happened on the last job, I've decided to let the dust settle for a couple of weeks. That means you won't be getting any cash from me for a while, okay?'

Prime was raging inside.

Had Mercer really just described the cold-blooded murder of his colleague as a "little accident"?

In a whining, subservient voice Prime said, 'Listen Gary, I really can't do this anymore. This arrangement of ours has got to stop. I simply can't afford to give you any more information after what's just happened, I'm really sorry.'

Mercer shook his head slowly.

He reached out and put his left hand on Prime's shoulder and said softly, 'Don't worry Noel, don't worry.'

In a flash he grabbed a handful of Prime's hair and smashed his face forward and down on to the walnut dashboard. It was done so quickly that Prime didn't even have the time to put his hands on the dashboard.

Prime's face hit the dashboard hard, before it was jerked backwards again.

He could feel blood trickling down from his smashed nose and pain at the back of his head where Mercer still tightly gripped a handful of his hair.

Mercer leaned over and said menacingly, 'No Chief Inspector Prime, what you meant to say, was that you can't afford NOT to pass information on to me. Do you think all I'm talking about is that stupid video of you and that little tart all those years ago? If you don't play ball sunshine, not only will I bring you down career wise, but I'll happily make your wife and kids suffer in ways you haven't even dreamed of, not even in your worst nightmares. Do we understand each other, Chief Inspector?'

Prime was shocked and nodded furiously, 'Yes Gary, I'm sorry. I'm sorry okay. I'll do whatever you say, don't hurt my wife and kids, please.'

Mercer looked coldly at Prime, released his grip on his hair and with real contempt in his voice he said, 'That's better, now we understand each other. Now get the fuck out of my car. You're bleeding on the leather, you worthless piece of shit! I'll be in touch when I need something from you! Get out, Prime.'

Prime half fell out of the car, he regained his feet, turned and said groggily to Mercer, 'Was Stevie Key your driver?'

Mercer thought for a second before saying, 'Maybe. Why did you say was, not is?'

'Stevie Key was killed trying to outrun the police two days ago. The car he was driving crashed and burst into flames, he was killed outright, that's all.'

Without batting an eye lid, Mercer shook his head and said, 'No. I think I know who you mean, but he wasn't our driver. Now fuck off! I've got another meeting to get to back in Liverpool.'

Prime scuttled off back towards his own car, desperately trying to stop his nose from bleeding with a handkerchief.

He got back in his car and watched as Mercer drove out of the car park.

For some reason that he didn't really understand himself, Prime decided to follow him. Gary Mercer had long since moved from the house where the entrapment had taken place and Prime suddenly felt a real need to know where the gangster was living now.

As he followed Mercer at a discreet distance, Prime was in a state of total flux. He had no idea what he was going to do; he just knew that finding out where Mercer was living currently, would be necessary to the germ of a plan that was forming in his mind.

After a twenty-minute drive they had reached the Sefton Park area of Liverpool. Initially, it had been easy for Prime to follow Mercer in the heavy traffic of the city. The light was fading fast as Prime now followed Mercer into the well to do suburb. He was having to drop further and further back as he followed Mercer into Sefton Park, he was very relieved to finally see the left-hand indicator of the Mercedes come on.

He slowed his Granada and watched as the black Mercedes was driven onto the driveway of a large, detached bungalow.

Prime parked his car thirty yards from the bungalow and quickly wrote down the address; 63, Greenbank Drive, Sefton Park.

He was just about to drive away when he saw a familiar looking, gun metal grey, Porsche 911 pull onto the driveway of the same bungalow.

Prime was transfixed and watched the petite, red haired woman, as she got out of the sports car. Carrying a small, white holdall and dressed in a powder blue track suit, she walked quickly towards the front door. As she approached the door it was opened from inside and Mercer stepped outside. He smiled and embraced the woman, before kissing her passionately on the mouth.

Noel Prime was in a state of shock.

It couldn't be his wife, could it?

He scolded himself for being so ridiculous. There were hundreds of Porsche 911's in the city and thousands of red-haired women. She did look a little like Glenys, but it couldn't have been her, she was over in Wavertree at her yoga class.

Something inside Noel Prime was driving him to make sure.

He locked his car door, walked across the tree lined road and up the secluded driveway of the bungalow. It was getting dark now and the street lights hadn't yet come on. Prime kept to the shadows as he approached the Porsche on the driveway.

When he read the registration plate fixed to the back of the Porsche, it felt like somebody had smashed him in the face with a sledge hammer

G A P 1 1

Glenys Avril Prime.

He had purchased the personalised plate at the same time he had bought her the car, on her fortieth birthday last year.

Not really understanding why, or what he intended to do, Prime now found himself walking slowly towards the bungalow.

Stealthily, he approached the large bay window at the front of the property. There was a soft light emanating from that room and the curtains hadn't yet been drawn. Keeping low, Prime crept forward to the window ensuring he wasn't seen from within.

He peered in through the window and felt his legs buckle at the sight that confronted him.

Mercer and his wife were now both totally naked.

He was lying on his back on a large, white sheepskin rug in front of the coal effect, gas fire that was providing the soft light. Glenys was sitting astride Mercer with her back to the window. She was moving rhythmically up and down as they slowly made love.

Prime recoiled away from the window and sank to his knees on the flower bed. He could feel his eyes stinging as tears began to trickle down his face.

He was in a state of shock and thought to himself, how could she betray me like this?

Any thoughts of his own infidelity that had lured him into the clutches of Mercer in the first place had instantly been dismissed from his mind.

Feeling dizzy and nauseous, Prime got to his feet and staggered back across the road to his car. He got in and sat there in the darkness, still in a state of total shock at what he had witnessed.

Thoughts were now racing through his mind.

Was this the reason for the change he had noticed in her?

Had she been coming here ever since she first told him she was going to yoga class?

Instead of yoga, had she been having sex with Mercer?

In that single illuminating moment when he finally recognised the full extent of his wife's betrayal, Prime decided to act.

He started his car and drove around aimlessly, until finally he found what he had been looking for. The familiar sight of a red, public telephone box by the side of the road. He stopped the car, got out and walked over to the kiosk.

He lifted the receiver, then placed his bloodstained handkerchief over the mouthpiece, before dialling the number of the Murder Incident Room, that had been set up following the fatal shooting of Detective Sergeant Mayhew.

A young, female voice answered the call, 'Murder Incident Room, Detective Forbes. How can I help you?'

Gravelling his voice and speaking with a broad scouse accent, Prime said, 'The man you should be looking at for the murder of that copper is Gary Mercer. Did you get that? Gary Mercer.'

Prime then gave the detective the address where they could find Gary Mercer before refusing any of his own details.

When the young detective pressed him for his name, Prime slammed the phone down.

He got back in his car and drove slowly back to his home on Beauclair Drive, Wavertree.

He parked his car in the garage and walked into the house. He poured himself a large scotch and sat alone in the dark, pondering what to do about his cheating bitch of a wife.

CHAPTER 21

4.00pm 7ᵗʰ December 1987
La Asomada, Lanzarote

Micky Stone was just about to call for a taxi to take him from his villa to Arrecife airport when the telephone started to ring.

Feeling irritable he snatched up the phone, 'What!'

'Micky it's Gadge. Are you okay mate? You sound pissed off?'

'I'm on my way to the airport, I've had to cut short my trip this time, had a spot of bother with a cockney tart. Nothing I couldn't handle, but I think it's best if I come home for a bit. You know how it is mate.'

'What time's your flight?'

'I'll be landing in Manchester around ten o'clock tonight, why?'

'I've got some bad news mate. Stevie's dead. He crashed his motor when he left the scrapyard the other night. The funeral's tomorrow morning at eleven o'clock. Are you going to show up?'

Micky exclaimed, 'Fuck me!', before being quiet for a couple of minutes.

Finally, he said, 'Yeah, I'll be there Gadge. Which cemetery is it?'

'It's at the Toxteth Park Cemetery. You know, the one off the A562, over at Wavertree. It's a cremation, the service is due to begin at eleven. I've got to go now Micky, I've got some company here of my own, if you know what I mean?'

'Okay Gadge, good lad, get stuck in mate. I'll see you tomorrow. Thanks for letting me know about Stevie. He was a tosser, but he was a good lad!'

'I know mate, talk to you tomorrow.'

Micky ended the call and then dialled for a taxi.

The taxi would be ten minutes, so he got another cold beer from the fridge and walked out onto the balcony to take one last look at the sea.

He took a swig of the cold beer and grinned as he stared out across the ocean. He couldn't help wondering where Janice was?

CHAPTER 22

4.00pm 7th December 1987
Force Headquarters, Nottinghamshire

It had been over forty-eight hours since the attempted kidnap of Sir Jarvis Soames by Angela Hincks and her animal rights activists.

Hincks, two men and a woman had all been shot dead by Tom Naylor and Matt Jarvis, after they themselves had come under fire. The two Special Ops men had both reacted with deadly force and were now suspended pending an enquiry into the shootings by the Independent Police Complaints Commission.

Both men had made full and comprehensive statements to the CID detectives who were undertaking the preliminary enquiries into the fatal shootings.

Pending a full enquiry and the result of any IPCC findings into the incident, they would both remain on light duties at Nottinghamshire Police Headquarters where there was no chance of any interaction between themselves and the general public.

Effectively, they were suspended from normal duties until the IPCC confirmed there was no criminal case to answer and that given all the circumstances, the fatal shootings of the four animal rights activists had been justifiable.

Along with the rest of C Section, Tom and Matt had been called into the large briefing room at The Huts for this afternoon's full de-briefing on the Farnsfield operation.

As the men grabbed mugs of coffee or tea, they were all chatting about the de-briefing. Rumour had it that the Head of the CID was coming over to speak to the men personally.

Sure enough, five minutes later Chief Inspector Chambers entered the briefing room followed by Detective Chief Superintendent Neil Wilkinson.

Chief Inspector Chambers gestured for the men to sit back down.

It was the Detective Chief Superintendent who spoke first, 'Gentlemen, prior to your operational de-brief this morning, I want to show you a Crime Bulletin that was received from Merseyside Police this morning in respect of the murder of Detective Sergeant Brian Mayhew, during the cash in transit robbery at a Tesco store in Merseyside on the 21st of November. No doubt you will have seen and heard a lot of speculation and rumour surrounding this case. The national press and the media generally, are pushing out story after story about this horrendous crime. None of this speculation is helping the enquiry and I would urge you to totally disregard everything you've read or heard thus far in respect of this murder. Our colleagues in Liverpool have put together a comprehensive presentation marked for Police Eyes only, in the hope that somewhere in the UK there's a police officer who'll recognise someone or something that will assist them and enable them to take this investigation forward.'

He paused to let his message sink in before continuing, 'Gents, the bottom line is this; these bastards executed one of our colleagues in cold blood when he was already on the ground wounded and helpless. They could have made their getaway unhindered, but instead they chose to deliberately shoot dead an unarmed man. They need catching and fast.'

Jim Chambers now spoke, 'The enquiry team in Merseyside have sent out everything they have, including testament from eye witnesses along with good quality CCTV of the shooting itself. The eye witnesses have all been recorded on video reading accounts from their own witness statements, that way nothing has been lost in translation. They've been able to say it, exactly how they heard it. I'm telling you all now, the video of the shooting itself is extremely harrowing. Have you any questions before I play the video?'

The room remained silent, the men of C Section sat staring at the television screen with grim expressions set on their faces.

Jim Chambers stepped forward and pressed the Play button on the video recorder.

The first part of the video showed the crystal-clear images of the cold-blooded murder of the unarmed, off duty officer in graphic detail. The room was as silent as the grave as the enormity of what they were watching hit home to the assembled officers.

Detective Chief Superintendent Wilkinson gave a narrative as the film played out, 'Note how DS Mayhew had already been incapacitated by one of the armed robbers before the second one took it upon himself to fire the fatal shot. Notice also that the first robber has a very distinctive limp on his right leg, you can see how he struggles to move quickly around the scene. The detectives in Merseyside have spoken to an orthopaedic consultant surgeon, but he was unable to determine whether this limp is the result of a recent injury to his right leg or if it's a more permanent condition.'

Immediately after the video of the shooting, came the film of the eye witnesses reading their own statements. There were four witnesses in all, all were visibly upset as they read aloud their statements.

When it came to the turn of the fourth and final witness, a middle-aged woman with a shrill, screeching scouse accent, something she said made Tom stiffen in his seat. The hairs on the nape of his neck stood up and he felt a shiver run through him.

In her high-pitched sing song tone the woman was describing a comment made by the first robber after he'd shot Detective Sergeant Mayhew in the legs.

She stared directly into the camera filming her and shrilled, 'And then he turned to that poor man on the ground and said, "How do you like those apples hero? Move again and I'll put the next one in your head. Got it?"

I could see the poor man trying to get something out of his pocket, and I could see that he was trying to say something but I couldn't catch what he was saying. Then the other man fired his gun. It was just awful.'

At that point the woman started to break down in tears, her shock at what she had witnessed still very evident.

Tom had heard and seen enough.

The comment about apples, the pronounced limp on the right leg, the obvious connection to Liverpool, the general stature and height of the first shooter.

Was this cold-blooded armed robber, the same man he had fought his way across the Falkland Islands with? The same man who had effectively saved his life?

The video came to a stop and Jim Chambers stepped forward and retrieved the cassette tape.

The senior detective once again addressed the men, 'If there's anything that springs to mind having watched that, however tenuous you think it might be, please speak up. Like I said before, these bastards need catching fast before somebody else is killed or seriously injured. Thank you, gents.'

Jim Chambers announced there would be a ten-minute break before the de-brief on the Hincks shootings started. The Chief Inspector and the senior detective then left the briefing room and headed back to Jim Chambers' office.

As soon as the senior officers left the room the men began to discuss in animated terms what they had just seen and heard.

Tom slipped away from the general discussion and out of the briefing room. He quietly tapped on Jim Chambers office door.

'Come in', shouted Chambers.

Tom entered the room and was pleased to see that the senior detective was still with his Chief Inspector.

Jim Chambers said, 'Close the door Tom. What is it?'

'It's the bulletin boss. This is going to sound crazy, but I think I know the identity of the first armed robber. The man who fired the first shot at the sergeant.'

Neil Wilkinson was now fully attentive and said, 'Sorry officer, I didn't catch your name?'

'It's Pc Tom Naylor sir. I think I may have served with him in the Parachute Regiment, we fought in the Falklands together, that's where he got that limp. The expression he used about apples, it all fits sir. I think it's a man called Mercer. Gary Mercer.'

Tom realised he was waffling and was half relieved when Wilkinson held up his hand to stop him talking.

The seasoned detective smiled and said, 'Whoa! Take your time man. Start from the beginning. I want to know chapter and verse everything you can tell me about Gary Mercer.'

Jim Chambers said, 'Sit down Tom, just tell us what you know, okay?'

Tom sat down and began to recount how he'd first met Mercer, their service together in the Parachute Regiment, what had happened in the Falklands, how Mercer had saved his life and then sustained a serious injury to his right leg. The way in which the Gary Mercer he knew would constantly make the comment about apples. That he did it to such an extent that his nickname in the Regiment was 'Apples' Mercer.

Twenty minutes flew by as Tom recalled everything, he could about the scouse paratrooper.

When Tom finally finished talking, Neil Wilkinson took a deep breath, sat back in his chair and said, 'Thanks Tom. Okay, it's all a bit tenuous, but I appreciate you coming forward. After all I did ask for anything, however small or insignificant it might seem. I don't want you to repeat this conversation with any of your colleagues for the time being. I want this information to remain just between the three of us, until I can get in touch with my counterpart in Merseyside. I need to ascertain if this man, Gary Mercer, has ever come to their knowledge before. Understood?'

'No problem, sir. Will you let me know one way or the other please? I know normally that information would be none of my business, but like I said this man effectively saved my life. If he hadn't acted the way he did, I would have died down there. I would hate to think of him this way, if he's got nothing to do with this shooting.'

Wilkinson put his hand on Tom's shoulder and said, 'No problem Tom, I'll let you know personally, one way or the other. I know exactly where you're coming from. Many years ago, I fought in Malaya. I understand the brotherhood that exists between men who have served their country.'

'Thank you, sir.'

Jim Chambers said, 'Go and join your mates Tom. I'll be through in a minute or two. If they ask where you've been, tell them I wanted to talk to you about Hincks before we start the de-brief proper. Okay?'

'Ok boss.'

Tom stood and left the room, leaving the two senior officers alone.

Jim Chambers said, 'What do you think Neil?'

'If I'm being honest, I don't really know what to think. I'll get onto Merseyside straight away. If needs be, could you spare Pc Naylor for a month or so? One other thing, has he ever done any sort of undercover work?'

Jim nodded, 'He could be seconded out, but it would depend on what he was going to be asked to do. Tom's one of the two officers, currently on restricted duties following the attempted kidnap of Sir Jarvis Soames. He's the officer who shot Angela Hincks. As far as undercover work goes, he's recently completed an undercover training course, but he's never been involved in a live operation.'

Wilkinson nodded thoughtfully, 'Okay Jim. I'll be back in half an hour, as soon as I've spoken to Merseyside Police.'

CHAPTER 23

4.45pm 7th December 1987
Mayhew Murder Incident Room, Merseyside

The young detective tapped lightly on Detective Superintendent Greg Mitchell's office door.

A deep voice shouted from within, 'Come in!'

Dc Megan Forbes was new to the CID and was still somewhat in awe of senior detectives. This was her first murder enquiry and she was desperate to make a favourable impression. The CID was where she wanted to spend the rest of her police career and she was very keen to shine.

She half opened the door, peeked into the room and said quietly but confidently, 'Have you got a minute, sir?'

Greg Mitchell looked up from the papers he was reading and said, 'Of course Megan. Don't just stand there, come in. What is it?'

'I've been manning the Incident Room information line this afternoon and I've just logged a call I think you should know about.'

Mitchell put his paperwork down, sat back in his chair and said, 'Well don't keep me in suspense, detective.'

'It was all rather strange, sir. It was obviously somebody trying to disguise their voice. It was a male voice, he gave me the name Gary Mercer and told me that this was the person we should be looking at for the murder of the sergeant. I've checked on all the Incident Room systems and there is no record anywhere of a Gary Mercer. Does the name Gary Mercer mean anything to you sir?'

Greg Mitchell thought carefully before replying, 'I can't say it's ringing any bells for me Megan, but let's check all the other computer systems at our disposal, not just those we're using in the Incident Room. Do that first and see if it turns anything else up, okay?'

Megan Forbes nodded politely and said, 'Will do sir. I'll get on it straight away'

She turned smartly and left the office, closing the door softly behind her.

After the door closed Mitchell stood up and stretched.

He paced around his office, thinking.

Why the disguised voice?

Who was trying to tell us something?

Who was Gary Mercer?

He sat back down and glanced at the Crime Bulletin he'd recently sent out to every police force in the United Kingdom. He was desperate for the Bulletin to turn something up.

His enquiry was stalling rapidly.

What he didn't realise at that moment in time, was that within the next hour or two he would be hearing the name Gary Mercer again.

CHAPTER 24

5.45pm 7th December 1987
Mayhew Murder Incident Room, Merseyside

Detective Superintendent Mitchell glanced at the wall clock in his office. It was five forty-five, he'd been at work since six o'clock that morning and he would be back at his desk at the same time tomorrow morning.

Suddenly, Greg Mitchell felt like going home. He wanted to see his wife and kids.

There was something about this case that had struck deep into his soul. It had made him realise just how fragile his very own existence could be. Every time he tried to sleep, he kept having the same unnerving, recurring dream. The nightmare provoked thoughts that then continued to race through his head all day.

In the dream, it had been him walking into Tesco's off duty, him witnessing the robbery, him diving in to try and stop it happening, him feeling the blast of the shotgun, him lying cold and dead on the pavement.

He put on his jacket and was just about to switch off the office light when the phone on his desk began to ring.

Thoughts of home vanished.

He snatched up the phone, 'Murder Incident Room, Det Superintendent Mitchell speaking, how can I help you?'

'Superintendent Mitchell, this is Detective Chief Superintendent Neil Wilkinson, Head of Nottinghamshire

CID. I understand from your control room that you're the Senior Investigating Officer on the Brian Mayhew murder enquiry. I need to ask you a question in relation to the Crime Bulletin you recently circulated.'

'Ask away, sir', Greg Mitchell replied flatly, as he slumped back down onto his chair.

'Has the name Gary Mercer ever been put forward or come to light in any of your enquiries thus far?'

Greg Mitchell instantly sat bolt upright, his eyes wide open and alert, slightly breathless he replied, 'Well sir, up until a couple of hours ago, it hadn't. We received an anonymous tip off earlier today, advising us that we should be taking a look at him. I've literally just come off the telephone to the Regional Crime Squad to organise a twenty-four-hour surveillance on this man. It's due to commence at six o'clock tomorrow morning. Can I enquire why you're asking the question sir?'

'I'm just coming to that, Superintendent. I've an officer down here who served in the Parachute Regiment with a man named Gary Mercer. This particular Gary Mercer is a Liverpudlian, he has a pronounced limp from an old war wound picked up in the Falklands and he uses the phrase about apples constantly, he used it so much that his nickname in the Regiment was 'Apples' Mercer.'

Energised by what he had heard, Mitchell jumped to his feet, 'Sir, if it's okay with you I'd like to travel down to Nottingham to talk to this officer. When's he next on duty? Where's he stationed?'

'His name's Pc Naylor, he's stationed with our Special Operations Unit. He has been on duty today, but has gone home now. He'll be available for you to speak to tomorrow.

He's currently on restricted duties following a police shooting incident, that he's directly involved in and that's currently under investigation by the IPCC. What time can you get down here? I'll ensure that both Pc Naylor and his Chief Inspector will be available to speak with you.'

'I'll be on the first train down tomorrow morning sir, I'll call you straight back when I know what time that train arrives into Nottingham. Could you arrange for a driver to pick me up from the station sir?'

'No problem Superintendent. I know it all sounds a little tenuous, but you never know, stranger things have happened. Gary Mercer might just be your man. Talk to you later and I'll see you tomorrow morning at Headquarters.'

'Goodnight, sir.'

Greg Mitchell felt a surge of emotion course through his tired body.

Yes, it was tenuous, but what the Chief Superintendent had said was very true, especially with police work. Stranger things had indeed happened before. He could think of a number of heinous, despicable crimes that had eventually been solved on links a lot more tenuous than this one.

He opened the door to his office and shouted, 'Dc Forbes, I need you to organise me a ticket on the first train from Lime Street to Nottingham Midland Station tomorrow morning. Let me know the time of arrival into Nottingham as soon as you can. Thanks.'

Megan Forbes immediately reached for the telephone on her desk and shouted, 'Will do, sir.'

CHAPTER 25

11.00am 8th December 1987
Toxteth Park Cemetery, Liverpool

It had only been four days since Stevie Key had been incinerated in his Audi car following the crash on the motorway; as a good Catholic, his mother had insisted that her son's funeral was carried out quickly.

The fact that his charred remains were now in a polished oak box with nice brass handles waiting to be turned into ashes all over again, was an irony that had not been lost on quite a few of the unsavoury crowd gathered at Toxteth Park Cemetery to mark his passing.

As the crowd waited for the coffin to be carried into the crematorium by six po-faced pall bearers, there was a lot of chuckling and giggling by the rows of hard men that had gathered to remember Stevie, the joker.

Only the immediate family seemed to appreciate the sadness of the young man's passing. He may have been a hard nut, a villain with a broken nose, but he was also a mother's son and a brother to his three sisters.

Standing outside the crematorium, away from the rest of the crowd, Gary Mercer was one of the few men there who had bothered to wear a dark suit, shirt and black tie. He was also wearing a black Crombie style coat to keep out the cool wind and Ray Ban sunglasses that were hardly needed against the weak December sun.

The only other man wearing a suit, now approached Mercer and shook his hand.

Micky Stone was wearing a stylish, very expensive, charcoal grey, pin stripe suit, wraparound sunglasses, black shirt and black tie, but no overcoat. He shivered slightly against the freshening cool breeze that blew across the open spaces of the cemetery.

Mercer said, 'Bit colder than Lanzarote, eh mate?'

'Fuck me, yeah. Just a bit, I'm bloody freezing.'

'Why did you have to rush back?'

'Something and nothing Gadge. Nothing startling, just thought it might be a good idea to make myself scarce for a few weeks. You know what I mean lad?'

Mercer had no idea what his associate was gabbling on about, so he changed the subject and said, 'It's good that you could make it here for Stevie's send-off though.'

'Yeah it is. I wouldn't have wanted to miss it. Stevie was always a bit of a dickhead, but I got on well with the lad.'

'I know exactly what you mean mate. Stevie was a diamond, but he was always going to end up dead this way. Everyone knew that sooner or later he would end up wrapping a car of some description around a tree or an artic!'

Stone laughed out loud and said, 'Yeah, dead right, but we should both drink to the fact he had the decency to do it, when we weren't in the fucking car with him.'

Mercer joined in laughing with Stone as the two men made their way into the small crematorium to bid a final farewell to their friend and wheels man.

Neither man would have been quite so happy to see the covert surveillance team secreted in the nondescript van nearby, who were busy photographing and video recording their meeting. The detectives in the van were already wondering who Gary Mercer's smart acquaintance was.

The detectives continued to photograph and record the pair after the ceremony to despatch Stevie Key had concluded.

Outside the crematorium, Mercer took Stone away from the rest of the mourners and said, 'We're well and truly fucked now mate. Until I can find another driver, we won't be able to work. I've spoken to The Ace, he was definitely getting cold feet after you wasted one of his boys in blue, but I've put him straight on that as well as bending his fucking nose a bit.'

Stone smiled, 'Good. There's only one thing worse than a bent copper and that's a greedy bent copper.'

Stone paused before saying, 'Look mate, I'm still in holiday mode. I'm going to get a flight over to Spain or Portugal for a few days. If you do get another driver organised, give me a call. When I get to wherever I'm going, I'll call you with a number so you can contact me if you organise another job, okay?'

Mercer smiled, 'Okay Micky, you go and top your tan up, you can leave all the arrangements to me, as usual.'

Stone grinned back and said, 'You know you love all that logistics shit mate, it's what you do best. We could do with getting another job in before Christmas though, it would be a real shame to miss out on all those lovely takings. You take care mate. I'll be in touch with that contact number as soon as I land.'

The two men shook hands and went their separate ways.

The detectives watching, were overjoyed.

They had observed the meeting with rising levels of excitement as they watched the two suspects in animated discussion outside the crematorium. The conversation between the two men had all been recorded on video.

If luck was on their side and with a little help from a lip-reading expert, they may be able to ascertain what the conversation had been about and find out what the two men had discussed.

The most pressing enquiry was to quickly establish the identity of Gary Mercer's well-dressed associate.

CHAPTER 26

3.00pm 8th December 1987
Nottinghamshire Police Headquarters

Detective Chief Superintendent Neil Wilkinson walked into Jim Chamber's office, followed by Detective Superintendent Greg Mitchell.

Tom Naylor and Jim Chambers were already sitting down in the office waiting for the detectives to arrive.

Nervously, Tom leapt to his feet as a mark of respect for the two detectives' rank.

Neil Wilkinson said, 'Thanks Tom, take a seat and relax. This is Superintendent Greg Mitchell from the Merseyside force. He's the detective leading the hunt for the killers of Detective Sergeant Mayhew in Liverpool. He's travelled down from Liverpool this morning. He wants to talk to you about the information you gave to your Chief Inspector and myself yesterday.'

'Okay sir, I'll help in any way I can.'

With a friendly smile, the man mountain detective, extended his huge hand and said, 'Pc Naylor, is it?'

Once again Tom stood up, shook the detective's hand and said, 'Tom Naylor sir. I just hope I haven't wasted your time travelling down here.'

'Please, sit down Tom and tell me what you know about Gary Mercer.'

Once again, Tom recounted the story he'd told to his own senior officers the day before. As he listened to Tom talking, the grin on Greg Mitchell's face got broader and broader.

When Tom finally finished giving his account, the big scouse detective said, 'Thank you Tom. Right gents, as you know Gary Mercer is currently the subject of round the clock surveillance by the Regional Crime squad. On my way down here, I was contacted on my mobile phone by the head of their surveillance team and asked to contact them on a secure line as soon as I arrived in Nottingham. As soon as I arrived here at your headquarters, I made that call. The update I have just received was extremely positive and I now have some very exciting news. It would appear that earlier today Gary Mercer was followed to Toxteth Park Cemetery where he attended the cremation of a man called Stevie Key.

Key had been involved in a fatal car accident a few days ago. At the crematorium, Mercer met a man we have now successfully identified as being Micky Stone. Stone is a wealthy business man who owns a very successful scrap metal business in Tranmere. He's also a very violent individual with a real taste for hurting people. There are a number of violence related offences attributed to him, including firearms offences. I say attributed to him, because up to now we've never been able to successfully convict him on any charge. The same is also true for Gary Mercer, neither of them has any criminal record. The point I'm coming to is this; at their meeting they were seen to discuss the planning of an armed robbery. I've chosen my words carefully gentlemen. We have employed the services of a lip-reading expert from Liverpool University to view the video recording of the two men talking. She has been able to tell us that the two men were discussing "setting up another job". They also spoke about "the need to find a new driver" and also mentioned the words "takings around the Christmas period being good". Her interpretation of the entire conversation was that the men were planning another raid at a supermarket sometime around the Christmas period on the proviso that they could find a new driver, presumably a getaway driver. From our enquiries so far, there's every likelihood that their previous getaway driver, was this morning's crematorium customer, Stevie Key.'

Using the natural pause Tom Naylor said, 'That's good news sir, at least you're one step closer to nailing them.'

'You're right Tom, but I want to be closer than one step nearer. I understand that you've recently completed an undercover course. I would like you to consider meeting Mercer.'

'I've never done an undercover role as yet sir.'

I'm aware of that, officer. What I've got in mind isn't as such an undercover role, I want you to meet with Mercer as yourself and attempt to become the gang's new getaway driver. I think he'll trust you. I've heard the way you've described your close relationship, from the time you served in the Paras together. It sounds to me like there was a very special bond back then.'

'There was back then sir, but that's a very long time ago. I haven't seen him or spoken to him since I left the Regiment years ago. As soon as he finds out I've been a cop he won't want anything to do with me.'

'He just might, if he thinks you're a disgraced cop. If we can come up with a cover story, that makes him think you now despise the police as much as he does. A story that would make him think, that after the way you've been treated by the police you have every reason to hate them.'

Tom was silent.

Jim Chambers had been deep in thought listening to Greg Mitchell, but now he spoke, 'Greg, are you aware of Tom's current situation? Were you aware that he is currently under a suspension following the high-profile shooting of Angela Hincks?'

'I was aware of the incident, there's been enough press coverage. Obviously, I wasn't aware that Tom was involved personally as his name hasn't been in the coverage. What are you thinking?'

'I'm just wondering if there's a way we can use that situation to our advantage? What I'm thinking, would require the intervention of both Nottinghamshire and Merseyside Chief Constables. They would both need to approach the Home Secretary and request that she create a special dispensation that would cover Pc Naylor.'

Tom sat back in his chair, bemused.

This was all spiralling out of control. Chief Constables involved. A special dispensation from the Home Secretary, no less. Tom wondered if Jim Chambers was losing the plot?

Jim Chambers carried on, 'What I propose is this. We falsely accuse Pc Naylor of some wrongdoing or negligence over the shooting of Angela Hincks. As a result, the likelihood is that sometime in the future he's likely to face criminal charges. He feels betrayed and angry at his treatment and resigns from the force. He faces losing everything and walks out of his career and his home life. He goes off the radar, leaving everything he holds dear behind. This way his loved ones will be protected when these villains check out his story. They will definitely check him out, so it's got to be all or nothing. The Home Secretary will have to be involved from the outset because the profile of the Hincks shooting has been so high. The national press and the media will be all over the fact that Pc Naylor has resigned and could face criminal charges. It must be made clear to her that this is an operational necessity and at its conclusion, Pc Naylor will be reinstated and fully exonerated. There's absolutely no doubt that the shooting was justified and the early indications from the IPCC are that both officers will be totally vindicated in their actions to use deadly force.'

Tom was stunned and also very worried.

The plan was brilliantly simple, but was asking an awful lot of him. He was very well aware of his limitations when it came to undercover work. Then there was the personal relationship with his girlfriend Bev to consider. It was one thing having a special dispensation that would preserve his police career, there would be no such safeguard in place over his personal life.

To betray a loved one like that could spell disaster. There was every chance that his relationship with Bev would never recover and who could blame her.

Greg Mitchell turned to Tom and said, 'Well, what do you think Tom? Would you consider being involved if I can get the two Chiefs on board and they agree to approach the Home Secretary?'

Tom replied, 'I don't know sir.'

The big Merseyside detective leaned forward and pressed on, 'Nobody in this room is going to put any pressure on you to do this Tom. We all realise the enormous upheaval this will cause you in every aspect of your personal life, not to mention the physical danger you'll be placing yourself in. It can only be your decision one way or the other, but I'll need to know that decision today. If we're going to move on this we need to act fast.'

Tom had listened carefully to everything.

The image of the defenceless Detective Sergeant Mayhew being gunned down in cold blood was etched into his brain. He only had one choice and he made it quickly, 'Start the ball rolling sir, I'll do it. The Gary Mercer involved in the murder of Ds Mayhew isn't the same man who I served with, who saved my life. He needs putting away and if this is the quickest way to achieve that, then so be it.'

Greg Mitchell was instantly on his feet, 'Thanks Tom. I'll get started making all the arrangements. There's one other thing that you all need to be aware of, the lip reader who deciphered this morning's conversation between Mercer and Stone was also able to establish that Merseyside Police have a bad apple. There is a corrupt police officer who they only referred to as The Ace. It would appear that this person, has been involved in the planning of the robberies leading up to and including the one where Ds Mayhew was murdered. Because of this fact, I must insist that nobody outside of this room can know what has been discussed here. This is for the safety of both Pc Naylor and his loved ones.'

Great, thought Tom, this just gets better and better.

CHAPTER 27

3.00pm 8th December 1987
Southport Beach, Sefton

Chief Inspector Noel Prime had managed to maintain an air of normality around his home, ever since he had discovered his wife's secret affair just over thirty-six hours ago.

On the evening he had discovered the illicit romance he had already gone to bed before Glenys had returned home. He couldn't face seeing her. It would have been too much to bear, knowing she had come straight from spending time with Gary Mercer.

Instead, he had laid in bed with his back to her, pretending to be fast asleep when she came up and got into bed.

As he lay in the dark, wide awake listening to her rhythmic breathing as she slept, he swore he could smell Mercer's aftershave on her.

He stayed awake all night thinking about the situation and mulling over what he was going to do.

As tiredness overtook him, his mood became darker and darker.

Finally, at four o'clock that morning he got out of bed, got dressed and left the house. He couldn't stand to be in the same room with her any longer. Glenys would think nothing of his early start, she was used to him working ridiculous hours.

It was still dark when he had first got into his car. Aimlessly, he had driven around the city for hours until finally heading out of the city and taking the coast road.

Eventually, he found himself driving into Sefton. In the early afternoon light, he could see the sun reflecting on the shallow, still water on the top of the beautiful expanse of sand at Southport Beach. He had parked the car on the promenade and walked down onto the sand.

Taking off his shoes and socks, he had walked slowly towards the sea. As the sound of the small waves breaking on the shore got louder, he thought back to a time when his daughters were youngsters and recalled the happy times they had spent as a family, building sandcastles and paddling in the cold sea.

The sun was quite low in the sky, but it was weak and held no warmth. There was a bitingly cold wind blowing off the sea, that brought even more tears to his eyes.

Prime suddenly felt very cold, he could feel the tears running down his cheeks as he slowly trudged through the sand back to his car. He needed to warm up, he was shivering. He suddenly realised that he hadn't eaten for almost twenty-four hours. He needed food and a hot drink.

He brushed the sand from his feet and slipped his socks and shoes back on. Getting back in the car, he instantly felt warmer now that he was out of the clutches of that bitingly cold wind. He started the car, turned the heater up to maximum and drove slowly along the seafront until he found the Beachcomber Café.

The small, chalet style building was another place that held really fond memories for Prime. He and Glenys had often driven out to the Beachcomber Café when they were first married. They would drive out and have breakfast after nights spent making love, before the children had come along.

As he walked into the warm café, the woman who ran it was busy making frothy coffees for the three elderly ladies who were the café's only other customers.

She had looked at Prime, smiled and said, 'Take a seat Hun, I'll be right over to take your order.'

Prime had walked over towards the large windows and sat at a table that had views looking back out over the wide expanse of wet sand, towards the sea.

After briefly studying the chalked menu board on the wall behind the counter he had opted for the special, Shepherd's Pie with chips and peas.

He had asked the waitress to bring him a large mug of hot sweet tea straightaway, while he was waiting for the food, so he could warm up.

When the food finally arrived, he had struggled to eat it. He was ravenously hungry, but every mouthful made him feel nauseous. He just picked at the food, moving the minced beef around the plate with his fork. In the end he had given up on the idea of eating and just drank the hot sweet tea.

He had spent almost four hours sitting in the Beachcomber Café staring out to sea, ordering refill after refill of hot sweet tea.

As he sat there, he pondered on what he needed to do and how he could do it.

There was no way he would allow Glenys to continue to see Mercer and he found it impossible to forgive her betrayal. The fact that it was his own betrayal of her in the first place, that had led Glenys to Mercer was totally lost on him.

About a year before, Glenys had overheard her husband talking to someone on the house phone. He had abruptly hung up the call when she had walked into the room. Fearing that her husband was having an affair she had requested an itemised telephone bill from British Telecom.

When the bill finally arrived, she had taken it from the postman outside and taken it into the house secretly so her husband didn't see it. She had taken the letter upstairs to the bathroom and locked the door. Sitting on the edge of the bath staring at the letter she hardly dared to open it.

Eventually, she had plucked up enough courage. She opened the envelope and studied the bill. It showed several calls to the same local number. It was a number she didn't recognise.

She waited until her husband had left the house and then called the number. It had come as a total surprise to her when she heard a man's voice on the telephone answering the call.

When Glenys had said who she was and why she was calling, Gary Mercer had quickly explained that he was a business associate of her husband's and that he would gladly meet her to put her mind at rest, that nothing untoward was happening.

Glenys hadn't been entirely convinced of her husband's innocence so in an effort to seek further reassurance she had agreed to meet Mr Mercer at the Assheton Arms, a typically English pub in the sleepy village of Downham.

They had met the following week and after a couple of drinks, Mercer had once again explained to Glenys how he knew her husband through mutual business interests and that there was absolutely nothing for her to worry about.

That should have been that, but from that very first meeting, Glenys had been bowled over by the charismatic stranger who her husband had never mentioned. There was an air of mystery about the powerful looking man with the mop of blonde hair and bright blue eyes that she had found irresistible.

Four weeks later, Glenys called Mercer again. They had arranged another meeting at The Assheton Arms. Mercer had agreed to the meeting as he had found Glenys to be an extremely attractive, very sexy woman. There was something about a redhead with green eyes that he could not resist.

He also found that there was also something deeply satisfying about being able to flirt outrageously with the policeman's wife.

The meetings at the Assheton Arms became a regular thing and the flirting became more and more overt. Within three months they had become passionate lovers. They had been meeting in secret every week ever since and the sex for both of them had just got better and better.

At the beginning there was never any question that Glenys would leave Noel Prime, it was just that she longed for the adulation and attention that Mercer showed her when he explored every inch of her still young and firm body. If anything, her illicit affair had even improved her sex life at home with Prime.

She had felt confident enough to educate her boring husband and show him what it was she needed to be pleasured properly.

As far as Glenys was concerned, what her husband didn't know about wouldn't hurt him. He should have paid her more attention and not taken her for granted.

Sitting in The Beachcomber Café, Noel Prime stared unblinking out to sea, trancelike.

The woman in the café walked over to his table and said, 'Can I get you anything else Hun? It's almost five o'clock, I'll be closing up in ten minutes.'

Prime shook his head and drained the last of the tea in the mug, stood up and walked over to the counter to pay his bill.

Noel Prime had finally come to a decision, he had thought everything through and he now knew exactly what he was going to do, how he was going to do it and when.

The when was the easy part, he would deal with his cheating bitch of a wife tonight.

CHAPTER 28

9.00pm 8th December 1987
Beauclair Drive, Wavertree, Liverpool

When he had returned home to his beautifully furnished detached house in Wavertree, one of the more select suburbs of Liverpool, Noel Prime had behaved as though today was exactly the same as any other day

As he drove his car onto the driveway, he knew that Glenys would already be home; he needed to remain calm so she wouldn't suspect a thing.

Everything had to appear as though nothing was amiss.

He had walked into the house with a cheery smile and kissed her on the cheek, as usual.

Gone upstairs, had a quick shower and got changed, as usual.

When he came back downstairs, he had asked about her day, as usual.

He had then made them both a cup of coffee and explained what he was going to be preparing for their evening meal, as usual.

One thing that Noel Prime excelled at was cooking. He had a real passion for food and whenever his shifts allowed, he would always cook their evening meal

Tonight was going to be a very special night, so he'd decided to prepare her favourite meal.

A meat lasagne with garlic bread and a side salad of wild rocket and cherry tomatoes with shavings of parmesan cheese. Prime had decided earlier in the day that the condemned woman should enjoy her last meal.

During the meal they had savoured a glass of Amarone Della Valpolicella wine, it had always been her favourite red wine and was perfect with all Italian food. After the meal, Prime had topped up their wine glasses and the two of them relaxed in the lounge, sipping the wine, listening to a Luciano Pavarotti CD.

Prime read the Daily Telegraph while Glenys flicked through her latest edition of Cosmopolitan magazine.

Glenys put down the magazine, looked at the ornate carriage clock on the mantelpiece and said, 'I don't believe that Hun, it's almost nine o'clock already. I'm going to run myself a nice hot bath, my muscles are aching from all that yoga yesterday.'

Prime never changed his facial expression or his demeanour as he said, 'That sounds perfect sweetheart. Leave the door open, I'll come up and give you a nice back and shoulder massage in a little while.'

She smiled at him and before leaving the room, said seductively, 'Mmmm, that would be lovely darling.'

Inside he was raging.

How could she be so brazen?

She was laughing at him.

Muscles aching from all that yoga yesterday, really? Who did she think she was kidding? Did she think he was that stupid?

In about an hour's time, she would find out just how stupid he was. He was now even more determined to make her pay.

For now, he said nothing and just smiled to himself.

Prime put down his newspaper, got up out of the chair, walked into the hallway and listened at the foot of the stairs.

He could hear the bath taps running.

He heard her singing softly as she walked across the landing into the bedroom to get undressed.

He waited motionless and heard her light footsteps again, as she padded naked across the hallway.

Finally, the taps were turned off and he heard her get into the bath.

As soon as he was satisfied, she was soaking in the bath, Prime moved silently out of the house and into the garage at the side of the property. He found his tool bag in the garage and removed a large claw hammer from inside. He threw the hammer from one hand to the other, as though testing its weight.

A smile passed his lips, and his eyes glinted in the darkness. There was no going back now, it was time.

He walked back into the house, kicked off his slip-on shoes and slowly climbed the stairs.

As he negotiated each step, he passed pictures of his children, who were now young adults and living away from home at University. As he stared at their smiling faces, Prime felt a single tear trickle down his cheek as he fleetingly remembered happier times.

As quickly as that joyous thought had entered his brain, it was equally as rapidly dismissed and replaced by an ugly image of Mercer together with Glenys, copulating on the floor at Mercer's house.

As he dwelt on that devastating image of her betrayal, his eyes once again became cold and dark.

Prime continued his slow journey up the stairs to the landing.

He paused outside the bathroom.

The door had been left ever so slightly ajar, wisps of steam from the hot water, escaped through the small gap.

The water must be really hot, thought Prime randomly, as he slipped the wicked looking claw hammer into the waist band of his trousers. He could feel it snuggled tightly into the small of his back.

He took a single deep breath, opened the door and walked into the steamy bathroom. In the centre of the spacious room sat a huge, free-standing Victorian, cast iron bathtub.

Glenys had lit scented candles at various points around the room. The soft light from the aromatic wax was reflected back in honey tones off the glossy travertine tiles on the floor and walls. The bath had been filled almost to the very brim.

He stood quietly and took a moment to gaze at his beautiful wife as she lay naked in the hot steaming water. There were no bubbles, but the smell of scented oils in the hot water filled his nostrils and he breathed in the heady aroma, deeply.

He allowed his senses to analyse the beautiful smell. Camomile and Sandalwood, if he wasn't mistaken.

The sound of his wife's voice brought him out of his brief reverie.

'You're eager darling, are you going to join me in the bath?', she said seductively.

'Let me give those aching muscles a nice massage first sweetheart, then I will.'

Prime stood directly behind her head, looking down at her firm body just below the water.

She sat slightly more upright and forward, allowing her husband access to massage her shoulders and neck.

Prime dipped both his hands into the hot oily water and began gently caressing her back and neck. Very slowly, he massaged the trapezium muscles at the top of her shoulders. After a few minutes, he allowed his hands to slide from her shoulders down the front of her chest, cupping her ample breasts, gently squeezing them, before playfully teasing her rosebud nipples.

Her nipples instantly became harder against the palms of his hands, as they came alive under his sensual, soft touch.

Glenys closed her eyes and murmured, 'Mmmmm, that's beautiful darling.'

He watched her as she allowed her own hands to slide across her flat, toned stomach and down between her thighs.

He continued to caress her breasts as he watched her slowly teasing herself.

As he watched her nimble fingers, Prime found himself becoming aroused, the erection in his tight trousers was now almost painful. The added pressure on his trousers meant he could now feel the shaft of the claw hammer and its steel head nestling into the small of his back.

Instantly, a gross image of Mercer and his wife rutting on the floor like wild animals, forced its way into his mind.

As swiftly as it had arrived, his erection now vanished.

In a robotic voice Prime said, 'I think I'll join you in the bath now sweetheart.'

He withdrew his hands and dried them on a nearby towel.

Glenys didn't answer, her eyes were tightly closed as she neared her self-induced orgasm. The only sound that escaped her lips was a soft moan.

Suddenly Prime felt disgusted.

I bet she's thinking about that bastard, Mercer, right now, he thought.

Reaching behind him, he retrieved the heavy claw hammer from the small of his back and without saying a single word, he raised the hammer high above his head. He then brought the weapon down in a hard, vicious arc, directly onto the top of his unsuspecting wife's head.

In a wild frenzy, Prime continued to rain down blow after sickening blow. He continued to bludgeon Glenys long after she was obviously dead. It was only as his arm physically tired, that he finally stopped and surveyed the scene of carnage before him.

The barrage of heavy blows had forced Glenys under the water in the bath. The once clear, oily water was gradually becoming a darker and darker shade of crimson, as she bled out from the massive head wounds she had sustained.

The walls, floor and ceiling were all splattered with her blood, brain and fragments of bone.

With a look of incredulity on his face, Prime looked down at his own blood-stained hands. In his right hand he was still holding the blood-soaked hammer. The blood all over the metal head and wooden handle was glistening black, in the candlelight.

Uncurling his fingers, he allowed the hammer to slide from his grasp. He heard it clatter noisily onto the tiled floor. Without bothering to look at Glenys, he turned and walked out of the bathroom. As he neared the door, he passed the large mirror above the sink. Prime didn't recognise the blood-spattered face or the demented eyes of the individual staring back at him.

Very slowly, he closed the bathroom door behind him and walked across the landing to the master bedroom. This was the same bedroom he'd shared with his beloved wife for the last twenty years.

Trancelike, he walked into the en-suite shower room, stripped off and stepped into the shower cubicle. He allowed the hot water to cascade down onto his bloodied body. He watched, mesmerised, as the water on the floor of the shower turned into miniature whirlpools of crimson, before disappearing down the plughole.

Thirty minutes later, Noel Prime sat naked on his bed staring at the large bottle of Paracetamol capsules. It had always been his plan to kill his cheating wife and then kill himself, but now that the time had come to end his own life, he was having second thoughts.

Deep down, in the very depths of his soul, Noel Prime knew he was a coward.

There was a little voice inside his head that constantly whispered to him. Why should I kill myself? I haven't done anything wrong. She was in the wrong, not me.

The whispered voice, slowly became louder and louder, until it was a deafening crescendo.

The voice was screaming at him now.

You don't deserve to die!

She was in the wrong, not you!

Punish her, not yourself!

There was a deafening silence.

Finally, the voice gave Prime a calm, matter of fact instruction.

Put the bottle of pills away. You know you're not going to need them.

The voice became silent once again.

Prime got dressed, picked up the bottle of Paracetamol capsules from the bed and went back downstairs. He walked straight into the utility room and placed the capsules back inside the medicine cupboard.

He smiled as he closed the cupboard door. He turned, walked into the kitchen, switched the kettle on and made himself a mug of hot coffee.

Tomorrow was just another day.

CHAPTER 29

5.00pm 8th December 1987
Nottinghamshire Police Headquarters

Tom and Matt were sitting in one of the small side offices at The Huts. The only furniture in the room was a large wooden desk and two iron framed chairs.

Tom sat on one chair and Matt the other, staring at each other over the mountain of old reports that were piled high on the desk. It had sounded a simple enough task when the Control Room Inspector had instructed them to look for the written copy of a vehicle check that had taken place in the city centre some six months or less ago.

The 'or less' comment, that had been thrown in as an aside by the Inspector, effectively meant that they now had to wade their way through six months' worth of vehicle check reports, looking for one particular vehicle, checked on one particular day. There were literally hundreds of reports stacked on the desk, it was like looking for the proverbial needle in a haystack.

Matt grabbed another pile of reports from the desk and said, 'Fuck me Tom, the joys of light duties!'

Tom just nodded, his mind was elsewhere. Ever since the meeting with Detective Superintendent Mitchell, he had found it difficult to concentrate wondering if anything was going to happen in respect of his old friend, Gary Mercer. He was praying that he would get a cursory call from Merseyside

Police, telling him that Mercer had been eliminated from their enquiries. He didn't want to believe that someone he considered to be a true friend was capable of being involved in the horrific events he had witnessed on that video.

It had been a full twenty-four hours now since the big Merseyside detective had dropped the bombshell request that he had readily accepted.

As Tom reached for another report looking for the particular Ford Sierra the Control Room Inspector was interested in, he thought to himself that it must be the two Chief Constables who were stalling over some part of the plan outlined the day before by his Chief Inspector.

Suddenly, the door to the small office opened and Jim Chambers stuck his head round the door. He looked at Tom and said brusquely, 'Naylor, my office now.'

Tom didn't say a word to Matt, he just stood up, left the room and made his way along the corridor to the Chief Inspectors office.

He knocked once and waited.

Chambers shouted, 'Come in Naylor!'

Tom stepped inside and Jim Chambers said, 'Close the door and sit down Tom. I've just received word from the Chief Constable that your personal dispensation has been approved by the Home Secretary. She's sanctioned the operation because of the huge public outcry following the murder of Ds Mayhew. Are you still up for this Tom? No second thoughts?'

'None at all boss.'

'Right, this is how the plan's going to work. Tomorrow morning, I'll announce in front of your mates on C Section, that the initial report from the IPCC has indicated that they will be investigating some negligence on your part in relation to the shooting of Hincks. I will then elaborate and say that this has come to light following testimony from one of your colleagues on C Section. In other words, one of your mates on the Section has grassed you up to the IPCC. I'll go on to say that the IPCC are in possession of a statement that suggests you may have behaved in an improper, unprofessional way on the night of the shooting. Are you with me so far?'

Tom nodded.

Jim Chambers continued, 'When you've heard what I have to say, I want you to get seriously angry with your colleagues in the room. I want you to demand that they tell you the identity of the person who's stitched you up. Obviously, there'll be no takers because nobody has. When you're met with that wall of silence, I want you to single out Matt Jarvis and lay the blame on him. Get angry and say something like, he was the only person who was with you throughout the entire operation, it's got to be him. Obviously, Matt isn't going to be too impressed by this accusation. I don't care if this verbal altercation becomes a physical one, it will soon be broken up. This has got to look genuine, Tom. Are you okay with all this so far?'

Tom nodded and said quietly, 'Bloody hell boss, do you think this is going to work?'

'It's got to work, Tom. Like I said yesterday, for the plan to work, this has got to be an all or nothing scenario. You've really got to embrace this to pull it off. Just remember, the more genuine you can make this now, the safer everyone will be, long term. Okay?'

'Okay boss, I understand. Go on.'

'As soon as this brawl is broken up, I want you to immediately hand in your resignation to me, which I'll gladly accept. I'll tell you, in front of your colleagues, that I consider you to be a disgrace to the uniform and that you're extremely fortunate I'm not dismissing you. There'll be no notice to work through, I'll instruct you to hand in your warrant card there and then. You'll be unceremoniously escorted off the premises. After that's done, you must have no contact with police officers at all. I'm sure that Matt Jarvis will try and contact you to make amends, I know how close you two are.'

Tom looked down at the floor and Chambers continued, 'For this whole charade to work, it's vital that you just piss him off. Get abusive if you have to, just make sure he gets the message that you're done with the police service and the men who work for it. Tell him, that as far as you're concerned anyone who works in the organisation is a double dyed, back stabbing bastard who can't be trusted.'

Chambers paused momentarily, then with a serious edge in his voice he said, 'Tom, I hope you understand how vital and necessary this all is. If your story is to hold water when these villains in Liverpool start checking you out, it's got to be believable. Be under no illusion, these people will definitely be looking into your cover story, big time. If they find one thing wrong, the consequences for you will be dire and they could be just as dangerous for those who you hold dear.'

'What about my girlfriend? What do I tell Bev?'

'I can't help you with that, Tom. You're going to have to work out what you want to say for yourself. For her own safety, I suggest you end the relationship in as clean a break as you can. Hopefully, at the end of all this, she'll understand the reasons why you broke things off with her the way you did and that uppermost in your mind, was her personal safety. There are no guarantees that she will, so this is a huge risk to take with your own personal happiness. Are you sure you still want to go through with this?'

Having listened carefully to everything his Chief Inspector had said, Tom thought for a moment before giving an answer. As he weighed up the options, once again the image of the defenceless Ds Mayhew came flooding into his head and before he realised it, he could hear himself saying, 'I'm doing this boss. I've got no choice. Bev will understand, I know she will.'

'Okay Tom. I hope you're right, for both your sakes. Go home now and be back here at eight o'clock in the morning. I want to play out this charade with your Section colleagues first thing. You will need to be in Liverpool by late afternoon, tomorrow. You'll need to sort out whatever you're going to say to Bev tonight, so you can leave Nottingham tomorrow. Understood?'

Again, Tom nodded. He had always known that when this operation started things would move quickly, but even he was shocked at the speed things were moving now.

'One last thing Tom, take this telephone number and memorise it. This is the number for your undercover contact in Liverpool. You'll only ever refer to this person as "Bailey". As soon as you arrive in Liverpool tomorrow, your contact will be at the railway station waiting for you. They'll sort you out with everything you need for the job. If you're not contacted at the station, use this number, but only as a last resort, okay?'

Tom replied, 'Yes boss', and took the piece of paper containing the contact number. He stood up and started for the door.

Jim Chambers said, 'Good luck Tom. Stay safe and stay careful. Never forget that the people you're going after are murderers. I know that Gary Mercer was once your friend, possibly your best friend, but you've got to forget everything that's ever happened in the past. This man and his associates are stone cold killers, they'll not hesitate to finish you or your loved ones. It's vital that you remain on your guard at all times.'

'Thanks boss, don't worry about me. That video of Ds Mayhew is indelibly branded into my brain. I won't forget what these people are. See you in the morning.'

Tom walked straight out into the car park and got into his car.

He drove quickly out of the car park, not knowing what the future would hold.

CHAPTER 30

8.00pm 8th December 1987
Linby Village, Nottinghamshire

Bev was standing in the kitchen of the small cottage, she was busily washing the dishes from supper. She had decided to stay out of Tom's way, as he was in a very strange mood. He'd arrived home from work early and had spent the evening constantly snapping at her for the least little thing.

Hardly a word had passed between them as they sat and ate their evening meal.

Tom walked into the kitchen and said, 'Bev, for Christ's sake, leave the dishes, come and sit down. I think you and I need to talk.'

Bev dried her hands on a tea towel and followed him through into the lounge. She didn't like the sound of what Tom had just said, she could tell he was building up to something.

She felt sure that whatever it was that was troubling him, they would still be alright. Obviously, he was under a lot of strain after the shooting and she knew it had been playing on his mind, but she hoped they were still very tight.

As soon as they both sat down, in a matter of fact voice Tom blurted out, 'I think it's time we had a break from each other. This relationship just isn't working for me. I feel something's not quite right between us. I need to get out of this place for a bit and I need a break from you.'

Bev was stunned and sat open mouthed. This wasn't what she'd been expecting at all. She was shocked and hurt at the bluntness of his comment and more than a little angry.

How could he feel so little for her after all the time they had spent together to just want to leave like that?

The way he had steamrollered through her feelings was brutal.

She supressed her anger for the moment and said flatly, 'Is it something I've done? Is it the pressure you're under at work? What is it? Talk to me, Tom. That's the least you could do, this all seems so unfair.'

Tom averted his eyes and looked towards the ceiling away from her piercing gaze, 'It's all of that, Bev. I've just got this feeling deep down, that if we don't have a break from each other now, we'll drift apart and have no future at all. That's it.'

Finally, Bev did lose her temper, 'Oh! Just like that, yeah. That's it, is it? Who the hell do you think you are? I've supported you throughout this entire mess, putting up with your mood swings and your churlish ways. You need to remember one thing, Tom. I didn't pull the fucking trigger and shoot that woman, you did! It's almost as if you're blaming me for what happened. Well fuck you, I don't have to put up with any of this crap, I'm out of here. If by some miracle, you do manage to crawl out from up your own arsehole in the next twenty years and you think about giving me a call. Don't bother! I won't be answering! I'll be out of here in the morning. Have a nice life you arrogant shit!'

Bev stood up, ran from the lounge and up the stairs to the bedroom of the tiny cottage.

She knew the tears were coming and she didn't want him to see her crying. Her heart was breaking, she really loved Tom and she couldn't understand why he was acting in this way. It was as if he had suddenly become a different person. Where his heart had once been, all there was now, was a swinging brick. How could he be so cruel?

She was desperately hoping that he would follow her upstairs, so they could talk some more, she didn't want it to end like this.

There was no movement from downstairs, Tom remained seated in the lounge, not moving.

Bev was proud, she had meant every word of her tirade. She would move out in the morning.

She reached for the telephone next to the bed and called her best friend, Kate Jarvis, 'Kate, it's me', she sobbed, 'Is it alright if I come and stay with you and Matt for a few days? Me and Tom have just had the biggest row, I'm leaving him in the morning, but I've got nowhere to go at the moment.'

Kate responded gently, 'Of course you can come and stay sweetheart, you're always welcome here. You and Tom will be able to talk things through, won't you?'

'I honestly don't know. I don't think we will, not this time Kate. He's been so unbelievably cruel tonight, I can't talk that over with him. It's like he just doesn't care about us anymore. He's changed so much lately, right at this moment I never want to see him again.'

'I'm so sorry to hear that sweetheart. Look, you're obviously very upset, why don't you come over tonight, that way you can give each other some space? We can have a proper chat tonight and you never know, things might be different in the morning, okay?'

'They might. Thanks, I will. I don't want to stay here tonight anyway, it's too fraught. I'll throw some things in a bag and come over. Thanks again Kate, you're a star, see you soon.'

Bev put the phone down and began to throw some toiletries and clothes into an overnight bag. She never said another word to Tom, who hadn't moved from the settee in the lounge.

She walked out of the cottage, slamming the door on the way out.

Her tears and feelings of sadness had now quickly turned to anger and resentment.

How could he just throw away what they had?

Didn't he realise how special he was to her?

Obviously not, the arrogant prick. Well fuck him, it was his loss.

CHAPTER 31

8.00am 9th December 1987
Nottinghamshire Police Headquarters

At eight o'clock in the morning, Tom sauntered into the main Briefing Room at The Huts. The rest of his colleagues were already there, busy doing routine admin duties. It was an unwritten rule that officers on the Special Operations Unit were expected to parade on duty, twenty minutes before their shift was due to start.

Tom had deliberately reported for duty at exactly eight o'clock this morning. To all intents and purposes, he was late for duty.

There were a few raised eyebrows from his colleagues, as Tom ambled over to the hot water urn and poured himself a large mug of strong black coffee.

He was unshaven and looked as if he'd slept on the couch in the clothes he was still wearing. Part of this was very true, he had been on the couch all night, but sleep not a wink of it.

After the terrible way he'd ended things with Bev, he felt awful and ashamed of the way he had acted. He knew it was in her best interests, but he still felt like a complete arsehole. He'd downed the best part of a bottle of Glenmorangie single malt whisky. The alcohol hadn't made him feel any better about what he'd done.

He was still an arsehole.

Finally, he had dropped off into a fitful, alcohol induced sleep that lasted about twenty minutes before his alarm clock went off. Tom had reached for his self-use breathalyser kit. He had bought the device when he first went onto the Special Operations Unit. He needed to be able to gauge if he was fit to attend emergency armed response call outs, if he had been drinking the night before. It wasn't normally an issue, as there was always a section on stand by for emergency call outs.

If you were on standby, you didn't drink, simple.

There was just the odd occasion, when two or three sections would need to be called out for a firearms job. It was necessary to be honest. If you had been drinking the night before you did not attend.

He'd used it this morning, just to see if he was sober enough to drive to Headquarters. He was under the limit, but only by a fraction.

Ordinarily, he wouldn't have risked driving, but today he had no choice. He had to be in the Briefing Room at eight o'clock.

Tom sat down and took a sip of the strong, black coffee. He still felt physically terrible, his head was banging, his mouth felt dry and every time he belched all he could taste was stale whisky.

Chief Inspector Chambers came into the Briefing Room and said loudly, 'Gather round C Section, I've got some rather disturbing news. I've just received a report outlining the preliminary findings of the IPCC enquiry into the Hincks shooting. It doesn't make good reading, particularly for you Pc Naylor.'

Tom felt all eyes turn on him. He remained seated, looking down at the floor and took another swig of coffee.

Jim Chambers continued, addressing his pointed remarks directly at Tom, 'The IPCC have been informed, by some of your colleagues, that you acted inappropriately and unprofessionally on the night of the shooting. Would you care to enlighten me as to exactly what "inappropriately and unprofessionally" means, Pc Naylor?'

You could have heard a pin drop; the air in the room was now thick with tension.

Very carefully, Tom placed his mug of coffee on the floor between his feet. Without looking up from the floor and with real menace in his voice, he asked, 'What did you just say boss? Informed by some of my colleagues?'

'That's what the report says. I've got to say I was shocked myself, but it's definitely there in black and white. I think you've got some explaining to do, officer.'

Tom stood up, took a step forward and stared at Jim Chambers. He had stood too quickly; his head began to spin. He stared straight ahead, waiting for his head to clear, then he said quietly, 'So let me get this straight, one or more of these bastards in this room, think I was out of order on the night, is that right?'

'That's not what I said, Pc Naylor and you would do well to remember who you're talking to. Have some respect and adopt a less abusive tone, officer.'

Steve Grey now spoke up, 'You need to watch your mouth Naylor! Who are you calling a bastard? Nobody in this room's said a word against you. You need to wind your neck in mate.'

Tom was furious, with eyes blazing, he shouted, 'Well that's obviously not the case, is it Steve?'

He then rounded on Matt Jarvis, 'You're keeping very quiet Matt. You were with me throughout the entire operation. Come on, be a man, tell me to my face that what I did was inappropriate.'

Matt tried to plead his innocence, 'Honestly mate, I haven't said a word against you. I told the CID and the enquiry team that you had no choice but to shoot. I even told them I would have made the same decision and taken the same shots as you did!'

Tom was now raging, 'A fucking likely story! You're just out to save your own scrawny neck, you lying, gutless bastard!'

That was one insult too many for Matt Jarvis, he saw the red mist and leapt forward at Tom, landing a punch just above his temple. Tom responded swiftly and landed a couple of punches of his own to Matt's face, before both men fell to the floor, grappling, still throwing punches at each other.

Jim Chambers shouted at the rest of the Section who were looking on in amazement, 'Don't just stand there gawping, break it up now!'

Instantly, the two combatants were pulled apart.

Chambers shouted, 'Naylor. Get in my office, now!'

'Fuck you Chambers! I quit! I can't trust any of you back stabbing bastards. You can all go to hell!'

'If you want to quit, that's fine by me Naylor. As far as I'm concerned, you've always been a loose cannon. You're too much of a liability to be on this Unit or this Force. If you really want to quit, I want your hand-written resignation and your warrant card on my desk in ten minutes. If I don't see it within that time, I'm putting you on a disciplinary charge anyway. I want you gone, you're not fit to wear a uniform. Is that understood?'

'Oh yeah, that's all crystal fucking clear!'

Within ten minutes, Tom stood in front of Jim Chambers desk. He handed over a hastily scribbled, hand written resignation letter, his warrant card and his police key.

The door to the office was wide open so all his colleagues could hear the conversation.

Jim Chambers shouted, 'Sgt Turner. Get in here!'

Graham Turner appeared in the office instantly and Chambers said loudly, 'Right Naylor, you're out of here. Sgt Turner, escort this man off the premises. Drive him home and recover any items of police uniform or kit you see.'

Graham answered quietly, 'Yes boss.'

Chambers then turned to Tom and said, 'As of now you're no longer a member of the Nottinghamshire Police Force son, is that understood?'

'Don't son me! You and the rest of them listening out there, mean jack shit to me anymore. I can't trust a single one of you. You can stick this worthless job up your arse. I don't need to be driven home, my car's in the car park!'

Jim Chambers said, 'You can collect your car at a later date, after making an appointment. I can still smell whisky on your breath and I don't think you're fit to drive. Don't tempt me into breathalysing you.'

'Whatever. Let's get going then. I don't want to be in this rat's nest another minute!'

Chambers had one last parting shot, 'Sgt Turner, make sure that shit surrenders his passport to you. We don't want to have to go looking for him, if the IPCC do recommend criminal charges.'

A clearly embarrassed Graham Turner replied, 'Will do, boss.'

Tom walked out of the office and past the Briefing Room that was full of his shocked, C Section colleagues. He stepped inside the room, gave a rigid middle finger salute and said loudly, 'You lot can all bollocks!'

Tom felt the presence of Graham Turner behind him, 'Keep moving Naylor, don't make me carry you out of here.'

CHAPTER 32

5.30pm 9th December 1987
Liverpool Lime Street Railway Station, Merseyside

The ageing loudspeaker system on the train, crackled into life.

The nasal, robotic tones of the announcer proclaimed loudly, 'This train, from Nottingham Midland Station to Liverpool Lime Street, terminates at this stop. This is Liverpool Lime Street. All change, all change.'

Tom Naylor stood up from his cramped, uncomfortable seat in the second-class carriage and stretched. He glanced at his watch before retrieving his holdall and Bergen rucksack from the luggage rack above his head.

It was now almost five thirty, the train was thirty-five minutes late. Tom was worried that he had missed the scheduled meeting with his handler. He hoped that this Bailey character, whoever he was, was a patient bloke.

Bloody British Rail!

As he waited for the train to come to a stop, Tom reflected on the day's events. After being escorted from Police Headquarters by a stony-faced Sgt Turner, everything had happened at a lightning fast pace.

When they had arrived back at his cottage in Linby, Tom had handed any police uniform and equipment over to his sergeant, who he'd left standing outside on the doorstep.

The last thing he handed over to Graham Turner was his passport.

Sgt Turner had said tersely, 'Good luck mate', before offering his hand to shake hands.

With great difficulty, Tom had ignored his sergeant.

Graham Turner was a man he had the utmost respect for, he would have gladly run through a brick wall for the powerful sergeant. He desperately wanted to extend his arm and shake Turner's hand. Instead he had said nothing and just slammed the door.

After the sergeant had left, Tom began packing his bags. He packed carefully, he needed clothes that would help him blend in on the streets of Liverpool.

An hour after he'd arrived back at his cottage, Tom had received a telephone call from Chief Inspector Chambers.

Chambers told him that he'd just come off the phone to the force's Press Officer and that news of his resignation would be being pushed out to the press and other media later that day. Because of the high-profile coverage the Hincks shooting had already received, the Press Officer had told Chambers that she expected the story to be picked up by all the television news crews,

Chambers also informed Tom, he'd arranged for a local estate agent to place the cottage on the market. It was to be marketed as being up for sale, but viewings were to be by appointment only.

A 'For Sale' board would be put up the following day, so to all intents and purposes it appeared as though Tom Naylor was moving on, starting afresh somewhere else.

Tom had taken the time to go around the cottage, securing everything and emptying the fridge and the freezer of their contents before switching off and unplugging all electrical appliances.

As he had walked around the cottage, he noticed that other than a couple of holiday snaps they were both on, there was no longer any trace of his girlfriend Bev. She'd obviously taken advantage of his absence earlier that morning to return to the cottage and remove the remainder of her belongings.

With a heavy heart, he picked up one of the holiday photos and stared at the picture of a smiling, happy Bev. At that moment, he wondered if he would ever be able to win her back.

He had telephoned for a taxi to take him to Nottingham Midland Station, where he intended to catch the one fifty-five train.

That train was scheduled to get him into Liverpool Lime street at four fifty-five that afternoon. That would give him plenty of time to meet his handler at the scheduled time of five o'clock.

When the taxi had finally arrived, the thought that flashed through Tom's mind, as he closed and locked the cottage door, was how long would it be before he returned to the cottage as Pc Tom Naylor.

The train finally came to a full stop and passengers started to move towards the doors. He grappled with his heavy Bergen and holdall, got off the train and made his way along the platform to the station foyer.

He was looking for The Steam Engine coffee shop. This was the location for the rendezvous with Bailey.

Having found The Steam Engine, Tom walked in and went to the counter. He ordered a large coffee and a cheese and pickle sandwich from the bored waitress.

Having been served his coffee and food, he walked over to a large comfortable armchair, put his bags on the floor and his coffee and sandwich on the small table in front of the chair. He quickly looked around the café, before he flopped into the armchair. The place was quiet, almost deserted. There was a young couple, staring into each other's eyes as they both sipped hot chocolate. Obviously, love's young dream, thought Tom.

Apart from the waitress who had served him, the only other person inside was a young red-haired woman, casually dressed in blue jeans and a khaki combat jacket sitting at the far end of the café. She was sipping a coffee as she flipped through the latest edition of the Smash Hits magazine.

Tom gulped a mouthful of the hot coffee and took a bite of his sandwich. No sign of this bloke Bailey then. He decided to wait for half an hour in case he showed up. If nobody came, he would have to make a call to the number he had memorised.

Not the most auspicious start to an operation.

He cursed under his breath, 'Bloody British Rail!'

Tom finished his sandwich, rummaged in his holdall and retrieved the trashy novel he'd bought at Midland Station. He flipped open the book and settled down to wait. He had sat in the chair facing the door of the café so he could see any new arrivals.

Fifteen minutes went by and Tom began to get more and more concerned.

Where was this idiot Bailey?

His thoughts were suddenly interrupted, 'Can I get you a refill? That coffee must be cold by now?'

It was the red-haired woman who had been sitting at the far end of the cafe.

She smiled and said, 'I was getting a fresh one anyway, I thought you looked like you could do with one too. I was supposed to be meeting my boyfriend Tom at five o'clock, but I don't know if I've missed him or not.'

Tom smiled back and said, 'A coffee would be lovely, thanks. I'm supposed to be meeting someone here as well. My name's Tom, by the way.'

As the woman turned to walk to the counter, she flicked her hair to one side, looked back over her shoulder and said, 'Hi Tom, I'm Bailey. Do you take sugar in your coffee?'

He shook his head and watched her as she walked to the counter.

When she returned with the two cups of coffee, Tom motioned for her to sit in the armchair opposite. To the casual observer, it would look like a chance meeting between two strangers.

Care had to be taken because of the known leak that existed within the Merseyside force. The identity of that corrupt officer was still unknown. This was one of the tasks Tom had been given once he had met with Mercer. He was to try and establish exactly who had been passing information and intelligence to Mercer.

He took a sip of his fresh coffee and said, 'I'm really sorry Bailey, but the last person I expected to see was a young woman.'

'No offence taken, Tom.'

'Definitely none intended.'

'We'll finish our coffees, then I'll take you to the flats where your digs are. They're in the Georgian quarter of the city. They're quite nice, not luxurious but not a dump either. Once we get over there, I'll brief you fully, where we're up to at this point. I don't want to say anything out here, okay.'

'Sounds good to me.'

They made small talk for the ten minutes it took to finish the coffee, then Bailey said, 'You ready for the off then Hun?'

'Ready when you are.'

She smiled again and led the way from the café to the multi storey car park where she had a black Peugeot 205gti waiting.

A short drive later and they were at the rear of a small block of flats on Egerton Street in the Georgian quarter of Liverpool.

It was already dark, but it looked a nice area. There were no burned out cars or gangs of yobs loitering on the corner. It looked like the sort of place Tom would have chosen to rent himself.

He grabbed his bags from the boot and followed Bailey to the front of the building.

Access to the front door of the flat was up four stone steps. The area was called the Georgian quarter for a reason, the majority of properties in this part of the city all dated back to the Georgian period and this block of flats was no exception. In its heyday, the building would have been a phenomenal house owned by a doctor, a ships master or some other well-paid professional.

Now it was a block of flats.

Bailey took the keys from her coat pocket and said, 'Your flat's on the second floor of the three, it's really quite nice inside.'

Tom said, 'Let's go and see, shall we?'

The flat itself had two roomy bedrooms, a bathroom with a shower, a kitchen diner and a lounge. It was quite small, but clean, modern and comfortably furnished. The food cupboards and the fridge freezer were already stocked, there were even a few beers and a bottle of wine in the cooler.

Tom looked around his new home, 'This is all very nice. My cottage back home is about the same size as this.'

Bailey said playfully, 'We aim to please, sir.'

Now they were safely at the flat, Tom took the time to look at Bailey properly. His handler for the operation was probably a couple of years older than he was. She had long, straight, dark auburn hair, bright green eyes and a very pleasant smile. She was quite short and curvy with large breasts. Tom suddenly realised where he was looking and immediately averted his gaze, hoping that she hadn't noticed.

Tom dumped both his bags in the bedroom that overlooked the street at the front of the property and then joined Bailey in the living room.

Before he sat down, he asked, 'Can I get you another coffee?'

'No thanks Hun, I'm all coffee'd out, ta.'

Bailey retrieved a video cassette from an inside pocket of her combat jacket, she placed the cassette into the video recorder below the television.

She switched on the TV and played the video.

The first image that came on the screen was a current up to date photograph of Gary Mercer. Tom could see that Mercer hadn't changed that much, physically. There were a few more lines around the eyes, but basically, he looked the same as he did the last time he'd seen him in the Falkland Islands.

The next image was a surveillance photograph of Micky Stone.

Bailey pressed the pause button and said, 'This handsome chap is Micky Stone. He's a scrap metal dealer from Tranmere.

Although he prefers to think of himself as a successful businessman, in actual fact Stone is a cold-blooded, violent thug. We strongly suspect that he's the individual who pulled the trigger and gunned down Detective Sergeant Mayhew.'

Tom studied the face of Stone. Was this sophisticated man, dressed in an Armani suit, wearing a Rolex watch really the person responsible for the cold-blooded execution he'd witnessed a couple of days ago?

Bailey interrupted his thoughts, 'The rest of the video is the bulletin that was sent out to all forces. Do you want to watch it again Tom?'

'No thanks, it was chilling enough the first time. I won't be forgetting that anytime soon.'

'Our surveillance teams have been on Mercer for the last twenty-four hours, ever since the Home Secretary got involved. They will continue to provide twenty-four-hour, round the clock surveillance on both Mercer and Micky Stone, until they're either compromised or they're ordered off the surveillance by the Chief Constable. The only people in the Merseyside Police area who know you're here are the Chief Constable, Detective Superintendent Greg Mitchell and yours truly.'

There was that smile again. It was like looking at a young Barbra Windsor, but with red hair, Tom thought.

Bailey continued, 'We took over from the Regional Crime Squad surveillance team and from what they told us on the hand over and what we've already seen, it would appear that Mercer's very much a creature of habit. This could be a throwback to his military service, I guess.'

'It does stay with you Bailey, I'm exactly the same.'

'It seems that Mercer's football mad, in particular Liverpool FC mad. In the short time we've been watching him, he's already attended two games at Anfield, one of those was for a reserve team match. I understand from my briefing that you're a Liverpool fan as well, is that correct?'

'Definitely. I've always been a red.'

'That's a pity, I've always been blue myself', she giggled at her unintended double entendre.

Stifling the giggle, she continued, 'Anyway, Mercer always goes in the Kop end of the stadium, our enquiries show he's currently a season ticket holder. The next home game is against Coventry City this coming Saturday, in just three days' time. Superintendent Mitchell thinks it would be a good idea for you to get acclimatised to the city. To get yourself out at night, have a look around the place before you try and meet Mercer at the match. From previous surveillance, we already know that his routine before the game, is always a pre-match drink at The Albert pub. I don't know if you know the place Tom? It's a very small pub, that's literally right next to the ground.'

Tom nodded, 'I do know it, but I haven't been inside for years.'

Bailey continued, 'We think that would be the best location to try and engineer a chance meeting with Mercer. He does know you're a fellow Liverpool fan, doesn't he?'

'Yeah, he knows alright. When he was wounded on Mount Longden, he conned me into carrying his flag into Port Stanley on my Bergen. I thought it was just the Union Jack. It turned out to be a Union Jack flag, but with a bloody great, golden Liver Bird in the middle of it.'

Tom couldn't help but grin at the memory.

An unsmiling Bailey said, 'That's about it for now Tom. There's still no information on who the mole is or in which department they work. Suffice to say, we're endeavouring to make careful enquiries into telephone records for numbers used by Gary Mercer to see if there are any obvious numbers that relate to serving officers or civilian staff. In the meantime, you should do what the Superintendent suggested and enjoy the sights and sounds of this lovely, vibrant city. If you need anything, and I mean anything Tom, call the mobile number. I have it with me constantly and I'll always answer it. If for any reason I can't speak to you immediately, I'll always say, "Oh Gran, what are you like", before I make an excuse and hang up. I'll always call you back within two minutes. If I ever have to call you first, I will always start the call by pretending to be a cold caller from a double glazing firm called Deluxe Windows, unless it's a pre-arranged call, understood?'

'Understood.'

'There's a mobile phone for you to use, in a drawer in the kitchen, along with the instructions how to use it. Have you used one before Tom?'

'Yes, I have, thanks Bailey.'

'There's no need to thank me Hun, it's all part of the service. Now go and unpack, there's a very lively city waiting for you outside these doors. I'll call your mobile next Saturday morning at ten thirty, to let you know where Mercer is, so you can "bump into him", Okay?'

Bailey then rose to her full five feet three inches and stretched before making her way to the door.

She paused and said, 'Oh, there's one last thing Tom', she turned and handed him a brown envelope, 'There's a grand in twenties in here. If you need any more cash, don't hesitate to call the Bank of Bailey. Okay Hun?'

Tom smiled, 'Don't worry, if this city is half as good as you're painting it to be, I'll be in touch tomorrow for a top up. See you soon Bailey.'

Bailey left the flat and he closed the door after her. Suddenly, he was alone with his thoughts.

He decided to unpack his bags, take a shower and then get a cab into town for a bite to eat and a quiet drink. He did want to check out his surroundings, but at the same time he knew he was here to do a job. No way was he going out on the lash in a strange town.

As he started to unpack, his thoughts turned to the problem of meeting Gary Mercer.

How the hell was he going to engineer a chance meeting at the upcoming football match?'

CHAPTER 33

8.00am 12th December 1987
Oxton Village, Nottinghamshire

Kate Jarvis hugged her friend, with real concern in her voice she said softly, 'Come on Bev, you don't have to go. You know you're welcome to stay with us for as long as you want. It's only been three days since Tom left. We've got plenty of room and we both enjoy your company.'

Kate's husband Matt said, 'Kate's right Bev, why don't you stay a few more days at least?'

Kate was genuinely concerned.

Ever since Tom had left in such a blinding hurry, she had seen a steady decline in her best friend, as Bev spiralled into a deep depression.

Who could blame the girl? thought Kate.

The man Bev loved, the man who she thought loved her and was going to marry her, had just taken off after dumping her. That was after he had physically attacked his supposed best friend Matt, resigned from his job, throwing away his career.

Kate found it hard to believe that the Tom she knew, was capable of such cruelty and stupid behaviour. He had totally lost the plot.

Bev broke away from Kate's hug and said, 'It's no good me staying here, Kate. You two are so kind, but I've got to try and get on with my life. When Matt told me yesterday, that the cottage is now up for sale, that was the last straw. I'm not stupid Kate, if Tom had any intention of coming back here, he wouldn't be selling his home, would he? He obviously wants a complete break from here, from work and from me.'

Kate could see the tears beginning to well up in Bev's huge blue eyes as she started to walk out of the door towards her little Volkswagen Polo.

Kate shouted after her, 'Where are you going to stay sweetheart?'

'I'm going back to my Mum's for now. I spoke to her on the phone last night and explained what had happened. She was her usual supportive self, bless her. She gave me the "plenty more fish in the sea" speech. I know when I'm there, I'll just be able to get my head down, go to work and try to forget that heartless prick.'

'Okay Bev, but if you change your mind, just pick up the phone. You're always welcome here any time, day or night. If you just need a chat or someone to have a drink with, please don't hesitate to call me.'

'I will do Kate and thanks; you and Matt have been fantastic.'

Matt stepped towards the Polo carrying Bev's suitcase.

He placed the case in the boot of the car, embraced her and said softly, 'Something doesn't add up here Bev, all this is so out of character. The way he behaved that morning at work, just wasn't like him. I don't know what's going on, but there's got to be an explanation for all this upset.'

With real steel in her voice Bev replied, 'There's a very simple explanation, Tom Naylor isn't the man we all thought he was. I never want to see him or hear from him again. Promise me, that if he gets in touch with you, don't tell me.

I don't want to know. As far as I'm concerned, Tom Naylor no longer exists. I intend to get on with my life. I've cried my last tears for that selfish bastard. I really hope everything goes okay for you with the IPCC enquiry, Matt. Once I'm back on my feet and I've found a little place of my own, I'll invite you both over for a nice meal and a glass or two of a good red wine, okay?'

Kate stepped forward and hugged her friend, 'It's a deal Bev, I'm looking forward to that already.'

Bev got into her Polo, started the engine and drove away from her friend's house.

She knew she would have to drive by the little cottage at Linby to get to her Mum's house in Hucknall. The same little cottage where up until four days ago she had spent the happiest times of her life, with the man she loved and who in truth she still loved more than life itself.

As she drove by the cottage and saw the 'For Sale' board outside, she felt tears stinging her eyes. As the tears began to trickle down her cheeks a little voice in her head was repeating Matt's words to her. Yes, this was out of character, there did have to be an explanation.

At that precise moment in time, Bev knew that she couldn't cope with that thought. She immediately dismissed those thoughts as being the musings of a desperate woman, trying to cling to a hopelessly lost and unrequited love.

As she pressed her foot hard down on the accelerator pedal and sped through the village of Linby, the voice in her head was now screaming, 'time will tell, time will tell'.

CHAPTER 34

10.30am 15th December 1987
Egerton Road, Georgian Quarter, Liverpool

It was Saturday morning and in his small flat in Liverpool, Tom had just finished clearing away the mess from his cooked breakfast.

He had always been very self-sufficient; cooking and housework were not alien concepts to him. Being neat and tidy came as second nature, almost to the point of obsession.

He made himself another mug of coffee, switched on the TV and sat down in the lounge. He was flicking through the channels, when the mobile phone Bailey had given him started to ring. The ringtone was very strident and very annoying, he grabbed the phone from the coffee table and said quickly, 'Hello.'

A very happy sounding Bailey said, 'Good morning Tom, how are you enjoying Liverpool?'

Tom sat back in his armchair, 'I can't complain from what I've seen so far.'

'How do you fancy going down to Anfield later, to cheer on that red shite you support?'

Tom laughed, 'Don't mind if I do, I've got nothing else planned.'

'Let's face it Hun, it won't be difficult getting you a ticket the way that lot are playing at the moment.'

'Do I take it our man's on the move then?'

'Nuff said on the phone, Tom. I'll be over at your place in half an hour with an update. Oh, and Tom there's one more thing.'

'Go on?'

'Please don't try the "sorry you just caught me coming out of the shower" routine. Standing there dripping wet in a towel, neither of us have got time today, okay?'

Tom laughed, 'You should be so lucky. I've been up, showered and dressed for over two hours now!'

'Sad act!', laughed Bailey, before terminating the call.

Tom was already thinking about how to contrive a meeting with Mercer. It had been a long time since he last saw him. He couldn't just walk up to him and say, "Hello mate, fancy seeing you here. Oh, by the way, I've just quit my job as a copper in Nottingham".

He knew he had to get thinking, and fast.

Bailey had said that Mercer always went for a drink in The Albert before the match. The pub had to be the best location for any sort of contrived meeting. It would be crammed full of supporters; the bedlam inside would be the perfect cover.

He just had to think of a way to accidentally bump into Mercer.

That thought set off the germ of an idea.

He would need to play it by ear when he got inside the pub. Hopefully the right set of circumstances would present themselves and he would have an opportunity.

Exactly thirty minutes passed before the doorbell to the flat rang once.

'Obviously not the postman', muttered Tom and he chuckled at his own joke as he walked to the door.

He asked, 'Who is it?'

'It's me, Bailey. Hurry up. Open the door, it's frigging freezing out here!'

Tom opened the door and smiled when he saw her, 'I'm not surprised you're freezing, there's frost on the ground and that's all you're wearing. You'll catch your death.'

Bailey was wearing very short and very tight denim shorts, a small denim jacket over a thin, cream coloured, mohair jumper that was stretched tightly across her full breasts. A pair of knee length suede cowboy boots finished the ensemble.

She scowled at Tom's comment and said, 'Shut it Naylor! You sound like my Gran. Make yourself useful and put the kettle on sharpish, before I die of bleeding hypothermia!'

Tom walked into the kitchen chuckling, he thought to himself, this girl's a complete nutter!

Five minutes later, Bailey had been provided with a large mug, full of steaming hot coffee and a couple of slices of thick buttered toast. At first, she had just held the mug in both hands trying to thaw out a little, before wolfing down the toast.

After she had warmed up a little, the unlikely pair began planning the day's events.

'As you know Tom, Mercer and Stone are under twenty-four-hour surveillance. What you aren't aware of, is that the people doing the surveillance are not police officers.'

'I don't understand, how can that be?'

'Ever since the Home Secretary got involved, due to the public outcry over the detective sergeant's murder and the discovery that Merseyside Police have got a security breach, other agencies have been involved.'

'Other agencies?'

'The security services.'

Tom was shocked at the involvement people in high office seemed to have, in the planning of this operation.

Bailey continued in her soft Liverpool accent, that Tom was finding more and more alluring, 'Anyway Tom, all you need to know is that MI5 have a crack team of surveillance operatives watching Mercer and Stone twenty-four hours a day. You personally, will never see them or have any contact with them. Any information they gather that you need to know about, will be fed through me and I'll ensure you get it. As we speak, the team are currently following Mercer from his home address in Sefton Park into the city. He's dressed appropriately for the match and was seen to pick up his season ticket before he left the house.'

Toms eyes widened a little as he wondered exactly what level of surveillance was going on here.

Had they bugged his house? Were covert cameras in his house?

With the Home Secretary's personal involvement and MI5 operating, anything was possible. Tom was aware that ever since Mikhail Gorbachev had become the Russian president in 1985 and the cold war had gone into decline, MI5 had often turned to serious and organised crime operations in an advisory and on occasion operational basis.

Obviously, the high level of media attention and the outrage felt by the population over the very public murder of the police officer, had created the political will for the granting of the operation.

Tom was starting to feel the pressure cranking up. He was beginning to realise that he would be playing an integral part in the operation. It was very likely that the operation would result in success or failure, depending entirely on how he performed.

Christy Almighty, he thought to himself, what have I let myself in for?

In between taking big gulps of coffee, Bailey continued talking, 'It's very likely that at some time today, Mercer will be inside The Albert pub next to the ground. Have you come up with any ideas how you two can meet?'

'I've got the basis of a rudimentary idea in my head, but it will depend on who else is in the vicinity of Mercer for it to work. I've got to try and make it look like a complete fluke that we've bumped into each other after all these years. If it looks in any way contrived, Mercer will definitely smell a rat. He's nobody's fool, Bailey.'

'I'll leave it down to you to make that call, Tom. My advice would be, just go with the flow when you get inside the pub. Sometimes you can overthink these situations and they end up looking completely staged and false. Anyway, you need to ensure that you're inside The Albert, no later than twelve thirty. The intelligence we have, suggests that as a rule by that time, for most home games, the place is already heaving. You'll have to get in there and locate Mercer pretty quickly, time will be pressing. Good luck with this Tom. If for any reason it does all go to ratshit, the surveillance team will be inside the pub and they'll get you out of there. They'll only get involved, if it's a matter of life and death, to be more precise, your life or death. Any questions Tom?'

'Only one Bailey, are you a cop or a spook?'

'There you go, the one question I can't answer. Well I could, but then I'd have to kill you', she chuckled and stood up.

She reached into a pocket of the denim jacket and took out a ticket for the match. She put it on the coffee table and said, 'Here's your ticket for The Kop. If there's any drastic changes to Mercer's expected routine, I'll call you on the mobile. If you haven't heard from me by twelve thirty, take it as read that he's in The Albert. There's only one thing left for me to say.'

'Go on', said Tom

'Come on Coventry!'

She laughed loudly as she left the flat.

CHAPTER 35

12.30am 15th December 1987
Anfield, Liverpool

It was a crisp, cold day.

The cloudless sky was a powder blue colour and there was an ineffectual sun, trying unsuccessfully to warm the city below. Tom was extremely grateful for the extra warmth provided by the woollen, Liverpool FC scarf he had bought from the street vendor on the way to the football ground.

It had been over seven years since Tom had last been to Anfield to watch Liverpool play. He was already feeling that familiar buzz of anticipation and excitement. It was a heady mix that instantly transported him back in time, to when he was a young man and the game of football was so much more important to him.

Nowadays, like many other true fans, he felt the game had lost its way a little. It was far more commercialised now. Television companies were providing huge sums of money to the clubs for the rights to televise live matches. The players were becoming more and more mercenary, demanding higher and higher salaries for something that should have been a privilege to do.

Tom acknowledged the fact that his interest in football had waned at about the same rate as Liverpool's success. It had been a few years since Liverpool had been strong enough to steamroller other teams. This year though, there was a new confidence. A new manager, Kenny Dalglish, had brought the best out of his players and the club had so far enjoyed an unbeaten start to the season.

Because the team were doing so well, the crowds were much bigger. As Tom turned the corner towards the rear of The Kop, the iconic stand that every football supporter had heard of, he could see the small building that stood in the shadow of the massive football stadium.

This was The Albert pub, only die-hard Liverpool supporters ever dared to set foot in there, especially on match day.

Tom zipped up his black bomber jacket a little more, thrust his hands in his Levi jeans pockets and strode purposefully towards the door of the pub.

Before he reached the door, he could hear the fans inside chanting the same old Liverpool anthems he used to sing when he was younger.

Having a pint in The Albert pub before the game was part of the match day ritual for many supporters. It seemed like this was also the case for Gary Mercer.

Tom glanced at his watch, it had just gone twelve thirty. He'd received no call from Bailey, so Mercer must be inside the pub.

Taking a deep breath, he opened the door and walked in.

The Albert was very small and already contained upwards of seventy people. The punters were all male and all football supporters. The smell of stale beer that had been previously spilled, making the floor sticky underfoot, brought memories flooding back to Tom.

The layout of the pub inside, hadn't changed. There was one long room that had a single bar that ran from one end of the room to the other. It was standing room only, there were no chairs or tables. The place was filled with the noise of different conversations all being held at a loud pitch, as people shouted over each other, trying to make themselves heard.

Fans were already three deep at the long bar, desperately trying to be seen by the overworked bar staff so they could get a pint. Cries of, 'Here ya are mate!' could be heard constantly.

Pushing his way firmly to the bar, Tom quickly glanced around.

The noise inside was further added to by three large TV screens mounted on the walls. These screens were all showing recordings of previous Liverpool goals, being played on a loop.

Finally, Tom managed to elbow his way to the front of the bar and holding out a ten-pound note, he soon caught the eye of one of the bar staff.

Tom shouted above the din, 'Pint of Guinness please mate, get one for yourself.'

The barman grinned and said, 'Cheers mate, I'll take for half of lager, okay?'

Tom nodded as he took his change and the familiar black pint with the cream coloured head.

He took a big mouthful of the dark beer and could feel the warmth from the alcohol immediately as he swallowed. He turned to the barman and said, 'Cheers pal.'

As soon as he'd been served, he immediately found himself being pressured away from the bar, as other punters pushed their way forward.

As he drifted back away from the bar, Tom scanned the faces in the pub and eventually he found Gary Mercer.

Mercer was standing at the far end of the long bar.

He was wearing a long black Crombie style coat and a red polo neck sweater. He was drinking slowly from a pint glass that had recently been filled.

Quickly assessing the situation, Tom could see that standing immediately in front of Mercer and with his back to Tom, was a very fat kid with a mop of curly red hair.

The fat kid was holding a full, pint glass in one hand and a meat pie in the other. He looked to be about eighteen years of age, very fat and very out of condition. He also appeared to be drinking alone. He was biting large mouthfuls of the pie, before washing it down with a gulp of ale. His attention was fully focussed on devouring the meat pie he was holding.

Perfect, thought Tom.

Slowly but steadily, Tom made his way through the crowd towards the fat, ginger kid. As soon as he got directly behind him, Tom turned so that he now had his back facing him.

After having one last glance over his shoulder, Tom stepped back sharply, deliberately barging into the ginger kid.

The outcome was inevitable, the fat, ginger kid's beer slopped out of the pint glass and splashed all over Mercer's pristine, Crombie coat.

In a flash, Mercer had grabbed the kid by the throat and growled, 'What the fuck are you doing? You fat clumsy prick!'

The ginger kid tried to pull away from Mercer's vice like grip and squealed, 'It wasn't my fault mate! This dickhead behind me, barged into me!'

Tom turned and said instantly, 'Who are you calling a dickhead? You fat fucker!'

Mercer finally let go of the ginger kid's throat and turned away. Leaving the youngster staring with real menace in Tom's direction, 'I'm calling you a dickhead! You fucking dickhead!'

The threat sounded ten times more aggressive when it was delivered in the kid's thick scouse accent.

Tom moved onto the next step of his hastily thought out plan, held up his hand and said, 'Look mate, it was an accident, let me buy you another pint.'

He already knew what the response was likely to be and the fat, ginger kid didn't disappoint him.

'Fuck the beer mate! You need to show some respect. I'm gonna bust you up!'

Tom saw the expression on the kid's face change. He'd witnessed this very subtle change of expression on countless men's faces immediately prior to them throwing a punch or kicking out.

Whichever way the fat, ginger kid's attack was going to manifest itself, Tom knew it was imminent.

Tom allowed his own pint glass to slip from his hand, then using both hands he shoved the kid hard in the chest, knocking him off balance and backwards. The only thing that stopped him hitting the floor was Gary Mercer. This time the remnants of the meat pie the kid was still holding, went all down Mercer's stonewashed denim jeans.

Once again Mercer grabbed the ginger kid and growled, 'Are you deliberately having a go at me or what?'

The fat, ginger kid struggled to get out of Mercer's grip and shouted, 'Fuck off Grandad!'

Without saying another word, Mercer smashed his forehead straight onto the nose of the ginger kid. The effect was devastating and the youngster dropped instantly onto the pub floor.

Although Tom had initially thought the ginger kid was drinking alone, he could now see two more spotty, adolescents making their way from the toilets towards the trouble. Both were obviously on a mission to help their friend. The first of the two youths, wearing a black hoody and a Liverpool beanie hat had seen Mercer deliver the crushing head butt and was raising an empty Budweiser bottle above his head, intent on smashing it down onto the back of Gary Mercer's head.

Tom stepped past Mercer, grabbed the arm of the youth and prevented the downward path of the bottle. Having blocked the attack, Tom then drove his right foot through the knee cap of the youth, dropping him to the floor. Ginger kid's other mate, having seen his two friends already dispatched to the ground, thought better of it and retreated back towards the toilets.

Everything had happened in a flash and Tom smiled as he heard a familiar cry from Gary Mercer who was now standing over the unconscious ginger kid, 'How do you like those apples, you fat, ginger twat!'

Mercer then turned to face Tom for the first time and said, 'Thanks mate, I think that bottle of Bud was destined for my fucking head. Let's get out of here, the bizzies will be barging in soon, and I for one want to see the match today. Head for that door over there, mate.'

Mercer nodded towards what looked like a fire escape door.

Tom followed him towards the fire door that was operated by a push bar. The sound of shouts and broken glass could be heard above the din, as fight after fight, began to break out behind them. The chaos inside the bar had all been sparked from the one incident Tom had engineered. Mercer lent on the push bar and using his shoulder, shoved the fire door open. The heavy door opened out into an alleyway.

Once they were both outside, Mercer shut the door behind Tom, before bending over, placing both hands on his knees and taking a deep breath.

Mercer then stared hard at Tom, 'Do I fucking know you?'

'Don't think so, mate.'

'Yeah I do. It's Tom 'fucking' Naylor isn't it?'

Tom, acting slightly stunned and bewildered said, 'Yeah, I'm Tom Naylor.'

'Tom, you dozy git, it's me Gary. Gary Mercer.'

Tom allowed a huge grin on his face and said, 'Fuck me! Gary Mercer. I should have guessed it was you, with that crack about apples to the ginger ninja back there.'

Mercer grinned and said, 'What the fuck are you doing in Liverpool mate?'

'I thought it had been too long since I saw the 'Pool, so I came up here and got a ticket.'

'Where's your ticket for, mate?'

'The Kop, where else?'

'That's great, I always stand on The Kop. We can watch the game together, have a couple of beers and a catch up. Fuck me Tom Naylor! It's been years mate.'

'Yeah it has, all the way back to the South Atlantic.'

'Fuck me yeah, the Falklands. Come on Tom, let's get out of here. You can tell me what you've been up to, since we beat up the Argies.'

Mercer laughed out loud and headed towards the turnstiles that led into The Kop. As Tom followed behind Mercer, he saw the first of the Police vans arrive outside The Albert. He watched, as officers jumped out of the vans and ran inside the pub, to try and control what had now turned into a fully fledged free for all inside. Tom could hear the sound of smashing glass and shouts from inside as boots and punches flew in.

Tom could only imagine the mayhem inside.

An image came into his head of the barman who had served him, cowering behind the bar trying to dodge the flying glasses and bottles that were being launched around the pub.

Oh well, thought Tom, just another Saturday afternoon in The Albert.

Both men made their way to a central position behind the Kop end goal, about halfway up the massive stand. They stood immediately in front of one of the many crash barriers, so when the crowd came pouring down the stand the movement would stop before they were swept along with the crowd. These were prime positions where everyone wanted to stand. Mercer threatened the two men that were already standing there, ordering them to move. The two strangers thought better of arguing with the aggressive Mercer and moved quickly away to stand somewhere else.

As they took their positions, with their backs resting on the metal crash barrier, Mercer grinned and looked directly into Tom's eyes, 'I don't believe this. After all these years, my old mucker Tom, here in Liverpool. Are you just up for the day or what?'

'To be honest Gary, it's a bit of a long story. I'll give you the short version so I don't bore you to death mate. I've just rented a small flat across town. I want to make a fresh start. I've got into a bit of a shitstorm with my previous occupation. I think I may have to bail out of the UK for a while, if you get my drift. I've come up here to clear my head, think things through and hopefully make some fast money, just in case I do need to skip overseas in a hurry.'

'Jesus Tom. That sounds like some serious shit. The last I heard from one of the old Regiment guys, was that you'd drifted over to the dark side and joined the bizzies.'

'That's true mate, I did. It was one of the biggest mistakes of my life. I don't know about you mate, but when I got back from the Falklands, I couldn't settle. Just to get back some enthusiasm for soldiering, I tried to join the SAS, but I did my ankle halfway through selection and failed. I couldn't face going back to the Regiment, so I bought myself out and left. In no time at all I was bored rigid, so I joined the Old Bill. It was alright for a bit and I got onto their firearms response teams. It was a nightmare after that, you just wouldn't believe how different it was to the army. They're all looking after number one, there's no teamwork. I don't know if you saw it on the news or in the papers about that animal rights woman who was shot dead by the cops in Nottingham. Well that was me mate. I shot the silly bitch and now I've got the Independent Police Complaints people all over my arse trying to prosecute me for doing my job. If that wasn't bad enough, I've just found out that my so-called colleagues, the treacherous bastards, have all given statements against me.'

'Bloody hell mate, the snide bastards.'

'The bottom line is, I could end up in jail for a long time. I quit the force there and then and legged it up here.

If I have to, I'll keep going. There's no way they're throwing me in jail for this mate. The biggest problem I've got is the bastards have confiscated my passport. That's the reason I need something to earn some fast readies. If I do make the decision to fuck off, it's going to be expensive, but there's no way I'm going to jail mate, no fucking way.'

'Fuck me Tom. Whatever possessed you to join the fucking police force anyway? Being in the cops has always been a job for losers.'

'I don't know mate. What I should have done was stayed in the army. Anyway, that's enough about me whinging on, how's the leg these days?'

'It's not too bad Tom. I've still got a bit of a limp, but it doesn't really stop me doing anything.'

'What have you been doing for work since the Regiment binned you mate? Oh fuck! Sorry mate, no offence intended.'

'None taken Tom. You're dead right, the fuckers did bin me. I nearly lost my leg, fighting for Queen and country and no fucker gave a damn. So now I don't give a damn about any other fucker.'

Tom didn't push it. He realised it was early days and he didn't want to appear to be too keen to know about Mercer's business.

'Fuck 'em all, eh Gary? That's what I say. Are the pies still any good? All that aggravation with the ginger kid and his mates has given me a bit of an appetite.'

Mercer smiled, 'Still the same Tom Naylor, always thinking about your belly. It's a wonder you're not twenty stone and as fat as that ginger fucker back there. Stay here mate and save our place, I'll go and get them. What do you fancy?'

'A great big, fuck off, meat and potato pie would be good, with a big mug of Bovril. I'm fucking freezing!'

As Mercer began to push his way through the crowd, Tom looked around the famous old stadium, as fans began to pour in through the turnstile. Kick off time was fast approaching.

He soon lost sight of Mercer as he made his way beneath the stand to the refreshment areas.

So far, so good, thought Tom.

He glanced around him trying to spot the team of MI5 operatives who would obviously still be watching them.

He wondered to himself how the surveillance team had fared in the fracas he had engineered in The Albert.

As soon as he went below the stand and out of Tom's view, Gary Mercer took out his mobile phone. He quickly glanced around him, before he punched in a number that was on speed dial.

Holding the phone tightly to his ear he said, 'Stone, are you back in the country yet?'

A weary sounding Mike Stone answered, 'I got back this morning, why what's wrong?'

'Nothing's wrong mate, I think I might have found the answer to our driver problem. Before I make any decisions, I'm going to need you to check a few things out for me. Be at Fat Sam's Café, first thing tomorrow morning, okay?'

'Okay Gadge, but what the fuck's going on?'

'I'll tell you in the morning when I know a bit more. Don't worry tight arse, I'll buy the breakfasts. Cheers mate.'

Mercer ended the call and made his way over to the refreshment stand.

He smiled at the young girl serving and said, 'Alright there Hun, can I have two of your famous, meat and potato pies, please. Oh, and two Bovril's as well luv, ta.'

CHAPTER 36

7.00pm 15th December 1987
Egerton Road, Georgian Quarter, Liverpool

'Thanks for the lift back mate', Tom said as he got out of Mercer's black Mercedes.

'No problem, it was on my way. Listen Tom, we'll have to go out for a beer and another chat soon. There's a business associate of mine I want you to meet, between us we might be able to sort you out some work round here. It'll be well paid work, cash in hand. We can go into all the details another time. It's been great to see you again mate, the dust up in The Albert was just like old times.'

Tom nodded and said, 'A bit of work would be brilliant mate. Yeah, it's been good to see you too.'

He shut the door, stepped away from the car and shouted, 'To the Regiment!'

Mercer wound the window down, laughed and said, 'Yeah, the Regiment. See you soon, Tom.'

Mercer wound the window back up and sped off into the night.

As he walked down the road towards his flat, Tom reflected on the day.

If he was being honest, he'd enjoyed being in his ex-army colleague's company again. It really was just like old times. They had chatted passionately about the football, jumping about like lunatics on each of the three occasions Liverpool had scored. The mood in the massive stadium was a happy, celebratory one as Liverpool cruised to an easy victory. Tom had even enjoyed joining in the singing and chanting with his old friend.

Towards the end of the second half, Tom had noticed a subtle mood change in Mercer. He began asking more direct, searching questions about his private life. He had asked questions about where he lived? Who his friends were that had betrayed him? Who his girlfriend was? If he had one? What did she think of him leaving Nottingham in a hurry?

He had begun to feel that Mercer was interrogating him, pumping him for information.

Tom had tried hard to answer the questions as nonchalantly as he could, so Mercer wouldn't realise he had recognised the fact that he was being questioned hard.

As he walked along the quiet street, his mobile phone ringtone broke the silence.

Tom grabbed the phone from his pocket, 'Hello?'

'Good evening sir. This is Deluxe Windows, have you ever thought about upgrading your windows?'

'It's okay Bailey, I'm alone.'

Bailey said quickly, 'Tom, don't go straight back to the flat. Meet me in the Duke of Wellington pub on Firmar Street. Do you know where I mean? Its just around the corner?'

'Yeah, I know where it is. Is everything okay?'

'See you there in ten minutes.'

She had terminated the call.

Tom walked down the road until he came to the junction of Firmar Street. He saw the Duke of Wellington pub across the road. It looked a sad, old place. A typical back street pub, that was on its last legs. Even a few of the letters had disappeared from the pub name. It was now the uke of Well ton.

It had only just gone seven o'clock, the pub was empty. Bailey was sitting on her own in a small booth at the far end of the pub sipping half of lager. The denim shorts had gone, she was now wearing black trousers and a mustard coloured anorak.

Far more sensible for this weather, Tom thought.

He got himself a pint of Guinness and walked over to the booth.

As soon as he'd served Tom, the barman went into the other bar, they now had the place to themselves.

Tom sat down next to her, took a swig of his Guinness and said, 'Well this place is hopping.'

'Tell me about it. What a dump.'

Cutting direct to the chase, she looked squarely at Tom and said, 'How do you think everything went today?'

'I think it went okay. We got on like a house on fire. It was just like old times. He did get into some serious questioning later on, asking about my recent past and stuff like that, but I don't think there's a problem. He's going to introduce me to a business associate of his about some cash in hand work.'

'I knew this would happen. Have you heard yourself?'

'What do you mean?'

'Got on like a house on fire. Just like old times. Get real Tom. This isn't the same man who was your Regiment buddy. You've got to remember who you're dealing with here. Mercer and Stone are killers, they're not your new best mates.'

'I know that', said Tom tersely. He could hear the tone of his own voice and the irritation in the reply.

'Listen to me Tom, as soon as Mercer went for the pies today, he was straight on his mobile phone to Micky Stone. We were able to eavesdrop on one half of their conversation.'

Once again, Tom was amazed at the level of surveillance that was in place.

Bailey continued, warming to her theme now, 'As you already know, Stone's the man we suspect of actually shooting dead, Ds Mayhew. Mercer will be getting Stone to check out your story. He'll be delving deep into your background. If, everything checks out to their satisfaction then maybe, just maybe they'll ask you on board as the driver for their next job.'

'I get what you're telling me Bailey, I'm being careful, alright?'

'For God's sake Tom, you've got to resist the temptation to contact anybody back home in Nottingham. Stone's a complete psycho, he'll readily torture to obtain information for Mercer and if we're right about the murder of Brian Mayhew, we already know he's willing to kill as well. I'm not saying that this will be the approach he's going to use, but you've got to remember that he's more than capable of doing so. You said he was questioning you quite hard at the game. Did you tell Mercer anything about individuals back home?'

Tom was quiet for a few seconds, staring at his pint.

He thought about the questioning by Mercer earlier and how he'd answered those questions. He thought about the information he'd given about his girlfriend Bev. He'd told Mercer her name, where she worked, what she looked like, virtually everything.

Things were starting to make sense.

Of course, Mercer would want to check that the situation

in Nottingham was just as he had described it. He would be an idiot not to check, and Tom knew only too well that Gary Mercer was definitely not an idiot.

Finally, he said quietly, 'I've told him chapter and verse about Bev, my girlfriend.'

Bailey was thoughtful for a minute, then she smiled and said, 'Okay. In one way, that's a good thing. We can take it as a given, that Stone will definitely be checking her out. Hopefully, Bev will tell him what an arsehole you are. How you've just walked out, leaving her high and dry without even having the decency to let her know where you've buggered off to!'

A now subdued Tom said, 'Is Bev in any danger, Bailey?'

'Have you spoken to her since the day you left Nottingham?'

'I haven't spoken to her since the night she walked out of my cottage after I'd broken off the relationship.'

'That's good. Look, I'm not going to lie to you Tom. Yes, she could be in danger, but as of this moment we'll be watching over her at all times.'

Tom slowly drank his beer and wondered again at the wisdom of what he'd got himself involved in.

In an effort to lighten the obvious tension in the room, Bailey said, 'Anyway, I'd like to congratulate you on that little stunt you pulled in The Albert today. It was perfect, worked like a charm.'

'Were you inside the pub?'

'Was I in there? It was me who served you your pint of Guinness. Thanks very much for the half of lager by the way, very generous of you.'

Tom grinned, 'You're very welcome.'

Bailey laughed, 'You see, my powers of disguise are second to none.'

Tom felt better and smiled.

She continued, 'Seriously, one of the guys who was in the pub, has got a lovely shiner from the brawl that started after you and Mercer had dived out the fire escape, but apart from that it was perfect. Who knows, you may have a future in this kind of work?'

'I don't think so', he replied quickly.

'Drink up Tom, it's time we both went home. Try not to worry about what's going on back home. We'll take care of Bev, I promise.'

CHAPTER 37

11.00pm 15th December 1987
Hoxton Street, London's East End

Jeff Wicks grabbed the last can of Kestrel super strength lager from the sixteen pack he had bought earlier that evening. Angrily, he yanked the ring pull from the top of the can and swallowed huge gulps of the strong beer.

He was already very drunk.

It was where he wanted to be, when he was drunk, he could no longer feel the pain.

He'd been in an alcohol induced haze for a week now. If it wasn't strong lager he was drinking, it was bottles of vodka.

He was sitting in his small bedsit above the Shifaz Kebab shop. The smell of the spicy meat, cooking on the huge spike below, was an ever-present odour in the flat. He had got used to the aromas after being there for two years. In his present condition he couldn't smell anything anyway.

Following the shooting in Farnsfield, he had been quickly interviewed by the local CID and a statement obtained. He'd then been driven by the Nottinghamshire CID, back to his home station in Woolwich. He had barely walked through the door of the station when his Chief Superintendent had called him into his office.

In his written statement, he had made certain allegations against the Nottinghamshire officers involved in the shooting. In particular against Pc Naylor, the officer who had shot Angela Hincks.

His senior officer was very unhappy about the statement Wicks had provided and had asked the detective to reconsider his evidence. When Wicks had refused, the Chief Superintendent had asked him exactly how closely he had become involved with Hincks?

Wicks refused to answer any more questions and said he would only talk to the IPCC investigating team. His frustrated senior officer had then ordered the undercover detective to go on indefinite leave, until after the IPCC had concluded their investigations.

Wicks had then walked out of the police station and returned to his small bedsit overlooking Hoxton market. He had seen nobody from the police since. There had been no welfare visits from the federation, no visits from colleagues, fuck all.

He had stayed in his flat, watching the news with interest. Only venturing out to get cigarettes, alcohol and the newspapers. The story of the shooting and the subsequent resignation of Pc Naylor had made the national press.

Wicks had wondered if the resignation was a tactic by the Nottinghamshire force to counter the allegation he had made in his statement. Whatever the reason, if Naylor thought that by resigning, he could get away with the crime he had committed, he was very much mistaken.

Wicks looked at the wall of the small bedroom in his flat that was now covered in newspaper clippings and photographs.

He was determined that the people responsible for Angela's death, would pay for what they had done.

He would see to it personally, if he had to.

He didn't trust the IPCC to carry out an impartial investigation. He knew that the whole thing would be swept under the carpet as soon as possible.

He drained the last of the lager, let out a huge belch and threw the empty can onto the floor. It joined the others in the pile on the floor.

He staggered from the bedroom into the kitchen, where he retrieved a half bottle of Smirnoff vodka from a Waitrose bag on the kitchen table. He unscrewed the cap and took a gulp. He gasped as the fiery liquid scorched the back of his throat.

He staggered back into the bedroom, still clutching the bottle.

He stared at the wall of press cuttings.

Right in the centre of the collage, was a black and white photograph he had cut from The Daily Telegraph business section. It was an image of Sir Jarvis Soames. His smirking, bloated face looked out above a headline about the upsurge in the share price of UK Pharmaceutical Ltd.

Shares in the company had soared in value, following the launch of a new drug to combat migraine headache.

He took another swig from the bottle and said angrily, 'I haven't forgotten about you, Sir Jarvis "fucking" Soames. I promised Angela that you'd pay for killing Jennifer. Everything you do, everything you've ever done, is all about making money. Don't you know that money's the root of all evil, you fat, egotistical bastard!'

The words of his tirade were badly slurred because of the alcohol, but his eyes blazed with a manic passion as he said them.

He slumped down on the bed, still staring at the businessman's face on the wall. He drank another gulp of the vodka and said quietly, but with the same anger, 'You first, then that bastard, Naylor!'

CHAPTER 38

9.30am 16th December 1987
Fat Sam's Café, Liverpool City Centre

The warmth inside the small café felt very welcome after the bitter cold of the Baltic weather outside. There was condensation on all the windows and the gorgeous smell of freshly fried bacon filled the air.

There was a general clamour as people ordered their food and the hard-pressed kitchen staff shouted orders that were ready.

It was one of Gary Mercer's favourite places in the entire city.

It was a haunt for villains. Everybody knew everyone else. A stranger would stick out like the proverbial sore thumb in here.

The owner of the café, Fat Sam Tanner, had himself served a twelve-year prison sentence for an armed robbery back in the sixties. Rumour had it, that the café had been set up using the hidden proceeds from that last robbery.

Gary Mercer and Micky Stone were sitting in their usual seats, next to the steamed-up windows at the very front of the café. Both men had ordered the full English and large mugs of tea.

The full English in Fat Sam's Café, was something to behold. It was a massive plateful of bacon, sausage, black pudding, fried eggs, beans, mushrooms, tomatoes and fried bread.

Customers could feel their arteries hardening as the delicious fried food was placed on the table in front of them.

It really was the food of the Gods.

Mercer finished chewing a mouthful of sausage, then said to Stone, 'So how was the Algarve mate?'

'Very nice, very sunny. I cracked off with this gorgeous bird from Birmingham on the first night. Well I say gorgeous, she was fit as fuck until she opened her gob! I don't know what it is about that frigging accent, but it's such a turn off. It does my head in!'

Both men laughed.

Stone took a swig of his hot, strong tea and said, 'Anyway, you didn't fetch me down here just to eat breakfast and talk bollocks about my shagging exploits on holiday. Why all the urgency? What's so important that you needed to see me here this early?'

'I think I might've found the answer to our driver problem. The only problem being, the guy's an ex copper.'

Stone looked at Mercer as if he'd gone totally mad.

He almost choked on a mouthful of fried egg, before spluttering, 'Are you off your fucking head, mate?'

Mercer was unconcerned by the outburst, he'd expected Stone's reaction to be exactly this.

He leaned forward and said conspiratorially, 'Listen Micky, I'll personally vouch for this guy. I served with him in the Falklands. He's an ex Para, extremely cool under fire and a very handy lad. If it wasn't for him, I would've probably lost my leg back then. I'm telling you, he's a stand-up bloke. You've got to trust me on this.'

Micky Stone was having none of it, 'No I don't have to trust you on this, Gadge. I don't care if he saved yours, your granny's and any other fuckers life in the Falklands! I'm not working with ex-filth and that's that.'

Stone began wolfing down his breakfast again, indicating that as far as he was concerned, the conversation was over.

As if to reinforce the point he said, 'Pass me that red sauce, Gadge.'

Mercer handed him the plastic sauce bottle that was shaped like a giant red tomato.

As Stone went to take it from him, Mercer gripped the bottle hard, so Stone couldn't take it from him. Their eyes met and Mercer said under his breath, 'Listen Micky, you work with the filth every time we go out on a fucking job, or have you conveniently forgotten about The Ace? Just hear me out, okay?'

Stone snatched the sauce bottle and said quietly, 'Go on then, spill.'

'From the sounds of it, this bloke's been stitched up. From what he's told me, he's been turned over by the cops himself. He was working on the police firearms teams in Nottingham, when he shot dead some mad bitch. They're setting him up to be the fall guy for a fucked up operation and it looks as though he may have to serve time for the shooting. I'm telling you Micky, at this moment in time, he hates the cops more than we do.'

Stone shovelled more bacon in his mouth and said, 'Now that's not possible. Nobody hates cops more than me.'

Mercer continued, 'There's a simple reason why I've asked you to come over this morning. I want you to travel down to Nottingham, on a digging expedition. When I was talking to this bloke, I got chapter and verse from him about loads of things. He told me all about his ex-girlfriend, where

210

he used to live, the whole job lot. I'll tell you everything he told me about his life, then I want you to spend the next few days in Nottingham checking out his story. If just one small thing doesn't look right, I'll bin the whole idea and we'll never have to set eyes on him again. Although if the prick is lying, it might be good to mash him up a little bit.'

Stone said, 'Mashing him up a bit, is the first sensible thing I've heard you say so far.'

Mercer ignored the remark and continued, 'If what he's told me is true, he could be a massive asset to us. He's very sharp, quick on the uptake and knows how to handle weapons. He can be a right nasty bastard when he has to be and he drives motors like Nelson Piquet. Think about it for a minute Micky, not only that, he knows how these firearms cops work as well. You never know mate, one day we may just come up against these blokes. He could be really good news for us.'

'Yeah, and he could also be your worst fucking nightmare. A couple of questions, how come he's just happened to meet you again? Don't you think it's a little weird after all these years?'

'I've already told you. He's on his toes. He's come up to Liverpool to get away from everything that's happening down there. He just wants to make some quick cash, no questions asked. He's already told me he's not bothered what he has to do to get it. The cops have confiscated his passport, so if everything does come on top, it's going to be very expensive for him to get suitable fake documents to get out of the country. At the end of the day, he's like the rest of us, he doesn't want to go inside. He didn't ask to meet me, we literally bumped into each other in The Albert at the match.'

'Very convenient.'

'It wasn't like that Micky, we ended up in a scrap with some tossers in there. He didn't even recognise me.'

Having finally finished the last of his gargantuan breakfast, Stone put down his knife and fork, took a long drink of tea from his mug and said, 'Okay Gadge, start from the very beginning. What's this shithead's name?'

'His name's Tom Naylor.'

'Right, I want to know everything you can tell me about this Naylor, but especially I want to know about his ex-bird. If this is all bullshit and there's a weak link in his cover story, my gut tells me that it will come from his ex-girlfriend. That's where he would've fucked up.'

'I think you're probably right, but listen to me Micky, I want this job to be done in a subtle way. If you go down to Nottingham with all guns blazing and start breaking people or generally fucking things up, it's not going to be worth bothering. Do you understand me?'

'Come on Gadge, you know me. Subtle and sophisticated should be my middle names.'

'Yeah, and it's exactly because I do know you Micky, that I'm telling you.'

'Okay, okay, I hear you Gadge. Subtlety all the way. Start talking about Pc "fucking" Plod then, the quicker you tell me what you know, the quicker I can get down to that rat's nest they call they Nottingham.'

CHAPTER 39

9.00am 17th December 1987
Beauclair Drive, Wavertree, Liverpool

Chief Inspector Noel Prime was just finishing his breakfast. As usual the night before, he had set two places.

Two dishes, two plates, two cups, two of everything.

This morning, he had prepared two bowls of porridge and made two cups of coffee, as usual only one breakfast had been eaten and only one drink touched.

As he cleared the uneaten bowl of porridge down the sink, he thought to himself that his wife really must start to eat something soon.

The fact that his wife was still upstairs in a bath full of cold bloody water, laying in exactly the same position as she had been, ever since the night Prime had smashed her head in with a claw hammer, wasn't registering in his rapidly unhinging mind.

Having tidied the kitchen, he finished getting ready for work, slipping on his highly polished shoes and buttoning up his uniform tunic. He was quickly ready for another day in charge of the Merseyside Police Control Room. He'd noticed, over the last few days, how people were starting to look at him differently. How distant some of his colleagues had become. How suddenly, everyone was concerned for his health.

He grabbed his car keys from the table in the hallway and made his way out of the front door. He walked briskly down the driveway to his car. He could already see his neighbour waiting for him alongside his car. She was an elderly spinster and a nosy, busy body he'd never liked. As he neared his car, she leaned over the short privet hedge and said, 'Good morning Mr Prime, how's your lovely wife? I haven't seen her for over a week, is she okay?'

Without looking at the woman Prime snapped, 'Gone to stay with her mother in Leeds for a while. Expecting her back in a week or two. Can't stop, late for work.'

His nosy neighbour tutted at his rude, brusque manner and carried on trimming the low hedge that separated the two driveways.

Prime started his car and reversed slowly off the driveway. As he backed the car down towards the road, he could see his neighbour staring at him. He smiled and whispered aloud through gritted teeth, 'Fuck off, you nosy old cow!'

Having reversed his car onto the quiet road, he then gunned the engine and drove off at speed down the street.

He had only gone about three hundred yards when his mobile phone began to ring. Prime stopped the car and answered it. 'Hello, Noel Prime.'

'It's Mercer. We need to talk, today.'

Just the sound of the man's voice, made his blood run cold. Prime's head was suddenly filled with images of the awful night that had led to his wife's violent death at his hands.

Glenys making love with Mercer.

The make believe, romantic last dinner he had prepared for her.

His wife pleasuring herself in the oily, scented bath.

The carnage after he had battered her to death.

As the different images whirled around his mind, he suddenly felt physically sick. He felt a little of the porridge he'd recently consumed rise into his mouth. Fighting the urge to vomit, he swallowed the regurgitated food and said quickly, 'Haven't got time today, sorry.'

His voice sounded clipped, as he tried to stifle the overwhelming sense of panic, he felt hearing Mercer's voice.

Mercer wasn't in the mood for a discussion and said angrily, 'I'll see you at the usual place in Stanley Park, the bench near the band stand at one thirty today. Make sure you're there and on time dickhead, or the next time you see me, I'll be bouncing your head off the fucking pavement. If that thought isn't enough to bother you, just remember that it's only a short drive from here to Sheffield University where your kids are. I can always go and have a discussion with one of them if you'd rather.'

Prime felt an inner rage building and suddenly found his voice. He roared down the phone, 'Don't you go near my kids, you evil bastard.'

Mercer's reply was calm and equally menacing, 'Shut the fuck up Prime, just make sure you're there. Stanley Park, one thirty, today.'

He ended the call.

Prime started his car and continued his commute to work.

He was seething, but he knew he would be at the meeting in Stanley Park.

What choice had he got?

None.

CHAPTER 40

1.30pm 17th December 1987
Stanley Park, Liverpool

Prime glanced nervously at his watch, it was almost one thirty. Where was Mercer?

He took a sip of tea from the polystyrene cup he'd purchased from the café in the park when he had arrived. The strong, sweet tea was already lukewarm and tasted disgusting.

He emptied the contents onto the ground and threw the cup beneath the park bench he was sitting on.

'Tut tut! Just look at all that unnecessary litter and you a policeman as well. You should know better officer!'

Prime almost jumped.

He hadn't seen Mercer approaching the park bench from behind him.

As Mercer sat on the bench next to Prime, he said, 'Nice of you to come Mr Policeman.'

'What do you want', spat Prime.

'Less of your fucking attitude would be a good start. What's got into you lately? Has Mrs Prime finally seen the light, fucked off and left you on your own for good?'

'You leave my wife out of this. I'm on my own for a bit that's all. She's gone to stay with her mother for a few weeks. What do you want that's so fucking urgent? I thought we'd agreed no more jobs for a bit.'

Mercer growled, 'Get this through your thick head, I say when we're doing jobs again, got it? In the meantime, the reason I wanted to see you is this, I want to know if anyone's been asking about me. Have you heard my name being mentioned or have any checks been done on me?'

Prime slipped into his well-rehearsed lie, 'I haven't seen anything about you, if anybody had been doing checks on your name, they would have to come through me, seeing as how I'm the person responsible for the administration of the Police National Computer in this force. Nobody's looking at you Mercer.'

Mercer's name had cropped up on a couple of routine checks ever since Prime had made the anonymous phone call giving his name to the incident room.

Mercer continued, 'One other thing. Have you heard the name Tom Naylor being mentioned? He's an ex-cop from Nottingham.'

This really was a surprise to Prime.

He shook his head, 'No. I haven't heard that name before. Do you want me to keep my ear to the ground and if I hear anything let you know?'

'Well yes, obviously. I wouldn't have mentioned it otherwise, would I?'

Mercer then put a mocking tone in his voice and asked, 'How come wifey has gone to stay at her Mum's then? Have you two lovebirds had a fall out?'

Prime said stiffly, 'That's really none of your business. Now is that it? I've got to get back to the office.'

Prime stood up ready to leave.

Mercer enjoyed the fact that he could make the senior police officer dance to his tune. He made Prime stand there for a full two minutes before saying, 'Yeah, go on then Noel, fuck off back to work. I maybe in touch sooner rather than later about another job. Your usual cut will apply.'

Mercer remained seated on the bench as he watched Prime walk down the hill towards the car park. He really did despise that little weasel of a man. At least he now knew why Glenys hadn't been round.

He'd been genuinely concerned when she hadn't turned up for the meeting, they'd arranged the last time they were together.

What had started out as a sordid little affair had gradually developed into something much more meaningful. They had both gradually become more and more absorbed by each other. The affair was becoming all-consuming for both of them. Mercer knew that in the very near future, he would be asking Glenys to leave Prime. It was obvious she was deeply unhappy in her marriage and only stayed with her husband out of a sense of duty.

Now that her children were grown up and away at University, he knew that when he asked the question, her reply would be yes.

He wanted to do one more job. A really big earner. He would then be set up financially and would ask her to leave Prime. It was their dream to leave Liverpool for somewhere a long way away. They had often lay in each other's arms and talked at length about living in Canada. A house in the wilderness, with snow-capped mountains as a backdrop, overlooking a vast lake was their dream.

Over the last few months, they had begun to discuss starting a new life together, which at the beginning would have seemed impossible. It was a measure of how their feelings for each other had grown.

Mercer wasn't a great fan of the love word, but he believed they had both fallen deeply in love with each other. Being together permanently was the obvious next move, it was bound to happen sooner rather than later.

All he needed was that one last big job, that's why he was so keen to bring Tom Naylor on board.

To achieve their dreams, he needed a driver, pure and simple.

CHAPTER 41

6.00pm 19th December 1987
Mansfield, Nottinghamshire

Micky Stone settled back in the soft leather seat of his BMW. He'd parked on Kings Mill Lane, a small side street that overlooked the entrance to the main Mansfield Ambulance Station.

The station was right beside the very large Kings Mill Hospital that was listed as being Mansfield's main hospital, but was actually situated in the neighbouring town of Sutton in Ashfield.

It was now his third day in Nottinghamshire. The previous two days had been spent checking up on the background story given by Mercer's old army mate, Tom Naylor.

So far, everything Naylor had told Mercer, had checked out.

One of the first things Stone had done when he arrived in Nottinghamshire, was to visit the cottage that Mercer had described. He'd found it quickly enough in the small village of Linby and had seen the 'For Sale' board in the front garden. He'd taken the time to visit the estate agents and arrange for a viewing of the property.

He'd viewed the cottage the next day with the young female estate agent. He spent most of his time flirting with the pretty brunette, but at the end of the visit, he was satisfied that the cottage was genuinely up for sale and it wasn't just a bogus 'For Sale' board in the garden.

While he was inside, viewing the property he had noticed the photographs of a young couple that had been left on the sideboard in the lounge. It had been a fair assumption to make, that the pretty blonde in the photographs was Naylor's girlfriend, Bev Wilson.

Naylor had let slip to Mercer, that his girlfriend worked as a Paramedic at Mansfield Ambulance Station.

Stone had watched the same blonde woman from the photograph at the cottage, going into the ambulance station just before ten o'clock that morning.

It was now approaching six o'clock in the evening and Stone was hoping that Bev Wilson would be finishing her shift soon and going for a drink with her colleagues. His plan was to follow her from work and if she went into a pub to go inside and strike up a casual conversation with her. If she didn't go for a drink, his plan was to follow her home and doorstep her, pretending to be a journalist after some information on Naylor.

If that didn't work, he would have to come up with some other bollocks. Whichever way he did it, Stone needed to check out Naylor's girlfriend or ex-girlfriend whatever it was now, to be absolutely sure his story held water, before he went back to Liverpool and spoke to Mercer.

Just after six o'clock, Stone spotted Bev Wilson leaving the ambulance station. He watcher her as she walked towards the car park at the front of the building. She was walking alongside two other women and they were all engaged in an animated conversation. All three were laughing and giggling as they reached their respective cars.

As the three cars pulled out onto Sutton Road heading towards Mansfield, Stone started his car and quickly slipped in behind them.

As the small convoy approached the first public house, Stone smiled to himself as the indicators on all three vehicles came on and the cars were driven into the car park of The Sir John Cockle pub.

He drove his car into the car park and watched as the three women got out of their cars and made their way, still giggling towards the pub doors.

Stone was confident that most women found him attractive, he was hoping that Bev Wilson would be no different.

He followed the women into the pub and was surprised at just how busy it was, it was still early, but the pub was full of young drinkers. He quickly spotted the three women waiting to be served at the far end of the bar.

Stone walked over and stood beside them. He made eye contact with Bev before turning to the young barman and saying, 'Lime and Soda mate, thanks.'

It was Bev who spoke up, 'Excuse me. We were here first!'

Stone slowly turned, looked directly at Bev, smiled and said, 'I do apologise ladies, I thought you'd already been served. I didn't mean to barge in, you must think I'm pig ignorant. By way of an apology, let me get this round of drinks. It's the least I can do.'

Bev's two companions were instantly attracted by the chiselled good looks of the softly spoken stranger.

Lynn said immediately, 'That's very nice of you. Jack Daniels and Coke for me, ta.'

Bev said, 'Just a minute Lynn.'

She then turned to Stone and said, 'There's really no need, we're alright, thanks.'

Bev's other work colleague, Mandy interjected, 'Come on Bev, he's only trying to apologise.'

Mandy turned to Stone and said, 'Please excuse my friend Bev, she's having a bad day. A white wine and soda would be very nice, thanks.'

Bev shrugged her shoulders in resignation and half smiled at Stone.

Stone smiled back and said, 'Well Bev, looks like you've been out voted. What can I get you?'

'A glass of red wine would be great thanks, a Merlot if they've got one. Sorry if I sounded a bit abrupt, but I'm just totally off men at the moment.'

'I'm sorry to hear that', he said in a very non-committal way.

When the drinks arrived, Bev and Mandy thanked Stone and made their way over to a table near the windows at the front of the bar. The table was in a dark recess of the bar and had four comfortable, tub style seats around it.

At the bar, Lynn took her Jack Daniels and Coke from Stone and said, 'Thank you. Look, why don't you come and sit with us if you're on your own? There's nothing worse than drinking alone.'

Stone smiled and held eye contact with Lynn, 'If you're certain your friends won't mind, that would be very nice. I've only stopped off for a quick drink, but a little friendly conversation would be good. Thanks.'

'You're more than welcome, where's that lovely accent from', flirted a very interested Lynn.

Stone followed Lynn over to the table and as he sat down with Bev, Lynn and Mandy he said, 'It's a scouse accent. I'm down here on enquiries from Liverpool.'

Mandy put down her glass and said, 'Enquiries? That sounds very official. What are you a cop, or something?'

Stone chuckled, 'Is it that obvious ladies? I don't know why they don't just give me a blue light and sirens to go with this suit.'

Bev scowled and said, 'That's all I need, small talk with a bloody cop!'

She stood up and said, 'I'm off to the ladies.'

Mandy said, 'Hang on a minute Bev, I'll come with you.'

Stone turned to a very attentive Lynn and said, 'Looks like your friend Bev isn't too impressed.'

She leaned forward and whispered, 'Don't mind her, she's just had a very painful split from her bloke. He's a copper too.'

'What, a divorce?'

'No, they weren't married. I think Bev was hoping that might be on the cards later this year though. It was all very sudden; her bloke just took off after getting in some very serious shit at work.'

'No way. That's unbelievable, the poor girl.'

'Don't worry about her, er sorry, what's your name?'

'My apologies. My name's Jake.'

'I'm Lynn, by the way. Anyway, as I was saying, it gets worse. The two of them had a massive row and he kicked her out. He's now apparently put his house up for sale. The worst bit is, Bev doesn't even know where he's gone. I think she's getting over him now though. She's already been on a couple of dates. She's a bit that way inclined, if you know what I mean? Anyway, that's enough about Bev. Where are you staying while you're down here?'

The last bit about the dates and Bev being a loose woman was a lie, but Lynn could sense that this dark, enigmatic, handsome stranger was a little bit too interested in Bev.

Lynn fancied a bit of this action for herself.

Stone said, 'I've been staying at the Premier Inn at Worksop, but I'm travelling back to Liverpool this evening. I was just heading for the motorway but fancied a quick drink before I got going. In fact, I really must be hitting the road soon.'

Lynn quickly scribbled her telephone number onto a beer mat and said, 'Let me give you this. If you're ever down this way again, give me a call. I've got my own place and it's a lot more comfortable than a Premier Inn, if you know what I mean.'

Stone knew only too well what she meant, but Lynn was nothing like his usual type. She was far too plain and frumpy for his taste.

'Thanks Lynn, that's so kind of you. Please apologise to your friend Bev for me. I didn't mean to upset anyone. I should be back down this way in a couple of weeks, I'll definitely be giving you a call, if you're sure?'

Stone leaned forward and gave her small peck on the cheek before standing up to leave.

A breathless Lynn said, 'Are you sure you have to drive back tonight? Why don't you come and stay with me tonight? Then drive back to Liverpool tomorrow morning.'

'I would have loved to Lynn, but I've an appointment I can't break at eight o'clock in the morning. Like I said though, I'll be back down here in a couple of weeks' time. I promise you, when I'm back we'll spend a few days and more importantly, a few nights together.'

Stone winked at her, smiled and said, 'How does that sound Lynn?'

Lynn could feel her face flushing, she smiled her best seductive smile and said, 'That sounds wonderful Jake. You won't be disappointed. Call me as soon as you arrive.'

'Bye Hun', said Stone as he walked out of the pub.

Lynn breathed in deeply, cherishing the waft of Paco Rabanne aftershave as he walked by.

He's drop dead gorgeous, she thought.

As Stone walked across the car park towards his BMW, he quickly tore up the beer mat that Lynn had so carefully written her phone number on.

Mercer would be pleased. It looked like his blast from the past mate checked out.

Stone picked up his mobile phone and dialled the number for Mercer.

It was answered straight away and Stone said, 'Gadge. Its Micky. Everything about this bloke Naylor, checks out down here. I'll see you at eight o'clock in the morning for a chat. Where do you want to meet?'

'How about the motorway services just outside Ellesmere Port on the M53?'

'Okay Gadge, I'll see you there around eight this morning.'

Stone terminated the call.

As he slowly drove out of the pub car park, he never noticed the three cars that slipped into a very loose convoy behind him as he headed back along the A38 towards the M1 motorway.

He'd been in Nottingham long enough, he couldn't wait to get back home to Liverpool.

Back inside the Sir John Cockle pub, Bev and Mandy returned to the table and saw that the mystery man had gone.

As the two women sat down Mandy laughed and said, 'Where's he gone? It didn't take you long to scare that one off.'

A disgruntled Lynn snapped back, 'For your information, Jake will be staying at my place in two weeks' time.'

Bev said, 'I wouldn't bank on that Lynn, he's a cop, isn't he? My money says, you'll never lay eyes on him again.'

'They're not all like your Tom', said Lynn sharply.

Bev stood up and said, 'That's it. I'm going home. Bye girls.'

Mandy turned to Lynn and said, 'Look what you've done now, big mouth!'

'Oh, just finish your drink Mandy. I'm sick of her moping about, the world doesn't revolve around Bev "bloody" Wilson.'

Lynn slumped back in her chair and took a long drink of the Jack Daniels and coke that Jake had bought her.

She drifted away and thought about everything she would be doing with him in a couple of weeks' time.

She breathed in deeply and could have sworn she could still smell his aftershave.

CHAPTER 42

1.00am 20th December 1987
Egerton Road, Georgian Quarter, Liverpool

It was almost one o'clock in the morning.

Tom was in bed but in that sleepless state, not quite awake but only semi-conscious of your surroundings.

When his mobile phone suddenly rang, he was instantly wide awake and grabbed it from the bedside cabinet.

Flicking on the lamp at the side of the bed he said, 'Hello?'

It was Bailey, there was a sense of urgency in her voice when she said, 'This is Deluxe Windows.'

'Bailey? It's okay, I'm alone. What's up?'

'Are you awake Tom? I need to see you right now.'

'Is something wrong? Is Bev alright?'

Tom could hear the panic in his own voice.

Bailey heard it too and she answered gently, 'Bev's fine. I'll be at yours in three minutes. Don't put any lights on, just open the door. I don't think I'm being watched, but better safe than sorry. Okay?'

'Okay.'

He unlocked the door, sat on the sofa in the living room and waited in the dark for Bailey to arrive.

Exactly three minutes later he heard her slowly come in through the unlocked door, closing it softly behind her.

'Tom, it's only me', she whispered, 'Where are you?'

'I'm in here', said a still shell-shocked, but wide-awake Tom.

Bailey sat down on the sofa next to him and he said, 'Well? What was so bloody urgent? I'm shitting myself here, what's happened?'

'Micky Stone has spent the last few days in Nottingham and has spoken with Bev. Don't worry, she's fine and the surveillance teams have now followed Stone back to Liverpool. She hasn't been touched and is fit and well. It looks like Mercer sent Stone down to Nottingham to check your story. We think your cover's still intact. If that's the case, then things should start to move pretty quickly now. We think the reason Mercer checked you out, is because he's looking to recruit you to be their driver on the next cash in transit robbery. We know Mercer had a meeting arranged at Stanley Park yesterday, but sod's law kicked in and the surveillance team had a malfunction on one of their vehicles. For over an hour we didn't have eyes on Mercer. The meeting took place during that one-hour black hole. It could be that he met with his source in the Merseyside Police. It would make sense. If he's taking the trouble to check you out in Nottingham, he'll be asking his source the same questions here. He'll be trying to ascertain if your name's being spoken about within the police.'

'So, do you think my covers blown? Am I still safe, or what?'

'Short answer. I don't know. I just needed to give you a heads up on what's been happening. If I'm right, I think Mercer will be contacting you sometime either today or at the latest tomorrow. He'll be wanting to set a job up quickly. Christmas is just around the corner and he'll want to make a score while the takings are so huge.'

'So, you think things are moving forward?'

'I think so, yes.'

'Great. I can't wait to get out of here and back to normality.'

'There's one other thing, Tom. As the getaway driver, you'll be expected to provide the car or cars for the job. If you're left to your own devices, then great, we'll provide you with high powered cars that have all kinds of sophisticated surveillance and tracking devices on board, that will remain undetected. If they want you to steal the cars while they're with you, just do it. The Home Secretary's already granted you an immunity from prosecution, within reason.'

'I'd better brush up on my car stealing techniques', grinned Tom.

Bailey handed Tom a shoe box and said, 'I've brought you some different training shoes to wear. Inside the sole of the shoe is a very small magnetic tracking device. Once you've stolen a car, just slip the device under a wheel arch when you get the chance. We'll then be able to track your location. Our surveillance teams should be on you anyway, but in case we have another fuck up like yesterday, this provides you with some insurance. Okay?'

'Okay. How was Bev when she met Stone?'

'By all accounts, very pissed off. She only stayed for half a drink with two of her girlfriends, before going back to her mother's house.'

Tom was thoughtful and there was a long silence before Bailey said, 'Are you okay? Are you still up for this job? We can pull the plug any time you want.'

'I'm fine Bailey. I just want to get this done, go home and try to resurrect some semblance of a normal life.'

Bailey placed a comforting arm around his shoulders and said, 'It'll soon be over, I promise. Don't worry, you and Bev will be fine.'

'Do you really think so? What about you Bailey? Is there anyone special in your life that puts up with this shit all the time?'

'Not at the moment, but who knows, one day there might be. Right now, I need to focus on the here and now. Come on Tom, you've got to stay switched on and strong to see this through. I'm not going to lie to you, the nearer you get to the actual armed robbery, the more stressful and dangerous this is going to get.'

'I know. I'm sure I'll be fine and thanks for the heads up.'

'In that case, I'm off. The trainers are over there. Don't worry I'll see myself out.'

She slipped out of the door and disappeared into the night.

CHAPTER 43

6.30am 20th December 1987
Motorway Services, M53, Ellesmere Port

Micky Stone blew on the large mug of scalding black coffee, before carefully taking a sip. He was sitting in the motorway services just outside Ellesmere Port. The place was a shithole and had definitely seen better days. The food hall comprised of a dingy coffee shop and a scruffy looking Wimpy Bar. Stone had avoided the burger place and sat in the coffee shop, gazing out of the window at the motorway traffic speeding by.

It was still early and the services were very quiet.

That all changed dramatically, as a coach load of Scottish schoolchildren heading south to London on a school trip suddenly descended into the food hall.

As Stone watched the noisy mixture of adolescent boys and girls, with a growing disdain, he was relieved when they all dived straight into the Wimpy Bar.

Obviously, burgers not coffee was their thing.

'Eyeing up schoolgirls now, are you? You big nonce!', said Mercer.

He had slipped in and sat down opposite Stone, while his attention had been diverted by the excited, squealing kids.

Stone grimaced, 'Fuck right off Gadge! That's not even remotely funny. You know exactly what I think about kiddie fiddling bastards!'

Mercer grinned, 'I'm only pulling your leg mate, don't be so fucking touchy. Anyway, enough of all that bollocks, tell me what you found out in Nottingham?'

'Basically, everything about Tom Naylor checks out. How you described it to me, is how it actually is. Nobody down there knows where the fuck he's disappeared to, not even his bird. He's really shit on her by all accounts. They were living together in a cottage he owns and talking about getting married next year. Anyway, it seems they had a blazing row, he kicked her out, put the house up for sale and then fucked off.'

'What about the trouble he's in at work, that shooting he spoke to me about at the footy?'

'That's all genuine too. He really did waste some animal rights twat who was carrying and now it appears he shouldn't have shot her. This has been all over the news mate. The rumour down in Nottingham is that the people making enquiries into her death are making progress, and any day now they're going to announce that this was an unjustifiable shooting by your man Naylor. The worst thing is, this has all come about because of what the other cops, his supposed mates, have said to the enquiry. Basically, your man Naylor is in big shit and looks like going down for a long stretch. Did he tell you they've confiscated his passport?'

'Yeah, he did and I told you when I briefed you before you went down there. Weren't you listening?'

'Oh yeah, I remember now you did tell me that. Sorry mate, I'm knackered. I drove back late last night and have hardly slept. Anyway, whichever way you look at this situation, it would appear that your mate's well and truly up shit creek.'

'So, you said. While you were down in Nottingham, I've had The Ace check him out this end as well. Nobody in the force has been talking about, or even mentioned Tom Naylor's name. No one's been looking at you and me either, so I think we're good to go for another little tickle before Christmas. Are you up for that Micky?'

'Definitely, one hundred percent. When are you thinking?'

'Well, Christmas is fast approaching and the goose, as they say, is getting very fat. So, for that matter are the Tesco Superstores at either Crosby or Preston. One of those two will be our next job. The pre-Christmas sales are currently getting under way now. In a couple of days, the takings at either of those stores are expected to exceed over half a million pounds. We'll be there waiting, ready to take out the security van when it's collected those massive takings. The only question is, do we take Tom Naylor along as our driver?'

'If we're going in two days' time, that doesn't give us much time for planning.'

'Don't worry, I've been planning this job for some time. I want this to be a spectacular success. I want a massive pay-out on this one, I've got some big plans and I need a big score. Things are almost in place, but I'm still waiting for your answer mate. Are you okay with Naylor driving?'

'Truthfully, I can't say I'm over the moon about it Gadge, but if you vouch for him then I'm willing to go along with it. Like you said before, The Ace has always been the difference for us and with this guy on board as well, it'll be like double protection. You say he's really switched on and he knows exactly how the filth think, it could be a nice bonus for us.'

'That's settled then. I'll call him later this morning and set a meeting up for this afternoon around two o'clock. How about we get him over to your scrap yard? I'll tell him on the phone that it's a genuine business proposition. A chance to earn some fast off the books cash, helping a mate of mine?'

'Yeah that sounds okay. Different business people are often at mine for one thing or another. We'll also be out the way of any prying eyes, when he's told about the actual job.'

Mercer smiled and said, 'I just hope he agrees to drive the fucking car after we tell him what our plans are.'

'Well if he doesn't, the scrap yard's the perfect place for grassing bastards to disappear without a trace', said Stone.

'If he lets me down and bottles it, the people of Nottingham won't be the only fuckers who don't know where Tom Naylor's disappeared to.'

Both men laughed at the joke, but both were deadly serious at the same time. Once Tom Naylor was aware of what they were planning he would either be in or he'd be a dead man walking.

The crushing machines in Stone's scrapyard would have a much softer object to dispose of.

CHAPTER 44

7.00am 20th December 1987
Farnsfield, Nottinghamshire

Sir Jarvis Soames hated early morning starts.

He cursed his private secretary for scheduling a meeting in Birmingham at nine o'clock that morning. It would mean they would have to be leaving his palatial house in Farnsfield, no later than seven o'clock.

His mood had been foul, ever since he'd been told by the pilot of his private helicopter the night before, that the aircraft was temporarily out of action as he was still waiting for a part to arrive. He needed to carry out the repair to a minor defect on one of the navigational systems, damaged recently during a very wild, electrical storm. Until that had been rectified the aircraft was grounded.

The appalling news about the helicopter, meant that he now faced a very tedious, two-hour car journey to Birmingham for a one-hour meeting.

He stood in the expansive kitchen, put his hands on his hips and bellowed, 'Andris!'

His harassed and chastened manservant, instantly appeared in the kitchen. He said quickly, 'Yes, Sir Jarvis.'

'Have the car outside the front of the house in ten minutes. We need to leave soon. Get a move on man!'

Soames shouted at and bullied his manservant and chauffeur for no other reason than he could, and because he enjoyed doing it.

Andris, didn't really care about the verbal abuse and bullying nature of Soames. While ever he got to live like a king, in Soames' beautiful, luxurious home, he could easily put up with his master's petulant tirades. If he had to put up with some bullshit from the arrogant prick now and then, so what.

Andris Kalnietis had made his way to Britain five years ago onboard a merchant ship bound for Hull from the Port of Ventspils.

As soon as the ship had unloaded its cargo, the crew were allowed to go ashore on a nine-hour pass. Andris Kalnietis, had immediately made his way to the railway station and caught the first train bound for London. He had no intention of returning to either his ship or his homeland.

Kalnietis had fallen on hard times, when he first arrived in London. He had no papers and led a very hand to mouth existence. It was a tough existence for the gay, effeminate Latvian.

Eventually, he had no choice but to join the rent boys that plied their sordid trade around Piccadilly Circus.

His life changed when he was picked up by a very famous, fashion designer who was taken by the angular good looks of the slender Latvian.

Andris then spent the next three years as a virtual sex slave of this man. It was a hellish existence, but at least he was off the streets and lived comfortably. The only problem for Andris was the rough style of sex that the man demanded with increasing regularity.

One particular evening, the fashion designer hosted a lavish party at his palatial home in Richmond, Surrey. One of the guests at the party was the wealthy industrialist, Sir Jarvis Soames. Soames had requested to stay overnight after the party had ended as he had business in the capital the following morning.

Andris had been asked to serve drinks to party guests throughout the evening. The overtly homosexual Soames was immediately smitten by the tall, willowy waiter and spent the night talking casually to him, while getting more and more drunk.

As the night wore on and the drink flowed, Soames eventually persuaded the fashion designer to allow him to take the Latvian with him to his room for the night.

The sex had been the best that Soames had ever experienced and the following morning, in the cold light of day he had made an obscene offer to the fashion designer to allow Andris to become his manservant.

It was a cash offer so huge, the fashion designer had readily accepted. The truth of it was that he was tiring of the Latvian anyway and had planned to turf him backout onto the streets after the party.

He wanted fresh meat.

Andris was effectively sold between the two men.

To all intents and purposes, he had now become the property of Soames and left with him that morning, taking the few belongings he had with him.

At first Andris was sceptical, but he was content to bide his time and wait. As soon as he saw the magnificent house where Soames lived, he accepted his lot.

Unlike his previous employer, Soames was a very undemanding, lazy lover who was happy for Andris to take the lead on every occasion the men had sex.

This arrangement was perfect for Andris and he now thoroughly enjoyed his life, living in the lap of luxury.

Exactly ten minutes after receiving the order from Soames, Andris had parked the powder blue, Bentley Mulsanne S, directly outside the grand oak doors of the Georgian Manor House.

Driving the beautiful car was yet another perk for Andris.

He'd always loved cars, but had never been able to afford one. Now he regularly drove one of the most prestigious cars in the world. Soames never drove anywhere, so Andris virtually had the use of the car at all times. He was even allowed to drive it when Soames was away on business.

He really loved the car and would have been quite happy to give up half of his very generous wages, just to drive it. As it was, he got to drive it for free.

When he saw the front door of the house open, Andris jumped out of the car and opened the rear offside door. Soames always liked to sit immediately behind the driver.

The fat businessman waited impatiently for his chauffeur to open the door and he blustered, 'Come on Andris, for fucks sake move yourself! The traffic will be terrible today and I've got to be in the Jewellery Quarter of Birmingham by nine o'clock.'

Andris said nothing, but gently closed the door after Soames had got in.

Within minutes the sleek, pristine car was being driven slowly down the private driveway and out onto the winding country lanes that surrounded the village of Farnsfield.

Neither Andris or Sir Jarvis, noticed the powerful, black, Yamaha motorcycle that slowly followed their progress as they weaved their way through the deserted lanes.

As they approached a blind T junction, Andris brought the vehicle to a stop in order to take a good look before emerging from the junction.

As the car stopped, he glanced to his right and was startled to see a black motorcycle right at the side of the driver's window.

The look of surprise on Andris' face, instantly turned to one of abject terror when he suddenly realised what he was seeing. He was looking directly into the barrel of a self-loading pistol that was pointed straight at his face.

Before he had time to cry out, or raise his hands in some futile gesture of self-protection, the glass in the driver's door shattered into a million pieces.

The first bullet fired from the gun went through the glass and smashed into Andris' forehead just above his right eye. The second bullet, fired immediately after the first, went straight through the right eye, causing a fountain of blood to erupt from the smashed eye socket.

As the two shots shattered the still morning air, the field next to the lane that had been full of resting crows, suddenly erupted in a cloud of black as the large birds rose as one into the air, disturbed by the sudden crack of the gunshots and the breaking glass.

After initially being thrown backwards by the impact of the bullets, Andris had rebounded forward off the plush seats, finally coming to rest with his devastated head pressing against the car horn on the centre of the steering wheel. The constant noise of the blaring horn further disturbed the silence of the early morning countryside.

The motor cyclist, very calmly placed the motorbike on its stand, walked the single pace to the car and reached through the smashed window. He pulled the dead chauffeur away from the steering wheel, stopping the noise of the horn.

The silence was now deafening.

Lifting the visor slightly on his full-face helmet, the motorcyclist turned to face the shocked and whimpering Soames.

He pointed the gun at his face and said softly, 'You. Out of the car. Now.'

Soames was paralysed by fear and did not move a muscle.

The gunman said, 'Get out of the car now, or I'll kill you where you're sitting. Move!'

There was a lot more volume and menace in the final word; it spurred Soames into movement.

Shaking visibly, he obeyed the command and slowly eased himself out of the luxurious car, smearing the blood of his slaughtered chauffeur along the top of the cream leather seats as he did so.

Once out of the vehicle he stood terrified with his head bowed in front of the leather clad motorcyclist, who now ordered, 'Get on your knees, pig.'

Soames resorted to the only bargaining tool he'd ever known and spluttered quickly, 'Please, I don't know who you are. I haven't seen your face. I can make you wealthy beyond your wildest dreams, just please don't shoot me. I'll give you anything you want.'

'Why would I want your wealth? Don't you understand Soames? Money is the root of all evil? No, the only thing I want from you, is to watch you take your dying breath.'

The very brief conversation was over.

Slowly the gunman raised his pistol, aiming directly between the small, piggy eyes of the wealthy businessman who was now weeping openly and who had lost all control of both his bladder and bowels.

Two shots in rapid succession again echoed around the quiet country lanes, as the gunman fired two shots from point blank range into the face of Soames. The close-range shots effectively removed a large portion of the back of the businessman's skull and sent a plume of blood and brains across the narrow lane in a deadly arc.

Soames slumped backwards in slow motion, leaving his legs twisted beneath him in bizarre shapes.

The motorcyclist smiled as he surveyed his mornings deadly work and dropped the visor of the helmet back down.

He placed the still warm gun, back inside his black leather jacket, straddled the motorbike and pressed the electric start button. Instantly the powerful machine roared into life and the gunman rode steadily away, leaving a scene of utter carnage behind him.

The carrion crows that had erupted from the field at the noise of the first gunshots, now circled slowly overhead. They already recognised the possibility of food below, as an ever-increasing pool of dark red blood seeped out from Soames' shattered skull.

The big, black birds would very soon settle around the dead knight of the realm and begin picking at the morsels of brain and flesh, that had been scattered over the country lane, like some massive, overblown road kill.

CHAPTER 45

11.00am 20th December 1987
Nottinghamshire Police Headquarters

Chief Inspector Jim Chambers slammed the telephone receiver back down onto its cradle. He was raging. He had just been informed of the murder of Sir Jarvis Soames and his chauffeur on a country lane, just outside the village of Farnsfield.

How could this have happened so soon after the previous unsuccessful kidnap and murder plot?

That attempt by armed animal rights activists had only failed thanks to the intervention of the Special Operations Unit, when the armed officers had shot dead four of the six people attempting the kidnap, including the leader of the group, Angela Hincks.

Chambers knew that today's murders would be thoroughly investigated. He'd just come off the telephone, after speaking to Detective Superintendent Chris Mahoney, who had been tasked with investigating the cold-blooded, assassination style killings.

Unsurprisingly, Mahoney had wanted to know everything about the SOU operation that had taken place just over two weeks ago, to see if there was any possible connection between the kidnap attempt and today's tragic events.

The Chief Inspector gave Superintendent Mahoney everything he had about the setting up of the operation and the decision his officers had made to use deadly force. He had then had no choice, but to refer the senior detective to the Independent Police Complaints Commission who were currently looking into the multiple shootings to establish whether or not the SOU officers had acted appropriately and more importantly within the law when they made the decision to fire the fatal shots. It would be up to the IPCC how much information from individual officers' statements they provided for the Farnsfield investigation.

The main reason for Jim Chambers' anger and frustration was that there was now a real danger of serious interference into the sensitive operation being undertaken in Merseyside.

Pc Tom Naylor was currently deployed in an undercover role working towards the arrest and conviction of the gang responsible for the murder of Det Sgt Mayhew during an armed robbery.

Chambers knew that once the press got wind of these murders in Farnsfield, they would try and link Pc Naylor, who had recently resigned from the force, to this latest atrocity.

They would no doubt be asking the question; had the disgraced former police officer killed again to try and silence any possible witnesses to the original shootings?

It was all rubbish, but Chambers was experienced enough to know how the press worked when trying to sensationalise a story.

For obvious reasons, nobody knew the current whereabouts of Tom Naylor, except for a very few high-ranking officers.

Jim Chambers leaned back on his office chair and muttered aloud, 'What a friggin' nightmare.'

The telephone on his desk started to ring again, he picked it up and said wearily, 'Chief Inspector Chambers.'

'Jim, it's Chris Mahoney again. I've just had Chief Superintendent Dilks from the Metropolitan Police on the phone, apparently the detective who was working undercover to infiltrate Angela Hincks mob has gone missing. He hasn't been seen since the day of the shootings at Sir Jarvis Soames' house. He was taken back to the Met by our lads and was immediately placed on gardening leave pending the result of the IPCC enquiry by Chief Superintendent Dilks. He hasn't been seen since he walked out of Woolwich Police Station later that afternoon.'

'Are you thinking that he could be connected in some way to the murders earlier today?'

'I asked Mr Dilks exactly the same question Jim, the short answer is a definite yes. When they couldn't contact Dc Wicks by phone, Chief Superintendent Dilks sent two detectives round to his bedsit in Hoxton. When they knocked on his door, they couldn't get any answer. Fearing for his welfare they asked permission from the control room to break into the flat. There was no sign of Jeff Wicks, turned out he was long gone.'

'So how does that help your enquiry Chris? Am I missing something here?'

'There was no sign of Wicks at the flat, but what the detectives did find was a stack of information about Sir Jarvis Soames, including his itinerary for this week. From what they've found inside the flat in Hoxton, Dilks now believes that Dc Wicks was in way too deep. The detectives have found all sorts of incriminating stuff in the bedsit, diaries and other papers, where he constantly expresses his undying love for Angela Hincks, the woman your guys shot dead. Apparently, an entire wall in the bedroom was covered in photographs and press cuttings from the newspaper's coverage of the Hincks case. It's like the bloke has become besotted by her and her cause, which turns out to be one of revenge, pure and simple. Angela Hincks blamed Soames for the death of her daughter, back in July last year. I think there's every chance that if we can locate Jeff Wicks, we'll find our Farnsfield assassin.'

'I hope you're right Chris, you've no idea how much we need an early resolution on this case. There's a hell of a lot going on behind the scenes, that's all linked to this case.'

'Would you care to enlighten me exactly what that might be, Chief Inspector?'

'Sorry sir, no can do at this time. Please don't try and pressure me into telling you anything by pulling rank, Superintendent. If you do, I'll make a phone call to the Chief Constable and get your wrists slapped.'

The detective laughed and said, 'I wouldn't dream of trying to do that Jim. I'll keep you posted on any updates I get about Dc Jeff Wicks.'

'Thanks Chris, the sooner the better please.'

CHAPTER 46

1.00pm 20th December 1987
Linby Village, Nottinghamshire

It had been an easy task to find out exactly where Tom Naylor had been paying his rates. For an experienced detective, following a financial trail to locate somebody was an everyday task. Once he'd found the address, he then cross checked that address for any other names who were resident there.

This check had yielded the name Beverley Ann Wilson.

He had driven to the village of Linby and quickly found the small cottage, where until very recently, Tom Naylor had been living.

He'd been disappointed to find that the cottage was now up for sale. He made enquiries with the estate agent and was informed that all viewings were to be arranged and carried out with their staff, as the vendor was not available to show people around.

This had been a significant setback as he was hoping to get to Naylor this way. He had quickly changed his tactics. Abandoning the idea of getting to Naylor through the estate agents, he had returned to Linby today to ask people who were resident in the village. It was a very small place, he felt sure that he would be able to glean some information from neighbours, as to the current whereabouts of Naylor.

At the fourth cottage he tried, which was no more than fifty yards from Naylor's cottage, he struck gold.

The grey stone cottage was beautiful, but it had the tell-tale hand rail by the front door, that told him whoever lived here was elderly. He knocked loudly on the solid oak, front door and heard a woman's voice inside, 'Just a minute, I'll be with you shortly.'

After a moment, the door was opened by an elderly woman who politely asked, 'Yes, what is it?'

He was dressed very smartly in a tweed jacket, grey crew neck sweater and dark brown, corduroy trousers. He smiled affably before saying, 'I'm so sorry to disturb you, but I wondered if you could help me?'

The woman was taken by the tall, handsome stranger with the impeccable manners and soft brown eyes, she gushed, 'I most certainly will, if I can. What's the problem?'

'Thank you, that's very kind. My name's Harvey Drake, I'm a novelist. You may have seen some of my books, I write turn of the century romantic dramas and I'm looking to buy an idyllic country retreat, where I can write without being disturbed. May I just say, that this is a beautiful cottage, the best in the village. The reason I knocked on your door, is because I noticed that the cottage down the lane is up for sale. I wondered if you could tell me who's selling it and how I could get in touch with them? I've phoned the estate agents and they aren't being very helpful at all.'

He pointed down the lane towards the cottage owned by Tom Naylor.

Squinting into the distance, the old lady said, 'Oh, you mean the policeman's cottage. I haven't seen him or his girlfriend for a while. I did notice there was a man looking around it the other day with a young lady. He looked a bit too flash for this village, so I've been keeping my fingers crossed he doesn't buy it.'

He smiled broadly and said, 'That would be a shame. All the more reason for me to get moving then. I did think there would be others interested in the cottage, this is such a beautiful little village. Maybe, I could get in touch with the owner through his work? You mentioned he was a police officer?'

'He is, but I have absolutely no idea where he works. To be perfectly honest, I used to talk to his girlfriend Bev, more than him. She is such a lovely girl, so very helpful and so pretty. She works as an ambulance driver over at Mansfield. She always helps me to sort out an ambulance, whenever I need transport to Kings Mill Hospital. Unfortunately, I have to get into the hospital more and more these days, but that's just one of the joys of getting old, I suppose.'

He knew he was in business.

There wouldn't be that many ambulance stations at Mansfield, it wasn't a huge town.

He smiled at the old lady, 'Thank you so much, you've been so helpful. I'm sorry I didn't catch your name?'

'It's Mrs Paveley, Vivienne Paveley. It's been a pleasure; good luck, I hope you get the cottage and we become neighbours.'

'Me too, it's been wonderful to meet you. Be seeing you. I think I'll have one last look around the cottage before I go.'

He walked back down the lane to the cottage owned by Naylor.

He made his way to the rear of the property, out of sight from Mrs Paveley's cottage. He knew she would be watching him through her net curtains.

Once round the back, he found a suitable window and forced entry. The window frames were wooden and very old, with no locks. It was an easy task to force his way in.

He quickly made his way around inside the small property, looking for anything that may help him.

In the lounge he saw the same photograph that Micky Stone had used to help him identify Naylor's girlfriend. He picked up the six by four-inch frame, ripped off the back and removed the photograph, stuffing it into his jacket pocket.

There was nothing else of use, so he made his way to the same window, climbing back out the same way as he'd got in. He walked round to the front of the property and saw the net curtains at Mrs Paveley's cottage start to twitch. He waved at the twitching curtain and immediately the curtain was pulled to one side and a beaming Mrs Paveley waved back.

He had parked his car about two hundred yards away in the car park of the Horse and Groom pub.

As he began to stride out towards the pub, he couldn't help smiling.

A plan was starting to come together in his mind.

If he couldn't find Naylor, there was still a way he could make him pay dearly for what he'd done.

CHAPTER 47

2.00pm 20th December 1987
Delta Scrap Metal, Rock Park Road, Tranmere

The noise from the car crushing machine was horrendous.

The screech of tortured metal as the saloon car was crushed down to a one metre by one metre, square block of solid metal was actually making Tom Naylor's ears hurt.

He turned to Mercer and shouted above the din, 'What the fuck are we doing here?'

Mercer said nothing, his head was down and he carried on walking towards the portacabin in the far corner of the massive scrap yard.

Once they reached the building, Mercer turned and said, 'I've brought you out here to meet a friend and business associate of mine, to see if you want to join a little business venture of ours. You keep telling me you need some fast cash. Well, if you agree to join us, I can promise you the cash doesn't come any faster, but you've got to decide right now. Once you step through that door, you're in and there's no way out. If you make the decision to go inside, there's no backing out. You'd have certain knowledge, that I couldn't allow you to leave with. You've been a good mate Tom, and I want you to know exactly where you stand. Do you understand what I'm saying?'

Tom bristled with anger, 'Are you threatening me, Gary?'

'Not at all. This isn't a threat in any way shape or form, I'm just giving you the facts of life here and telling you straight. We're not fucking about here mate. If you go into that office, you're well and truly in. This is your last chance to say no. If you don't want to go into business with us, turn around now and fuck off back to wherever it was you came from!'

Tom could see this was no joke and that Mercer was deadly serious. He also knew him well enough to know that when he was in this mood, nothing would stand in his way. Their friendship would count for fuck all.

He'd been waiting for this invitation, but now it was being offered he was understandably wary and not a little scared by the situation.

In order to buy himself a little time to compose himself he said, 'Before I decide if I'm in or out, there's a couple more things I need to know.'

Mercer growled, 'Go on?'

Tom grinned and said, 'How much cash? How fast can I get it?'

Mercer's face creased into a wide smile and he clapped Tom on the back saying, 'More than enough to get you out of your little predicament with the law and get you overseas with a nice wedge that will last you a good few years. If all goes to plan, you'll have it in your sweaty little hands by tomorrow night.'

Tom smiled, turned the handle on the door of the portacabin and walked inside.

As soon as he walked inside, he was met by the muscular figure of Micky Stone.

Mercer said, 'Tom, this is my associate Micky Stone. This is his scrap yard.'

Tom offered his hand which Stone took and shook firmly. He didn't let go and maintained his grip. Squeezing Tom's hand, he said menacingly, 'Tom Naylor is it? Gadge has told me a lot about you. He tells me you were a good lad when you were in the Para's, but then you went over to the dark side. Why the fuck are you here, Tom?'

Tom was shocked by the venom in Stone's voice and pulled his hand away firmly, breaking Stone's grip.

They had literally just met and it was as if Stone genuinely hated him.

Stone acted and looked as though he wanted to kill him on the spot.

Mercer smiled and said, 'Take it easy you two. Tom's made his decision and he knows what will happen if he tries to back out now. Micky, there's something else you need to know about Tom; don't try to scare him, it won't work. Okay?'

Tom decided it was time to put down a couple of markers and to take this meeting by the scruff of the neck.

He stared at Stone and said, 'Look, I don't need to prove anything to you Stone', he turned to Mercer and continued, 'And I certainly don't have to prove myself to you Gary. Whatever it is you're planning, I'm up for it. I'm not a fucking choir boy and I realise that what you're planning isn't going to be earning either of you any Businessmen of the Year awards, so can we cut to the fucking chase! I want to know exactly how it is I'm going to get rich enough to get the fuck out of here!'

Mercer roared with laughter, 'Do you see what I mean Micky, this boy's a fucking Rottweiler.'

Stone didn't laugh, he didn't smile. He just glared at Tom, having taken an instant dislike to him.

Mercer broke the tension between the two men by saying, 'Fuck this, let's get down to business. You two are starting to do my fucking head in.'

An hour later and Tom had been totally briefed on the next armed robbery Mercer was planning. They had reached the stage where small problems and final questions were being ironed out.

Mercer directed a comment at Stone, 'I want no fucking disasters this time. We take the usual weapons, but we only use them as a last resort. Got it?'

Stone stared at Tom and muttered, 'It was the last resort last time, with the added bonus that it was a copper.'

Mercer ignored the comment from Stone and turned to Tom, 'Tom, you're staying with me at my place tonight. We'll go out and rob the cars we need this evening and get them stashed out of the way. I want to be out early doors tomorrow morning, checking the locations to make sure there's no unseen obstacles. I want to be sure everything's still okay before hitting the security van tomorrow night.'

Tom said, 'You've covered everything, except for one major detail, where are we hitting?'

Stone scowled, 'Just like a fucking bizzie! Always asking questions.'

Mercer looked squarely at Tom, 'You'll know when we get there. It'll depend on what The Ace can tell me tomorrow. What he says will determine which store we hit.'

Tom frowned, 'What the fuck's The Ace?'

Once again Stone had to comment, 'It's not what, it's who. He's our secret weapon, the reason why we never get our collars felt.'

'That's enough, Micky', said Mercer sharply.

Mercer then turned to Tom and said, 'The Ace is somebody who provides us with up to date information that makes our job a whole lot easier. That's all you need to know. I'm the only one who deals with The Ace. Now if there's nothing else ladies, we've all got work to do.'

The meeting over, Tom walked with Mercer back across the scrapyard towards his car, he could feel Stone's eyes boring into his back.

As the two men got into the car Tom grinned and said, 'I've got a very strong feeling that your friend Stone, doesn't like me much.'

Mercer was deadly serious, 'A word to the wise Tom, don't ever cross Micky Stone. He's a fucking psychopath. He'll kill you without batting an eye lid. Now you're on board with us, I'm going to let you into a little secret, Tom. This blagging is going to be my last job. I want one last big score, so I can retire abroad. I've had enough of working with that lunatic. I've got plenty of dosh stashed away and after this last job, I'll be set fair.'

'You never know mate, after the job I might go down to the Costa del Sol as well. We could be neighbours. I'll be just along the beach in the next villa.'

'Not going to Spain, Tom. I don't mean any offence, but no one will ever know where the fuck I'm going.'

'No offence taken, Gary.'

CHAPTER 48

6.00pm 20th December 1987
Mansfield, Nottinghamshire

It was the end of yet another long shift for Bev Wilson.

She leaned against her locker, let out a long sigh, bent down and unlaced her heavy work boots. She placed the boots in her locker before stripping off the one piece, green overall that made up her Paramedic uniform. The uniform was still clean, so she hung it back in the locker, it would do for tomorrow.

She slowly got dressed in her civilian clothes, she felt dog tired and ravenously hungry.

It seemed like the days' shift had gone on forever.

She'd been on the road since six o'clock that morning and had answered countless calls. Now the shift was over, all she could think about was getting home to her Mum's house, having a nice hot shower, getting something to eat and then bed.

She desperately needed to sleep.

Thank God, I've got the day off tomorrow, she thought.

Five minutes later and Bev walked out of the Ambulance Station building and into the dimly lit car park. It was already dark outside, but it felt very mild for the time of the year.

The street lighting was poor and she never noticed the smartly dressed man standing across the road watching her every move.

He'd been waiting patiently all that afternoon and into the evening. He was still clutching the crumpled photograph he had stolen from the cottage in Linby, earlier that day.

The photograph he was holding, was an old holiday snap of Bev and her boyfriend Tom. It had been taken in Crete that summer, in happier times. In the photograph, she looked tanned and happy, smiling in the bright sunshine.

The man glanced down at the photo and then looked across the road towards Bev. It was no good, in this light and at this distance he couldn't be sure.

He needed to get closer.

As Bev reached her bright yellow Volkswagen Polo, she was startled by the sudden appearance of the man, who was now standing directly behind her.

Seeing her jump, the man quickly apologised, 'I'm so sorry, I didn't mean to make you jump. I just need some directions. I was told that there's a really good chip shop near here. This is the ambulance station, isn't it?'

Recovering her composure Bev said, 'Yes, this is the ambulance station, but the fish and chip shop's still quite a way away. It's called The Barracuda Fish Bar and it's at least a quarter of a mile down this road, towards town. Just keep walking in that direction. The chip shop's right opposite the Sir John Cockle pub. You really can't miss it.'

'Not too far then. Thanks ever so much, sorry if I gave you a fright.'

The stranger strode off into the night heading for the chip shop.

Bev shouted after him, 'No problem, enjoy your fish and chips.'

He was smiling broadly as he walked away.

It was definitely her, that murdering bastard Naylor's, lovely girlfriend.

Her little yellow car stood out a mile. It would be so easy to spot her again.

He was smiling, because he knew that it would soon be time to teach Pc Tom 'fucking' Naylor, exactly what it was like to suffer an irreplaceable loss.

CHAPTER 49

1.00am 21st December 1987
Crosby, Liverpool

Tom Naylor glanced at his watch, it was now almost one o'clock in the morning. He was exhausted, but still wide awake.

He was cruising the back streets of Crosby with Gary Mercer. They were on the hunt for suitable, high-powered cars to steal.

Mercer was driving and had been actively engaged in anti-surveillance techniques ever since leaving Stone's scrap yard in Tranmere yesterday.

Tom knew there was no chance that the surveillance team, however good they were, would still be following them. It would have been impossible for them to remain undetected had they stayed on the surveillance and continued to follow Mercer.

Mercer had used every trick in the book; travelling around roundabouts twice, signalling one way before turning the other, driving knowingly into cul de sacs to see who followed, suddenly coming to a stop without signalling. He had done everything he could to make sure they weren't being followed.

Tom was right.

The team tasked with following Mercer, had quickly reported exactly what was happening to the control room.

They had been just as quickly advised to abandon the surveillance. The people in charge of the operation in the control room, were fully aware that Tom was in possession of a covert tracking device. They were all pinning their hopes on resuming the surveillance operation on the successful deployment and activation of that device.

Until Tom was able to activate the tracker he had been given by Bailey, he was effectively on his own.

The planned robbery necessitated the theft of two high powered cars.

One was to be parked up and left on a car park behind an empty pub. The abandoned pub was the perfect location for the first change getaway car as it was situated in an area of the city that was only a two-minute drive from each of the supermarkets that were the proposed targets.

This vehicle was to be the first change car.

Immediately after the job, was one of the most dangerous times for the gang of armed robbers. It was the time when they were most likely to be challenged. The positioning of the first change car was vital.

Provided nobody was in hot pursuit, they would head directly to the car park of the derelict pub, once safely out of sight they would quickly change out of the overalls and high visibility vests worn during the robbery.

The first getaway car and the clothing would then be disposed of by dousing them in petrol and setting fire to them.

Mercer had chosen the disused pub car park so they wouldn't be observed at this first change over.

The plan was then to drive the second getaway car to a derelict warehouse, where they would also torch that, ensuring that no forensic evidence was left for the police.

Mercer would leave his own car at the warehouse the night before the robbery. This car would then be used to drive the three of them and the proceeds of the robbery back to the safe house in Toxteth.

The safe house was a small flat on a sinkhole estate where the Police presence was non-existent. As soon as they were at the flat the cash would be split three ways and the men would go their separate ways, for good.

It was a simple plan, but a good one. It had been tried and tested and had never been found wanting.

Mercer was always meticulous in his planning and this job was no different.

Each of the three men knew their individual roles during the robbery.

Tom was the getaway driver and would never get out of the vehicle. He would keep the engine running at all times and at the first sign of any police presence, he would wait exactly ten seconds for the other two men to get back in the car before driving away. It was agreed by all three men that anyone not back in the car after ten seconds, would be left behind.

Micky Stone would be the first of the gang to confront the three security guards.

As usual, he would be armed with a pump action, Remington shotgun that had a shortened barrel and a folding metal stock. His job was to gain control of the guards. Mercer would be armed with an identical weapon and he would assist Stone to control and contain the guards

As soon as the security guards were on the floor and controlled, Stone would retrieve the hard-plastic boxes that contained the days takings and place them into the boot of the getaway car.

While he was loading the cash boxes into the boot of the car, it would be down to Mercer to control all three security guards and any passers by that might want to intervene like last time.

There would be no shots fired unless absolutely necessary and once the cash boxes were in the boot there would be no delay in making good their escape.

From start to finish, the entire robbery should take no more than one and a half minutes.

All three men knew the score and were happy with the plan.

Tom would stay with Mercer overnight at the safe house in Toxteth and be joined there by Stone on the morning of the job.

It would be down to Stone, to carry out the necessary anti-surveillance techniques he had learned from Mercer, before he drove to Toxteth to ensure he wasn't followed.

They would remain in the flat at Toxteth until four o'clock. That was the time Mercer would receive the information from The Ace that would determine which store they were going to target. The gang would then make sure they were in position to intercept the arrival of the security van at the targeted store at five o'clock.

Mercer had carried out detailed recces of both superstores. He had painstakingly carried out getaway timings and rehearsed the various routes from both of the stores to the car park of the empty pub and then onto the disused warehouse. He was happy that whichever target The Ace decided upon, both stores were suitable, achievable targets, especially when all police resources would be diverted from the area by The Ace.

They still needed to steal the two cars and time was pressing.

It was Tom who saw the car first. He said quietly, 'There's one Gary, did you see it? A BMW M3 on that side street we just passed. They go like shit through a goose, very rapid.'

'I'll pull over, so we can nip back and check it out.'

Mercer parked the car, both men got out and walked back down the poorly lit side street. The metallic blue BMW was obviously somebody's pride and joy. It was highly polished and looked in mint condition, obviously very well maintained.

Mercer grinned, 'This will do nicely Tom, can you boost it?'

'Yeah, no problem.'

Within a matter of seconds, Tom had opened the door and was reaching below the dashboard to expose the ignition wires. He touched two wires together and the powerful engine burst into life.

Hearing the engine start, Mercer quickly walked back down the side street and got back in his own car.

Keeping the revs down to a bare minimum so residents weren't alerted, Tom very quietly closed the car door. He slipped it into first gear and crawled slowly out of the side street, barely allowing the engine to tick over. As soon as he was clear of the side street, he drove off down the street followed by Mercer.

Half an hour later the stolen BMW had been stashed in the car park behind the derelict pub and both men were back in Crosby, looking for another car to steal.

After ten minutes of cruising back streets they spotted a slate grey, Subaru STD parked on an ungated driveway.

Mercer said, 'There you go Tom, that Subaru on the drive. That would be perfect for the actual robbery. Not too flash and very quick.

Tom got out of Mercer's car and crept down the driveway.

Once again, it took him no time at all to get into the car and hot wire the ignition.

Within twenty minutes of the Subaru's engine bursting into life, they were back at the disused warehouse. As Mercer parked his own car at the rear of the warehouse, Tom took the opportunity, while he was alone, to remove the covert tracking device from within his training shoe and place it under the rear wheel arch of the Subaru.

As he reached under the wheel arch, he activated the tracker and heard the satisfying clunk as the magnetic strip on the back of the device stuck to the metal wheel arch. He then drove the Subaru to the rear of the warehouse and picked up a waiting Mercer.

Mercer's car was now hidden under a tarpaulin ready for the journey back to the Toxteth flat, after the job.

Mercer walked over to the Subaru and said, 'Budge over Tom. I'll drive us back to the flat, it's easier than giving you directions.'

Tom said nothing, climbed over the gearstick and sat in the front passenger seat.

Mercer gunned the engine and said, 'Is there plenty of petrol in it?'

'There's enough for what we need.'

'How does it drive?'

'I reckon its fine, very torquey. See what you think.'

As Mercer drove away from the warehouse and headed for Toxteth, he said quietly, 'I don't know about you Tom, but I'm knackered. I think as soon as we get back to the flat sleep's the order of the day.'

Tom felt drained after the days events and said simply, 'That sounds good to me, mate.'

As they drove into the Toxteth estate, Mercer said, 'I'll park this little beauty a couple of streets away from the flat. There's an old people's complex where we can leave it, it should be safe there. We don't want it getting nicked, do we?'

With a dead pan expression on his face, Tom replied, 'Are there thieves in this area of Liverpool, mate?'

Mercer laughed out loud, 'Very funny, you daft sod. We've got a busy day coming up. This time tomorrow, we'll both be very rich men.'

Tom grinned, 'Amen to that Gary. I can't wait to get my hands on some readies, I've had enough of this shithole. I need to get a moody passport organised sharpish, I'm ready for some fun in the sun.'

CHAPTER 50

2.00am 21st December 1987
Covert Operations Control Room,
Merseyside Police Headquarters

Detective Superintendent Greg Mitchell walked in and looked around the small, sparsely occupied, covert control room.

The control room had been set up in secret, at the commencement of the operation to catch the killers of Ds Brian Mayhew. Unless actively involved in the operation, nobody employed by Merseyside Police knew of its existence.

It had been set up this way, after it was discovered that the Merseyside force had a leak.

Seeing his boss walk into the room, one of the handpicked control operators waved to attract his attention and said, 'Good news, boss. We've finally picked up a signal from Naylor's tracking device. It's coming from a Subaru, that's parked up on a right shit hole estate in Toxteth. That's the good news. The bad news is, there's no way the surveillance teams can plot up on the car while it's parked up on that estate.'

Greg Mitchell listened carefully, then said, 'What are the thoughts of the surveillance team? Have they done a drive by?'

The strain of the covert operation was beginning to take its toll on the big detective. He realised the question he had just asked was a stupid one, as the control operator had just told him that the vehicle couldn't be observed.

The control operator, showing a great deal of tact and awareness of the strain on his boss simply said, 'They've only been able to do a single drive by boss. They were able to identify the vehicle the tracking device is attached to, but that's all they could do. At the time they did the drive by, there was nobody with the vehicle. Unfortunately, the location is such that it's just not possible for the surveillance team to set up observations on the vehicle at this time.'

Greg Mitchell realised what the control operator had done to spare his blushes and said, 'Thanks for that Tony. Could we just monitor the signal? Has the surrounding area been staked out? That way we can pick up the vehicle as soon as it moves from its current location.'

'The surveillance team have just confirmed that they've already thrown a cordon around the perimeter of the estate and they, like us, are monitoring the tracking device. They're confident, that as and when the Subaru moves, they'll be in a position to locate it and start a surveillance without being detected.'

'That's the plan then Tony. I want to know the instant that bloody Subaru moves. Okay?'

'Right you are, boss.'

CHAPTER 51

5.30am 21st December 1987
Toxteth Estate, Liverpool

Try as he might, Tom had been unable to sleep.

The anticipation of what he was about to do had plagued him throughout the small hours. The seedy flat where he and Mercer had spent the night was on the second floor of a traditional three bed semi, that had been turned into flats.

The place reeked of mould and damp, it was sparsely decorated with just the bare essentials of furniture. The two single beds were fairly new, but because the duvet covers had remained on the top of the mattresses in the unheated flat for so long, they felt cold and damp.

The flat only had a single bar electric fire in the living room and the tiniest storage heaters in the bedroom. Neither the fire or the heaters appeared to work.

It reminded Tom of his army days where he'd often spent cold, sleepless nights shivering under the stars. As both men had battled against the cold to try and find some sleep, at one point Mercer had commented that they'd been warmer down in the Falklands.

Tom looked at his watch, it was still only five thirty.

Suddenly, there was a loud bang on the door of the flat.

Mercer muttered, 'For fucks sake, I'd just dropped off.'

Both men looked at each other questioningly, who the fuck was banging on the door at this hour?

They weren't expecting Micky Stone to arrive at the flat until seven thirty that morning.

Warily, Mercer picked up one of the shotguns from the table in the living room. Without making a sound he made his way to the door of the flat, being careful to avoid creaking floorboards as he approached.

He looked through the fish eye peephole in the door and exclaimed angrily, 'What the fuck's he doing here already?'

Mercer unlocked the door to let a wide-awake, Micky Stone into the flat.

Angrily Mercer said, 'What the fuck are you doing here so fucking early? We said be here at seven thirty!'

Stone was hyper. He was buzzing. He was definitely on something; his pupils were large and he was skittish.

He burst into the bedsit, staring wild eyed at Tom, he said, 'There's been a change of plan, Gadge. Basically, I don't trust this fucker! We either do this my way or I'm out and the jobs off!'

Mercer looked across at Tom, who just shrugged his shoulders with a resigned air. He then turned back to Stone and raged, 'Exactly what do you mean, Micky, "either your way or the jobs off"? Who the fuck put you in charge, you lairy shit!'

Stone glared back, 'I mean it Gadge, I've brought over another motor to do the job in. I'm not going in any motor he's provided.'

'I was with him last night when we both nicked the car, you fucking idiot!'

Stone shook his head, 'I don't care. My mind's made up on this mate!'

Mercer continued, 'Look at the fucking state of you. What are you on?'

'Never mind.'

'I hope you made sure you weren't followed here, you dumb prick. I'm warning you now, if you were and the cops are onto us, I'll kill you right here, right now. I don't believe I'm hearing this shit! What the fuck's wrong with you Micky?'

Now it was Stone's turn to fly into a rage, 'I'm not fucking stupid! Of course, I made sure I wasn't followed. I'm deadly serious about this, Gadge. I don't want to use the car you nicked last night. I've just got a bad feeling about this prick.'

Tom had been insulted once too often by Stone. He knew he would have to take him to task over it, or risk looking weak. If he said nothing, he ran the risk of losing Mercer's respect.

He stood up to face Stone and with real menace he said quietly, 'Listen Stone, I don't really know you, but out of respect for Mercer, I'm willing to let that last comment go. You need to hear this, because I'm only going to say it once. If you continue to slag me off, like I'm not even in the same room, you and me, we're going to have a big fucking problem.'

He saw Stone's eyes glance fleetingly towards the two shotguns that were now back on the table, directly in front of where Tom stood.

Stone was too far away to grab either of the guns.

He glared back at Tom and said, 'Are you threatening me, dickhead?'

Tom stayed calm, placed a hand on the folded stock of one of the Remington pumps and said through gritted teeth, 'I don't do threats, you muscle bound piece of shit! Insult me once more and I'll drop you.'

Mercer reacted with lightning speed.

He snatched the other shotgun from the table and levelled it in the direction of Micky Stone and Tom Naylor.

He growled under his breath, 'Only this gun is loaded you pair of idiots! For Christ's sake, what the fuck is wrong with you both? In a few hours' time we're all going to be very rich men. After this job you'll never have to see each other again. I'm sick of all this macho bullshit!'

The tension in the room was palpable, Tom still had his hand on the other shotgun.

Mercer said menacingly, 'Micky, you calm the fuck down. Tom, let go of that weapon, right now. I mean it.'

Tom let his hand slip from the shotgun and shrugged his shoulders, he said, 'Listen Stone, I don't have a problem trusting you even though I don't know you. Gary says you're okay, that's good enough for me. I just need the money from this job and I need it fast. I've already got all the shit I can handle, without all this crap as well. You can use whatever car you fucking like for the job, I don't give a shit. When this job's done, you two will never see me again.'

Having said his piece, Tom turned his back on Stone and Mercer.

Mercer looked hard at Stone, who stared back before shrugging and saying, 'Alright Gadge, I'll calm down. I still don't like you Naylor, we'll be using the car I've brought over, not whatever piece of shit you boosted last night.'

Mercer grinned and placed the Remington pump on the table, 'You moody pair of twats, it's like working with Mancs! This car you've brought over Micky, what the fuck is it, an Aston Martin V8 Vantage?'

Missing the humour in Mercer's statement, Stone said flatly, 'No, it's an Audi Quattro.'

Stone continued, 'Another thing Gadge, I don't want to hang around in this shit hole all day either. Can't we go to the motorway services in a while and get some food? I'm fucking starving.'

Mercer said, 'Alright, I agree this place is a shit hole, but we need to keep our heads down. We'll stay here until two o'clock, then go to the services. We can get a bite to eat before I make the call to The Ace. For fucks sake, is everybody happy now?'

Stone grinned and nodded.

Tom shut his eyes and tried to get some elusive sleep.

As he closed his eyes, he was praying that somehow the surveillance team would be able to locate them again. As things stood, without the tracker device which was still under the wheel arch of the Subaru they were no longer using for the job, Tom knew he was on his own; he was well and truly fucked.

Unless things changed dramatically over the next few hours, later that day he would be left with no choice but to commit an armed robbery.

What none of the men in that damp, stinking flat knew at that time, was that circumstances beyond their control were about to dictate exactly which car they would be using to do the robbery.

CHAPTER 52

5.45am 21st December 1987
Toxteth Estate, Liverpool

Jimmy Seed and Merv Sadler were both teenage scallies who were always up to no good. They were a pair of wide boys who wouldn't hesitate to steal anything they could get their thieving hands on.

Jimmy was the older of the two by three months and was therefore the leader. He was seventeen years old, tall and skinny with a mop of black hair that sat on the top of his head. He kept the sides of his head shaved, as he thought it made him look cool. He was wearing scruffy black jeans, dirty Nike trainers and a black Donkey jacket over the top of a dark blue Everton FC hoody.

Merv was the polar opposite of his best friend.

He was short and skinny, but had a pronounced pot belly. His dark hair was long and unwashed. He was also wearing a hoody beneath a dark purple, kagoule that he'd borrowed from his older sister. He didn't own a coat and it had looked like rain when they had set out on the rob earlier that night.

They had been out on the streets since two o'clock that morning, looking for something, anything to steal. They were both desperate to raise some cash. They were beginning to rattle and needed to score soon.

Heroin had always been their poison and they hadn't had a fix for eight hours now.

They had tried to break into a couple of sheds, looking for power tools they could flog at tomorrow's car boot sale down at the Welfare in Crosby. They managed to get into one of the sheds, but the fucking thing had been empty. All that effort for fuck all.

It was almost getting too late to be out on the rob. It was still dark, but before long people would start to be out and about on the streets. They would either be coming home from a night shift or beginning their day and setting off to work.

Either way, with people up and about, time was running out for the two petty thieves.

It was always people that were the problem, never the police. Both of the lads knew, that the likelihood of being disturbed by the police on this estate was virtually non-existent.

The cops only ever drove through the estate in their diesel cars. The two scallies could hear the loud, throbbing of the diesel engines coming from three streets away. They always had ample time to hide away and watch them drive past.

As they trudged disconsolately, through the old people's complex on the way back to their shitty houses they both realised that the likelihood of them finding anything at this late hour was virtually nil.

The prospect of rattling without their much-needed fix of heroin was looming large.

Suddenly, Jimmy perked up and became very alert. His jet-black eyes glistened in the reflected glow from the orange street light.

He said under his breath, 'Do you see what I see, Merv?'

Merv Sadler was already starting to rattle quite badly, as he suffered the first pangs of withdrawal.

Almost incoherently, he mumbled, 'No. What do you see?'

Jimmy grinned and said, 'Over there, parked under the street light. All shiny and bright'.

He reached inside his Donkey jacket pocket for the threadbare pair of gloves and the flat headed screwdriver that was his breaking tool of choice.

Trying hard to take an interest, Merv looked out from under the hood of the Kagoule and said, 'Do you mean the motor?'

'Yes, I mean the fucking motor! Get your gloves on you dingbat.'

Suitably gloved up, both youths sidled over to the unattended Subaru.

Looking in through the driver's door window, Jimmy made a startling discovery, 'This fucker's already been hotwired, Merv. Try the door mate.'

Merv immediately tried to open the passenger door and grinned wildly as it opened.

He chuckled, 'It's fucking jackpot time!'

In a flash, Jimmy was inside the car and reaching for the already exposed wires to start the car.

As the engine fired into life, Merv jumped into the passenger seat and began hooting and hollering loudly as Jimmy drove off down the street.

Jimmy shouted above the din, 'Merv, shut the fuck up daft lad! You're giving me a fucking headache. I know a bloke over in Southport, who'll pay handsomely for this little beauty.'

He laughed and continued, 'This time tomorrow mate, you and me will be smacked off our tits!'

At the thought of that prospect, Merv let out a low whistle, then sat quietly with a manic grin on his face. The pangs of withdrawal were instantly forgotten.

A quarter of a mile away, just off the estate, several car engines suddenly started up as the radios inside them crackled into life.

The control operators calm voice said, 'All units be advised, target vehicle is moving. The tracker shows it's heading along Bass Street towards its junction with Grosvenor Road.'

The surveillance team quickly got into position. Minutes later, they saw the grey, Subaru as it was driven off the Toxteth estate. The lead car of the team drew alongside the target car and discreetly checked out the occupants, before overtaking and moving away, allowing the next vehicle in the convoy to continue the follow.

'Alpha to control, permission.'

'From control, go ahead Alpha.'

'I think we've got a problem. The two occupants in the target car look to be about sixteen. It looks like a couple of little tow rags have nicked the car again.'

Detective Superintendent Greg Mitchell had been informed of the developing situation and was now standing behind the operator in the control room.

Angrily, he shouted, 'Bollocks, that's just what we don't need.'

He turned to the operator and said, 'Tony, tell the surveillance team to back off, but to keep the target vehicle in view. Get onto the Force Control room, tell them you're a concerned member of the public who's following a new looking Subaru that's being driven erratically by a couple of kids.'

Tony said, 'Will do boss.'

Greg Mitchell went on, 'Tell the surveillance team that as soon as they see the Traffic mobile stop the target vehicle to move in closer and observe the arrest of these twats. I don't want any of the surveillance team involved with the arrest, but I want that tracker removing from the target vehicle before it goes back to the owner. Is that understood?'

'Yes boss, no problem. I'll see to it.'

The big detective realised that he now had a major problem. He had an inexperienced undercover officer mixed in with a gang of ruthless armed robbers and absolutely no idea where he was. He also knew that another armed robbery was imminent, but had no idea where and when that armed robbery would take place.

He put his hands behind the nape of his neck, interlaced his fingers and said aloud, 'Fucking marvellous!'

He stormed out of the control room and into his office.

Slumping down in his chair, he snatched up the telephone on his desk and quickly dialled a number.

The phone was answered on the third ring, 'Jim Chambers.'

'Chief Inspector. It's Greg Mitchell in Liverpool. I'm sorry to call you at this ungodly hour, but we've got a serious problem that could well jeopardise Pc Naylor. I think you should get over to Liverpool as soon as you can, the situation seems to be developing quickly. Obviously, I can't say too much on this line, but things are getting dangerous for your man.'

Jim Chambers was instantly wide awake, 'Okay Greg, thanks for the call', glancing at his bedside clock he continued, 'I'll drive over this morning, I can be in Liverpool at ten o'clock. Can you arrange for somebody to meet me in the long stay car park at Speke Airport, they can then drive me into your covert command centre.'

'Will do Jim, I'll explain everything properly when you get here.'

Greg Mitchell terminated the call and sat back in his chair, he was deep in thought. He didn't dare think about what the next twenty-four hours may bring. Self-doubts now smashed their way into his subconscious. Why had he ever thought that putting such an inexperienced officer undercover with this gang was a good idea? Surely it was only ever going to end in disaster?

Meanwhile, back out on the Southport road, Jimmy Seed was suddenly aware of blue lights flashing in the rear-view mirror of the Subaru.

He slowed the car down and muttered, 'Fucking hell, shit happens!'

In the passenger seat, Merv was oblivious to the flashing lights and mumbled, 'Are we nearly there yet, Jimmy?'

Jimmy stopped the stolen car and said, 'Shut up Merv, you dickhead!'

CHAPTER 53

10.00am 21st December 1987
Speke Airport, Liverpool

Bailey glanced at the clock on the dashboard of her car, the time was just past ten o'clock in the morning.

Chief Inspector Jim Chambers was late. She had parked up in the long stay car park of the new South Terminal as arranged between Chambers and Detective Superintendent Greg Mitchell.

She had parked at nine thirty that morning, facing the main entrance. The last thing she wanted to do was miss the senior officer's arrival at the car park.

Strictly speaking, mundane, transport jobs were well outside of her remit, but she had found herself volunteering to pick the Chief Inspector up from the airport.

There was something about Tom Naylor, that was beginning to occupy her thoughts more and more, although she would never admit as much.

Ten minutes passed slowly by, then a dark blue, Audi estate car pulled into the car park. The Audi was being driven by a middle-aged, grey-haired man who was travelling alone.

Even though she had already committed the registration number to memory, Bailey quickly checked the number she'd been given by Greg Mitchell.

Sure enough, this was the Chief Inspector from Nottingham.

She waited for him to park the Audi, then casually strolled over to the vehicle and tapped on the driver's door window.

Jim Chambers wound the window down halfway, smiled amiably and said, 'Can I help you?'

Bailey smiled back and said, 'Yes sir. It is Chief Inspector Chambers, isn't it?'

'Yes, it is.'

'Good morning sir. My name's Bailey. Greg Mitchell asked me to pick you up from the airport and provide you with transport to the covert operations centre.'

'Marvellous. Let's get cracking, shall we? Are you the Bailey that's been looking after Pc Naylor on this operation?'

'Yes sir. I've been acting as his liaison between agencies.'

'How's he doing?'

'So far, he's acquitted himself brilliantly, but we're fast approaching the crunch time on this operation now.'

Chambers nodded, threw his overnight bag into the boot of Bailey's black Peugeot 205gti, got into the passenger seat and was driven at speed away from Speke Airport.

As she drove, Bailey briefed Chambers on the recent events that had precipitated the telephone call from Greg Mitchell. She explained the direction the undercover operation appeared to be heading and that another armed robbery was imminent. They believed this robbery would definitely take place within the next twenty-four hours.

Bailey explained how Tom Naylor had become accepted into the gang and that he would probably be their getaway driver on the forthcoming robbery.

As she provided Jim Chambers with detail after detail, she was impressed by how quickly and easily the Chief Inspector assimilated all the information he was being given.

The Chief Inspector from Nottingham may look like everybody's favourite uncle, she thought to herself, but underneath that avuncular exterior the man was as sharp as a tack.

Jim Chambers didn't interrupt as he was thoroughly briefed. He sat quietly and listened carefully to what he was being told. He was deeply concerned about the welfare of his officer and was beginning to harbour doubts about the wisdom of the entire operation.

As he listened, it appeared that everything that could go wrong, had gone wrong. To get the operation back on track and Tom Naylor safe and out of there in one piece, was going to take a huge slice of good fortune from somewhere.

Right at this moment in time, he just couldn't see where that luck was going to come from.

As Bailey drove her Peugeot into the car park of the covert operations centre, Jim Chambers was a very worried man.

CHAPTER 54

2.00pm 21st December 1987
Motorway Services, M58 near Liverpool

Tom drove the Audi Quattro, provided by Stone, into the busy car park of the services on the M58 motorway, not far from Aintree.

Mercer had chosen those particular services as they were the nearest to the potential targets at Crosby or Fazakerley. There was a very large Tesco store at each of those locations and it would be one or the other they would be hitting later that afternoon.

All three men were wearing non-descript, navy blue fleece jackets over the top of blue boiler suits. The two Remington pump action shotguns and ammunition were in a holdall, hidden beneath the high visibility tabards and black nylon ski masks safely locked away in the boot of the car.

Everyone was pleased to finally be out of the depressing flat in Toxteth. It was only as they emerged from the dirty, damp safe house that they realised just how bad it stank inside.

As they walked down the road to the Audi, each of the men had breathed in deeply, dragging the fresh air into their lungs. For Tom, leaving the flat meant another step closer to being involved in an armed robbery. There was nothing he could say or do about the choice of car. Anything he said or did to try and persuade the other two men to use the Subaru, would have looked extremely suspicious.

It was the Audi or nothing.

He got in the car and started the engine. He deliberately chose a route that that took him past the old people's centre, where they had left the Subaru. He was amazed to see that the grey Subaru was no longer there.

Maybe the surveillance team had removed it? Maybe there was somebody watching over him after all?

It gave him a glimmer of hope that just maybe all was not lost.

The drive out to the services on the motorway had been uneventful.

Tom parked the car in a quiet corner of the car park and the three men got out and began walking towards the food hall.

Micky Stone was extremely happy about being at the services. He was almost childlike in the way he couldn't conceal his excitement.

As he walked towards the food hall, he loudly exclaimed, 'I'm well up for this! They've got one of those new Burger King restaurants here. I went in one the last time I was in London, the burgers are fucking awesome!'

Tom was incredulous.

Stone was about to commit a violent, armed robbery where there was every likelihood that extreme violence would be used and here he was getting excited over a burger. This man is definitely not playing with a full deck, thought Tom.

Mercer, on the other hand, was very quiet, he looked pensive and thoughtful.

As the three men walked into the brand-new Burger King restaurant, Stone made his way to the counter and said, 'I'm fucking starving. What does everyone want? I'll get them, my treat.'

Mercer said, 'Just coffee for me, Micky.'

Tom quickly studied the garish menu boards on the wall, then said, 'Thanks Micky, I'll try one of those Whopper things, I think. Oh, and a coffee, ta.'

Stone was grinning like the proverbial kid in a sweetshop, 'No problem lads. You sure you don't want any food, Gadge?'

Mercer just shook his head.

It appeared to Tom, that all the animosity Stone had shown towards him the night before had now vanished.

Tom was relieved, he felt stressed enough without having to worry about Micky Stone holding a loaded pump action shotgun while he was unarmed and vulnerable.

He still didn't trust the muscle bound, scrap metal dealer and was determined to watch him like a hawk throughout the time he was in his company.

While Stone stood in the queue to get the food order, Tom and Mercer made their way over to the far side of the seating area, they kept going until they were well away from any other customers and couldn't be overheard.

As they sat down, Tom said under his breath, 'Is he always like this before a job? It's like he's on drugs or something?'

Mercer nodded, 'Every fucking time. I don't know if he's on the gear, Tom. I genuinely think he just gets his rocks off doing it. Let's face it, he must do it for the adrenalin rush or something. It's not like he needs the money, the bloke's already a millionaire.'

'He's a nut job, Gary.'

'Like I said before Tom, this is my last job. I can't stand to be around that lunatic anymore. He was hyper for three days after shooting that poor sod last time. To be honest, it was that job, that made my mind up about packing it all in. It was so sickening. I'd already shot the bloke in the legs; the geezer was badly wounded lying on the pavement. He was no threat to us, he was out of it. That nutter, just blew him away for the sake of it. Me and you mate, we've both killed people, plenty of people, but it was always a necessity. For us it was duty. We were at war and it was kill or be killed, nothing more, nothing less. What he did, he did for pleasure. He really enjoyed pulling that trigger. I'm telling you mate; Micky Stone is one seriously sick bastard.'

Tom quickly changed the subject as he saw Stone approaching the table carrying a tray full of food and drinks.

As well as Tom's food, Stone had ordered himself two huge burgers with everything on them and two large bags of fries.

Tom grinned and said, 'Christ Micky, you weren't joking when you said you were starving. You won't be able to move when you've scoffed that little lot.'

Stone grinned back, showing a mouthful of half chewed burger, 'Just a snack boy, just a snack.'

Tom laughed and shook his head, 'Fuck me Micky, you're an animal!'

Mercer took a sip of his coffee and said seriously, 'Alright you two, enough of the fucking about. Let's start getting switched on, shall we? I'll go and make the phone call to The Ace in a minute, then we'll know which target we're going to hit. Does anyone need to go over anything one more time?'

Without waiting for an answer, he continued, 'I'll go through it one more time anyway. From here, we'll drive over to the disused pub and make sure the second car's still okay. From the second we get there, we wear the gloves and the ski masks. Make sure you keep these on from start to finish. You'll only pull the ski mask down just before we hit the security guards. Micky, you and I will have the pumps, Tom you won't be tooled up. You're strictly the driver and I want you fully focussed and concentrated on that. Whatever shit may be going down outside the car, you don't get involved, okay?'

Tom nodded.

In a way he was glad he wasn't going to be armed. It was one less thing to worry about. Being involved in an armed robbery was bad enough.

He still had a niggling worry about Stone having a shooter though. At the end of the job, when they were all at the warehouse, he knew he would need to stay aware and stick close to Mercer.

Even though Stone appeared happy enough today, there was just something about the bloke that Tom didn't trust.

Mercer continued with his final briefing, 'Usual plan Micky, you'll intercept the guards as they emerge from the store with the cash boxes. There'll be three guards to grip on this occasion. Each one will be carrying two cash boxes. They normally emerge from the store together, thinking there's safety in numbers, actually that just makes them an easier target for us. Anyway, get them controlled and on the ground quickly in whatever way you have to, okay?'

Again, there was that manic grin from Stone, 'Don't worry about a thing Gadge, I'll have them eating out of the palm of my hand in no time.'

Mercer continued, 'If there's any problems, I'll assist you controlling the guards. I'll also deal with any have a go heroes, that are intent on making a name for themselves. As soon as they're gripped, we scoop up the cash boxes as quickly as possible and get the fuck out of there. As usual boys, speed's the key. If The Ace has done his stuff, the cops shouldn't be a factor, but we still need to be in and out of there as quickly as possible.'

Mercer now looked squarely at Stone, 'Most important. We don't shoot unless we fucking well have to. Do you understand me Micky?'

'No problem Gadge', said Stone as he chewed another mouthful of burger.

'For the last time, does everybody understand the ten second rule?' asked Mercer.

Both men nodded.

'Just to be crystal clear then and so nobody's in any doubt. If it all comes on top and the filth do show up, Tom counts ten seconds and then bugs out. Anyone who's not in the car gets left behind, everyone okay with that?'

Again, Tom and Stone nodded.

Mercer said, 'After the job, we drive to the disused pub and provided there's no fucker in hot pursuit, we leave the clothes and masks in the car. Keep your fucking gloves on! I'll then set fire to the Audi and everything in it. We then take the second car to the warehouse. At the warehouse we transfer all the cash into my car, then torch the second car. Then it's back to the flat at Toxteth for a count up and divvy up, before we all fuck off into the sunset. Any questions?'

Tom spoke up, 'Just one. What's the plan if someone is in hot pursuit?'

Stone growled, 'You lose them, dickhead!'

Mercer said calmly, 'Really Tom, with the information

I'll get from The Ace, there'll be no hot pursuit. Trust me, it's not an issue. After he's done his stuff there won't be a cop within ten miles of the job. Right, if there's nothing else I'll go and make that phone call.'

Mercer took one last drink of his coffee, then stood up and walked outside to make the call, leaving Tom and Micky Stone alone.

Quick as a flash, Stone's mood suddenly changed.

He leaned across the table and glared at Tom, 'You'd better not fuck up. You're just the driver, it's fucking easy, a monkey could do it. Just get us in there and get us out again.'

Tom said through gritted teeth, 'Don't you worry your little head about me Stone. You just concentrate on what you've got to do, alright? In a few hours' time you'll never have to see me again.'

'I won't be sorry about that, Naylor. As far as I'm concerned, once a bizzie always a fucking bizzie.'

Tom ignored the taunt and turned away, sipping his coffee.

As the time for the robbery was fast approaching, Tom was starting to try and formulate a plan of action. There was no way he could back out. He knew if he tried, he would be killed on the spot. He just had to go through with the job and hope that the surveillance teams were somehow still watching over them.

Three minutes later, Mercer returned to the table, 'Right gents. The job's definitely on. Let's have another drink then get over to the disused pub to check the second car. I'll brief you about the location at the pub. The security van will be arriving at five o'clock so we've only got a couple of hours to get sorted and make sure we're there to relieve them of all that lovely cash.'

CHAPTER 55

4.30pm 21st December 1987
Beauclair Drive, Wavertree, Liverpool

Chief Inspector Noel Prime, was in a daze as he parked his car on the driveway of his beautiful home in the plush suburb of Wavertree. He had walked around in a permanently befuddled and bemused state ever since the night he'd murdered his wife, after discovering she was having an illicit affair.

He was just existing from day to day. Every day was the same, he was going through the motions, not really functioning. He was drifting through life like an automaton and now found it impossible to show or feel emotion anymore.

Deep inside his soul, he knew his life was effectively over.

He had been sitting alone in his private office, just outside the main Merseyside Police control room, when he'd received the expected telephone call from Gary Mercer.

Mercer had been his usual arrogant, bullying self and had made the expected demands in relation to the armed robbery that he and his criminal associates had planned for this afternoon.

That call was over an hour ago.

As soon as Prime told Mercer, that from four thirty onwards he would divert all police resources away from the area of Crosby, the decision had been made. It would be the

Tesco Superstore at Crosby, on the outskirts of the city that would be the location for the planned armed robbery.

Prime knew the security van that collected the takings would be arriving around five o'clock. He was also aware that the takings after the pre-Christmas trading would provide the biggest haul of cash yet.

Ordinarily, this would have excited him as he looked forward to his cut of the ill-gotten gains. Over the years he'd been paid handsomely by Mercer, for the information he had provided and for diverting the police away from the location of their criminal enterprise.

Now, with his wife Glenys dead, none of that counted for a thing.

He was no longer interested in the material things in life. Money meant nothing to him anymore.

As far as Noel Prime was concerned, he'd got nothing left to live for anyway.

Before he dealt with that burning issue, there was still the small matter of Gary Mercer and his gang to deal with. This time everything was going to be different. Far from diverting the police he would ensure that the police would be there to take them down.

He would finally have his revenge.

Prime had gone way beyond the point where worrying over whether or not the armed gang grassed him up, became an issue.

He would wait another five or ten minutes, then make an anonymous call into the Incident Room that had been set up to investigate the murder of Detective Sergeant Mayhew.

It would be the easiest thing in the world to make that all important telephone call. He had all the knowledge. He would be able to outline the details of where and when the armed robbery was about to take place.

The Incident Room would quickly pass on that information to the Force Control Room who would immediately despatch armed police units to the location to intercept the armed robbers.

With any luck, Mercer and his cronies would all be shot dead by the police marksmen as they resisted arrest.

Prime walked into his house, bolted the front door behind him and stepped into the comfortable lounge. He plonked down into his favourite armchair and stared at the ornate carriage clock on the mantlepiece above the fireplace.

The ticking of the clock was the only thing he could hear and as the hands moved slowly round the clock face, the ticking seemed to get louder and louder.

He waited until the hands of the clock showed exactly four forty-five in the afternoon. In just fifteen minutes time, the security van would be arriving to collect the takings at Crosby. He had left it late to make the call, because he wanted Mercer to be actually on the pavement holding a weapon in the act of committing the robbery, when the armed police arrived.

Slowly, he picked up the telephone from the coffee table next to his armchair and dialled the number for the Incident Room.

On the second ring the call was answered by a young woman, 'Hello, Incident Room. How can I help you?'

Disguising his voice by placing a handkerchief over the handset, Prime said, 'I've got some very important information for you. The same men who shot and killed your copper are just about to commit another armed robbery at the Tesco Superstore in Crosby.'

Before the young woman could respond to what she was being told Prime said urgently, 'Don't ask me any questions, you haven't got time. All you need to know is that in fifteen minutes time at five o'clock, the murderers of that copper will be committing another armed robbery at the Tesco Superstore in Crosby. They're going to be armed with shotguns. You need to get armed police to that location now!'

Having said his piece, Prime quietly replaced the telephone on its cradle. He stood up and walked the few paces across the spacious lounge to the mahogany cabinet, where he kept his drinks. He poured himself a huge measure of whisky and returned to his arm chair, carrying the crystal glass tumbler in one hand and the bottle of Glenfiddich in the other.

He sat down and began to contemplate his future.

Carefully, he placed the bottle of Glenfiddich down onto the coffee table, next to the three packets of Paracetamol tablets. Each packet contained forty tablets. More than enough to do the job.

Prime knew what he was going to do. The only question left for him to answer, was when he should do it.

There's really no hurry, he thought to himself.

He took a long drink of the fiery Scotch.

As he felt the empowerment from the alcohol course through his veins, he suddenly smiled and said out loud, 'Fuck it! I've still got time to enjoy my drink and enjoy the downfall of that bastard Mercer, as well.'

CHAPTER 56

4.55pm 21st December 1987
Tesco Superstore, Crosby, Liverpool

It was now rapidly approaching five o'clock and Tom Naylor drummed his fingers nervously on the steering wheel of the Audi Quattro. Above the noise of the engine, he could hear the steady breathing of the two men on the back seat of the car, directly behind him.

Tom had parked the getaway car, three parking bays away from the side entrance to the superstore. It was this small door that the security guards would use when collecting the enormous pre-Christmas takings.

There was a very fine drizzle starting to fall. It was already dark and the lighting in this area around the store was poor.

There was none of the powerful lighting that illuminated the front of the store so brightly. Here there was just a single, ineffectual, white light located directly above the side entrance,

There were no other cars parked in the vicinity of this side door. It was too far from the main entrance; because it was quite a walk from here to the front of the store, genuine customers tended to avoid the area.

Stone had noticed Tom drumming his fingers and said mockingly, 'What's the matter Naylor? Is your fucking bottle going, or what?'

To stop the nervous drumming, Tom gripped the steering wheel tightly. He hissed under his breath, 'Don't you worry about me Stone. Just make sure you don't take your time grabbing up those cash boxes!'

Mercer growled quietly, 'Knock it off you two. Here comes the security van now. It's showtime!'

Tom could now see the navy blue, armoured Transit van making its way slowly across the almost empty car park.

As the security van came to a stop directly outside the side door, Mercer and Stone ducked down on the back seat. As the guards got out of the vehicle all they saw was a lone car with just the driver sitting inside. For all they knew, he was just another disgruntled husband waiting for his wife to finish up the last of the essential Christmas shopping.

Tom watched through the drizzle covered windscreen as the three security guards got out of the rear of the van. Even though the view was distorted by the water on the windscreen, he could see that all three men were very large individuals. They were all carrying far too much weight around their midriff than was ideal. Fitness obviously wasn't a pre-requisite of getting this job, thought Tom.

The three men wore the security company's uniform of black trousers, and a maroon coloured NATO style sweater. They also wore NATO helmets that were the same maroon colour as the jumpers. That was the only protection they had against an attack.

It's nowhere near enough, thought Tom.

The three men walked confidently from the van over to the side door and knocked loudly. The door opened slightly and after one more cursory look around them, they stepped inside and closed the side door.

'They're inside', whispered Tom.

Instantly, Mercer and Stone sat bolt upright and began loading the Remington pump action shotguns. Both weapons were secured by lanyards around their necks, which meant they could be hands free if they needed to be. Stone also slipped a cord around his neck that held a pair of small bolt croppers. He would need this tool to cut the chains of the handcuffs that secured the cashboxes to the guards' wrists. It was the quickest and easiest way to free up the cash boxes.

Tom looked at the bolt croppers and realised that they were probably the same pair, Stone had used to sever the fingers of a helpless guard during the last robbery.

At least this area appeared to be devoid of members of the public who might want to play the hero this evening, thought Tom.

After what had happened during the last robbery and the murder of Brian Mayhew had been splashed all over the media for days, he didn't think that anybody would be so keen to have ago this time.

The side door opened again, Tom hissed, 'Down!'

Mercer and Stone instantly dropped down on to the back seat again.

From the back-seat Mercer whispered, 'Don't forget Tom. Wait for the door to close behind them first, before you give the word to go. I don't want them to be able to get away by going back inside through the door.'

Tom said, 'Okay.'

Mercer said aggressively, 'Everybody, masks on. Now!'

The three men pulled down the black ski masks, so only their eyes were now showing.

As soon as the last guard was out of the side door and the door was closed behind him, Tom shouted, 'Now! Go! Go! Go!'

Instantly, Mercer and Stone were out of the car, bellowing orders and threats to the stunned guards. In a matter of seconds, the three men were lying prone and submissive on the cold, wet ground.

Stone allowed his shotgun to hang on the lanyard and began moving swiftly between the downed guards, deftly using the bolt croppers to cut the cash boxes away from their wrists. The heavy blades of the croppers went through the handcuff chains like a knife through butter.

Mercer stood in front of the guards, pointing the lethal, menacing looking pump action shotgun at each one in turn. Calmly, barking orders at them, telling them to remain still and to do exactly as they were told.

Tom pressed the boot release catch on the car and Stone began hurling the heavy plastic cash boxes into the large boot of the Audi Quattro.

After the fourth box had landed in the boot, Stone grabbed the shotgun from around his neck and took his turn controlling the guards, while Mercer threw the last two remaining cash boxes into the boot.

Watching the robbery unfold from inside the car, Tom noticed how Stone's whole demeanour suddenly changed as soon as the weapon was back in his hands.

He instantly became more and more agitated and extremely aggressive towards the helpless guards.

As the last of the cash boxes landed inside the boot, Mercer slammed it shut. The sound of the car boot slamming seemed to spur Stone on to become violent. He stamped down hard onto the hand of one of the guards, grinding the man's fingers down onto the concrete pavement.

The man pulled his hand away sharply and cried out in pain.

Stone immediately began to scream at the helpless guard, 'What did you fucking call me? You worthless maggot!'

He began to kick the man hard in the ribs and levelled the loaded shotgun at his head.

Mercer shouted, 'Leave it! We need to get out of here. Now!'

Stone wasn't listening.

It was either that, or he was lost in his own hostile aggressive place. He totally ignored Mercer and instead began stomping up and down in front of the now terrified guards, screaming abuse at each of the men in turn and pointing the shotgun at their ashen faces.

It was Mercer who saw them first.

Five dark coloured saloon cars were racing across the car park towards them, with just their sidelights on.

Forgetting about Stone, Mercer jumped into the front passenger seat next to Tom and shouted, 'Drive! Forget the fucking ten second rule! Leave that mad bastard where he is, the cops are all over us. Get us out of here now Tom!'

Knowing that Mercer was still holding a loaded shotgun, Tom instantly gunned the engine and took off in the opposite direction to that of the oncoming cars. Now that he could see them in the rear-view mirror of the Audi, he recognised them as being unmarked, armed response vehicles.

Thank God for that, he thought to himself.

Hearing the revs on the getaway car engine, suddenly roar above his shouting, Stone turned and saw the Audi being driven away at speed.

As the Audi was driven at speed over the car park, Stone pointed his shotgun in its general direction and screamed, 'You pair of bastards, I'll fucking kill you both!'

Before Stone had the chance to discharge his weapon, the first of the unmarked police cars was skidding to a halt alongside the attacked security van. As soon as the vehicle came to a stop, armed officers leapt out of the car and began barking instructions at Stone.

The first officer out of the vehicle squatted by the front wheel, raised his weapon and shouted, 'Armed Police! Put your weapon down. NOW!'

Stone ignored the order and raised his pump action shotgun in the direction of the black clad, armed response officers.

As soon as Stone levelled his weapon, the sound of two sharp cracks echoed around the car park.

The kneeling officer, recognising that Stone had become a threat to life, instantly fired two rounds from his Heckler and Koch Mp5.

The first bullet smashed into the armed robber's left shoulder, spinning him around. The second round struck him lower down the left forearm, causing the Remington pump action to fly from his grasp and clatter onto the pavement.

Stone fell to the ground, where he lay writhing in pain from the two bullet wounds. In between his agonised moans, he was muttering, 'You fucking pair of bastards, I'll have you for this.'

The armed response officers moved in to arrest Stone.

They quickly assessed the armed robber's injuries and realised that neither bullet wound was life threatening. Both were flesh wounds; the biggest problem would be to control any shock caused by the injury. Stone was handcuffed and left on the floor until the Paramedics arrived. He was kept under constant observation to ensure his physical state didn't deteriorate further. The Remington pump action shotgun was left in situ on the floor for Scenes of Crime officers to photograph.

The first priority was to make the area safe. Once that had been achieved, the second goal was to preserve and gather any evidence that had been left at the scene.

While two officers constantly watched over Stone, other officers helped the shocked guards to their feet.

Three of the five, armed response cars had continued across the car park in pursuit of the getaway car. Within three minutes, Tom had managed to evade the last of the pursuing vehicles, by driving through a pedestrian underpass. The sides of the Audi had screeched along both the walls of the underpass causing extensive damage to the bodywork, but not affecting the function of the vehicle.

The armed response vehicle driver had refused to follow the getaway car through the underpass and Tom had sped away from the area with no one still in pursuit.

Five minutes later and Tom drove the wrecked Audi onto the car park at the rear of the disused pub. As he jumped out of the getaway car, he considered tackling Mercer there and then, but knowing he was still in possession of a loaded shotgun, he decided to bide his time.

Tom knew he would get an opportunity at some stage, but this wasn't it. He was well aware that Mercer was still full of adrenalin. He knew the ex-paratrooper would still be extremely alert and would respond quickly to any threat.

Both men worked quickly to transfer the cash boxes from the boot of the Audi into the boot of the second car. They then undressed and threw the outer clothes they had worn during the robbery onto the back seat of the Audi.

Mercer grabbed two overalls and a can of petrol from the boot of the second car. Both men quickly donned the new overalls, before Mercer lobbed the full petrol can at Tom and said, 'Torch it mate!'

Mercer had never once let go of the pump action shotgun.

Tom began to splash petrol over the interior and exterior of the Audi Quattro.

Mercer shouted, 'Step back!' as he used a disposable lighter to set light to a rag. He then hurled the blazing rag inside the car.

The Audi was instantly transformed into a raging fireball.

Both men then jumped into the BMW, as Tom drove away from the burning wreck, he said quietly, 'Stone was taken down. I saw him drop in the rear-view mirror. He was shot.'

Mercer stared, unblinking through the windscreen, 'It serves the nut job right. I don't know what the fuck he was playing at. Without him fucking about playing the big man, we could have all been out of there before the cops even arrived.'

'I don't get it Gary, I thought you said the cops wouldn't be an issue. We only got out of there by the skin of our teeth.'

'It's got to be that bastard Prime, who's set us up. I thought he'd been acting fucking weird lately.'

'Who the fuck's Prime?'

'Never you mind Tom. Get us back to the warehouse as quick as you can. It's got to be that bastard who's grassed us up, it couldn't be anyone else. When we get to the warehouse, I want you to stay with the money until I get back. I need to go and have a word with that treacherous bastard.'

As soon as they arrived at the disused warehouse at Aughton Park, Mercer got out of the BMW and walked quickly to his own car that had been previously stashed there.

He got in, started the engine, wound the window down and shouted above the engine noise, 'Tom, wait here until I get back. What I've got to do won't take long, but it needs sorting right now. Get all the cash boxes out of the boot and stack them over there. Don't torch the motor until I get back, it will just attract attention. As soon as I'm back, we'll take the cash to a different safe house in Croxteth, one that Stone doesn't know about. If he's still alive, I reckon he'll grass, especially after we left him behind. While I'm gone, make a start getting everything together that needs torching. I won't be long.'

Mercer then sped out of the warehouse, leaving a bemused Tom behind him.

Tom was deep in thought.

He recalled the name Mercer had mentioned in anger. Prime, had to be The Ace.

Whoever this Prime character turned out to be, Tom didn't expect him to survive the visit from Mercer. Before driving off, Mercer had said he needed to talk with Prime, but he had very purposefully taken the pump action shotgun with him.

He had seen Gary Mercer with that look in his eye before.

CHAPTER 57

5.25pm 21st December 1987
Aughton Park Industrial Estate, Liverpool

As Mercer raced away from the warehouse, he was raging.

It had to be that bastard Prime, who had set them up and brought the armed cops in to arrest them.

The burning question racing through Mercer's brain was, why?

What had caused the change in Prime?

It couldn't be the death of the cop during the last robbery. Prime was too much of a greedy bastard to let that bother him. No, it was definitely something else.

As he drove through the windswept, deserted streets, questions began to flood into his brain.

How come Glenys had suddenly stopped coming around?

What was it Prime had told him, Glenys had gone to stay with her mother?

Hadn't she once told him, that both her parents were dead?

He dropped the car down a gear and revved the engine hard, gunning the engine as he followed the road signs for Wavertree.

Suddenly, things became clear for Mercer. Somehow this was all connected to his relationship with Glenys Prime.

Had Prime found out about their relationship?

That would certainly explain the change in his attitude the last time he had seen him.

Had Glenys finally told him?

Mercer had planned this moment for a long time. He would finally be able to leave Liverpool with the woman he loved and start afresh somewhere else.

He had already made tentative plans, looking at properties in Canada. He recalled the long talks with Glenys, after they had made love. How they both wanted to live in the semi wilderness of the wide-open spaces in Canada.

He felt a surge of excitement pass through him, but this was quickly replaced by a nagging doubt.

Why had Prime told him the bullshit story about her going to stay with her mother?

Had something happened between her and Prime?

Mercer could feel a volcano of rage building inside him now. If Prime had harmed one hair on her head, he would make him pay.

He was now driving through the tree lined suburb of Wavertree, he could see Prime's house ahead in the darkness. It would soon be time for Prime to start talking. Mercer had a lot of questions that needed answers.

He wanted to know why the armed police had turned up at Crosby during the robbery? More importantly, he needed answers about Glenys.

As he drove along Beauclair Drive towards Prime's house, he was suddenly filled with dread. In that exact moment, he knew something terrible had happened to her and he glanced down at the loaded shotgun on the passenger seat.

CHAPTER 58

5.25pm 21st December 1987
Aughton Park Industrial Estate, Liverpool

As soon as Mercer had driven out of the disused warehouse and disappeared into the night, Tom ran outside to try and establish his bearings.

The industrial estate was dark and poorly lit, drizzly rain was still falling. He had only ever been here in a car. Now he was on foot and in the dark, the entire estate looked completely different.

He knew that the warehouse they had chosen was on the very edge of the Aughton Park Industrial Estate. A lot of the other properties were like the one he was standing outside, boarded up and empty. The economic climate in this part of the north west was definitely on the decline.

Looking away from the industrial estate, Tom could see a run-down street of terraced houses. At the far end of that street, he could see a large white building that was lit up. He began walking towards the old building and as he got closer, he could see that it was actually a dilapidated, run-down pub.

The faded sign that hung from the wall declared the premises to be, 'The Black Prince'.

Tom walked in through the open, front door of the pub. The door itself was battered and hadn't seen a paintbrush in twenty years.

The interior of the pub was as depressing as the exterior.

In one corner of the public bar, two old men clutched pint pots that were half full of flat beer. They had their heads down, huddled over a game of dominoes.

There was a fat, middle aged woman perched on a bar stool wearing a woefully too tight dress, that bulged in all the wrong places. She had peroxide bleached blonde hair with black roots and wore garish, doll like make up.

She was leaning over the bar, flirting with a large, red-faced man who was wearing a sweat stained, white shirt that had ten days' worth of grime on the collar and cuffs. The shirt was unbuttoned, exposing a grey vest that still displayed the remnants of past fried breakfasts, down the front.

He was obviously the landlord of this salubrious licensed premises; he warily clocked Tom as he entered the bar.

The entire place reeked of stale cigarette smoke and even staler beer.

On the wall, directly behind the landlord, was a dog-eared poster that declared "Happy Hour" was between six and seven on week nights.

Not been much happiness in here lately, thought Tom, as he approached the bar.

The landlord eased his massive, fat frame off the stool he was sitting on and asked, 'Yes mate. What can I get you?'

With a concerned look on his face, Tom replied, 'It's an emergency mate, I need to use your phone to call for an ambulance. A mate of mine's had a bad accident down the road and he's bleeding like fuck.'

Tom had deliberately lied.

He knew that if he'd asked to use the phone to call the police, he would have been told to fuck off.

The fat landlord appeared to break out in a sweat at the effort of reaching below the bar to retrieve the dirty, yellowing telephone.

As he passed it over to Tom, he said, 'Ring three nines, it doesn't cost me anything then, alright mate?'

Tom nodded, grabbed the phone and quickly dialled the number for Bailey's mobile phone.

Not as stupid as he looked, the landlord quickly realised that Tom wasn't phoning three nines. He lurched over the bar, made a grab to try and snatch the phone back out of Tom's hands and said, 'That wasn't three nines you dialled! What the fuck are you playing at, you little shit?'

Tom was too quick for the now heavily sweating landlord and moved the phone out of his reach.

He gave the landlord a hard look and said in a menacing tone, 'Police business mate, now back the fuck up and crawl back onto your stool. Just leave it, alright?'

The landlord raised both of his large hands in a gesture of appeasement and whined, 'Alright, alright. There's no need to get heavy mate.'

Ignoring Tom, he plonked his fat arse back on the overworked stool, turned to the woman and in an overloud voice said, 'It's the fucking filth Doris! They just waltz in here thinking they own the bloody place!'

The woman tutted loudly and glared at Tom.

He ignored them both and waited for Bailey to pick up her phone.

Suddenly, he could hear Bailey's voice, 'Hello. Who's this?'

Tom said quickly, 'Bailey, it's me Tom. Listen, I think the cop who's been giving information to Mercer is a guy called Prime. I don't know where he works, but his name's definitely Prime. Anyway, Mercer's on his way to see him, I presume he's going to his house, wherever that is. He's got it into his head that it was Prime who grassed him up about the robbery today and he's going to sort him out. The thing is Mercer's still armed with a pump action shotgun that's identical to the one Micky Stone had when he was shot by the armed officers earlier.'

She replied calmly, 'Okay Tom. I'm in the covert ops room and I've put your call on the loudspeaker. As soon as we identify who Prime is, there will be a team of armed officers despatched to his home address. More importantly, where are you?'

'I'm at the Aughton Park Industrial Estate. I'm currently in a shithole pub called The Black Prince. The cash boxes from the armed robbery and the second getaway car are in a disused warehouse about a hundred yards from here.'

'Right Tom, stay where you are. There's a forensic team and a recovery team on their way to your location to deal with the getaway car and the cash boxes. I'm on my way to pick you up from the pub. The bosses here want me to take you straight to Prime's address, as soon as we find out where it is.'

'Get that armed team to Prime's house as soon as you can, Bailey. I've seen Mercer in this mood before and I don't fancy Prime's chances when he catches up with him.'

CHAPTER 59

5.45pm 21st December 1987
Beauclair Drive, Wavertree, Liverpool

Mercer was driving like a man possessed by the time he arrived at Noel Prime's house on Beauclair Drive, Wavertree.

He drove the car straight onto the driveway of Prime's house, before braking hard and screeching to a halt. He grabbed the shotgun from the front seat and got out of the car. He could see lights were on in the lounge at the front of the house. The curtains were open and he could see Prime sitting in an armchair.

The man was still dressed in his police uniform and wasn't moving.

Mercer ran around to the rear of the house. Without breaking stride, he kicked the kitchen door off of its hinges and marched straight inside the Chief Inspector's house.

He walked into the living room, where he found Prime still sitting in the same armchair. The reason for his stupefied state was obvious.

Immediately in front of him on the coffee table, was an empty bottle of Glenfiddich, to one side of the upturned bottle were three unopened packets of Paracetamol.

Mercer placed the shotgun carefully onto the settee and grabbed Prime by his shoulders, shaking him vigorously until he roused him out of his stupor.

Prime looked up through blood shot eyes. He was both surprised and angry to see Mercer standing in front of him.

He smacked his lips and said, 'What the fuck are you doing in my house, Mercer?'

Mercer was in no mood for polite conversation, he picked up the shotgun from the settee and smashed the metal stock of the weapon into Prime's mouth.

He glared at Prime and said menacingly, 'Are you surprised to see me, you double crossing, grassing bastard? Was I supposed to be arrested, or even better, shot dead by now?'

Prime spat blood from his injured mouth and spluttered, 'After what you've done to me, you piece of shit, if you'd been shot, it would've been no more than you deserve.'

'After what I've done to you? What are you babbling on about? I haven't done anything to you, except make you a very wealthy man for doing next to nothing.'

Prime suddenly lurched to his feet and feeling emboldened by the whisky he'd consumed, he said angrily, 'You're a thief, Mercer. You've always been a thief. I suppose you couldn't help yourself. You had to steal away the most precious thing I had, just because you felt like it and because you could. You've destroyed everything I ever had, just so you could enjoy a sordid, dirty little fuck.'

Up until that point, Mercer hadn't realised he was pointing the shotgun directly at the chest of Prime.

He lowered the weapon to the floor, staring into the whisky soaked eyes of Prime he asked softly, 'How long have you known about me and Glenys?'

Prime reached forward and grabbed the empty whisky bottle from the coffee table. He hurled the bottle across the room, narrowly missing Mercer's head.

The bottle smashed against the wall and Prime screamed, 'Don't you dare speak her name in my house, you bastard!'

Once again Mercer gripped the shotgun tightly and used the metal stock as a weapon. This time he crashed it into the forehead of Prime, knocking him backwards onto the floor and splitting his head open.

Prime lay dazed on the floor but said venomously, 'You'll never see her again Mercer!'

Suddenly the house was flooded with light.

Mercer reacted instantly and closed the heavy drapes, blocking out the light.

He then grabbed the plug of the television and ripped the cable from the back of the appliance. He used the cable to quickly tie Prime's wrists before picking him up off the floor and throwing him, trussed up, onto the armchair.

In his injured and drunken state, Prime no longer had any inclination to move. Blood was pouring down his face from the large gash in his forehead, making it difficult for him to see.

From outside the house, a loudspeaker suddenly blared out, 'Gary Mercer, this is the police. There are armed officers surrounding the house. We know you're in there. Leave your weapon on the floor and come to the front door immediately.'

Mercer turned to Prime and growled, 'Sit still and say nothing shithead.'

Instantly, the telephone started to ring.

Mercer knew it would be the police. He let it ring four or five times before he snatched it up.

He said calmly, 'This is Gary Mercer.'

The soft tones of a hostage negotiator came on the phone, 'Gary Mercer, my name's Inspector Ray Donovan. Is anybody hurt in there? Are Mr and Mrs Prime okay?'

'No one's hurt Inspector, but that will change very quickly if you don't get me exactly what I ask for. Is that clear?'

'As crystal Gary. What exactly do you want?'

'It's quite simple. I want a way out of here. If you haven't organised that for me in one hours' time, Chief Inspector Prime of the Merseyside Police will be a fucking dead man. Is that crystal too, Ray?'

'It might take a little longer....'

Mercer interrupted, 'Don't try all that bollocks on me! You've got one hour to get things sorted, from now!'

Mercer slammed the phone down and said to himself, 'Fuck it!'

CHAPTER 60

5.50pm 21st December 1987
Aughton Park Industrial Estate, Liverpool

Bailey had arrived at The Black Prince pub within ten minutes of Tom putting down the telephone in the pub.

As soon as Tom had ended the call, the fat, sweaty landlord of the pub snatched the telephone back from him.

He had pointed to the door and bellowed, 'Now get the fuck out of my pub!'

Tom had just grinned and walked outside to wait for the cavalry to arrive. He felt like a ton weight had been lifted from his shoulders.

Nobody, apart from Stone, had been hurt during the armed robbery. All the money that had been stolen was about to be recovered. The psycho, Micky Stone, was either dead or in custody and Gary Mercer was about to join him.

He leaned against the wall of the pub trying to shelter from the incessant drizzle and began to think of his life back home in Nottinghamshire.

He thought about getting his job back and moving back into his cottage, but most of all he thought about his girlfriend, Bev. He was still deeply worried that when he finally did get home, he wouldn't be able to win her back.

Bailey had driven like a maniac to get to the pub. Seeing Tom standing by the door, she had braked hard and her car had skidded to a stop outside the pub.

The vans containing the Cash Recovery team and the Scenes of Crime team arrived shortly after. Keen to get out of the drizzle, Tom jumped into Bailey's car and directed her and the teams of detectives back along the street to the disused warehouse.

From the front passenger seat, Tom watched as the detectives and the Scenes of Crime staff got to work at the warehouse.

Bailey said, 'Stay in the car, Tom. I've been instructed to get you straight over to Wavertree. The ops room have established that there's only one person named Prime working for the Merseyside Police. He's Chief Inspector Noel Prime, who is currently in charge of the Control Room.'

'Well that makes perfect sense', said Tom,

'It sounds like Mercer's already at Prime's house. His car was on the drive when the armed response team arrived at his home address in Wavertree. From what I've been told on my way here, it would appear that there's now an ongoing siege situation developing at Chief Inspector Noel Prime's house.'

As they drove through the wet streets of Crosby, heading across the city towards Wavertree, Tom was desperate for some answers from Bailey.

'So, who exactly is this Chief Inspector Prime character?', he asked.

'As I said, Noel Prime is, or rather was, the Chief Inspector in charge of the Merseyside Police control room. Obviously, he was in the perfect place to divert police resources from any planned robberies and to make sure no units would be in the vicinity to impede the armed robbers. Diverting police officers away from the impending robberies worked fine and

313

the police never got anywhere near the armed robbers. We think this same crew have been responsible for upwards of a dozen or so other robberies, where security vans have been targeted. The one thing Chief Inspector Prime and the robbers hadn't factored in, was the raw courage of the unarmed Detective Sergeant Mayhew. When he bravely intervened to try and protect the security guard he was off duty and just out getting the weekly groceries for his family.'

'Prime sounds like a right treacherous bastard', said Tom.

'I think it will be very enlightening when they do a full financial investigation into Noel Prime. I wouldn't be surprised if he hasn't been on the take for years.'

'What happened to Stone? I saw him go down as I drove away. Is he dead?'

'No, he was lucky. He was shot twice by the armed response officers, but hit in the shoulder and the arm. Neither wound is life threatening. He's currently in custody at Aintree University Hospital, where he's getting his wounds treated. Even when he was being transported to the hospital, it appears that he is already wanting to grass on Gary Mercer and a certain ex-copper called Tom Naylor.'

'Mercer thought Stone would grass us both up, if he was still alive.'

'What's happening at Prime's house now?'

'Mercer has taken the Primes hostage. He's making demands to try and get out of there.'

'The Primes?'

'Yeah, it would appear that Prime's wife may also be in the house.'

'Bloody hell, what a mess.'

'There's somebody else waiting to see you at Wavertree as well.'

'Who's that?'

'Your boss, Jim Chambers, is here. Greg Mitchell phoned him yesterday when you had dropped off our radar.'

'What do you mean, dropped off your radar? I thought you'd had me under surveillance all the time and that's why the armed cops had arrived in the nick of time at the superstore.'

'No, that's not how it went down. The Subaru you'd set up as the getaway car with the tracker on was nicked by a couple of kids this morning. We thought you knew, because you turned up later in a different car, the Quattro.'

'That's a long story, Bailey. Micky Stone didn't trust me one bit. Basically, from the outset he hated my guts. He brought the Quattro over this morning before the job and insisted that we used it instead of the Subaru that I had provided. The fact that Mercer was with me when I had nicked it, made no difference to that lunatic.'

'I see.'

'So how come the armed cops showed up bang on time?'

'There was an anonymous tip off telling us the time and location of today's robbery.'

'Prime?'

'It looks that way, only time will tell.'

'What deadlines has Mercer set at Prime's house?'

'He's said, if free passage out of the house hasn't been organised within one hour then Prime's a dead man.'

'Has Mercer mentioned Prime's wife?'

'Not as far as I know, why?'

'Because if she was in there, he would have done. You can bargain better with two lives than one.'

'Has anything been set up yet?'

'Not yet.'

'I think I should try and talk to Mercer when we get there. We both know he's never going to be offered a way out of there, don't we? You never know, he might just listen to me.'

'They might let you try, Tom.'

Tom sat in silence for the rest of the journey, trying to think of a strategy he could use, that Mercer might just listen to.

He knew it was going to be a virtually impossible task.

The Gary Mercer he knew, would never accept a life behind bars. He had told him often enough that he would never allow himself to be sent to prison and would rather die.

Gary Mercer would much rather go out shooting.

CHAPTER 61

6.00pm 21st December 1987
Beauclair Drive, Wavertree, Liverpool

Inside the house on Beauclair Drive, Noel Prime continually taunted Mercer.

Mockingly he said, 'You do realise that you'll never get away, don't you? You're going to be spending the rest of your life behind bars, where you belong'

Mercer waved the Remington pump action shotgun in Prime's face and said through gritted teeth, 'We'll see, Prime.'

Ignoring the shotgun, Prime sneered, 'They're not going to let you just walk out of here. You've already murdered a policeman. Those armed cops out there want you so bad, it's hurting them.'

'As you quite rightly say Prime, one cop's already dead, so another one won't make any difference, will it? Now, for the last time shut your mouth.'

Prime finally relented and sat quietly.

Mercer's mind was overwhelmed with thoughts, but the one thing that kept pushing its way to the front, was the comment Prime had made earlier about Glenys. He seemed to take a great delight when he had said, "You'll never see her again Mercer!"

What had he meant?

There was only one way to find out. He didn't really want to engage him in conversation again, having only just got him to be quiet, but he knew this was the only way to get answers about Glenys.

He looked hard at Prime and said quietly, 'What did you mean earlier, when you said I'll never see Glenys again?'

'You really are one thick bastard, aren't you? I meant exactly that. You'll never see my wife again, I've made sure of that.'

'What have you done? Have you sent her away? What's happening?'

A cruel smile played over Prime's face, 'You'll find out soon enough, you fucking idiot.'

Mercer felt a familiar rage building inside him and he was just about to smash the steel butt of the shotgun into Prime's mocking face, when the telephone rang.

The strident ring tone made him stop in his tracks.

He lowered the shotgun, grabbed the phone and turned away from Prime, 'Have you got my car ready yet?', he snapped.

'Gary, it's me Tom Naylor.'

Mercer was shocked to hear Tom's voice. He sat down in stunned silence with the telephone pressed against his ear. He couldn't quite believe what he'd just heard.

Tom spoke again, 'You've got it all wrong Gary. It wasn't Prime who grassed you up, it was me. I set you up. The only option you've got left, is to give yourself up. There's thirty or more, armed cop's out here. The house is totally surrounded and these guys out here, they would all like a piece of you. I know the only person responsible for killing that off duty cop, was Stone. I'll make sure everyone knows there was nothing you could do to stop it happening. Gary please, you've got to trust me on this. Give it up, let the Primes go.'

An incredulous Mercer couldn't believe what he had just heard. There was a long pause before he said, 'Trust you? Why did you do it Tom? I saved your life, why have you betrayed me?'

'What happened to that off duty cop was totally wrong. Stone had to be stopped. You know full well exactly what Stone is. He had to be stopped before he killed again.'

'Maybe I should've walked away before and yeah, I suppose I do know what Stone is, but let's get back to you. So, everything you told me was all bollocks. Tom Naylor isn't a grass, he's still a cop. Is that it, Tom?'

'Yeah, that's it Gary, I'm still a cop, doing my job. Please, give this up, let Prime and his wife out.'

'It's just Prime. I don't know where Glenys is. Let me think things through, Tom. There's one thing that's still puzzling me though. You say you set us up, but I can't work out how you got the armed response teams to the Tesco Superstore in Crosby. You had no way of contacting anybody and we definitely weren't followed after I'd told you which superstore we were going to hit.'

Suddenly, Noel Prime interrupted, 'What Glenys ever saw in you, I'll never know. You really are a very stupid man, aren't you? It was me, you idiot. I called the location of the robbery into the control room. I grassed you up Mercer, because you'd taken Glenys from me.'

Mercer forgot that Tom was still on the telephone. He turned and faced Prime, 'Where's Glenys?', he asked coldly.

Prime smirked, 'Where you'll never be able to pleasure her again.'

Mercer levelled the shotgun at Prime's face and snarled, 'Where is she? I won't ask you again.'

Prime tipped his head back and let out a guttural laugh, 'She's upstairs, having a bath.'

Mercer dropped the telephone and ran upstairs.

He looked inside each of the bedrooms, until finally he found the bathroom.

When he opened the door to the bathroom, the stench almost knocked him backwards out of the room.

Lying half submerged in the dirty, brown stained, bath water was the badly decomposing body of Glenys. She had the permanent rictus grin of death etched onto her rotting, bloated face.

A horrified Mercer looked around the room trying to take in the scene of carnage before him. He could see blood splashes all over the walls and he saw the vicious looking claw hammer, still on the tiled floor where Prime had dropped it.

With tears now streaming down his face, he shouted at the top of his voice, 'What have you done!'

He turned his back on the scene of utter carnage and stepped out of the bathroom.

Slowly he walked back down the stairs, his brain struggling to cope with the enormity of what he had just witnessed. With each step down the stairs he took, his grip on the shotgun got tighter. By the time he reached the foot of the stairs his hands were aching and his knuckles were white. It felt like he was about to crush the weapon in his bare hands.

He stepped back into the living room and in a voice trembling with emotion he asked Prime quietly, 'Why did you have to do that to her? She was the most beautiful, caring woman I've ever met. She deserved so much better than you.'

Prime allowed a cruel smile to play across his lips and sneered, 'Don't you understand? What happened to Glenys up there, is all your fault. She betrayed me, with you, the lowest form of scum on the planet. You left me with no other option, she had to die. It was you Mercer, you made me kill her.'

'She didn't betray you, you betrayed her. Don't forget Prime, I remember how we first met. The real reason she did what she did with me, was because you showed her no interest, no affection, no love. If it hadn't been with me, she would have left you soon enough anyway. Glenys had grown sick of your cold, indifferent manner. You always were a selfish, grasping bastard. Don't forget Prime, I know your history. I'm not letting you get away with this.'

Prime suddenly became angry and shouted, 'You just don't get it, do you? After I'd seen her with you, at your house, rutting like a pair of wild animals, I actually enjoyed smashing her cheating head in.'

Prime roared with laughter and little flecks of saliva sprayed all over Mercer's face.

Mercer wiped the spittle from his face and then slowly racked a cartridge into the breach of the shotgun. He levelled the barrel directly in front of Prime's laughing face and said, 'No more laughing, Prime.'

He squeezed the trigger of the shotgun and shot Prime full in the face, silencing that cruel, mocking laugh once and for all.

Mercer reloaded and fired again and again.

He carried on doing so until the magazine of the pump action shotgun was empty and there was nothing recognisable left of Chief Inspector Noel Prime's head.

Once his ears had stopped ringing from the shotgun blasts, Mercer could vaguely hear his name being called. He looked around and realised it was coming from the telephone handset he'd dropped on the floor when he went to look in the bathroom.

He picked up the phone and said, 'Hello.'

He heard Tom Naylor's voice, 'What's happening Gary? Is Prime dead?'

'Yes. He's stone dead, the prick. The selfish bastard killed his wife. He didn't have to do that, he could've let her walk away.'

'I don't understand, Gary.'

'Me and Glenys, we were in love. He took that all away and laughed about it. Well he isn't laughing now, mate.'

Tom silently cursed before saying, 'Put the gun down and come outside, Gary. It's not too late, we can sort something out. Please, do as I say mate.'

Mercer put down the phone, reached inside the pocket of his overalls and took out another shotgun cartridge. Very slowly and deliberately, he slid the cartridge full of buckshot into the magazine of the Remington.

He racked the cartridge into the breach of the weapon, picked up the phone and said, 'Tom, are you still there?'

'I'm still here Gary, are you coming out?'

'Nah, there's nothing worth coming out for. You know me, I'd go fucking ape in prison. There's only one thing left to do Tom, it's the old apples for me mate.'

Tom heard a loud bang as the shotgun was fired, then he heard the clatter of the shotgun as it fell to the floor.

Gary Mercer had sat in the armchair, placed the barrel of the shotgun beneath his chin, pulled the trigger and blown the top of his head off.

Tom put the phone down, turned to Jim Chambers and said, 'I think Mercer's just shot himself, boss.'

Chambers said, 'We'll soon find out Tom, the armed response team are preparing to go into the house now.'

CHAPTER 62

9.00pm 21st December 1987
Beauclair Drive, Wavertree, Liverpool

Three hours had passed since the armed response teams had made entry to the house and confirmed that Mercer had killed Prime and then shot himself. They had also made the grisly discovery of the decomposing body of Glenys Prime upstairs in the bathroom.

Standing outside the front of the detached house were Jim Chambers and Greg Mitchell; they looked on impassively as the last of the three bodies was removed from the house.

Jim Chambers said, 'How soon will Tom Naylor be able to go home?'

Mitchell looked thoughtful before saying, 'I don't see any reason why he shouldn't be able to go back tomorrow, Jim. He'll need to be fully debriefed and a lengthy statement obtained, but there's no reason why all that can't be completed by then.'

'As you can imagine, Tom's very keen to get back to Nottingham, he's got quite a few bridges to mend.'

'He did a great job up here Jim. To say it was his first ever undercover job, he acquitted himself very well. I'll be making sure my boss expresses our gratitude in writing to your Chief Constable. I'll make sure she lets him know how much the Merseyside Force appreciates his hard work and sacrifice. From what you've told me, I know things haven't been easy for him back home.'

Two undertakers in dark suits, wearing sombre expressions on their faces walked past the two senior officers. They were carrying the black plastic body bag, that contained the putrefying remains of Glenys Prime.

The two police officers maintained a respectful silence as her remains were carried passed them and in to the waiting van.

Chambers deliberately waited until the undertakers had placed the body bag into the back of the dark grey Transit van before saying, 'Thanks Greg, I appreciate that, the lad deserves that recognition. I was just wondering how your Chief Constable is going to handle the fallout from Noel Prime? A bent cop who murders his wife. That's going to take some time for the force to get over.'

'That's his problem, not mine, Jim. I catch criminals, I don't give a fuck about politics. As far as I'm concerned, Chief Inspector Prime was just as evil as Stone and Mercer. It was the greed of all three that led to the death of a very brave man. I couldn't care less about the reputation of Noel Prime, or the force in general for that matter.'

'That's exactly how I feel Greg. The politics of the police force was never something that concerned me. I try to rise above all that shit.'

'Come on Jim, my team can finish up here. Do you fancy a quick drink before I drop you back at your hotel?

'Sounds good to me, it's been a long day and I could murder a pint.'

CHAPTER 63

3.00pm 29th December 1987
Force Headquarters, Nottinghamshire

Tom was feeling very nervous, for the fifth time in as many minutes he checked that all the buttons on his uniform tunic were done up and that the bull on his boots looked immaculate.

Chief Inspector Chambers was standing next to Tom, he was also resplendent in full dress uniform.

Both men were waiting patiently outside the office of the Chief Constable. They had been standing there for ten minutes already. The Chief's secretary had let him know they were there. She'd told them ten minutes ago that he was on the telephone and it wouldn't be long before he called them in to the office.

Jim Chambers broke the nervous tension, 'Are you always this fidgety, Naylor?'

Tom grinned, 'No sir. Only when my career's on the line. Normally I'm fine.'

There was a loud shout from within the office, 'Come in!'

Tom Naylor followed Jim Chambers into the office, he closed the door behind him, then took his place standing at attention alongside Chambers in front of the large, dark wood desk.

The Chief looked over his wire framed glasses at them and said, 'Stand easy, gents. Pc Naylor, you can relax, it's very good news. I've just received confirmation from the office of the Home Secretary that you're to be reinstated as a Police Constable of the Nottinghamshire Constabulary forthwith. Now that we've received that news, it's just left for me to formally offer you your old job back on the Special Operations Unit. Is that where you still want to be stationed?'

'Definitely, sir.'

'Good, good. That's all settled then. I understand that you've already been informed that the IPCC have found you acted justifiably and within the guidelines of The Criminal Law Act when using deadly force during the incident at Farnsfield. With that notification comes the lifting of your temporary suspension from full duties, so as of today you can resume full duties. Do you have any questions, Pc Naylor?'

'No sir.'

'For your information the press officer has released a statement to the media earlier today outlining the findings from the IPCC enquiry. Okay?'

'Yes sir.'

'Finally, I'd like to commend you both for your efforts in bringing to justice an extremely dangerous gang of armed robbers, who had already shown their propensity for violence and murder. Pc Naylor, what you've been through was well above and beyond your normal duties. You should be justifiably proud of your efforts.'

'Thank you, sir.'

'Chief Inspector, I understand from my counterpart in Merseyside that this whole operation was your brainchild. I would like to express my admiration for the way you continue to think outside the box. Long may it continue.'

'Thank you, sir.'

'That's all gentlemen. Keep up the good work, both of you.'

That was their cue to leave the office, so both men snapped smartly to attention, turned and walked out of the office.

As they walked from the main Headquarters building back to The Huts, Tom grinned and said, 'If it's all the same to you boss, would you please refrain from thinking outside the box for a while. I don't think my nerves will take much more of it.'

'Very funny, Naylor. Not a word of that comment to the other lads, I'll never hear the last of it.'

'My lips are sealed, boss.'

'On a more serious note, how are things between you and your girlfriend now?'

'It's going far better than I expected boss. When I first got back from Liverpool, we had a long talk. She understands now why it had to be done the way it was. I think the visit she had from Micky Stone, made her see that it was the right decision to handle it the way we did. I think provided I don't make a habit of it, we'll be okay. She's already moved all her stuff back into my cottage, so that's got to be a good sign. It's still very much one day at a time though boss.'

'I'm really pleased to hear that, Tom. You two deserve to be okay. Will you be having a drink with the rest of C Section this evening, to celebrate your reinstatement?'

'I don't think so, not tonight boss. I want to get home on time, nice romantic meal, bottle of wine, the works. Me and Bev have still got a lot of things to talk through and a lot of catching up to do, if you know what I mean.'

'I know exactly what you mean, Naylor. I'm not that bloody old!'

Both men laughed.

Chambers then said, 'Try and make time for that drink later in the week Tom. I know that Matt Jarvis, in particular, is keen to clear the air and welcome you back onto the team.'

'Later in the week, definitely boss.'

CHAPTER 64

6.00pm 29th December 1987
Mansfield, Nottinghamshire

Bev Wilson walked out of the ambulance station and walked across the car park to her yellow Volkswagen Polo. It had been another long shift and she was tired.

It had been a very strange few months for her. Even now looking back, it all seemed like some surreal nightmare.

She really had thought that things were all over between her and Tom. She just couldn't understand the way he had suddenly changed, the dreadful mood swings and finally the separation that had almost broken her heart in two.

Now, it seemed as though none of that heartache had ever happened. All that pain and anxiety she had been feeling, had been washed away.

Of course, when Tom had first appeared at her mother's house after he'd arrived back from Liverpool, she had refused to listen to any of his pitiful explanations. The story he'd given her, trying to justify his outrageous behaviour was so outlandish, that you couldn't have made it up.

He had persevered and tried again and again to explain where he had been and why. Gradually, she slowly came to realise that his behaviour towards her and everything else that had happened, had played out that way for one reason only.

That single paramount reason was their safety.

Slowly she came to understand just how dangerous the people Tom was trying to bring to justice, actually were.

Even now, when she thought of the visit by Micky Stone and the conversation, she had with him, she shuddered. The way the gangster had casually chatted to her in the pub. How he had been so charming. When in actual fact, all he was doing was coldly assessing whether or not he should kill her boyfriend Tom.

It was too terrifying to even think about, but hopefully now they would be able to move forward and put all the stress of the last couple of months behind them.

It had been a long tiring day and Bev suddenly realised how much she was looking forward to driving home. She was actually relishing the prospect of the ten-minute drive back to the little cottage in Linby, that she was once again sharing with Tom.

Five minutes later and Bev was driving along the road between Annesley and Hucknall, towards Linby, towards home.

In the distance, just past the turn off for Newstead she saw a white Transit van approaching at speed from the opposite direction. What's his hurry, she thought to herself.

Suddenly, the large van swerved across the carriageway and was now heading directly for the front of her car.

There was no time at all for her to react and her last thought, before the massive impact, was to wonder why the driver of the van was smiling so broadly and looking so pleased with himself.

CHAPTER 65

6.45pm 29th December 1987
Linby Village, Nottinghamshire

Tom saw the car headlights flash through the windows of the cottage and heard the car come to a stop on the gravel driveway outside.

Not before time, he thought. How long did she expect him to keep her dinner warm?

Tom had just taken the dinner plates out of the oven when he heard the doorbell ring.

How many times will that girl forget her door key?

He shouted, 'I'm coming, just a minute, sweetheart.'

Quickly, he put the hot dinner plates onto the table and threw the oven gloves onto the work top, before making his way to the front door.

He opened the door and was shocked to see Matt Jarvis and Jim Chambers on the doorstep.

As soon as he saw the serious expressions on their faces, Tom instinctively knew why they were there.

He said, 'What's happened? Where's Bev? Talk to me Matt.'

Matt stepped into the hallway, followed by Jim Chambers.

Matt looked into Tom's eyes and said quietly, 'Bev's been involved in a car accident after she left work. I'm so sorry mate, she died on her way to the hospital.'

Tom felt his legs go weak, he felt physically sick, 'That can't be right. I only spoke to her an hour ago, she was just leaving work.'

Matt saw the colour drain from his best friend's face, so he very gently took him by the arm and ushered him into the small lounge, where he guided him to one of the armchairs.

Slowly, Tom half sat and half collapsed into the chair.

Matt sat down opposite him and said, 'It was a car crash, Tom. A stupid accident. A van swerved across the carriageway and collided head on with Bev's car coming the other way. She wouldn't have known a thing about it, mate.'

Jim Chambers stepped forward and said, 'Come on Tom, grab your coat. We'll drive you to the hospital.'

Still unable to comprehend what he'd been told, Tom stood up and walked robotically into the hallway.

He took his coat from the pegs on the back of the kitchen door, put it straight on, turned to face Matt and said, 'Come on then, let's go. I want to see her.'

The three men walked out to Chambers' car.

Tom was moving on autopilot. Not thinking, just breathing, existing.

He stood quietly in the darkness, waiting for Jim Chambers to unlock the car doors.

Matt shouted, 'Tom, where's your keys, I'll switch everything off and lock up.'

Tom thrust his hand into his coat pocket, his keys were still inside. He threw them across to Matt and said, 'Hurry up Matt, she's waiting for me.'

Matt quickly locked up and jumped in the car. The three men sat in silence as Jim Chambers drove quickly away from the cottage.

CHAPTER 66

7.15pm 29th December 1987
Kings Mill Hospital, Sutton In Ashfield, Nottinghamshire

As soon as Tom had arrived at the hospital, he'd been ushered into the relatives waiting room.

He had sat quietly with Matt and Jim Chambers for ten minutes, still desperately trying to come to terms with what was happening. The door opened and a young doctor came into the room, she looked sympathetically at Tom and said, 'Mr Naylor. Please follow me.'

Somehow, he managed to stand.

On legs that felt like jelly, he fell in behind the doctor and followed her slowly through corridors that held a dark atmosphere of suffering and reeked of disinfectant.

The doctor led him into a small room just behind the Casualty Department.

That's where he found Bev.

She was covered by a white sheet. The only part of her not covered by the sheet was one half of her face.

He stood in shock, staring at her misshapen, mangled body, covered and hidden by the sheet. He gasped to get his breath, as tears streamed down his face.

Tom had seen plenty of death in his short life, but this was different. This was a person he genuinely loved and with whom he had planned to spend the rest of his life.

Thoughts raced through his head.

The guilt over the abysmal way he had treated her just because of his bloody job.

What had all that been for?

All that wasted time, had any of it been worth it?

The young doctor placed a caring hand, gently on Tom's forearm and said softly, 'I'm so sorry Mr Naylor, we did everything we could to try and save her, but her head injuries were too severe.'

He just nodded.

He couldn't speak, his mouth felt dry, his Adam's apple felt like a rock in his throat.

He swallowed hard, stepped forward and placed a tender kiss on the one cheek he could see.

He said nothing.

The doctor placed a reassuring hand on his shoulder and said, 'Are you okay Mr Naylor?'

Of course I'm not bloody okay, he thought.

He just nodded, turned and walked out.

When he arrived back at the waiting room, Matt's wife and Bev's best friend, Kate, was waiting for him.

She rushed over to Tom and said tearfully, 'I'm so sorry Tom.'

Tom muttered, 'I know Kate', before sitting down heavily in one of the armchairs.

He felt drained.

He looked across the room and saw Matt and Jim Chambers having an animated conversation. Chambers, had obviously just told Matt something and Tom could see from his friend's reaction, that Matt had been totally shocked by what he'd heard.

Suddenly energised, Tom immediately stood and walked across the room.

He looked straight at Jim Chambers and said, 'What is it boss? What's going on?'

Chambers said, 'Try and stay calm Tom, this isn't going to be easy to hear.'

'None of this is fucking easy boss! Just tell me what's going on.'

'I've just been talking to the Traffic Department sergeant investigating the accident. The driver of the van involved in the accident was Dc Jeff Wicks. Do you remember him?'

'Of course, I do. The undercover cop who infiltrated Hincks' gang.'

'The sergeant has just informed me that from what witnesses are saying this doesn't appear to have been an accident. They're saying that the white van was driven deliberately head on into Bev's car.'

Tom exploded with rage and screamed, 'The fucking bastard! Where is he? I'll kill him!'

Matt grabbed his friend and said, 'It's too late for that Tom. Wicks was pronounced dead at the scene. He's gone.'

All the fire and energy instantly evaporated out of Tom, he dropped to the floor. Matt helped him to a seat and said, 'Come on Tom, I'll take you home.'

Regaining a little composure, he said, 'No. I need to go to Hucknall first. I've got to tell Sandra, Bev's mum, what's happened to her daughter. I don't want her to hear this news from a stranger.'

'Okay mate. Come on. Kate and I will drive you over there.'

Kate stepped forward, took Tom's arm and helped him walk from the waiting room.

As Matt was about to follow them out of the room, Jim Chambers grabbed his arm and whispered, 'Matt, just a minute.'

Matt said to Kate, 'Be with you in a second sweetheart, see you by the car.'

He turned to Chambers and said, 'What is it boss?'

'That Traffic sergeant told me a hell of a lot more Matt, but now isn't the time or place to tell Tom. A letter's been found inside the wreckage of the van that Wicks was driving. In the letter, Wicks has admitted the murder of Sir Jarvis Soames and his driver Andris Kalnietis. He's stated that he killed them both as some sort of half-arsed revenge for Angela Hincks being shot dead during the Farnsfield operation. He also vowed to get revenge against Pc Naylor. In the letter he spells out how he's going to make Pc Naylor know exactly what it feels like to lose a loved one.'

Matt was shocked, he said quietly, 'So let me get this straight. This so-called detective's way of obtaining revenge for the death of Angela Hincks, mad terrorist, was to kill my best friend's innocent girlfriend?'

'In the letter his reasoning is this; he says he couldn't live with the fact that the way he had betrayed Hincks had ultimately cost her, her life. In his warped mind, Hincks death was all the fault of Tom Naylor. I think when he's been unable to get directly to him, he's decided to target his nearest and dearest.'

'Bastard!' said Matt.

Chambers said, 'Tom doesn't need to hear any of this right now. It will be way too much for him to take in, especially after what they've been through as a couple recently. I want you to let him know that we're all here for him and that I personally will make all the necessary funeral arrangements with Bev's mum. Tell him, from me, that he's to take as long as he needs. Advise him to take some time away from here, away from work. Make sure he understands this, Matt. If he isn't very careful, I don't know if he'll be strong enough to come back from this.'

Matt nodded, 'I'll make sure he understands, boss.'

Grim faced, he turned and left the room.

CHAPTER 67

7.15pm 10th February 1988
Bamburgh Castle, Northumberland

It had been three weeks since his girlfriend, Bev, had been laid to rest. The service had been a simple one with only family and close friends in attendance.

Throughout the moving ceremony at the crematorium, Tom had found it impossible to even look at Bev's distraught mother.

He blamed himself for her death, he knew in his heart that would always be the case.

It didn't matter how many times, or how many different people tried to tell him otherwise, he would never change his mind.

Bev had died as a direct result of his actions, pure and simple. If he hadn't taken the decision to shoot Angela Hincks, his beautiful, innocent girl would still be alive today.

At the time of the service at the crematorium, there was still a real sense of anger that burned within Tom. That rage was aimed generally at the police service and more specifically against the Metropolitan Police. He couldn't understand why it had taken the Met so long to realise that he and his loved ones were in serious danger from their mentally unstable, rogue detective. That particular failing by them, had endangered not only him, but also everyone he cared for.

It had been Bev, who had paid the ultimate price for the Met's failure to spot the downward spiral into madness of their undercover detective Jeff Wicks.

At the service Tom could feel himself drowning in a desperate depression, he could feel it engulfing him and he knew he had to somehow try and eradicate those feelings or risk his own mental well-being for good.

After the funeral, Tom had found himself unable to go back to his cottage in Linby.

Ever since the fateful night when Bev had died, Tom had been staying at Matt and Kate's house.

The cottage had remained exactly the same as it had been, on the night he'd walked out of the front door with Matt and Jim Chambers, to go to the hospital and see Bev for the last time.

Following the service at the crematorium, as soon as he got back to Matt's house, Tom had gone upstairs, packed an overnight bag, got in his car and driven away.

He had told Matt that he needed to get away and spend some time alone. He had told his friend that he wouldn't be back until he'd cleared his mind.

Tom had driven to the motorway and then headed north.

He just kept driving through the night and eventually found himself in a small bed and breakfast in the picturesque village of Penicuik, just outside Edinburgh.

He had stayed at that small, guest house for a few days, never venturing out of his room, grieving quietly. Working things out. Trying to make sense of everything.

On the fourth day, he'd got out of bed, showered and got dressed. He ate a hearty breakfast, the first food of any description he had eaten in days, then paid his bill, got into his car and started to drive south again.

He had made slow progress.

Each day he only drove until he found a village or a town, he liked the look of. He would then stop, get out and have a look around before finding somewhere to stay for the night.

He didn't know it at the time, but he was healing himself.

With nothing else to think about, he was slowly beginning to come to terms with his loss. He knew he would never forget Bev, but he was beginning to understand that he could carry on with his own life.

It had been during one of the long nights in that small bedroom in the guest house at Penicuik, when he had suddenly realised that the last thing Bev would have wanted, would be for him to never stop grieving.

In life, she had been so vivacious, so energised, so full of life that the last thing she would have wanted for Tom, was to see him depressed and unable to cope.

So, that was how it had been for him over the last fourteen days or so. He had woken up every morning in a different village and slowly meandered his way south.

The night before, he had found himself arriving late into the coastal village of Bamburgh. He had parked up and booked himself into a bed and breakfast less than fifty yards from the famous Bamburgh Castle.

He had woken this morning feeling refreshed and rested.

He ate a full English breakfast and decided that as it was such a lovely morning, he would have a stroll along the beach before he hit the road again.

It was nearing ten thirty, when he stepped down onto the hard-packed yellow sand of the wonderful beach, that stretched as far as the eye could see in either direction.

It was one of those beautiful, clear sunny mornings.

The air was cold and crisp and there was hardly a breath of wind. The only sounds to be heard were the cries of the seagulls overhead and the small waves gently breaking upon the sandy beach.

Tom walked down to the water's edge and listened to the oceam rippling up onto the sand. The noise of the sea relaxed him, so he stepped back onto the drier sand and sat cross legged, looking out to the horizon.

Behind him was the imperious grandeur of Bamburgh Castle and as he looked along the coast to his left, he could just make out on the far horizon, the outline of the abandoned abbey on Lindisfarne, the Holy Island.

Tom breathed in the cool, cleansing air, drawing it deep into his lungs, he could smell the ozone and taste the salt from the ocean. As he savoured the breath-taking views along the coastline, he heard a familiar voice from behind him, 'Good morning Tom. How are you?'

Startled, he jumped to his feet and spun around.

Standing less than ten feet away, with her long red hair being ruffled by the gentle breeze, was Bailey.

Tom smiled, stepped towards her and said, 'Bailey! It's good to see you, but how did you find me?'

'Do you remember when we first met, you asked me if I was a cop or a spook?'

'Yeah, I remember that conversation.'

'Well let's just say, if I was a cop, I wouldn't have been able to find you', she grinned before continuing, 'I hope you don't mind me coming Tom? I don't want to intrude, but I had to know how you were doing? What happened to Bev, was so terrible. It had so many parallels to what happened three years ago, when my fella Damien, was killed on his motorbike at work. Back then, I took forever to make any sense out of what happened. I just haven't been able to stop wondering how you were coping with it all.'

'Firstly, don't ever think that I wouldn't be pleased to see you Bailey. Secondly, you are definitely not intruding. I'm not going to lie to you, I've been in a mess. I still have good days and bad days, today is very definitely a good day. Every day I still feel the same pain, but it's gradually becoming less intense. It doesn't make me struggle to catch my breath anymore, when I think about her. I can breathe normally now. Does that make any sense?'

'That's exactly how it was for me Tom. I still think about Damien every day, but these days the thoughts are good ones, happy ones, they're no longer always tinged with sadness and heartache.'

'I don't want to forget her Bailey, it really worries me that one day I'll wake up and she'll no longer be in my thoughts.'

'You'll never forget her Tom, you need to stop worrying that you will. Trust me, that's never going to happen, but it doesn't mean you can't slowly move on with your own life, either.'

Tom smiled, 'How did a red-haired girl from Liverpool ever get so worldly wise?'

She grinned back and said, 'Don't be so cheeky, Naylor! Us scouse girls have our moments, you know.'

Tom said, 'Do you fancy joining me for a stroll along the beach? So you can impart some more of your wisdom?'

'A stroll along the beach sounds wonderful. I happen to know there's a little beach hut café about four hundred yards that way, where we can get a nice hot brew and a sausage sandwich with loads of brown sauce on.'

'How do you know that?'

She smiled, 'I could tell you Tom….'

'I know, but then you'd have to kill me', he grinned.

They walked slowly along the beach holding hands, not in an intimate way like lovers, but in the same way caring friends would. Friends, who were looking to find some solace and comfort from each other.

As they walked Tom said softly, 'I'm so glad you came to find me.'

Bailey said nothing and just gently squeezed his hand.

CHAPTER 68

3.15pm 10th May 1988
Manchester Crown Court, Manchester

The Crown Court building in the centre of Manchester was packed to the rafters, it was standing room only. Today was the last day of the trial of Micky Stone, the sole surviving armed robber from the gang that had terrified the North West.

Stone was on trial for the murder of Detective Sergeant Brian Mayhew, as well as a series of armed robberies.

The cold-blooded murder had been a crime that shocked the nation. The media involvement covering the murder had been huge from the outset and the coverage of the trial had been on a similar grand scale.

The area outside the red brick court building was a throng of television outside broadcast units. Reporters from the newspapers and television alike, had behaved like sharks in a feeding frenzy, battling over a shoal of sardines.

Tom had felt like he'd been living his life under a spotlight for the last three weeks. Every morning when he arrived at the impressive court buildings, the press had harangued him with questions on the court steps. The reporters knew very well that he wasn't allowed to answer their questions while ever the trial was still ongoing, but still they persisted in bombarding him with a barrage of shouted questions every day.

The day before, the judge had completed his summing up and given directions to the jury. It had been one o'clock that afternoon when the jury had finally retired to consider their verdict.

During the trial, the defence team had been brutal with their cross examination of Tom Naylor. They had tried their very best to muddy the waters, accusing him of acting as an agent provocateur for the robbery at the Tesco Superstore in Crosby. They had also tried to shift the blame for the murder of Brian Mayhew onto the now deceased Gary Mercer. The judge in his summing up had reminded the jury of the crucial CCTV footage that provided the most damning evidence against Stone. He had purposefully instructed them to remember those images when thinking about the levels of culpability for each of the gang members.

All the evidence pointed squarely at Micky Stone.

The testimony of witnesses as well as that all-important CCTV evidence appeared to prove beyond all doubt that he was the person, solely responsible for the death of the off-duty police officer, but would the jury agree?

There was a buzz starting to circulate inside the imposing Crown Court building, as word spread that the jury were coming back into court.

As he sat quietly at the back of the court, Tom could feel his heart starting to beat faster. Any verdict from a jury of twelve good men and true could never be predicted with any certainty and Tom felt nervous.

The court usher suddenly shouted, 'All stand.'

Everybody in the crowded courtroom stood up and after a suitable pause, the door at the back of the court opened. His Honour Judge Benjamin Forsythe strode in, looking suitably stern faced, resplendent in his robes and wig.

At forty two years of age, Benjamin Forsyth was one of the youngest judges on the circuit and was considered by the establishment to be the rising star of the British legal system. It had been no surprise to anyone when he had been selected to preside over the trial of Micky Stone.

Finally, the men and women of the jury returned to the courtroom and took their seats.

Judge Forsythe turned to the jury and said, 'Members of the jury, have you elected a foreman to address the court?'

A short, squat man in his fifties with crew cut, grey hair who had taken the seat on the front right of the jury benches stood and faced the judge.

The man was impeccably dressed in a charcoal grey suit, white shirt and burgundy red tie. He looked into the eyes of the judge and answered confidently, 'Yes, we have, your honour.'

The judge now addressed the man directly, 'Thank you. Please respond to my learned clerk's questions.'

The clerk's voice now boomed out theatrically, 'Members of the jury, have you reached a verdict on all the charges in this case?'

The foreman replied, 'Yes we have.'

'On the first count, the murder of Brian Mayhew, how do you find the defendant? Guilty or not guilty?'

There was a slight pause as the foreman of the jury steadied himself.

In a clear voice he said, 'Guilty.'

Tom instantly felt a huge wave of relief rush over him.

He could hardly hear the clerk as he read through the rest of the indictments of robbery and firearms offences that Stone faced. Inside the courtroom there was now a general clamour as people voiced their reaction to the guilty verdict being given on the murder charge.

The noise gradually died down and the foreman could once again be heard answering with the word guilty as every indictment was put to him.

At the conclusion of the indictments, Judge Forsythe addressed the jury directly, 'Members of the jury, I wish to place on record my thanks to you all for your attention and diligence in what has been a very difficult, complex and often harrowing case to listen to. It hasn't been easy for anyone in this courtroom to watch some of the evidence that has been presented, so thank you for your efforts. You are now formally discharged from your duties.'

There was a slight rise in the noise levels of the courtroom as the jurors all stood and made their way out of the court.

Throughout the delivery of the verdicts, Stone had stared unblinkingly at Tom Naylor.

His Honour Judge Forsyth, now turned his attention to the dock. He looked directly at Micky Stone who had remained seated throughout the guilty verdicts.

The judge said loudly, 'Stand up, Stone.'

Still glaring across the courtroom at Tom Naylor, Stone slowly got to his feet.

Ignoring the Judge, Stone shouted at Tom, 'Are you proud of yourself Naylor? You betrayed your so-called best friend, the man who saved your life. You're a treacherous dog and very soon, you'll get what's coming to you!'

Judge Forsythe immediately intervened, 'Stone, one more word out of you and I'll have you removed from this court. I will have no qualms in passing sentence in your absence if you persist, now be silent.'

Momentarily, Stone shifted his gaze from Tom and turned to face the Judge.

Judge Forsythe continued, 'Stone, you've been found guilty on the charge of the murder of Brian Mayhew. I have found this case to be one of the most chilling, cold-blooded acts of violence against an innocent, defenceless bystander that has ever been my misfortune to hear. I consider you to be an extremely dangerous, evil individual and any sentence will need to reflect that. The sentence I am obliged to pass is a statutory one of life imprisonment, but in your case, I am stipulating that life in this instance means a minimum of thirty years. Take him down.'

Stone immediately attempted to climb over the rail of the dock, but was instantly restrained by the two burly prison officers who were standing alongside him in the dock.

He shouted from the dock, 'You're a dead man walking Naylor! Enjoy your moment of glory, you worthless shit. You're a fucking dead man! Do you hear me? A fucking dead man!'

He continued to shout threats and abuse as he was dragged out of the dock, down the steps and into the cell block below the courtroom.

Slowly, the packed courtroom cleared.

Finally, the only people left inside the courtroom were Tom Naylor, Jim Chambers, Greg Mitchell and the prosecution barrister, Mr Henry Chiltern QC.

In his plummy, home counties accent, Henry Chiltern QC said, 'Well gentlemen, I hope that's the last we hear from Mr Stone for many a year.'

Jim Chambers nodded, 'Let's hope so, sir.'

Chambers then turned to Greg Mitchell and said, 'What

about those threats Stone was making, Greg? Are they to be taken seriously?'

The big, scouse detective replied, 'I don't know at this moment in time Jim. I'll make the usual enquiries with the prison authorities to monitor what contact Micky Stone is having with people on the outside. In the meantime, you should be on your guard, Tom.'

Tom said, 'After what's happened recently, my guard's never down sir.'

Within an hour of the sentence being passed, Jim Chambers and Tom Naylor were in a car heading out of Manchester on the long, tiresome journey back to Nottingham.

Both men were quiet, occupied by their own thoughts.

Chambers concentrating on his driving and Tom gazing out of the window at the bleak, foreboding Saddleworth Moor as it flashed by.

Chambers broke the silence, 'I bet you're glad it's all over, Tom.'

'Definitely. I don't know if it will ever be completely over though, if you know what I mean? At least that maniac Stone is locked up where he can't do anyone any harm.'

'Did it bother you what he said about you and Gary Mercer?'

'No. When I spoke to Mercer at the end, I could tell he understood why I'd acted against him. He realised that it was all to do with Stone. He knew in his heart; exactly what sort of monster Stone was. He was as sickened by the murder of Mayhew as the rest of us. I don't know where it went wrong for Gary, I still think that deep down, he wasn't an evil man. A villain yes, evil definitely not.'

Keen to change the subject, Chambers said, 'Have you got anything planned for the weekend?'

'Not much boss. My friend Bailey, is coming down from Liverpool to stay for a few days. She's been down and stayed at the cottage for a few weekends now, we're getting on great. We've got a lot in common, she's been a great friend to me.'

'That's great Tom. I'm glad you feel able to start moving forward with your life. It's all too easy to let a single tragedy define the rest of your life. I can see that Bailey's good for you, Tom.'

'She is boss, she is.'

'What sort of name's Bailey, by the way? I don't think I've ever known anyone with that name before.'

Tom smiled, 'I don't think I have either boss, but it definitely suits her.'

Chambers reached for the car stereo and said, 'Let's have some music on, shall we?'

As Radio Two came on and the music of Phil Collins broke the silence, Tom looked out of the car window again. As he stared out of the window, Tom thought about the last time he and Bailey had spoken, they had talked right through the night about their future.

After everything that had happened, Tom was still undecided whether or not his future now lay as a member of the police force.

He still felt let down by the organisation.

The more he learned about Dc Wicks and his actions after the incident at Farnsfield, the more he felt the warning signs were there and should have been acted upon. He found it difficult to come to terms with the fact that if the police had acted sooner then maybe, just maybe, Bev would still be alive.

He didn't know if he still wanted to be part of an organisation that could let people down so badly.

In the coming weeks, he would have a decision to make.

He hoped that Bailey would still be around to help him make those decisions about both his career and his future generally.

As they had discussed the possibility of having a future together, she had been slightly more open about her own occupation, but not much.

Tom hadn't pressed her too hard. He could feel there was a real chemistry growing between them and he didn't want his problems, her job or anything else to spoil that.

He was just glad that she was there.

EPILOGUE

3.00am 10th July 1988
Linby Village, Nottinghamshire

Fat Man sat in his battered, old Mini Metro, in a layby no more than one hundred yards from Tom Naylor's cottage in the picturesque village of Linby.

From his vantage point he could see both the lounge window and the bedroom window. He knew that the windows he could see related to those particular rooms. The week before he had been inside the cottage to do his final recce.

He had waited for Naylor and his girlfriend to go jogging together and had then taken the opportunity to go in and have a good look around the cottage.

It always gave him a strange sense of power, that as a specialist locksmith he had the ability to virtually walk into any property without leaving a trace. The mortice lock on the cottage door had proved no barrier at all to his specialist skills.

As he thought back to the recce, he allowed his mind to wander and he thought of the moment he had watched Naylor and his girlfriend jog down the quiet country lane.

His thoughts focussed on the girlfriend; her long red hair, ripe, full breasts swaying as she jogged.

As those thoughts filled his head, he made his mind up there and then that after the main job had been taken care of, he would take his time and have some fun with Naylor's girlfriend.

The contract had come from his usual broker in Manchester. He'd been told that the client was serving a long stretch in Strangeways, but nevertheless he still wanted this particular matter sorting as soon as possible. The offer that had been made by the client was a very good one, well above the going rate.

Fat Man knew that it needed to be, he would need to stay well below the radar for a long time after this contract.

He had no issue that the target was a serving police officer.

As long as the money was right for the risk, it made no difference to him who the mark was.

He'd already been paid ten grand up front, with another forty grand to follow after the hit had been successfully accomplished. With fifty grand in his bank he knew he would be able to live like a king for a long time in Phuket, with as much sex as he wanted.

In Fat Man's case that was a lot of sex. The more depraved the better, as far as he was concerned.

As he sat in the car he listened to "Eleanor Rigby" by The Beatles.

It was almost ritualistic, whenever he worked, in the moments leading up to the actual hit, he would listen to songs by The Beatles.

As the final chords of the song played out, he looked down onto the passenger seat at the specialist tools of his trade.

The picks he had used to defeat the mortice lock, the blue latex gloves and most importantly the Glock 9mm self-loading pistol with silencer attachment.

He decided he had waited long enough, it was time for Tom Naylor to be despatched. As he started to screw the silencer attachment onto the barrel of the Glock, "Strawberry Fields Forever" came on the cassette.

He decided to wait for the song to finish, it would be so wrong to interrupt a Beatles classic.

The song faded out and finished. Fat Man turned off the car engine and put on the blue latex gloves. He was just about to get out of the car when the mobile phone in his boiler suit pocket began to ring.

He fumbled for the phone and muttered, 'Shit.'

Finally, he answered the phone, 'Yeah.'

He heard a familiar guttural voice on the phone, 'Have you done Naylor yet?'

It was that sing song Mancunian accent that he normally detested, being a born and bred scouser himself.

'No. Not yet. Why?'

'You might want to reconsider your position.'

'What do you mean?'

'There's a problem with the sponsor. He's been topped inside Strangeways nick. The word is, he picked a fight with some psycho cockney who stuck a chiv through his windpipe.'

'And why exactly is that my problem?'

'It's your problem because without the code he was going to give me after the job, I can't access your forty grand. It's left entirely up to you? If you still want to waste the pig, that's fine. All I'm saying is, you'll be doing the hit and taking down a copper, for ten grand not fifty.'

Fat Man was now deep in thought.

It was usually only ever strictly business with him.

The risk versus the reward, but in this case the red-haired girlfriend with the magnificent breasts was definitely a factor to consider. He really wanted to see her in the flesh, so to speak, before he put a bullet through her pretty face.

Suddenly, thoughts of the red-haired girlfriend vanished from his mind and he had made his decision.

He spoke quietly into the phone, 'I can't have people expecting me to do my thing for nothing. I don't want to be setting a precedent, now do I? No money, no job. This conversation's over.'

There was nothing else to be said and Fat Man ended the call, he unscrewed the silencer from the Glock and removed his latex gloves.

He leaned back in the car seat and said aloud, 'You're a very lucky boy, Tom Naylor. Who knows, maybe I'll catch up with you and your lovely lady some other time.'

He turned on the ignition of the Metro and drove away from the cottage.

As he drove down the lane, his all-time favourite Beatles track "Can't buy me Love" boomed out from the car stereo.

He sang along, ever so slightly off key, to the classic track.

THE COAL KILLER –
NOTTINGHAMSHIRE – 1984

The county's in the grip of a bitter, acrimonious strike called by the National Union of Mineworkers. Jimmy Wade is pure evil, he first killed at the age of eleven, he's now a coal miner in Nottinghamshire.

Mick Reynolds is in a hateful marriage and has a pathological hatred of women, he's a sergeant in the Metropolitan Police. When Reynolds is sent to police the strike, his duties. involve escorting Wade and other miners breaking the strike into work every day.

Thrown together by circumstance and recognising each other's murderous natures, they embark on a brutal killing spree, using Wade's natural cunning and Reynolds knowledge of forensics and police procedures to evade detection.

The two men are pursued in Nottinghamshire by Det Insp Flint and in London by Det Insp Johnson. The killers revel in playing games, taunting the police, ultimately intending to kill one of the detectives. As the police close in, the story reaches a thrilling and unexpected climax.

THE EXODUS MURDERS – NOTTINGHAMSHIRE – 1986

Two brutal murders are discovered on the same day at different ends of the county. Both the victims are men, and both have been mutilated and tortured before having their throats cut and being left to bleed to death. An identical series of letters and numbers has been daubed on the walls at both scenes using the victim's own blood.

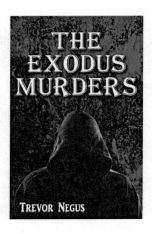

Detective Chief Inspector Danny Flint is now in charge of the newly formed Major Crime Investigation Unit and his fledgling team are tasked with finding the killer. After discovering the meaning of the code left at the murder scenes, Flint and his team realise they are in a race against time before the cold-blooded killer strikes again.

As the investigation reveals the killers' motive, the reason for the slaughter becomes apparent and the detectives realise that unless they can stop the killer one of their own is in mortal danger of becoming the final victim.

A DIFFERENT KIND OF EVIL –
NOTTINGHAMSHIRE – 1986

The body of a young boy is discovered at a secluded beauty spot in Nottinghamshire.

The post mortem reveals that the child had been sexually assaulted and suffocated. Chief Inspector Danny Flint and the MCIU begin an enquiry into the boy's death.

As their investigation takes them into a murky world of child exploitation at Children's Homes across the county, they are also tasked with investigating the escape of psychopath Jimmy Wade from Rampton Hospital. Wade was assisted in his escape by an obsessed and troubled young woman and has remained in hiding at the woman's remote woodland cottage.

He is fixated on achieving revenge against the people who abused him at Rampton and the detectives who tracked him down and convicted him. The two investigations set Danny Flint and his team their toughest test yet and stretch their resources and nerves to the limits. As the detectives close in on their quarry the story hurtles towards a thrilling and breathtaking climax.

TWO WRONGS

Nottinghamshire, 1987 Barry Tate the man who had controlled the distribution of illegal drugs across the county for over a decade has finally been jailed for life. With his vice like grip removed rival dealers strive to fill the void and violent drug related crime soars in the towns and cities of Nottinghamshire.

Standing in the way of this downward spiral into lawlessness are the Special Operations Unit, the armed response teams of Nottinghamshire Police.

This war on crime takes an unexpected and personal turn when the wife of a serving SOU officer is abducted. She is Kate Jarvis, the barrister responsible for the successful prosecution of Barry Tate. As the police struggle to keep up with developments a burning question is left unanswered. Can two wrongs ever make a right?

Coming Soon: The Cause
December 1990

The Londonderry Brigade of the IRA are engaged in a murderous bombing campaign on mainland Britain.

When a chance discovery in rural Nottinghamshire leads to the identification of the Active Service Unit responsible and the carnage is brought to a premature end the commander of the Londonderry Brigade plots a devastating revenge that will cause maximum embarrassment to the Nottinghamshire Police Force.

The unsanctioned plan to unleash a master sniper, nicknamed The Death Adder by the British Army serving in Northern Ireland, causes a huge rift between the hierarchy of the Londonderry and Belfast Brigades of the IRA.

A breath-taking pursuit over three countries follows, as the Police and Security Services race to identify and intercept the mysterious, deadly assassin before he can strike a devastating blow aimed at the very heart of the British establishment.

The Author – Trevor Negus

Trevor Negus is a retired Police Officer who spent 30 years working with Nottinghamshire Police. He worked both inner city and rural beats in uniform and spent the entire duration of the Miners' Strike of 1984 on a Police Support Unit.

He then spent six years as an authorised firearms officer and was a sniper on the Force's Special Operations Unit. The last eleven years of his Police career were spent as a detective on the CID, where he was involved in numerous murder enquiries. During his time on the CID he was trained as a specialist interviewer involved in the planning and interviews of murder suspects.

1st TRILOGY
BOOK 1) THE COAL KILLER
BOOK 2) THE EXODUS MURDERS
BOOK 3) A DIFFERENT KIND OF EVIL

2nd TRILOGY
BOOK 1) TWO WRONGS
BOOK 2) THE ROOT OF ALL EVIL
BOOK 3) THE CAUSE - coming soon